AN AMISH SINGING

AN AMISH SINGING

FOUR STORIES

AMY CLIPSTON

THORNDIKE PRESS
A part of Gale, a Cengage Company

Copyright © 2020 by Amy Clipston.
Scripture quotations marked NIV are taken from the Holy Bible, New International Version®, NIV®. Copyright © 1973, 1978, 1984, 2011 by Biblica, Inc.™ Used by permission of Zondervan. All rights reserved worldwide. www.zondervan.com. The "NIV" and "New International Version" are trademarks registered in the United States Patent and Trademark Office by Biblica, Inc.™
Thorndike Press, a part of Gale, a Cengage Company.

**LIBRARY OF CONGRESS CIP DATA ON FILE.
CATALOGUING IN PUBLICATION FOR THIS BOOK
IS AVAILABLE FROM THE LIBRARY OF CONGRESS.**

ISBN-13: 978-1-4328-8302-7 (hardcover alk. paper)

Published in 2021 by arrangement with The Zondervan Corporation LLC, a subsidiary of HarperCollins Christian Publishing, Inc.

Printed in Mexico
Print Number: 01   Print Year: 2021

CONTENTS

CONTENTS

GLOSSARY

ach: oh
aenti: aunt
appeditlich: delicious
bedauerlich: sad
boppli: baby
brot: bread
bruder: brother
bruders: brothers
bu: boy
buwe: boys
daadi: grandfather
daadihaus: small house provided for retired
  parents
danki: thank you
dat: dad
dochder: daughter
dummkopp: moron
Dummle!: hurry!
Englisher: non-Amish
fraa: wife
Frehlicher Grischtdaag!: Merry Christmas!

freind: friend
freinden: friends
froh: happy
gegisch: silly
Gern gschehne: You're welcome
Gude mariye: Good morning
gut: good
Gut nacht: Good night
haus: house
Ich liebe dich: I love you
kaffi: coffee
kapp: prayer covering or cap
kichli: cookie
kichlin: cookies
kind: child
kinner: children
krank: ill
kuche: cake
kuchen: cakes
liewe: love, a term of endearment
maed: young women, girls
maedel: young woman
mamm: mom
mammi: grandmother
mei: my
naerfich: nervous
narrisch: crazy
onkel: uncle
schee: pretty
schmaert: smart

schtupp: family room
schweschder: sister
sohn: son
Was iss letz?: What's wrong?
Wie geht's: How do you do? or Good day!
wunderbaar: wonderful
ya: yes
zwillingbopplin: twins

■ ■ ■ ■

HYMN OF PRAISE

■ ■ ■ ■

HYMN OF PRAISE

For my sweet Rico, with hugs and kisses

Featured Characters

Annie m. Emmanuel "Manny" Esh
|
Rosemary
David

Edna m. Harvey King
|
Calvin
Raymond

Louise m. Moses Smoker
|
Jay

Jean m. Merle Detweiler
|
Andrew
Samuel

Feenie m. Ira Lambert
|
Sharon
Ruby Sue

Dorothy m. Floyd Blank
|
Benjamin
Alice

Roselyn m. Alvin Bender
|
Biena
Darlene

CHAPTER ONE

Sharon Lambert sighed with contentment as she strolled with Alice and Darlene toward the field of horses and buggies waiting for their owners to start the trek home. The church service and community meal had been held at Alice's family's dairy farm, which meant Sharon could walk home from the Blanks' whenever she wanted.

The early April air was cool and crisp as she breathed in the scent of a rain-soaked pasture and enjoyed the warm sun that kissed her cheek. Springtime had made its way to Lancaster County, Pennsylvania, and when she glanced at the cheerful flowers in Alice's garden, they seemed to smile as if they'd invited the warmer weather just for them.

"I heard everyone is going to play volleyball over in Ronks this afternoon." Alice pushed the ties from her prayer covering off the shoulders of her yellow dress and white apron. "Do you want to join them?"

Sharon looked her way. With Alice's reddish-brown hair and mocha-colored eyes, Sharon had always considered her one of the prettiest young women in their church district. Today was no exception.

"I don't know." Darlene blew out a sigh and looked toward where her father and older sister stood talking to some neighbors. *"Mei mamm* hasn't been doing well since her treatment on Friday. I'm surprised *mei dat* was willing to leave her today, but he insisted the rest of the family come. We all wish patients receiving chemotherapy treatments could be around large crowds, but since their immune system is suppressed, she'd run the risk of getting *krank."*

"So she has some good days?" Sharon touched Darlene's arm as concern about the Bender family slid through her. She'd known Darlene and Alice since they were all in first grade together fourteen years ago. They were best friends, and she cared about their families too.

Sharon noticed Darlene's demeanor as Darlene looked at her sister and father again. Sharon had always envied Darlene's golden-colored hair and pretty brown eyes, too, but today she saw only the worry in her friend's eyes.

"Sometimes, but most days are tough." Darlene's voice wobbled, and Sharon gave her arm a little squeeze as her own throat dried.

"I'm so sorry," Alice said. "I know it's Sunday, so we can't help with chores today. But there must be something we can do to help out this afternoon."

"No." Darlene shook her head. "We'll be fine. Go have fun with our *freinden.*"

"What are you three doing today?" Cal King asked as he approached them with Jay Smoker and Andrew Detweiler in tow.

All around the same age, the six of them had always been friends, but over the past year, they'd become a tight group.

Sharon tried to clear her dry throat as she looked up at Jay. Although she was taller than Alice and Darlene, which they'd once confessed to envying, Jay still stood a few inches taller than her — about six feet.

Inwardly, she sighed a little. Although Andrew and Cal were handsome, too, lately Jay had stood out as not just good-looking but intriguing. At twenty-three, two years older than her, he was about the same height as his friends, but he somehow seemed even taller. And she'd noticed how well his light-brown hair and honey-colored eyes complemented his chiseled cheekbones

17

and enticing smile.

She'd always thought he was attractive when they were in school and youth group together, but he also seemed more mature these past few months. He'd seemed more serious as well, especially during church services.

"I was just talking about playing volleyball with everyone else at Katie Miller's *haus*," Alice said.

"Let's do something different." The words seemed to burst from Sharon's lips.

"Like what?" Jay's gorgeous eyes focused on Sharon's, and her heart did a little dance.

"I noticed Martha Bontrager wasn't in church today. I thought maybe we could go sing for her and brighten her day, so I asked her *sohn* if that would be okay. He said it would, and he promised not to mention it to her, so if we go, it will be a surprise."

Jay nodded before dividing a look between Cal and Andrew. "I think that's a *wunderbaar* idea. Don't you agree?"

"Absolutely." Cal lifted his hat and pushed back his golden hair. "Let's do it."

Sharon turned to Darlene, suddenly feeling guilty. Why had she suggested they sing for Martha when Darlene's mother was so ill? "We can sing for your *mamm* instead."

Darlene shook her head. "No, it's okay.

She likes it quiet after she has a treatment. She really doesn't want visitors."

"How is she doing?" Andrew asked.

"She's hanging in there. Anyway, I need to go check in with *mei dat* and *schweschder.*" Her smile seemed forced before she hurried off.

"Is she all right?" Andrew's dark eyes seemed full of worry. He was such a good guy.

"I'm not sure. She doesn't share much about what she's going through." Sharon turned toward where Darlene now spoke to her family.

Alice frowned. "Maybe her *mamm* doesn't want us coming to the *haus*, but let's ask Darlene soon if we can help them some other way."

"That's a *gut* plan." Jay stepped closer to Sharon, and his nearness sent her senses spinning. What was wrong with her? She'd known him since she was seven years old!

She saw Darlene nod at her father, and then she returned. "*Mei dat* thinks I should go singing with you. He just asked me not to stay out too long."

"Are you sure you don't want to go home instead?" Sharon asked. She didn't want Darlene to feel obligated to go with them.

"No." Darlene shook her head. "I want to

19

go with you. *Mei dat* and Biena said they'll take care of *Mamm* this afternoon. It's the Lord's day. Let's go to Martha's *haus* and bring her some joy."

Alice looked behind her. "Let's invite Dave too."

When Alice approached Dave Esh and said something, Sharon saw him stick his hands in his pockets and look down, shaking his head. Alice frowned and nodded before returning to the group. Dave had always been a part of their activities until a tragedy occurred last winter, but Sharon wasn't surprised he wouldn't come.

"He said he can't go." Alice looked back at Dave as he made his way toward the knot of buggies. "I was hoping he'd say *ya.*"

"Dave has been best *freinden* with Cal and me forever," Jay said, and then he turned to Cal. "We won't give up on him, right?"

"*Ya,*" Cal said. "That's right." But Sharon thought Cal looked a little less sure about that.

"I just need to let *Mamm* and *Dat* know I'm going." Sharon hurried to where her parents were talking to friends by the barn. She hoped Jay would wait for her and give her a ride to Martha's house. The thought of sitting beside him in his buggy sent a thrill racing through her.

She stood near her family a little impatiently until her mother noticed her, but she didn't want to interrupt her conversation.

"Sharon!" *Mamm* finally said. "Are you and your *freinden* going to play volleyball this afternoon? I heard that was the plan for all the young people today."

"No." Sharon jammed her thumb toward the buggies. "We're going to go sing at Martha Bontrager's *haus* since she wasn't in church today. Her *sohn* said it would be okay."

"Oh. I think she'll like that." When it looked like she wouldn't be interrupting either, *Mamm* got *Dat*'s attention with a hand on his arm. "Ira, Sharon and her *freinden* are going to go sing at Martha Bontrager's *haus*."

"That's awfully nice." *Dat* smiled. "Be home for supper, though."

"I will." Sharon looked at her sister, who'd joined them. "What are you doing this afternoon?"

Ruby Sue nodded toward a group of teenagers behind her. "I'm going to play volleyball. *Mei freinden* and I are leaving in a few minutes."

"Be careful," Sharon told her before waving good-bye to her family. "I'll see you all later." She rushed back to where Alice was standing with Andrew by his buggy. "Where's everyone else?"

Andrew opened the passenger-side door. "Jay said he had to run home for a minute, and Darlene and Cal just left for Martha's. Hop on in."

"Oh." Sharon tried to disguise her disappointment as she maneuvered into the back of the buggy, doing her best to swallow a frown. She'd really wanted to ride with Jay.

Alice and Andrew sat on the front bench seat as Andrew guided the horse down the rock driveway toward the main road.

"*Danki* for coming with me to Martha's," Sharon said as the horse *clip-clopped* down the road. "While I was praying in church today, I felt moved to do something more meaningful than play games this afternoon."

Alice looked back at her. "I'm glad you suggested this."

Andrew nodded while keeping his eyes on the road. He was the quiet one in their group. When Jay and Cal joked and horsed around, Andrew just smiled as he looked on. Sharon often wondered what he was thinking.

"Martha's *sohn* thought she'd appreciate company. She must be lonely since Herman died. It's only been six months," Sharon said as Andrew guided the horse onto Martha's street.

"I'm sure you're right," Alice said.

Andrew guided the horse into the driveway that led past the main Bontrager house to Martha's small, whitewashed *daadihaus* at the back of the dairy farm. As the horse approached the little building, Sharon spotted Martha sitting in a rocking chair on the front porch.

Cal was tying his horse to a post beside the house as Darlene made her way to Martha. Andrew halted his horse beside Cal's, and Alice and Sharon climbed out of the buggy to join the other women.

"Good afternoon, Martha," Sharon called as she and Alice climbed the porch steps. *"Wie geht's?"* Sharon took in Martha's bright smile amid the many wrinkles that lined her face.

"I'm well. What brings you all here today?"

"We wanted to see you since you weren't in church today," Sharon said.

"And we thought we might sing for you too," Alice chimed in.

Martha clapped her hands together. "What a blessing! I prayed for some company, and the Lord has provided it for me. And I would love to hear you sing." She looked past them as Andrew and Cal joined them. "You brought your handsome boyfriends too."

"Oh no." Sharon laughed as Alice and Darlene shook their heads. "We're all just *freinden.*"

"My Herman and I started out as *freinden.* You never know." Martha pushed herself up from the rocking chair and then hobbled toward the front door with the aid of a cane.

"Let me help." Andrew opened the door wide for her.

"Danki." Martha gazed up at him, and with her tiny frame, she looked like a child next to him. She touched his arm. "You're a *gut bu.*"

Sharon looked at Alice, and they shared a grin.

Martha beckoned them to follow her. "Come into the kitchen. My daughter-in-law brought me *kichlin* from the bakery yesterday."

"May I help you get them out?" Sharon offered as she stepped to the counter.

"Ya." Martha pointed to a box. "The *kichlin* are there."

"What can I do?" Darlene asked.

"I'll help too," Alice said.

Martha directed them to plates, napkins, and glasses, and soon they were all eating oatmeal raisin cookies and drinking milk,

24

crowded around the small kitchen table with the aid of folding chairs Cal and Andrew brought from a tiny utility room.

"How have you been?" Cal asked Martha between bites of a cookie.

Martha turned toward the window that looked out over a vast green pasture dotted with cows and outlined by a white fence. "I miss my husband. We were together nearly seventy years." She sighed. "It seems strange to wake up alone and then spend the day longing to tell him things."

Sharon glanced at Alice, who looked at Martha with the empathy Sharon had come to appreciate from her.

"But God is *gut.*" Martha's expression lightened. "After all, he sent you all to see me today. That's just what I needed."

Darlene smiled. "Sharon suggested we come, and we loved the idea."

"You're all so thoughtful. I didn't sleep well last night, so I was too tired to get to church. I seem to have trouble sleeping now that Herman is gone." Martha's wrinkled hand shook as she picked up a cookie. "Now, what are you all going to sing for me?"

Sharon's friends all turned their gaze to her.

"What do you think?" Alice asked.

Sharon bit her lower lip as her favorite hymns clicked through her mind. "How about we start with 'Rock of Ages'?"

"*Ya,*" Andrew said, and their other friends nodded in agreement. "You sing the first verse, and then we'll join in."

Sharon closed her eyes and smiled as the Holy Spirit filled her with warmth. Yes, she belonged here, sharing the Lord's love with this dear, lonely woman.

If only Jay were here to sing with them . . . Where was he?

CHAPTER TWO

Jay blew out a sigh of relief when he spotted his friends' horses tied up next to Martha's house. He glanced down at his fresh pair of trousers and rolled his eyes.

When he told Andrew and Cal he had to go home first, covering the evidence the best he could with his hat, he couldn't bring himself to admit that just as Sharon left to talk to her family, he'd noticed he'd dropped peanut butter spread on his trousers during lunch. He'd tried to get the spot out in the bathroom, but that just made it worse. Not only was the spot then wet, but the peanut butter spread smeared.

He couldn't imagine going to Martha's like that. So he'd hurried home, changed, and hoped his friends would still be there when he arrived.

He was grateful they all wanted to do something today. He needed to get his mind off his loss. His grandfather had died almost a month ago, but he still missed him to the depth of his soul. He'd been more than his grandfather; he'd been one of his best friends and his greatest confidant. Jay felt lost without his sage counsel.

Putting those thoughts aside, Jay secured his horse and then jogged around to the front of the little house and up the porch steps. He raised his hand to knock on the screen door but then froze when he heard a single beautiful voice singing inside.

His heart seemed to turn over in his chest as he took in the lyrical tune and angelic voice singing "How Great Thou Art."

His lips turned up in a smile. That had to be Sharon. He'd caught her singing "Jesus Loves Me" with one of the toddlers in their church district a few weeks ago, and he was struck by the beauty of her voice. But he'd noticed more than her singing voice lately. He'd seen her in a whole new light.

They'd known each other since she started school when she was seven and he was nine. As the years went by, he'd always found an easy friendship with her. During the past couple of months, though, he'd found himself wondering if they could be more than friends. The feelings had seemed to come out of nowhere, and they'd stunned him. Was it even possible that Sharon could see him as someone to . . . love? Or would she reject that idea as a crazy notion?

He pulled open the screen door and stepped into the small family room. After navigating past the furniture in that tight space, he stood in the doorway of the kitchen to listen. Sharon was still singing alone, her eyes closed.

Jay was mesmerized, his own eyes glued to her face. With light-brown hair, baby-blue eyes, high cheekbones, and pink lips, she was so pretty. Had she grown more beautiful just this week?

Sharon opened her eyes and stopped singing when her eyes locked on to his. Her mouth closed, and then her cheeks turned bright pink as she glanced down at her lap — as pink as her dress against a white apron.

What did that mean?

"Jay!" Martha said, her greeting enthusiastic. "How nice of you to come. Please sit down and sing with us."

Cal grinned at him. "It's about time you got here. We saved you a chair."

"Sorry I'm late." Jay cleared his throat and entered the kitchen. The empty chair was next to Sharon. *Perfect.* He smiled to himself as he sat down next to her. "Hi," he whispered. "I'm sorry I interrupted you."

"It's no problem." She gave him a little

shrug and then looked across the table at Alice, who seemed to give her a strange expression.

"We have *kichlin.*" Sharon pushed a plate of cookies toward him. "Would you like some milk?" She popped up from her chair. "I'll get you a glass."

"Oh, you don't have to —"

"I'm *froh* to." Sharon took another glass from a cabinet and brought it to the table. "Here you go."

"*Danki.*" He poured himself some milk. "You sounded amazing."

She waved off the compliment. "I lost my place . . ."

Had she been about to say more? That she lost her place when she saw him? Maybe she felt the same growing attraction between them he did. Was it even possible for her to care for him after being just his friend nearly her whole life?

"Should we start over? Or should we try a different hymn?" Alice asked.

"Have you sung 'Peace Like a River' yet?" Jay asked.

Sharon turned and blessed him with a sweet smile. "Oh. One of my favorites."

"Mine too." He returned her smile, and he was certain something special passed between them. He felt the sudden urge to ask her if she'd like a ride home so they could talk alone.

"Great," Alice said before she gave them the first note. It was a blessing so many of his friends had perfect pitch.

Everyone joined her as Martha nodded her head along with the beat. He discreetly leaned a little closer to Sharon and enjoyed the lovely lilt of her voice.

They sang and talked with Martha until it was close to suppertime, when Sharon stood and started gathering glasses and plates. "We'll clean up before we leave, Martha."

Alice scooped up the napkins and utensils, and Darlene lifted the plate, now empty of cookies. Soon all three of them were at work.

Martha pushed back her chair, and both Jay and Cal jumped up to help her as she stood. Andrew handed her the cane. Then Martha looked up at Jay and patted his cheek with a frail hand. "I appreciate that you all came out to see me today."

"It was Sharon's idea." When Sharon turned from the sink and gave him a shy smile, warmth seemed to rise from some new place in his heart.

"May we make supper for you before we leave?" Darlene made the offer as she dried a plate Sharon handed her.

"No, *danki.*" Martha shook her head and

leaned against the counter. "*Mei sohn* and his family insist I share meals with them." A smile broke out on her lips. "I suppose they're afraid I'll leave the burner on under a pot and burn down the *haus.*"

Jay and his friends laughed.

"They keep asking me to move in with them, too, but I enjoy my privacy here."

When the kitchen was clean, they told Martha good night and then filed outside.

Jay turned to Sharon. "Could I give you a ride home?"

Her pretty eyes widened as she nodded. "That would be nice."

Alice sidled up to them. "Could I ride with you, too, Jay? Since my farm is beside hers?"

"Oh, of course." Disappointment threatened to strangle his excitement, but he managed to keep his expression pleasant.

"Have a *gut* week at the store." Cal patted Jay's back.

"You too. Sell a lot of horses for your *dat.*" Jay shook Andrew's hand. "I hope you have a *gut* week at your *dat*'s furniture store."

"*Danki.*"

Darlene asked Cal for a ride, then they both waved good-bye to everyone before climbing into his buggy.

When Jay slipped into his buggy with

Sharon on the bench seat beside him, his happiness returned. At least he could enjoy having her there during the short ride home.

"That was fun," Alice said from the back as Jay guided the horse toward the road. "I think Martha enjoyed it."

"I do too." Jay snuck a peek at Sharon, who was smiling as she gazed out the windshield. He took in her profile and tried to commit it to memory.

"I'm so glad we went," she finally said. "First, I just kept feeling like we needed to do something meaningful this afternoon, and then during the second sermon, it was as if God put the idea to sing for Martha in my heart." Sharon looked at Jay, and her expression grew sheepish. "Does that sound *gegisch*?"

He shook his head as he peered out at the rolling patchwork of green on the farms they passed. "I don't think it's silly at all."

"I don't either," Alice piped up from the back.

"Have you ever felt led to do something?" Sharon asked him.

"I have." Jay opened his mouth to share a story, but he was cut off by Alice.

"We need to do this more often," she said. "We should sing for more church members who are alone or *krank*."

Sharon turned around and nodded. "I agree."

Jay once again longed to be alone with Sharon so they could really talk. Maybe he could give her a ride home after church in two weeks. Or if they all sang for someone before then, he could ask her if she needed a ride and maybe ask Cal to give Alice a ride.

"How is your family doing?" Sharon's question broke through his thoughts. "I'm so sorry about your *daadi*."

"We're okay. We really miss him, but we're leaning on God's comfort. *Danki*."

"Of course," she said. "How's business at your *dat*'s lawn ornament store?"

He glanced toward her and found her looking at him rather intently. "It's *gut*. This is the start of our busy season, and we get a lot of rush orders too. We're already selling quite a few wishing wells and lighthouses. We had to hire more carpenters to keep up with the demand."

"That's exciting." Sharon tilted her head as if studying him. "Do you like making lawn ornaments?"

"I do." He nodded. "I like working with my hands."

"Do you think you'll take over the business someday?"

"I hope *Dat* will ask me to when he's ready to retire. After all, I'm his only *kind*, and of course, his only *sohn*. At least I hope he does instead of asking one of *mei onkels*."

"I'm sure he will." Sharon looked out the side window at the traffic rushing by.

He merged onto a road that would lead them to Alice's farm first. "How's your *dat*'s dairy farm doing?"

Sharon shrugged. "Well, I think it's fine. *Dat* seems *froh,* and he has two farmhands to help him."

"*Mei bruder* helps *mei dat* on our farm," Alice announced from behind them.

This time Jay was startled by Alice's voice. He'd almost forgotten he and Sharon weren't alone in the buggy.

Sharon's smile faded slightly. "I used to wonder if *mei dat* regrets not having a *sohn,* since Ruby Sue and I don't help with the farmwork as much as a *bu* would. We mostly help *Mamm* in the *haus.*"

Jay was struck by this comment. Could a father truly regret not having a child the "right" gender? Wasn't each child a gift from God?

"I doubt that," Alice said. "Your *dat* is so loving and patient. He adores you and Ruby Sue."

"I suppose." Sharon's smile returned. "Do you like being an only *kind*, Jay?"

He shrugged. "It's all I've ever known, so I'm not sure if I like it or dislike it. And I have a lot of cousins, so I'm never lonely, especially at family gatherings."

"That makes sense."

Jay spotted Alice's farm ahead of them and Sharon's in the distance. The ride with Sharon would soon end, and disappointment gripped him almost as hard as he gripped the reins. But at least he'd have a few minutes alone with her.

"*Danki* for the ride," Alice said as the buggy moved up her rock driveway.

"*Gern gschehne.*"

Jay halted the horse by her back porch, and Sharon jumped down from the buggy to help Alice make her way out. She gave her friend a quick hug. "See you soon."

Alice waved at Jay. "*Danki* again."

He waved back. "Have a *gut* week."

Sharon returned to the buggy as Alice climbed the back-porch steps. Then as his horse started down the driveway, Jay wished he could just keep riding around Bird-in-Hand with Sharon at his side.

"Do you have any special plans this week?" she asked as his horse *clip-clopped* up the street toward her father's farm.

"Just work, as far as I know."

"Oh." She looked at him and smiled again. "I appreciate the ride home."

"Anytime." He guided the horse into her driveway and halted it by the back porch before angling his body toward hers. "Let me know if you want to sing for another church member. I'd love to join you."

"Of course. We need your voice. Singing wouldn't be the same without you, Cal, and Andrew."

His smile wobbled at the mention of his friends' names. Did she like one of them? She'd accepted his offer for a ride, but maybe she would have preferred to ride home with Andrew or Cal. He ignored the threatening jealousy and concentrated on her sweet smile.

He was glad he did. Somehow, it felt as though it was meant for only him.

Sharon pushed the buggy door open and stepped out.

"Remember. Call me if you want to get together to sing again this week," he said.

"I will. Be safe going home." She pushed the door closed.

He lifted his hand in a wave and then started his journey home.

He smiled as he recalled his afternoon with Sharon and their friends. He could still hear her beautiful voice singing "How Great Thou Art." He would be so blessed to have her as his girlfriend. But how could he ask her for a new relationship after all these years? And what if she said no? That would make everything awkward between them.

The questions lingered in his mind as he stowed the horse and buggy in the barn before entering his house. He left his boots and hat in the mudroom and stepped into the kitchen, where his father sat at the table. His mother carried a warmed dish from the oven, and Jay's stomach gurgled with delight at the delicious smell he recognized as chicken and broccoli casserole — his favorite!

"How was your afternoon?" *Mamm* asked as she placed the casserole on a hot pad she'd placed on the table.

"It was *gut.*" Jay crossed to the sink and began washing his hands.

"What did you do?" *Dat* asked.

"Sorry I didn't tell you before we left." *I was distracted.* "We visited Martha Bontrager and sang for her." Jay turned to face his parents and leaned back against the counter as he dried his hands with a paper towel.

"I'm certain she enjoyed that," *Dat* said.

"She did." Jay tossed the paper towel into

the trash can and then took his usual seat, his parents on either end of the table.

After a silent prayer, *Dat* scooped a pile of casserole onto his plate and then scooted the dish to Jay.

"You made my favorite, *Mamm. Danki.*" Jay grinned at his mother before placing a mountain of casserole on his own plate.

"Of course. I told your *dat* it was your turn for a favorite meal. Didn't I, Moses?"

"That's right." *Dat* held up a forkful of casserole as if to toast her. "You're a *gut mamm,* Louise!"

Mamm grinned and reached for the casserole dish. "So I made it last night after you went upstairs to your room to read. I'm surprised you didn't smell it baking. Who all went to Martha's today?"

"The usual group — Cal, Andrew, Alice, Darlene, Sharon." He smiled as he said her name. "It was Sharon's idea to sing for Martha. I told her to let me know if she wants to sing for more members of our church district."

Dat pointed his fork at Jay. "That's a *wunderbaar* way to serve the Lord." His smile faltered a little. "Your *daadi* would be *froh* to hear you're helping others like that."

"*Ya,* I agree." Jay nodded. "And I hope we do it again soon."

In fact, he longed to spend a lot of time with Sharon while also serving the Lord.

Chapter Three

"So I'll cherish the old rugged cross . . ." Sharon sang the following afternoon as she hung towels on the clothesline that ran from the back porch to a tree near the pasture. "Till my trophies at last I lay down . . ."

Ruby Sue appeared beside her and joined in. "I will cling to the old rugged cross and exchange it someday for a crown."

Sharon smiled down at her sister, who shared the same light-brown hair and blue eyes Sharon had inherited from their mother. At eighteen, Ruby Sue had a beautiful, sweet voice that matched a kind and thoughtful personality and her pretty face. "You have a lovely singing voice."

"No, you do." Ruby Sue picked up another towel and handed it to Sharon. "I finished cleaning the bathrooms, and *Mamm* told me to see if you needed any help out here."

"*Danki.*" Sharon added the towel to the line.

"Did you have fun yesterday?"

Sharon took the towel from Ruby Sue. "I did." She bit back a smile as she recalled how handsome Jay had looked, how he'd sat beside her at Martha's house. And how he'd listened and smiled at her in the buggy during their ride home. She had to admit, she'd had to fight against being a little frustrated Alice was in the back seat.

Oh how she hoped she and Jay could be more than friends someday!

But she pushed those thoughts away and took the washcloth her sister held out to her. "And you played volleyball while we were at Martha's?"

Ruby Sue's face lit up. "*Ya*. At Gretchen Zook's *haus*. It was a combined event, so we met members of youth groups from Ronks and White Horse."

"How fun."

"It was." Ruby Sue picked up another washcloth and a hand towel. "I had a *gut* day. The weather was perfect."

The back door opened, then clicked shut as *Mamm* joined them. Although her hair had hints of gray, she still looked young and full of life to Sharon. "I meant to remind you earlier that we're hosting supper for another *Englisher* group Wednesday night. It's a large group — twenty."

Ruby Sue's eyes widened. "Twenty?"

"That is a lot," Sharon said.

"I know." *Mamm* smiled. "But these suppers are always a blessing to our family. I was so grateful when Tiffany from Lancaster Inn first called to ask if we would host a group of tourists who wanted to visit an Amish home. And I'm thankful we have an extra-large kitchen here to accommodate this larger group. Not only do I enjoy preparing meals for our guests but the extra money is a great help to your *dat,* even when the dairy farm is doing well."

"Are we going to make our usual barbecue meat loaf?" Ruby Sue asked.

Mamm shook her head. "No, I think we need to introduce more variety. You never know when a guest might decide to come back with *freinden* or family." Then she counted off what she wanted to make on her fingers. "I was thinking baked chicken, noodles, homemade *brot,* fruit salad, corn, and a crustless spinach quiche. For dessert we can make shoo-fly pie and whoopie pies. And, Sharon, you should make your *appeditlich* German chocolate *kuche.*"

"That sounds perfect." Sharon hung two more hand towels on the line and then looked out toward Alice's farm. "I think we'll need some extra help, though. Should

I invite Alice and Darlene to come?"

"That's a great idea," Ruby Sue chimed in. "Do you think the *Englishers* will ask *gegisch* questions again this time?"

Sharon rolled her eyes. "Like asking why we have a stove instead of using a fire pit in the backyard?"

"Or if we use deodorant!" Ruby Sue cackled. "I can't believe someone asked me that last month."

Mamm shook her head. "Well, if they want to know something, they'll ask." She headed for the door. "I'm going to start a shopping list. We'll have to get all our supplies for the supper tomorrow. You two finish the laundry and then start dusting."

"Okay, *Mamm,*" Sharon said as Ruby Sue handed her the last towel. "After we finish, I'll call Alice and Darlene. Hopefully they'll be free and willing to help us."

"It will be fun to have them here," her sister said.

"*Ya,* I think it will."

"Everything smells *appeditlich,*" Alice announced as she and Darlene strode into Sharon's kitchen late Wednesday afternoon.

"*Ya,* it does," Darlene said. "I hope you're going to save some of that *kuche* for us."

Sharon heaved a sigh of relief when she

looked up from the counter, where she was frosting her German chocolate cake. "I'm so glad you're both here. And we made enough food for the guests and us too. But it is possible this *kuche* will be gone. I'll make us another one soon."

"Put us to work." Alice gestured around the room. "What can we do?"

Mamm pointed to the utility room off the kitchen. "Ruby Sue, why don't you and the girls get the folding tables and chairs? Let's see . . . for twenty guests, we'll need four tables and, of course, enough chairs to supplement our regular kitchen chairs."

Sharon glanced at their wooden table, now shoved against one wall. That was where they set out most of the food before serving it.

The oven timer buzzed, and *Mamm* hurried over to turn it off and check the baked chicken. "Oh dear. We're running out of time. Our guests will be here soon."

"I'm almost done with the *kuche,* and then I'll help." Sharon spread the last of the coconut pecan frosting as her sister and friends returned with the tables and chairs.

The food was ready, and the tables were set, just as car engines rumbled into the driveway.

"Sharon," *Mamm* said. "You made a mess

of your apron. Go change."

Sharon glanced down at her black apron. Splotches of frosting dotted it. "Oh. I'll be right back."

She dashed upstairs and pulled off the dirty apron before covering her blue dress with a fresh one. She checked the mirror to make sure her prayer covering was straight and then hurried down the stairs to the kitchen, where her friends were carrying glasses to the tables.

"Welcome," *Mamm* said to two middle-aged couples, the first of the *Englishers* stepping into the kitchen from the mud-room. *Mamm* always had guests leave their outerwear near the back door. "We're so glad you're here today."

"What's next?" Sharon asked Ruby Sue.

"Here." Her sister handed her a crystal pitcher of water. "Fill the glasses on that far table and work your way toward me. I'll start here."

As Sharon carried the pitcher to the table, she smiled at a couple who looked to be in their late twenties. "How are you today?"

"We're fine," the man said.

The woman gave her a wide smile. "We were so excited when the inn manager told us we could eat in an authentic Amish home. This is such a treat for us. And the food smells delicious."

"Thank you. I hope you enjoy it." Sharon finished filling the glasses and then stood by the counter with her sister and friends as all the guests took seats. Several folks looked to be in their forties, and a few looked to be in their sixties or seventies.

When everyone was seated, *Mamm* stood in front of the tables. "Good evening. I'm so glad you could all join us for supper tonight." *Mamm*'s smile was bright as she clasped her hands together. "Let's start by introducing ourselves. My name is Feenie, and these" — she gestured toward Sharon and Ruby Sue — "are my daughters, Sharon and Ruby Sue." Then she swung a hand toward Sharon's friends. "And we're grateful our friends Alice and Darlene are here to help us serve. Now, tell us where you're from and if it's your first time visiting an Amish home." She pointed to the first table to the left. "Why don't you start?"

A gentleman with dark skin and horn-rimmed glasses shifted in his seat. "I'm Bob Davenport, and this is my wife, Samantha." He nodded toward a petite woman wearing a pink sweater beside him. "We're from Philadelphia, and this is our first time visiting any Amish home."

"And we're excited to be here and taste

that food," Samantha chimed in with a husky voice. "It smells divine."

A few of the other guests nodded in agreement, and Sharon shared a smile with Alice. Then she leaned back against the counter while the other guests introduced themselves and shared their Amish Country experiences.

When everyone had been heard, *Mamm* said, "Let's say a prayer, and then we'll start serving the meal." She bowed her head, and before she closed her own eyes, Sharon saw that all the guests had followed suit.

"Dear Lord, thank you for bringing our new friends here today to share this meal with us. We ask you to bless this food to the nourishment of our bodies. And please be with our guests as they make their way back to the inn tonight. In Jesus' holy name, amen."

When *Mamm* lifted her head, she said, "We'll now serve your meal, starting with a fruit salad."

Sharon and the others each delivered a bowl of fruit salad to a table. Once that course was finished, they followed with the crustless spinach quiche, bread, chicken, and noodles. As she refilled glasses during the meal, always asking if she could bring more food, Sharon chatted with the guests.

When the main courses had been consumed, they cleared the tables and delivered slices of the German chocolate cake and shoo-fly pie as well as whoopie pies, along with mugs of coffee.

Mamm pulled a stool over to the tables and sat down as the guests began eating. "While you enjoy your dessert, I'll be happy to answer any questions you have about our life here."

Sharon and Alice joined Ruby Sue and Darlene at the sink, where Ruby Sue had already filled the sink with soap and water and lowered soiled dishes, quietly scraped first out of earshot.

"How long have you lived here?" a young man seated in the back asked.

Mamm sat up straighter. "This dairy farm has been in my husband's family for four generations. We moved here when we were married, and his parents moved to a small house on his sister's farm, which is only about a mile away."

"Is it true that the Amish don't build churches?" another woman asked.

"That is true. We take turns worshipping in each other's homes or barns every other week."

"I've heard many Amish families have ten or more children." The woman in the pink

49

sweater looked at Sharon and Ruby Sue. Sharon thought about her closest friends' families as her mother answered that some families do, but many do not. God provided what he saw best.

"Do you really not have any electricity? Or do you have secret light switches everywhere?" One of the older men asked this question as he looked around at the several gas lamps dotting the kitchen.

Ruby Sue spun to face Sharon, who bit back a smile.

"Some Amish have solar-powered lights, but we don't have any on our farm." *Mamm* kept a relaxed smile on her face.

"I've seen some reality shows on television about the Amish, and they feature youth going through a running around time," a middle-aged man with a bulbous nose and a gruff voice began. "I'd like to ask about that."

Sharon mustered all her strength to prevent a groan from escaping her lips. She looked at her mother, who continued to give the man a serene smile.

"What do you want to know?" *Mamm* asked.

"Is it true that some Amish youth go wild?"

Sharon's body began to shudder with a

50

mixture of frustration and disgust.

The man waved his arms around widely. "The Amish on that show act so pious, but then their youth try drugs and all sorts of terrible things before they join the church, like —"

"Why don't we sing a song for you?" Sharon said loudly, determined to interrupt his inappropriate and rude tirade. She felt all the eyes in the room turn to her as she stepped to her mother's side.

Sharon cleared her throat and looked at Alice, whose eyebrows were raised as she stared at her. "How about one of my favorites? It's called 'Farther Along.' " After clearing her throat, she began the first line and nodded at her friends and Ruby Sue, hoping they'd join her.

Thankfully, Alice and Darlene came closer and began singing in near perfect harmony. Sharon noticed the guests listened intently, but then she closed her eyes and allowed the Holy Spirit to fill her. She felt she was not only singing of God's blessings but sharing the gospel.

When the song ended, the guests smiled and applauded, and a fresh kind of happiness rolled through her. She glanced at her mother, who grinned and nodded encouragement.

"Why don't we all sing a song together?" Sharon asked. "How about 'Jesus Loves Me'? Do you know that one?" She began the song, and when almost everyone joined in — including the rude man — the room filled with their voices. Relief loosened the frustrated knots in Sharon's shoulders. This seemed to be the perfect way to handle the large crowd — and avoid disrespectful questions about her community at the same time!

"Thank you again," Sharon called as the last guest stepped onto the back porch. Then once the door clicked shut behind them, she left the mudroom and dropped into the closest kitchen chair. "Thank goodness it's over."

Ruby Sue sat down beside her. "I think you're brilliant, Sharon."

"What do you mean?"

"The way you distracted that rude man was amazing." Her younger sister beamed.

"I agree," *Mamm* called from the stove, where she was removing the leftover chicken and noodles from where she'd kept them warm in the oven.

Darlene touched Sharon's shoulder. "It was perfect. You caught everyone off guard when you started singing. They seemed surprised at first, but then they loved it. I even saw a few of the women join in when we sang 'Farther Along.' "

"And they all seemed to enjoy singing 'Jesus Loves Me,' " Alice added.

Sharon sat up straighter. "I was afraid you'd think I was *narrisch,* but I couldn't stand to hear that man talk about our community that way. Surely *Englishers* know those television shows aren't real. No true Plain person would participate in that."

"You did the right thing," Ruby Sue said. "You not only brought the conversation back to a good place but to Jesus and the gospel."

"You did." *Mamm* passed out clean plates and utensils, all they needed to enjoy a buffet once the guests were on their way back to the inn. "Let's eat and then finish cleaning so we can get some rest."

"Is it safe to come in? I'm starving," *Dat* joked as he stepped into the kitchen. At fifty, he had deep-blue eyes lined with wrinkles and dark-brown hair streaked with gray. Sharon had always admired his easy sense of humor and loud, boisterous laugh.

"You missed all the fun," Ruby Sue said as *Mamm* handed him a plate too. "One of the guests asked an inappropriate question, and Sharon redirected the conversation by starting a sing-along."

"Really?" *Dat* gave Sharon a wide smile. "*Gut* for you. What a great idea."

"*Danki, Dat.*"

After they'd all eaten, *Dat* said, "I'll help with the chairs." He grabbed an armload of them from Darlene and carried them to the utility room.

Once all the work was done, Sharon walked Darlene and Alice outside to meet Darlene's driver.

"*Danki* for helping tonight. You were a blessing."

Sharon hugged them and gave each one an envelope. They'd balked when *Mamm* first mentioned paying them for their help. But arguing with Feenie Lambert was useless.

"It was fun," Darlene said.

"Let us know the next time you have a large crowd," Alice said.

Sharon waved as Darlene's driver backed out of the driveway, and Alice started down the street with a flashlight guiding her way.

When Sharon stepped back into the kitchen, she found her parents and sister sitting at the table now again in the center of the room. "When is the next supper?"

"Next Friday," *Mamm* said.

Sharon smiled as she imagined what the

evening would be like. These suppers were a lot of hard work, and they never knew how a guest might behave, but she found herself looking forward to a new opportunity — singing. After they ate, her mother could field their questions like she always did, but then Sharon could lead the group in another sing-along. She'd choose selections she thought might be familiar to them.

Next Friday couldn't arrive soon enough!

Shouts and cheers echoed as a group of young people gathered around a ping-pong table in Andrew's family barn on Sunday afternoon. The sweet scent of rain mixed with hay filled the air and wafted over Jay.

He turned toward the crowd just as Cal hit the ball, and it shot up in the air and then landed on the other side of the barn. Laughter exploded as Cal took a dramatic bow.

"Cal always swings the paddle too hard," he said. Then he turned to Sharon, who sat next to him on a bench.

She chuckled, and her face lit up with a gorgeous smile.

Jay angled his body toward her. "Where's Darlene today?"

"Her *mamm* wasn't feeling well again today, and Darlene thought she should stay home."

"I'm sorry to hear that."

"*Ya,* me too. I've been praying for them. I've offered help, but Darlene insists her *mamm* doesn't want anyone but family in the house. That leaves all the work three women used to do to only two — Darlene and Biena. To say nothing of their supporting Al in the family's dry goods store."

They sat in silence for a few moments as he wondered what to say next.

"How was your week?" he finally said.

He had been delighted when Sharon followed him to the bench and sat down beside him. He'd spent the past week thinking of her, even while building lawn ornaments in his father's store. He'd hoped she'd call and suggest they sing for a member of their church district some weekday evening, but that call never came.

Yet his hope was ignited when Andrew suggested he host a youth gathering to play games today. Since it was an off Sunday without a church service, they had all met in the early afternoon for a picnic lunch. And when the light rain started, they set up the ping-pong tables in the barn.

Now Jay couldn't take his eyes off Sharon's beautiful face. He was mesmerized.

"I had a *gut* week." She picked up her cup of iced tea and took a sip. "I had my usual chores to do, of course." She shrugged. "You know — laundry, cleaning, sewing. And we hosted another group of *Englishers* Wednesday night. Darlene and Alice helped us since the group was so large."

"Really?" He rested his arm on the back of the bench. When his hand brushed her shoulder, he was almost certain he felt her shiver. "What did you serve?"

"Let's see . . ." She looked adorable as she glanced up at the ceiling. "We made baked chicken, noodles, *brot,* fruit salad, corn, and a crustless spinach quiche. Then for dessert we offered shoofly pie, German chocolate *kuche,* and whoopie pies."

"German chocolate *kuche.*" He rested his hands over his heart and gave a dramatic sigh. "Tell me it had coconut pecan frosting."

"It did. That's how I always make it." She nodded, and the ties to her prayer covering bounced on her slight shoulders. Then she tilted her head. "Let me guess. That's your favorite."

"No." He held up his index finger. "It's my *absolute* favorite. There's a difference."

Her smile grew coy. "Are you asking me to make you a German chocolate *kuche*?"

"Maybe."

She laughed and swatted his shoulder. "I'll

make you one. You just have to ask."

"Okay." He folded his hands as if to beg. "Sharon, would you please make me one of your amazing German chocolate *kuche*?"

"*Ya,* I will." She laughed again, and he relished the sweet sound. "Now, tell me about *your* week."

He looked down at his lap and then back up at her. "I built quite a few big wooden planters. And a few wagons too. The days were long, but it's *gut* for business, right?"

"Hey, Jay!" Cal called. "Are you going to sit there all day? Or are you going to play?"

Jay bit his lower lip to suppress a frown. He'd rather talk to Sharon all day, but he couldn't admit that out loud. At least, not yet. If he seemed too eager, he'd run the risk of scaring her away.

He turned to her. "Do you want to play ping-pong?"

She shrugged. "Sure."

"Great." Jay stood and then waited for Sharon to approach the ping-pong table first.

With a smirk, Cal tossed Jay a paddle. "Let's see how *gut* you are."

Jay nodded. "Let's go, Cal."

The afternoon flew by as Jay enjoyed playing several ping-pong games, especially when Sharon was his partner. When it was time to go, he helped Andrew stow the tables and then joined Sharon where she stood with Alice and Cal at the entrance to the barn. Glancing outside, he could see the rain had stopped, but large, gray clouds still clogged the sky.

Jay had been eager to ask Sharon if he could give her a ride home, but he hadn't found the right moment all day. Now was the time to ask.

"Sharon," he began, and she turned toward him. "Would you like a ride home?"

"Oh." She glanced at Alice and then back at Jay. "I just asked for a ride with Cal. He not only brought Alice and me today but he's already taking Alice home. You know how close together our farms are."

He forced a smile. "That makes sense. I guess I'll see you soon, then."

"*Ya.* I hope so. I'll have to get you that German chocolate *kuche.*"

"Right." His heart warmed at her sweet smile. "Take care."

Jay waved good-bye to his friends and then headed for his horse and buggy.

As he started his trek home, he found himself stuck on the idea of asking Sharon's father for permission to date her. Excitement thrummed through him as he imagined beginning the journey as a couple.

She'd seemed content to talk with him today, and she'd offered to make him a cake, but would she give her old friend a chance at something more than friendship?

"You can just drop me off here," Sharon said as Cal guided his horse up Alice's driveway. "I don't mind walking home."

"All right." He halted the horse at the top of the driveway.

"*Danki* for the ride." Alice hopped out of the buggy and Sharon climbed out of the back.

"Thanks, Cal." Sharon waved at him.

"See you all soon." Cal winked and then guided his horse back to the road.

Sharon started down the driveway. "Have a *gut* —"

"Wait a minute." Alice grabbed her arm and pulled her back. "Is there something you're not telling me?"

Sharon squinted her eyes. "What are you talking about? You know I tell you everything."

"Uh-huh." Alice folded her arms over her chest as she gave her a look of disbelief. "You and Jay were practically glued together today. When did he ask your *dat*'s permission to date you?"

"What?" Sharon held up her hands. "No,

no, no. We're not dating. Besides, I doubt he sees me as anything more than a *freind.*" *Though I'm hoping that could change.*

Alice snorted. "Please. I'm not blind. It's obvious he likes you."

Sharon dropped her arms.

"I can tell when you're analyzing, Sharon. What's on your mind?"

"Why do you think Jay would want to date me after knowing me as only a *freind* for so long?"

"Do you like him?"

Sharon nodded. She might as well admit it. "Lately, I've realized I do. But, again, why would he like me after all this time?"

"Why not?" Alice gestured at her. "You're *schee* and sweet. And you know each other well. It actually makes sense. I'm sure he's going to ask to date you. If you can imagine him as more than a *freind* now, why couldn't he imagine you the same way?"

Sharon swallowed a happy squeal at the thought. "I hope you're right."

"You let me know when he asks." Alice gave her a quick hug. "I'm excited for you. Have a *gut* week."

"You too." As Sharon started down the road toward her house, she imagined being Jay's girlfriend, and her stomach fluttered. If only Alice were right in her assessment of

Jay's behavior. Sharon prayed she was, but wouldn't that be too good to be true?

Jay lost himself in images of Sharon's pretty face as he sanded pieces of a lawn windmill in his father's workshop two days later. The familiar sweet scent of wood and stain filled his senses as hammers banged, saw blades whirred, and air compressors hummed.

He smiled to himself, unable to stop thinking about his conversation with Sharon at Andrew's gathering. He had to work up the courage to ask her father's permission to date her on Sunday after church. He couldn't wait any longer —

"Does that piece of wood you're staring at hold the answers to your most complicated problems?"

"Huh?" Jay dropped his sanding block and turned to face Cal, who was grinning. "What are you doing here?"

Cal sat down on a stool. "I was in the area running errands and thought I'd stop by. So . . . tell me. What's on your mind?" He lifted a fresh bottle of water from Jay's toolbox and opened it.

Jay shrugged and then opened a bottle of water too. "Nothing. We're just busy." He gestured around the shop crowded with carpenters. "As you can see."

Cal eyed him with suspicion. "Nice try."

Jay pulled up another stool and sat. He fingered his bottle of water, which crinkled in protest as he debated being honest with his best friend.

"It must be *gut* if you can't find the words." Cal's signature grin was back.

"Fine." Jay sat up straighter and cleared his throat. "Do you think Sharon would date me if her father gave me permission to ask her?"

Cal blinked, then shook his head as if Jay had just slapped him. "You want to date Sharon?"

"Does that come as a surprise?"

"Well, you've known her forever. Why are you suddenly interested in her as more than a *freind*?"

"Why not?" Jay set his bottle on his workbench. "She's *schee,* sweet, easy to talk to, and a great *freind.* True, I hadn't thought of her as more than a *freind* until just recently. She just seems different now."

"Sharon is the same *maedel* she's always been." Cal gave him a knowing look. "Maybe she's not different. Maybe you are."

"Wow." Jay laughed. "You've become quite the philosopher."

Cal shrugged as he drank more water.

"I've always been one, but you never noticed."

"Do you think she'd go out with me?"

"I think so. You two were getting along well at Andrew's on Sunday."

"That means you noticed we were talking more."

"I did. But the only way to find out if she likes you that way is to ask her." He finished the water and tossed the bottle into a nearby trash can. "Talk to her *dat* if you're serious about asking her out."

"Of course I will. I would never go against our community's rules." Jay's thoughts turned to his grandfather. "*Mei daadi* told me it's important we keep our traditions and pass them on to the next generation. I'll never do anything that would make him ashamed of me."

Cal stood. "Well, I'd better get going before *mei dat* thinks I ran off to Florida for the spring." He shook Jay's hand. "I'll see you Sunday. Keep me posted about you and Sharon."

"Keep it a secret just in case she says no."

"Nah. I'll rent a billboard out on Old Philadelphia Pike. Then everyone will know." Cal gave a wink. "See ya."

Jay chuckled as his friend walked toward

the showroom. He could always count on Cal to make him laugh.

"Welcome to our home. We're so glad you came this evening," Sharon told the group of six guests as they sat at two folding tables Friday evening. Her mother had suggested Sharon be their host for the evening.

Sharon had spent the day helping clean and prepare for tonight's guests, all the while imagining singing hymns for this group. She hoped they would want to join in too. She felt as though her soul over-flowed with happiness when she sang. Not only did it put her in a great mood but it was her favorite way to pass time when she took care of chores. It made any task fun, even scrubbing floors and washing windows.

"Let's go around the room so you can introduce yourselves and tell us if you've visited an Amish home before," Sharon said, following her mother's lead.

After the *Englishers* introduced them-selves, Sharon, Ruby Sue, and *Mamm* all served the meal — barbecue meat loaf, green bean casserole, homemade bread, a lettuce salad, and Jell-O salad. Then they brought out slices of carrot cake and red velvet cake before delivering mugs of coffee.

"Normally we answer questions now, but

I was wondering if anyone would like to sing hymns first," Sharon said.

Mamm shot her a surprised look.

"Oh, that would be nice." A young woman with a pierced eyebrow said.

"Great." Sharon sat down on a stool. "What songs do you like?" she asked her.

"How about 'This Little Light of Mine'?"

"I love that one too," Sharon said, then began to sing. "This little light of mine . . ." Her heart danced with bliss as nearly everyone joined in.

After they'd sung two more songs, the guests finished their desserts, asked a few questions, and then said good night.

"How did it go?" *Dat* asked when he walked in from the family room.

Mamm looked over her shoulder. "It went well."

"Did you hear? Sharon led another sing-along," Ruby Sue announced as she gathered dishes.

"Did you, now?" *Dat* asked. "I guess I was out in the barn."

"*Ya,* I did." Sharon lifted a serving platter. "It was fun, but I think I like singing to people with *mei freinden* more." She looked at Ruby Sue. "Although we could sing a duet when we host a supper."

"Oh. No. I'd be too *naerfich.*"

"Why do you like singing with other people better?" *Mamm* asked.

"It's as if we're making a bigger impact then. And I love feeling a part of a community when I sing with a group."

Mamm and *Dat* shared a look.

"What did that look mean?" Sharon asked as concern skittered through her. Had she said something wrong?

"It means we're impressed by your commitment to serve the Lord with your gift of singing — and by encouraging your *freinden* to do the same," *Dat* said.

Sharon smiled. "Will you allow me to invite them to sing with me at these suppers, then?"

Dat looked at *Mamm,* and they both nodded.

"That's *wunderbaar.*" Sharon clapped her hands. "I can't wait to tell them about it on Sunday."

CHAPTER FIVE

Standing in the Glick family barn after the church service, Jay shoved his hands in his pockets. Then he took them out and rubbed his chin as he watched Ira Lambert talking to Robert Glick.

Conversations swirled around him as the other men of their congregation began converting benches into tables for the noon meal. Jay had spent most of the service envisioning himself asking Ira's permission to date Sharon. In each scenario, Jay was cool and confident, knowing exactly what to say.

But now his mind had drawn a blank. He had no idea what to say as his confidence deflated like a balloon.

Taking a deep breath, he forced his legs to move forward and approached Ira and Robert.

Ira finished what he was saying and then turned to him. "Hi, Jay. How are you?"

"I'm well. Hi, Robert." Robert nodded at Jay and then excused himself.

Jay pointed to the barn door. "Could I talk to you in private?"

"Of course." Ira headed outside with Jay, and a cool spring breeze moved over them. "It's a *schee* day, isn't it? Not a cloud in the sky."

"It is." Jay jammed his shaky hands into his pockets again and tried to recall the speech he'd rehearsed in his mind. What had he been going to say?

"What do you need?" Ira's smile was so easy and friendly. Sharon had indeed inherited her father's sunny personality.

"I want to discuss Sharon with you."

"Oh?"

Jay swallowed. "I've known her since I was a little *bu,* and she's always been *mei freind.* Lately, though, I've realized just how special she is, and I think God is leading me toward her in a new way. She's a *wunderbaar maedel.*"

When Jay heard a slight tremble in his voice, he paused to clear his throat. "What I'm saying is I want to get to know her better. May I have your permission to date her? I promise I'll always treat her with respect." He pressed his lips together as Ira's eyebrows careened toward his thinning hairline,

70

then a smile slowly dawned on his face.

"I'm *froh* to give you permission to date my Sharon." Ira's expression was warm. "I have a feeling she'll be *froh* too."

"*Danki,* Ira." Jay shook his hand as relief flooded through him.

Ira patted his shoulder. "Now, you go ask her."

Jay turned and spotted Sharon and Alice carrying platters of food toward the barn. Sharon looked so beautiful in that light-blue dress that always complemented her eyes, and her smile was as bright and welcoming as the azure sky.

Sharon was everything he'd ever longed for in a girlfriend. But was Ira right? Would she give him a chance to be more than a friend?

His shoulders tightened. He'd have to ask the Lord to not only give him the courage to ask Sharon to be his girlfriend but grant him the right words.

Then, silently, he prayed.

Sharon left the Glicks' kitchen with Alice and Darlene after they finished helping with cleanup. Her pulse ticked up when she spotted Jay close by, standing by his buggy with Cal and Andrew. He looked so handsome dressed in his black Sunday suit and his

71

crisp, white dress shirt and black vest. The sun beating down on his head gave his light-brown hair a golden hue and made his brown eyes seem warmer. She smoothed her hands down her white apron and hoped she looked presentable.

"So what are we going to do today?" Cal asked as they approached.

Alice and Darlene turned toward Sharon as if she were the activity director for their friend group. Perhaps she was.

"I heard a group is playing games over at Henry Lapp's *haus,* but could we go sing for Earl Yoder instead? He's been very *krank* with pneumonia, but *mei mamm* heard he's starting to feel better. He might appreciate a visit." Sharon met Jay's gaze, and when he smiled, her body relaxed.

"Visiting Earl is a great idea," Jay said, his tone warm as his eyes stayed fixed on hers.

Sharon felt captured in his gaze, just as if they were standing alone. She longed to discover what was rolling through his mind as his eyes intensely bore into hers.

"What are we waiting for?" Alice announced, breaking through Sharon's thoughts. "Let's go. Earl lives only a few blocks away."

"Sharon, will you ride with me?" The direct manner he'd asked the question caught her off guard.

"Ya," she said. "I'd like that."

"Great." He opened the passenger side door of his buggy, and she climbed in.

She glanced at Alice, who winked at her before directing Darlene toward Cal's buggy.

In a few moments, Jay sat beside her as he led his horse toward the road. She sat up straight and once again smoothed her hands over her apron and dress as she tried to think of something to say. She was finally alone with Jay, but she was also tongue-tied. She glanced at his handsome profile and took in the muscle flexing in his jaw. Was he upset or nervous?

She settled back in the seat and crossed her arms over her waist. "Was it still busy at the shop this week?"

"Ya." He kept his eyes on the road as he spoke. "Were you busy this week too?"

"I was." She angled her body toward his. "We hosted another supper at our *haus* for *Englishers.*"

"Oh? How did that go?"

"It went well. I started something new. Instead of answering their *gegisch* questions, at least right away, I led them in singing songs. I did that last week, and it went well. So I tried it again."

He didn't respond. It was as if he were distracted by something. But what?

Quiet fell between them, and the *clip-clop* of the horse's hooves, whirr of the buggy wheels, and hum of the passing traffic filled the buggy.

Sharon glanced at Jay again and found him gripping the reins with such force that his knuckles were white. She took a trembling breath and then searched for the nerve to ask him what was going on.

"Is everything all right, Jay?" She'd managed to keep her voice steady — but barely.

"Ya." He sounded slightly hoarse as he kept looking straight ahead. "I talked to your *dat* earlier."

"You did?" She blinked as confusion took hold. "Why?"

His Adam's apple bobbed as he continued to study the road ahead. "I wanted to ask his permission." He paused and licked his lips. "I was wondering if I could date you."

Sharon's mouth dropped open. Had she heard him correctly? Or had she just imagined those words? Her heart seemed to trip over itself before exploding into a gallop. She wanted to speak, but she couldn't find the words, and silence spread between them.

Jay halted the horse at a red light and then turned toward her, his expression looking

74

pained. "That was a mistake. I completely misread how you feel about me. I'm sorry." He held up his hand. "Forget what I just said, and let's just be *freinden*. I didn't want to make you feel uncomfortable or —"

"No, no, no!" She shook her head. "You're misunderstanding. I'm just stunned. I didn't think you thought of me that way, that you would want to date me. I just wanted to believe you would."

His expression warmed as his shoulders visibly relaxed. He reached over and took her hand in his, and she relished the feel of his skin against hers.

"Sharon, you've always been a *gut freind,* but lately I've seen you in a different light. And I find myself craving more than friendship with you. I'd be honored if you'd be my girlfriend."

"Actually, I'm the one who'd be honored."

His lips lifted in a smile. "Is that a *ya?*"

"Ya."

"Danki." He moved his thumb over the back of her hand, and she quivered at the intimate touch.

A car horn tooted behind them, alerting Jay that the light had turned green.

"Whoops." He gave a little laugh as he guided his horse through the intersection.

Sharon couldn't stop smiling as they

continued their short journey to the Yoder farm.

When they arrived, Sharon and Jay met their friends by the front porch before climbing the steps and knocking on the screen door.

Earl's wife appeared. Wearing thick glasses and with a gap between her front teeth, Miriam had a friendly expression. Sharon guessed she was in her midfifties.

"Hello there. What brings you here today?"

Sharon glanced at Alice, who gave her a nod as if asking her to speak for them.

"We heard Earl is better but still recovering, and we wondered if we could sing for him."

Miriam's smile widened. "How lovely. Just yesterday he was saying he'd enjoy some visitors." She beckoned them into the house. "Join us. I made a cheesecake this week, and I'd love to share it with you."

Jay held the door open, and Sharon followed Miriam into the family room. Earl sat in a recliner, covered in a blue-and-gray quilt with a Lonestar pattern. He looked weak, and his light eyes were rimmed with dark circles.

"Earl, weren't you just saying you were hoping for some company?" Miriam asked as she led them all to his side. "Well, here you go. Some nice young folks want to sing for you."

"Hi, Earl." Sharon gave him a wave as she stepped closer to the recliner. "We hope to cheer you up."

Earl raised a hand and gave a tentative smile to Sharon and her friends. "How nice to see you all."

"How are you feeling?" Jay shook Earl's hand.

"A little better." Earl coughed, and it sounded as if it rattled up from deep in his chest. "The medicine seems to be working. I'm not wheezing as much."

"I'll put on *kaffi* and get the *kuche* ready," Miriam said.

"Do you need help?" Sharon asked.

"No, no." Miriam waved her off. "You all came here to sing, not work in the kitchen."

"What should we sing first?" Darlene looked at Sharon.

Sharon turned to Jay for guidance. "What do you think?"

Jay studied her for a moment and then said, "I enjoyed hearing you sing the first verse of 'How Great Thou Art' as a solo for Martha."

"We all did," Cal said.

"Okay." Sharon closed her eyes as the

77

words came to her, and then she began to sing.

She opened her eyes when her friends joined in for the second verse, and then she smiled. What lovely harmony they created. She looked at Jay and found him watching her as he sang along. Her chest fluttered, recalling how nervous he'd seemed mere minutes before.

She was Jay Smoker's girlfriend. It still felt too good to be true!

They sang four more hymns for Earl and Miriam before they joined Miriam in the kitchen for cheesecake and coffee.

After visiting for a while, they thanked her for the treat and said good-bye to Earl, then headed out to the waiting horses and buggies. Jay, Andrew, and Cal stopped to talk by Cal's buggy while Sharon and Alice made their way to Jay's buggy.

"That was fun," Darlene said as she joined them.

"It was." Alice gave Sharon a suspicious smile. "Now update us on what's going on with you and Jay."

Sharon peeked at Jay and found him deep in conversation. She turned back to her friends and kept her voice low. "On our way here, Jay asked me to be his girlfriend."

Darlene gasped as Alice grabbed Sharon's

arm and squealed.

"That's *wunderbaar!*" Alice said.

"Shh!" Sharon looked at the guys and found them still talking. "I don't want him to hear us gushing."

"I'm so *froh* for you." Darlene gave her a quick hug. "You two will be great together."

"Danki." Sharon grinned. "I'm really excited."

Alice gave her a knowing expression. "I'm not surprised." Then she smiled. "Darlene is right. You two will be great together."

Jay strode over to them. "Are you ready to go?"

"Ya." Sharon snapped her fingers when she recalled what she'd wanted to ask them all. "On Friday we're hosting another supper for a group of *Englishers.* I was wondering if you would all come and help me sing for them."

"That would be fun. I'll even come early to help. I'll ask *mei mamm* to be sure I'm free," Alice said.

Darlene gave a tentative smile. "I'd love to, but I'll have to see how *mei mamm* is doing."

"I'll check my schedule," Cal said.

Andrew nodded. "I'll do the same."

"Great." Sharon turned to Jay, who wore an unreadable expression. "Do you think you can come?"

He hesitated for a moment, and then he said, "We can talk about it in the buggy."

"Okay." She nodded, but she was curious. Then she turned to her friends. "I'll see you all soon. Be careful going home."

They all said good-bye before climbing into the buggies and heading their separate ways.

"Did you enjoy singing for Earl?" Sharon asked as Jay's horse and buggy moved down the street.

"I did." Jay nodded as he glanced at her, then cleared his throat. "So tell me . . . Why do you sing for *Englishers*?"

She paused, surprised by the question. "Because I love singing, and it's a way to share the gospel." She took in his serious expression. "Does that bother you? You didn't say anything earlier when I told you about it."

He stared out the windshield as she admired his handsome profile.

"I . . . I guess I didn't hear you. I was working up the courage to ask you to be my girlfriend." He smiled, but his smile quickly faded. "I'm just not sure it's a *gut* idea to sing for them."

"Why wouldn't it be?"

He gave a half shrug, lifting one shoulder.

"I just feel our singing is for our community, not something we should share."

She blinked as his words rolled around in her mind. She opened her mouth to protest his words but then pressed her lips together. He was entitled to his opinion, even if she didn't understand it.

"You told me before that you serve baked chicken at these meals you host," Jay said. "What else do you like to serve?"

He was changing the subject. Maybe he just needed some time to think over her request. Surely he'd see her point and come around.

"Barbecue meat loaf, or sometimes a casserole or roast beef . . ." Sharon continued talking about menus as he maneuvered his buggy toward her house. But disappointment over what he'd said weighed on her shoulders.

Jay halted the horse near her back porch and then turned to her. "May I walk you to the door?"

"That would be nice."

They climbed out of the buggy, and when he threaded his fingers in hers, goose bumps traveled up her arm.

Once they reached the back door, he smiled down at her. "I had a nice afternoon." He ran his finger down her cheek.

"I did too."

He leaned down, and her breath stalled in her lungs. She was about to receive her first kiss! Jay's lips brushed her cheek, and she sucked in a breath at the brief contact.

"I'll see you soon," he whispered in her ear, sending shivers cascading down her back.

"Good night, Jay." The words came in a rush.

He gave her hand a gentle squeeze before loping down the steps.

Soon his horse and buggy were headed toward the road, and she leaned back against the doorjamb and released an excited yelp. She couldn't be more thrilled as happiness rained down on her.

CHAPTER SIX

"My friends and I would like to sing for you while you enjoy your dessert," Sharon said as she stood in front of the group of sixteen *Englishers* Friday evening. They were eating either peanut butter or lemon meringue pie — or a slice of both.

Sharon had been excited when her mother told her another large group was coming, and the meal had gone almost perfectly. Andrew and Cal arrived early enough to set up the tables and chairs while Alice and Darlene helped finish preparing the meal.

They were ready for the guests when they came around five o'clock. Each of the visitors had been pleasant and showered them with compliments. The roast beef, baked potatoes, corn, egg noodles, and salad had all been a hit. So had their desserts.

But disappointment nipped at Sharon. Something was missing.

Jay hadn't joined them. He'd stopped by

to see her earlier in the week, but he didn't mention the supper tonight, and neither had she. Surely their discussion about singing for *Englishers* wouldn't have kept him away.

"What are you going to sing?" Ruby Sue asked, pulling Sharon from her thoughts.

Sharon turned to her sister. "What do you suggest?"

Ruby Sue touched her chin. "How about 'Take My Hand, Precious Lord'? Your *freinden* should know the words."

"Oh *ya*," *Mamm* chimed in. "That's one of my favorites."

"Okay." Still thinking of Jay, Sharon forced a smile. "You start, Ruby Sue. You can do it."

A flicker of panic crossed her sister's face, but when Sharon told the guests they were about to sing, Ruby Sue cleared her throat and began.

Sharon and her friends all joined in, and their little choir filled the kitchen with the Lord's praises.

If only Jay were standing beside her, offering his voice too.

"I think that went well," Cal said as he folded a table later that evening.

"It did." *Mamm* washed, while Alice dried. "*Danki* for helping us. I'll give you each

84

some of the profits."

"You don't need to do that," Andrew said. "I just enjoyed spending time with you all. And I enjoyed your food."

"That's not right," Sharon said, protesting as she set a stack of dried plates in a cabinet. "You all helped, so we can split it."

Cal waved her off before picking up the table. "We're just glad we could, right, Andrew?"

Andrew nodded before lifting another table and following Cal into the utility room.

"Are you okay?" Alice asked Sharon as she dried a glass.

"*Ya,* I am. I was just hoping Jay would come, although he never told me for sure that he would." Sharon tried to shrug, but the disappointment ran deeper than she wanted to admit.

"You should check our voice mail," Ruby Sue suggested as she swept the floor. "Maybe he left you a message."

Sharon hesitated.

"Go now." *Mamm* nodded toward the door. "See if he did."

"Okay." Sharon pulled on a sweater in the mudroom and then stepped out into the cool April night.

As her shoes crunched the rock path, she glanced up at the bright stars peppering the dark sky, and then she pointed the bright-yellow beam of the flashlight toward the phone shanty. Walking by one of the large barns, she spotted a lantern shining from where her father was settling their animals for the night.

She stepped into the small shanty and set the flashlight on the counter, then picked up the phone receiver and dialed for voice mail. She punched in the code and listened as a message began.

"Hi, this is for Sharon." As Jay's voice filled her ear, warmth swirled in her chest. "This is Jay. I'm sorry I won't make it tonight. We got a rush order for three wooden benches for a local restaurant, and *mei dat* asked me to stay late. I hope your supper goes well. I'll talk to you soon. Bye."

As a voice told her they had no more messages, Sharon held the receiver against her chest. Disappointment stole her euphoria. While she was grateful to know that Jay had cared enough to call, she was still frustrated that he hadn't come.

She made sure she'd deleted Jay's message and then hurried back into the kitchen, where the men were restoring the wooden kitchen table and chairs to their rightful place as the women continued cleaning.

Ruby Sue stopped sweeping crumbs into

her dustpan and looked at her. "Did he call?"

"He did." Sharon began slipping the rest of the leftovers into storage containers. "He had to work late because his *dat* took a big rush order for some wooden benches."

"Oh." Ruby Sue clucked her tongue. "Maybe he can come next time."

"*Ya,* maybe." Sharon turned toward her friends. "Would you all be willing to do this again?"

"Absolutely," Cal said, and Andrew nodded in agreement as they each pushed a chair under the table.

"Just let me know when." Alice set a handful of forks into a drawer.

"I can come if *mei mamm* is feeling okay," Darlene said as she wiped down a counter.

"How is your *mamm,* Darlene?" *Mamm* asked.

Darlene shrugged. "Today was a bit better. Some days are worse than others."

"Please let us know if you ever need anything," *Mamm* said. "We mean that sincerely."

"*Danki,* Feenie. And I'd definitely like to sing here again. This was fun."

"I'm so grateful you all came." As Sharon set a stack of containers in the propane-powered fridge, she thought about Jay. He was telling the truth about his father asking him to stay late at work. She was sure about that. But had the misgivings he expressed about singing for *Englishers* kept him away as well?

On Sunday afternoon two weeks later, Sharon pushed the porch swing into motion, closed her eyes, and breathed in the warm May air as she sat beside Jay on her back porch. Then she looked out to where the cows had all congregated in her father's green pasture.

She picked up her glass of iced tea and glanced at Jay. He looked so handsome in his light-gray shirt and dark trousers. Smiling, she recalled how he'd stopped by to see her at least twice each week and called her every other day to see how she was doing. She felt close to him as they explored their new relationship, and she was excited to be his girlfriend.

Still, it bothered her that he hadn't attended either of the suppers her family had hosted, even though their friends had. She longed to know if he still felt that singing for *Englishers* was wrong, but she'd been afraid to ask him. She was so happy about their relationship that she didn't want to risk a disagreement — at least not yet.

"It's the perfect afternoon." Jay reached over and took her hand.

She smiled at him, but her question about the singings lingered at the back of her mind, threatening to steal her happy mood.

"And I'm very spoiled with this *appeditlich* German chocolate *kuche.*" He held up a plate with a large piece of the cake. "It's superb."

"I'm so *froh* you like it."

He seemed to study her. *"Was iss letz?"*

"What do you mean?"

"I can tell something is bothering you." He pointed to her forehead with his free hand. "Your skin puckers right there when you're upset about something or you're trying to figure something out. Which is it?" Concern flashed over his handsome face. "Have I done something to upset you?"

She looked down at her lap as she gathered her thoughts. Maybe she did need to get this out in the open. She met his gaze. "I'm not upset with you, but I don't understand why you've never come when my family has hosted a supper."

"I've told you. I've been working late filling rush orders for work. They just keep coming, and *Dat* needs my help."

"I know." She looked down at the skirt of her lavender dress and then up at his curious face. "I'm just disappointed that you can't be here when the rest of our *freinden* are. I like it when we're all together."

He released her hand as he blew out a sigh, and a thread of worry twisted in her belly. She braced herself for some defensive words.

"Okay. I just still don't know how I feel about singing for *Englishers,*" he began. "It feels wrong to me, and that's another reason I've been staying away from your suppers."

She nodded slowly. "But I still don't understand why. How could singing about God's glory ever be wrong?"

"Because we're called to be separate from the world. *Mei daadi* used to talk about how serious it is for us to follow those rules. That's what makes us Amish, and if we don't keep our traditions for the next generation, we'll cease to exist." He gestured widely. "That's why we don't have electricity or phones in our homes." He pointed at her dress. "And that's why we dress the way we do and don't drive cars. We're separate. We're Plain."

"But what does that have to do with singing? Where in the Bible does it say we can't sing for others?"

He shook his head. "You're not hearing me."

"I am, Jay." Her voice rose with her frustration. "But I believe we should share the gospel, and I think singing hymns to people who may not be believers is a *gut* way to do that."

"I disagree." He rubbed his chin. "I think singing for *Englishers* is a performance that cheapens how we worship."

She pressed her lips together but then responded. "I respect that we disagree, but I still want you to be a part of this. Won't you please come?" She took his hand in hers. "Won't you at least give it a try? You have such a nice voice. We sound so much better when we all sing together. Please, Jay? Please? For me?"

His lips twitched. "How can I resist that *schee* face?"

She lifted her eyebrows as a smile overtook her lips. "Does that mean you'll give it a try?"

"*Ya,* if it makes you *froh.*"

"It does." She nodded with such vigor that the ribbons from her prayer covering bounced off her shoulders. "We're hosting one on Thursday."

"Okay." His smile faded as his gaze grew intense. Then he leaned forward and touched her lips with his, sending heat roaring through her veins. She leaned into the kiss, savoring it as her heart thrummed.

"I'll do my best to be there." His voice was husky next to her ear, and she shuddered with delight. "I really care about you, Sharon."

"I've always cared about you." She cupped her hand to his smooth cheek.

"I'm sorry I was blind for so long."

He settled back on the swing, and she rested her head on his shoulder as contentment settled in her. She'd just received a real kiss from Jay Smoker! Oh, how she was blessed.

"I'll ask *mei dat* if I can leave work early on Thursday," he said. "Then I can help you set up for the meal too."

"Danki." She smiled up at him. Now the supper would be perfect!

"I think we're ready," *Mamm* said as she surveyed the folding tables set for the guests and platters that lined the kitchen table.

"Everything looks and smells *wunderbaar,* Feenie," Alice said as she stood beside Sharon. "I think it's going to be a great meal."

Sharon leaned back against the counter and folded her arms over her chest as she looked at Cal, Andrew, and Alice. She'd hoped tonight would be perfect, but it wasn't.

First, she'd burned an entire sheet of oatmeal raisin cookies just before her friends arrived, and the smell still lingered in the kitchen despite the open windows and the delicious scent of pot roast mixed with chocolate chip cookies and banana bread.

To make matters worse, Darlene's mother had a bad day, which meant that Darlene and her family were having a challenging time, and she had to stay home. And then Jay didn't show up. Maybe his father couldn't let him go early after all, but Sharon had to wonder if Jay would find some excuse not to come even if he had.

"He'll be here," Alice whispered as if she could read her thoughts. "He was probably just delayed. You know this is his busiest time of year at work, and he has to help his *dat*."

Sharon sighed. "I know."

Alice gave her shoulder a gentle squeeze. "Don't give up faith."

Soon the guests arrived, and Sharon helped serve the meal after her mother went through the introductions.

She tried to focus on their guests, but her eyes kept moving to the windows as she hoped to catch a glimpse of Jay.

■ ■ ■ ■

Jay looked at the clock on the wall and ground his teeth. He was late, very late, for the supper at Sharon's house. Guilt crawled onto his shoulder and dug its talons into his already sore muscles. He'd hoped to leave early, but then his father received the rush order for three wishing wells from the motel on Old Philadelphia Pike, just after most of the carpenters had left for the evening. Out of loyalty to his father, Jay had offered to stay despite his promise to Sharon.

He had to get to her house before he broke her heart. He had to make sure Sharon knew she was his priority, or he might run the risk of losing her. The notion sent icy fear slicing through him.

He set his tools in his toolbox and then made his way to the office at the front of the shop, where his father sat at a desk staring at a stack of paperwork. With dark-brown eyes, graying brown hair, and a matching beard, *Dat* had always reminded Jay of his paternal grandfather.

Oh, how he missed his *daadi*! He had always been around to help Jay with a project or talk about anything from God to their friends in the community. His grandfather had been a mentor alongside his father when he was learning to build the wooden creations they sold at the store. *Daadi* had always been there when he needed him.

"Dat," Jay said, and his father jumped with a start as he looked up. "I didn't mean to disturb you, but I'm late for a supper at Sharon's *haus.*"

"Oh." *Dat* looked at the clock on the wall above his desk and then back at Jay. "Why didn't you tell me you had plans for tonight?"

"I wanted to help you with that wishing well order, but I'm really running late. Is it okay if I just come in early tomorrow?"

"Ya, ya." *Dat* waved him off. "You go. Be safe on the road."

"Danki." Jay hustled out of the shop and toward their house, which was behind the store. He had to get changed and hurry to Sharon's. He just hoped she would forgive him for being late.

After the *Englishers* had finished their supper, Sharon, Alice, and Ruby Sue brought out the desserts while her mother answered questions about their community.

When the guests ran out of questions, *Mamm* turned to Sharon and asked in a low voice, "Are you going to sing now?"

"Ya." Sharon looked at her friends as an idea took root in her mind. "Why don't we do something different tonight? Why don't we sing a traditional Amish hymn?"

Alice raised a reddish-brown eyebrow. "Which one?"

"How about *'Das Loblied'*?" She picked up a copy of the *Ausbund,* the Amish hymnal, sitting on the counter behind her.

Cal and Andrew looked at each other and then faced Sharon, both nodding.

"Ya, that sounds *gut,"* Ruby Sue said, agreeing with them.

"Okay." Sharon looked at their guests. "We'd like to sing a traditional Amish hymn for you called *'Das Loblied.'* It's a hymn of praise we sing during our church services. We have a young man in the congregation serve as song leader, meaning he starts each line, and then the congregation joins in." She held up the *Ausbund.* "This song, along with other traditional Amish hymns, is included in our hymnal, which is called the *Ausbund."*

"Tell us what the song means." The question came from a young man probably in his midtwenties. He had bleached-blond hair that stuck up as if he'd added quite of bit of hair gel to it before coming.

Sharon opened the *Ausbund* to the hymn and began translating. " 'O Lord Father, we bless thy name, thy love and thy goodness praise.' " Then she shared the rest of the English words for verses one, two, three, and four.

"It's beautiful," a teenaged girl wearing a T-shirt with a cat on it said.

"Thank you." Sharon turned to Andrew and Cal. "Who wants to be the song leader?"

"He does." Andrew pointed to Cal, and everyone chuckled.

"Okay. No pressure." Cal cleared his throat and then began to sing.

All her friends and Ruby Sue joined in, and Sharon closed her eyes as she lost herself in the words of the familiar hymn.

Jay couldn't believe his ears as he opened the back door and stepped into the mudroom. The words to *"Das Loblied"* filled the air as Sharon's beautiful voice rang out above the others. It was bad enough that she and his friends were singing for *Englishers.* But to make matters worse, they were sharing a hymn of praise sacred to the Amish church! Anger raced through his veins, causing his jaw to clamp shut so tightly that it ached. His grandfather would never approve of this!

He entered the kitchen, and his eyes locked on Sharon as she sang with Ruby Sue and his friends. Then he looked at the *Englishers.* They were watching his girlfriend sing as if she were a street performer.

This was wrong! *So wrong!*

Jay took in a gush of air through his nose as resentment boiled in his chest. He couldn't stand here and watch this. He'd already been concerned about singing for the *Englishers,* but sharing this precious hymn was too much. He had to leave.

He looked at Sharon, who was no longer singing, but he didn't care. He turned on his heel and stalked out of the kitchen, through the mudroom, and out the back door. Sharon wasn't the *maedel* he'd thought she was. Perhaps it was time to end their new relationship. He wasn't even sure about being friends after this.

As he strode toward his buggy, his anger transformed into disappointment and anguish, breaking his heart with each step.

CHAPTER SEVEN

Sharon had stopped singing when Jay abruptly turned and stomped out of the kitchen. He'd come in with his face twisted in a deep scowl, and now she heard the back door nearly slam shut.

What had she done wrong? He knew they'd be singing tonight. Confusion whisked through her as she looked at Alice, chased by worry.

Alice motioned toward the door and mouthed *Go*.

"Excuse me," Sharon muttered as she weaved past the tables of *Englishers* and then ran outside, sprinting toward Jay's horse and buggy just as he started toward the road. Her heart felt as if it might beat out of her chest.

"Wait! Jay, wait!"

The horse stopped, and Jay climbed down from the buggy.

"Jay!" She ran over to him, then paused

just long enough to catch her breath. "What happened? Why are you leaving — and looking so angry?"

His eyes sparked. "Was it your idea to share *'Das Loblied'* with outsiders?"

"Ya." She shrugged despite her apprehension. "I thought they might be interested in hearing one of our traditional hymns." She could hear the tremble in her voice.

"Why would you share something so sacred to our community — and convince our *freinden* to do it too?" He pointed toward the house. "What were you thinking?"

"I'm thinking singing our hymns to others is more meaningful than sharing how our stoves work." The words flew out of her mouth as she defended her actions, her heart. "What's wrong with singing hymns of praise for outsiders? Aren't we called to spread the *gut* news about Jesus?"

He shook his head. "I don't understand you. We're supposed to be separate. That's what makes us Amish."

"Are you saying it's wrong for *mei mamm* to host *Englisher* suppers?"

Jay hesitated. "I won't criticize your *mamm*. It's not like she's sharing how the Amish worship."

"But I'm not breaking any rules. It's just

a hymn. I'm only sharing what makes us Plain. I'm not doing anything sinful or degrading."

He took a step back. "I think we need to take a break."

"What?" Her voice broke. "You're breaking up with me over a hymn?"

He glared at her. "I need to go."

"Jay, wait." She ran after him and reached for his arm, but he eluded her grasp. "I'm sorry this upset you. Come inside and we'll talk about it, okay?"

"I've had a long day, and I'm tired." He looked down at the ground and then up at her again. "We'll talk another time."

As she watched him climb into his buggy and leave, Sharon pressed a palm to her chest as if it could somehow stop her heart from splitting in two.

Jay's body thrummed with irritation and misery as he unhitched his horse and led it to the barn. Then he stood at the horse's stall for a moment and took deep breaths as he recalled Sharon and his friends singing for those strangers.

How could Sharon believe it was acceptable to share something so sacred with *Englishers*? Had he ever truly known her if she would do something so blasphemous? And what would *Daadi* say about this? He always said "*Das Loblied*" was his favorite hymn. It had reminded him of when he was a boy and his father was the bishop of the community. He'd been honored when he was called to serve as song leader and start the first line of each verse. And because the hymn meant so much to his precious *daadi,* it was special to Jay too. What was Sharon thinking?

"Jay?" *Dat* came toward him. "Why are you home so early? Was the supper canceled?"

"It should have been," Jay muttered as he kicked a stone with the toe of his shoe.

"What do you mean?"

Jay leaned back against the barn wall and fingered his hat. "I went, but I couldn't stay." He explained how Sharon had been singing for *Englishers,* but he was never comfortable with the idea. Then he shared what he'd heard earlier, as well as his argument with Sharon. "I can't believe she would do something like that. I thought I knew her, but she's not the *maedel* I believed she was when I asked her to be my girlfriend. And she's even influenced our *freinden,* including my best *freind!*"

To his surprise, his father seemed more confused than disturbed. "Are you saying you're upset because Sharon and your *frein-den* were singing *'Das Loblied'*? And that's why you argued with Sharon?"

"Right."

"Jay, your *mamm* and I have always appreciated that you take your beliefs seriously. You've never given us any trouble. Nor have you ever strayed from the community. While some of the *buwe* in your youth group got their driver's licenses and purchased loud sports cars, you joined the baptism classes and became a member. And I'm glad you did that. We never had to worry that you would leave the church or leave our family." *Dat* paused and fingered his beard. "But at the same time, sometimes I worry that you're *too* serious."

"What do you mean?" Jay bristled at the comment. "A man my age *has* to be serious. And I've always worked hard for you. When your other employees leave for the evening, I stay an hour or two later to work on a rush project."

"I know." *Dat*'s expression was warm as he touched Jay's shoulder. "But I think you're overreacting in this instance."

Jay's anger roared to life. "How can you say that? *Daadi* always told me how important it is for us to adhere to the rules. He said that's what makes us Amish and that's what sustains our culture. And I think singing for —"

"*Mei dat* was very conservative, and I always respected him for that. After all, his *dat* had been the bishop. That's how he was raised."

"Are you saying he was wrong?"

"No, but just think about this for a moment. Sharon and your *freinden* sang a hymn of praise. What if an *Englisher* who was struggling with his faith was at the supper, and the hymn brought his heart back to God? Wouldn't that be a miracle?"

"You're completely missing my point, *Dat. Daadi* would never have approved of what they did." Jay tried to shove away his festering frustration. "I'm going inside."

As he made his way to the house, Jay shook his head. His father thought he had overreacted, but in his heart, he knew his instincts were right. Now more than ever, he needed to honor what his grandfather taught him.

Sharon's lower lip trembled as she stood at the back of the kitchen and listened to her friends sing "Jesus Loves Me" with the *Englishers*. She had tried to sing along, but her voice wobbled as a swelling lump clogged her throat.

She was heartbroken. Why would Jay break up with her over this? How could he be so furious with her when she was trying to spread God's love through singing?

When the singing was done, the guests left, and her mother, sister, and friends dove into the leftovers. Sharon sat down at one of the clean tables, not wanting to be rude. But she needed this evening to end so she could run up to the privacy of her bedroom and allow her tears to flow.

"Are you okay?" Alice whispered in her ear. Ruby Sue was there too.

Sharon shook her head.

"What happened?" Ruby Sue asked.

"I can't talk about it now." Her voice cracked.

Mamm brought a stack of plates to the table.

"Do you want to talk about it?" The sympathy on *Mamm*'s face nearly caused now-pooling tears to leak from Sharon's eyes.

Sharon glanced behind her at Cal and Andrew and then looked back at *Mamm* before shaking her head.

"Okay." *Mamm* touched her hand. "I'm here to listen when you're ready."

"Danki." After everyone had eaten, Sharon focused on washing dishes while *Mamm*

dried, Ruby Sue wiped down the tables, and Alice swept the floor. *Dat* had gone to bed.

When the tables and chairs were stowed, Andrew and Cal said good night, but before he left, Cal looked at her with a question in his eyes. Did he know how strongly Jay felt about their singing to *Englishers*? After all, the two men were best friends. Maybe he'd believed Jay hadn't come to the suppers because he was just busy at work. But did he know why Jay had stalked out tonight? She didn't think so.

Once they'd left, Sharon leaned over the sink and allowed her tears to break free.

"Ach, mei liewe." *Mamm* rubbed her back. "What happened?"

"Sharon!" Ruby Sue rushed over and touched her arm. *"Was iss letz?"*

Alice was soon at her side. "Did you and Jay argue?"

"We basically broke up." Saying the words aloud sent a shock wave of agony through her chest.

"Ach, no!" *Mamm* took Sharon's hand and steered her to the sofa in the family room.

Ruby Sue and Alice sank into the wing chairs across from them.

Mamm handed her a tissue. "Take a deep breath and tell us what happened."

Sharon wiped her eyes and blew her nose.

Then she shared her conversation with Jay while the women stared at her with disbelieving expressions.

"I just don't understand," Sharon said. "How could singing a hymn be a sin? Why would he get so upset when we're just sharing a tiny piece of our culture? We're not accepting money for singing, either. The money the *Englishers* pay is for the meal, not the singing. We're not using our hymns as entertainment. We're just sharing God's Word." She looked at *Mamm*. "Do you think I'm terrible?" She sniffed as more tears filled her eyes.

"No, no." *Mamm* touched her cheek. "If I thought what you were doing was wrong, I would tell you. Your *dat* and I wouldn't allow our *kinner* to do something we considered sinful. I agree with you completely."

Sharon looked at Ruby Sue and Alice, and the pity in their eyes was almost too much to bear. "What do you think?"

Alice shook her head. "I think he's completely wrong."

"*Ya.*" Ruby Sue's nose wrinkled as if she smelled something foul. "I think he's *narrisch.*"

Sharon chuckled despite her anguish. "What can I do to fix it?"

"Give him time." *Mamm* patted her knee.

"Let him calm down and then talk to him."

"Okay." Sharon stood. "All this crying has worn me out. Let's clean up the kitchen so I can get to bed."

Later, Sharon walked Alice out to the back porch. "*Danki* for helping tonight."

"*Gern gschehne.*" Alice hugged her. "Don't give up on Jay. Pray for him, and then talk to him. Everything will be okay."

"I hope you're right."

"You know I am." Alice gave her a little wave. "*Gut nacht.*" Clicking on her flashlight, she started down the driveway toward her farm.

After showering, Sharon slipped on her nightgown, then turned off her lantern and crawled into bed. As she stared at her dark ceiling, she opened her heart to God.

"Please, God," she whispered, "help me figure out what to say to Jay to make him realize that I would never disrespect our culture. Please grant me the words to explain that I only meant to do your will and not use our culture for my own means. Help Jay and me find a way back to our special relationship."

Then she rolled onto her side and wished for sleep.

Jay slammed his hammer onto the workbench the next morning and then picked up a screwdriver.

When he turned back toward the windmill he'd been making, he found Cal watching him with his chin lifted and his arms folded across his wide chest.

"If you banged that hammer down any harder, you'd probably leave a dent in that workbench," Cal quipped.

Jay leaned back against the wall and eyed his best friend with suspicion. "What do you want, Cal?"

"That's a nice greeting." Cal sat down on a stool and pointed to the one across from him. "Why don't you have a seat so we can have a little chat?"

"I don't have time," Jay grumbled as he turned back to the windmill.

"Sure you do. Sit."

Jay narrowed his eyes. "If you're here to lecture me about last night, you can save your breath."

"You'd better believe I'm here to discuss last night. You acted like a complete *dummkopp.*"

Jay froze. Had Sharon told everyone what they discussed? Had she always shared their private conversations?

"Why would you come into Sharon's *haus,* glare at all of us, and then stomp outside?

109

What were you thinking? Why would you embarrass Sharon that way? What could we have possibly done that upset you so much? Or were you just angry with her for some reason?"

"She didn't tell you why I was upset?"

"No, but she came back inside and looked like she was going to cry. In fact, she looked that way for the rest of the evening." Cal gestured wildly. "What did you say to her? What could she have possibly done to deserve your making her that upset?"

For a moment, Jay mentally breathed a sigh of relief knowing that Sharon had kept their conversation private, at least from his best friend. But that didn't make up for her singing their hymn of praise to the *Englishers* like some entertainer.

"Well?" Cal's voice rose. "What do you have to say for yourself?"

"I don't have to explain myself to you, but I will tell you what upset me. I was furious to hear you all singing *'Das Loblied'* for those *Englishers* as if it were some ordinary song instead of a hymn that's important to our culture. It was blasphemous and sinful. That's why I told Sharon she's not the *maedel* I thought she was. She's influenced all of you, and I told her we need a break."

Cal's eyes widened as if they might pop

out of his head. "You can't be serious."

"I'm *very* serious."

Cal leveled his gaze with Jay. "You're going to lose her."

The words punched him in the center of his chest. But he dismissed the feeling and pushed on. "I can't act like it's okay to parade around our beliefs as entertainment."

"You know what, Jay?" Cal began. "Sharon really cares about you, and you're being blinded by whatever this conviction is. You need to think about what you're doing. She's about spreading the gospel, not using our beliefs to sell meals. And if you can't see that, you're missing out on the bigger picture of what these suppers truly are." Then Cal stood. "And if you're going to be mad at her, you might as well be mad at me and the rest of our *freinden* too. See you later."

Before Jay could respond, Cal was gone, and Jay was left alone in the big, noisy shop, confused — and near panic. Was he ready to lose Sharon over this? Could he even lose his friends? He felt very strongly, but he wasn't sure about the cost.

No. His heart ached so much that the pain brought tears to his eyes, but he had to stand his ground.

CHAPTER EIGHT

"Kaffi?" Holding a carafe, Sharon made her way down the long table in the Swarey family barn and filled coffee cups for the men.

She looked toward the end of the table, where Jay sat across from his father, Moses, and anguish erupted in her chest once again. She'd spent most of the church service trying to avoid eye contact with him after their gazes tangled. His stony eyes had quickly looked away, and his rejection ripped through her heart like a jagged knife.

She moved along the table, forcing a smile as she drew closer to Jay. How she wished she had chosen to fill cups at the next table to avoid him.

But why should she avoid him? After all, she'd done nothing wrong!

When she reached him, she stood behind his chair, pushing her shoulders back as she mustered all the courage she could.

"Kaffi?" She held up the carafe.

112

Jay's back and shoulders went ramrod straight.

"*Ya,* please." Moses reached across the table and handed her his Styrofoam cup. "How are you, Sharon?"

"Fine. *Danki.*" She filled his cup and then handed it back to him, working to keep her wobbly smile on her lips.

Moses looked at his son. "Do you want *kaffi,* Jay? Sharon is standing right behind you, waiting for you to make a decision." His words were measured, as if they held a hidden meaning.

Jay didn't turn to look at her. "No, *danki.*"

Oh how she wanted to scream *Look at me, Jay! Look at me!* She was certain her stare could burn a hole in his back.

"You two enjoy your lunch," she said as pleasantly as she could. Then she moved on to the next table, her heart crumbling a little more with each step.

Once she'd filled all the cups as requested, she hustled out of the barn and nearly crashed into Alice and Darlene, who were each carrying trays of food.

"Are you all right?" Darlene's eyes went wide.

Alice gasped. *"Was iss letz?"*

"I just saw Jay, and he won't talk to me. He wouldn't even look at me in there, and

113

when he looked at me in church, he nearly glared. I don't know how to fix this."

"Let's think of a way." Darlene looked up at the blue sky as if it held the answers. "I've got it. What if we all sing for Martha again this afternoon? I noticed she wasn't in church, and when I asked her *sohn* about her, he said she was feeling too tired again."

"That's a great idea," Alice said. "Invite Jay to come with us. It will force him to be civil to you."

A tiny spark of hope ignited in Sharon's chest. "All right. I'll tell my parents about our plans and then ask him after we eat lunch."

As she walked toward the kitchen to refill the carafe, she prayed the plan would work.

After nearly inhaling her lunch, Sharon slipped outside alone, determined to catch Jay. She spotted him near his buggy; she'd learned to recognize his horse long ago. He was stepping back from Cal and Andrew, as though he was about to leave.

She quickened her pace. "Hi." She gave them all a little wave. "Alice, Darlene, and I are going to sing for Martha Bontrager today. Her *sohn* said she was too tired to come to church again. Would you all like to join us?"

"Ya." Andrew nodded and glanced at Cal, who also agreed.

"Great. Would you like to come, Jay?" Her hope sank when he frowned.

"I can't. I'm sorry." Jay opened his buggy door.

"Why not?" Cal's tone seemed harsh as he glowered at his best friend.

Jay's glare seemed to challenge Cal's. "I have work to do."

"On a Sunday?" Cal took a step toward him. "It's a day of rest, remember? Or are you not following the Amish rules?"

Sharon blinked and turned toward Andrew, who grimaced.

"Fine. I'll rest. At home." Jay turned to Sharon. "Sorry. Have a *gut* time."

The distance in his eyes made it hard for her to breathe for a moment. How could they go from being so close to near strangers in the blink of an eye?

As Jay climbed into his buggy and then guided his horse to the road, she stood cemented in place, frozen by his casual dismissal.

"He said no?"

Alice's voice was behind her.

"Ya."

"Don't blame yourself. He's the one with the problem." Cal nearly spat out the words.

115

"He told me how he feels, but you did nothing wrong. And today he didn't seem to want to talk to any of us."

Sharon turned toward him. "If I did nothing wrong, then why does it feel like I ruined everything between us?"

"You didn't." Darlene touched Sharon's shoulder. "Let's go see Martha."

"Okay." Sharon allowed her friend to steer her to Cal's buggy, but she couldn't keep her eyes away from Jay's buggy as it drove away.

Sharon couldn't bring herself to sing along as her friends sang "Rock of Ages" and Martha moved her head to the beat of the song.

Instead, she stared down at the wood grain on Martha's small kitchen table while her mind replayed her brief and heartbreaking conversation with Jay. Her heart couldn't accept that he had just disregarded her as though she were an annoying child instead of someone he seemed to have cared for only a few days earlier.

How could he forget all the feelings he said he had for her? He'd told her he cared. He'd even kissed her! Didn't any of that mean something to him? Hadn't she been important to him?

"Sharon?"

"Huh?" Sharon's head snapped up to find Martha smiling at her. "I'm sorry. Did you say something, Martha?"

"Ya." Their friend pushed a plate of macadamia nut cookies toward her. "Take a *kichli.* It will make you feel better, sweetie."

"Danki, but I'm not hungry." Sharon tried to smile, but her lips refused to tip up. She longed to leave. Once again she craved the privacy of her room at home, where she could cry into her pillow until she ran out of tears.

"Why don't we sing another one?" Darlene said. "How about 'Farther Along'?"

Sharon stood. "I really need to be going."

Her friends looked up at her with surprise etched on their faces.

"You all stay. It's not a long walk." She started for the back door.

"Wait, *mei liewe."* When Martha struggled to stand, Andrew and Cal jumped up from their seats and assisted her. *"Danki, buwe.* Help me go outside with Sharon. I think we need to have a woman-to-woman talk. In private."

Sharon nodded. "That would be nice, Martha."

Andrew and Cal helped Martha out to the porch, where she and Sharon sat down, side by side in matching rocking chairs.

"Now, Sharon," Martha began as soon as they were alone, "tell me what's burdening your heart."

Sharon pushed her chair into motion as she tried to put how she was feeling into words.

"Is it about a *bu*?" Martha asked.

Sharon nodded.

"Did he break your heart?"

"*Ya*, he did." She summarized their disagreement. "I tried to explain that we were just sharing the Word of God and not doing anything wrong. My intentions were always *gut*." She turned toward Martha, who was staring out toward a pasture.

"Do you think I'm terrible?" Sharon gripped the arms of the rocking chair as she awaited Martha's response.

"No, I don't." She shook her head and then offered a warm smile. "Herman and I had disagreements plenty of times, and sometimes we wouldn't speak for a day or two." She reached over and patted Sharon's arm with her frail hand. "You two will work it out."

"But he broke up with me. He dismissed me today as if I were a meaningless acquaintance. I think it's over."

"I don't think so."

"Why not?"

Martha gave her a knowing look. "I could sense how he felt about you when you two were here last month."

"How?"

"It was the way he watched you. The way he gazed at you as if you were the only *maedel* in the room." Martha gave a sigh. "My Herman used to look at me that way."

With her whole heart, Sharon wanted to believe Jay still cared for her, but merciless doubt plagued her. "Martha, I don't mean to disrespect you, but I think you might be wrong. If I were important to Jay, how could he just throw away our relationship as if it meant nothing?"

Martha turned toward her again. "Sometimes *buwe* can be *gegisch.* You can't give up on him or your relationship. Give him a little more time, and he'll realize he's wrong. Just pray for him and have faith that God will guide his heart."

"I hope you're right."

"I am." Martha patted her arm again and then nodded toward the door. "Would you ask those nice *buwe* to help me back inside? I think I'm ready for a nap."

Sharon summoned Cal and Andrew, and they assisted Martha back inside the house.

After Sharon, Darlene, and Alice cleaned

up the kitchen, they all said good-bye to Martha and then headed outside. Darlene elected to ask Cal for a ride home, and Sharon and Alice climbed into Andrew's buggy.

Sharon stared out the window, then she closed her eyes and sent up a silent prayer.

God, please guide Jay's heart back to me. I miss him, and I have a feeling he misses me too. Please find a way for us to work out our differences and build a stronger relationship through our love for you.

Then she hugged her arms to her chest and tried to hold back threatening tears.

"I need to make a phone call. Would you please run the register for a few minutes?" Jay's father asked when Jay entered the showroom of their store.

"Of course." Jay slipped behind the counter and smiled as a couple who looked to be married and in their thirties approached him. "Good morning. How may I help you?"

The man pointed to the display of wooden lighthouses. "We'd like to get one of those. The blue one in the front."

"All right." Jay told them the price and rang it up. "Where are you two from?"

"New Jersey," the woman offered as she

pushed a red curl away from her round face. "It's our first time here, and we've had a lovely time."

"Welcome to Amish Country." Jay took the man's cash and gave him change and a receipt. "What's been the best part of your trip?"

The woman looked at her husband, and they shared a smile. Then she turned back to Jay. "We had a meal at an Amish home the other night, and it was delightful."

Jay's stomach clenched as he handed the man the receipt. "Really?"

"It was so different from what we expected," the man said as he closed his wallet. "We thought the opportunity would just be an excuse to eat more delicious Amish dishes, but it was so much more."

"That's right," his wife chimed in. "After we ate, they answered our questions, and then they sang for us. It was just fantastic. I felt as if the Holy Spirit was touching my soul as these young folks sang hymns we knew and then this lovely Amish hymn."

Jay's mouth dried.

"What did she call the hymn, Lee?" The woman snapped her fingers and glanced at her husband again. "Do you remember?"

"She said it was a hymn of praise," he told Jay.

"Das Loblied." Jay could hardly get out the words.

"That's it," she said. "We came here expecting to do some shopping and eat some great food. I was pleasantly surprised to also find myself spiritually moved by this place. You all have a wonderful culture. I'm so grateful we've been able to experience it. It's been a blessing to us."

"It truly has. Thank you." The man left the counter and picked up their lighthouse.

"You have a great day." The woman gave Jay a wave and then followed her husband toward the exit.

As Jay watched them go, confusion plagued him. Was Sharon right to share their hymn of praise? But what would *Daadi* say?

God, help me understand what I should do.

CHAPTER NINE

On Friday morning, Jay examined the wooden lawn windmill he'd just finished making. It wasn't his best work, but it was adequate.

"Great job."

Jay turned as his father stepped into his stall. "*Danki.* It's not perfect, though." He pointed to the roof. "See that slat there? It's slightly crooked, and the stain isn't quite as even over here."

Dat scrunched his nose as he examined it. "I must need glasses, because I don't see the imperfections you're talking about." Then he turned toward him. "You know, Jay, that's your whole problem."

"What?" Jay took a step back.

"You're always looking for imperfections where there aren't any. This is a prime example." *Dat* gestured to the windmill. "This is perfect. In fact, I think it's your best work. It might be the best windmill our

123

shop has ever created."

He pointed at Jay's chest. "But you choose to see what's wrong with it instead of the beauty that's here. I'm certain the customer who takes this home will cherish it for years, but you'll still think about what you did wrong instead of what you did right."

Speechless, Jay stared at him.

"Is that what went wrong with Sharon?" *Dat* said, pushing his point. "Did you expect something she couldn't give you? Maybe perfection? A perfection you've defined on your own?"

Jay gaped at him. "*Dat,* I —"

"Can you honestly tell me you don't miss her? Because when I saw you with her at church, before you broke up with her, you looked happier than I'd ever seen you."

"I miss her all the time." The confession came out in a dry croak.

Dat's expression warmed as he stepped toward him. "So what are you waiting for? If you don't go after her, another young man will snatch her up. I think your *daadi* would have agreed that Sharon is a *wunderbaar maedel.* I also think he would say that singing for *Englishers* is a way to share the gospel and isn't a danger to our Amish beliefs and culture. Not even when they hear one of our own special hymns."

Jay nodded as God's answer to his prayer echoed in his mind. *Go after Sharon! Don't lose her! Ask for her forgiveness!* "You're right. I need to start by making a phone call."

Dat pointed toward his office at the back of the shop. "Take your time."

Jay dashed into the office and closed the door. He took a deep breath as a plan filled his mind. And then he dialed the number for Cal's horse farm.

After a few rings, a voice picked up. "King's Belgian and Dutch Harness Horses. How may I help you?"

"Cal?" Jay asked. "Is that you?"

"Jay?"

"*Ya*, it's me." He closed his eyes and pinched the bridge of his nose as he searched for the right words. "I'm sorry for being such a jerk to you."

Cal snorted. "Keep going. I'm listening."

"You were right. I was too hard on all of you. You weren't being disrespectful by singing *'Das Loblied.'* I was completely wrong, and I want to make it up to you all."

"Including Sharon?"

"No. *Especially* Sharon. When is the next supper at her *haus*?"

"It's tonight. Will you come?"

Jay picked at a loose piece of wood on the

125

corner of his father's desk. "I want to. Do you think I should?"

"*Ya.* I think you should."

Jay blew out a sigh of relief. "Would you do me a favor and not tell her? I want it to be a surprise."

"All right."

"I'll see you tonight."

"Hey, Jay."

"*Ya?*"

"I'm glad you're back to your old self. We've all missed you."

"*Danki,* Cal."

"See you later."

Jay hung up just as his father came into the office.

"How did it go?" *Dat* asked.

"I called Cal and found out Sharon's family is hosting a supper tonight. May I leave early so I can be there on time?"

Dat smiled. "Of course you may."

Jay stood and strode toward the door. Then he stopped, spun, and faced his father. "*Danki* for helping me see the light."

Dat shook his head. "That wasn't me. I'm sure it was God."

"I know you're right." Jay nodded, and then he rushed to his stall to create a gift for Sharon. He wanted to show her how much he cared.

126

■ ■ ■ ■

"I think everything is ready," Sharon said as she looked at the tables set for their eight guests. "I hope they'll like the parmesan chicken with rice."

"I'm sure they will." Alice's arms encircled her shoulders. "*All* the food looks perfect."

"*Ya,* it does." Cal grinned at her.

Sharon let her gaze linger on Cal. He'd been grinning nonstop since he arrived, and she couldn't figure out why. It was as if he knew something she didn't, and it was really annoying. Why wouldn't he share his secret with her?

"They're here," *Mamm* announced as she came into the kitchen. "I heard the cars coming up the driveway. Let's get ready to greet them." She touched Sharon's back. "You did a *wunderbaar* job on the chicken and rice. I'm sure it's going to be a hit."

"I hope so."

Mamm touched her cheek. "I know you're still upset about Jay, even angry now after his rejection on Sunday. But everything's going to be fine. Just trust God."

Sharon nodded, and then she turned toward the door as Ruby Sue led the guests inside. "Good evening. Welcome to our home."

Jay climbed the back steps of Sharon's house. He'd hoped to be there early, but he had to wait for his gift to dry.

He glanced down at the birdhouse he'd created with love and care. He'd designed the rectangular box with the sloping roof to keep the rain off the birds. He hoped this little gift would go beyond his apology, would show her that he wanted to try again, and he'd do better this time. He would cherish her, be patient — and stop being so critical.

He reached the top step and heard voices floating out through the open windows. He stopped when he heard her sweet voice carrying out from the kitchen.

"This next hymn is called *'Das Loblied,'* and it's a hymn of praise we sing on Sundays," she said.

He set the birdhouse on the small table on the porch and then pulled open the screen door and walked into the mudroom, where he stilled and listened as Sharon explained how a song leader would start each line and then the rest of the congregation would join in. Then she shared the translation of the words in English. When she began to sing, Jay stepped into the kitchen and stood quietly. Her voice was like a balm to his soul. He took in her beautiful face and lyrical voice.

He knew at that moment that he loved her, and he needed her in his life. God had led him to her, and he prayed for the hundredth time today that she would allow him to be her boyfriend again.

Sharon looked at him, and their gazes locked as she continued to sing. He smiled and raised a hand in greeting, but her expression remained serious.

Then he glanced at the *Englishers* sitting at the tables, and they all seemed mesmerized by her voice. They listened with what seemed like reverence, as if they were worshipping God as they heard the holy words. He was reminded of what the couple in the store told him about their experience here.

And Jay now saw for himself what Sharon had been trying to tell him — she was glorifying God and sharing the gospel by singing these hymns. She was doing what they were called to do — serving God in all things.

Jay looked at Cal and found him smiling at him. He nodded, and his best friend returned the gesture. Then Cal joined in the singing, which prompted Andrew, Darlene, Alice, and Ruby Sue to join in too.

Sharon turned to Jay, and he gestured for her to follow him outside. She pursed her lips but then slipped away from the group and came toward him.

His body trembled with a mixture of worry and hope as she followed him out to the porch. He hoped he could remember the speech he'd practiced during the ride to her house.

She spun toward him and slammed her hands on her small hips as she glared at him. "What are you doing here?"

"I came to apologize." He held up his hands as if to surrender. "You were right. You're doing nothing wrong by singing *'Das Loblied'* to the *Englishers.* I've realized you are doing God's work. I could tell they were moved tonight. The hymn was touching their hearts."

She lifted one eyebrow. "So now you've decided I'm not sinning when I sing?"

"No, you're not. And I'm sorry. I hope you can find it in your heart to forgive me." He sucked in a breath. "I've been so wrong, and I'm embarrassed. The truth is *mei daadi* was very conservative. But even if he would have disagreed with singing our hymn of praise for *Englishers,* I realize now he would

130

have been wrong. We're called to share the gospel."

She nodded. "I agree."

"And I've missed you. This time without you has been torture, and I'm sorry for hurting you. I want to start over. I want to make it up to you and show you that I'm no longer the critical *dummkopp* I was."

He reached for her hands, and she allowed him to take them. "The truth is I love you, Sharon. I can't imagine my life without you. If you give me another chance, I promise I'll cherish you and treat you right. I'll show you that I can do better. I'll do my best to never hurt you again."

Her eyes misted as he went on.

"You once asked me if I ever felt led to do something." He took a deep breath. "I absolutely have. In fact, I've felt God leading me to a future with you."

She took a shuddering breath, and then a tear rolled down her cheek. He released one of her hands, and she quickly wiped the tear away.

He released her other hand and picked up the birdhouse, then handed it to her. "I made you a gift. I was late because I had to wait for the finish to dry. It's not much, but I thought you might —"

"I love it." She turned it over in her hands.

"It's the most *schee* birdhouse I've ever seen."

"I'm so glad you like it. While I made it, I imagined that one day we'll have a *haus* of our own. But for now, this one will have to do."

Another tear fell. "*Danki*, Jay. It will be beautiful in my garden. I've missed you so much." She gently placed it back on the table, then dabbed her cheek.

"Will you give me another chance?" He searched her eyes.

"*Ya*, of course."

"*Danki*." He stepped closer, then leaned down and kissed her. When their lips touched, bliss rolled through him, setting his nerve endings aflame. When he broke the kiss, he rested his forehead against hers. "*Ich liebe dich*, Sharon. I'll cherish you always."

She smiled up at him. "I love you too. Will you come back inside and sing with us?"

He took her hand in his. "I'd be honored to."

Sharon smiled as she sat on the glider beside Jay Sunday afternoon. The rest of their friends surrounded them as they ate chocolate chip cookies and drank iced tea while enjoying the bright, sunny afternoon.

She looked out at her father's green, rolling pastures and listened to the birds singing in nearby trees.

"I think we should expand our singing ministry," Alice said as she sat on a rocker next to Cal's.

"What do you mean?" Andrew asked. He'd plopped down on the steps.

"We should invite more people to join us."

"That's a *gut* idea," Jay said.

Sharon smiled at him. "I agree." She glanced toward the birdhouse Jay made for her. He'd hung it on a tree before he left Thursday night. The birdhouse was the perfect addition to her rows of colorful flowers. She laughed when she spotted a cardinal sitting on the roof. "Look. There's a bird on the *haus* you made."

Jay glanced at it and smiled. "I'm so glad."

Sharon leaned her head on his shoulder and breathed in his familiar scent. She'd been so taken aback when Jay appeared in the kitchen Thursday. But that's when she realized why Cal had been grinning at her — he'd known Jay was going to join them.

After their talk on the porch, Jay had come inside and sung with them. He also stayed after their friends left, and they talked on the porch until late in the evening.

"I'm going to invite Dave to join us," Alice said. "I think singing would help him heal after what he's been through."

"I agree," Darlene said. "I'll try to think of more people we can ask."

"Hey," Jay whispered in Sharon's ear, sending a shiver dancing up her back.

She looked up at him. "What?"

Ich liebe dich," he said in a low voice.

"I love you too."

Jay gave her hand a gentle squeeze, and she felt as if she were floating on a cloud. She was so grateful that Martha had been right, that Jay had realized he'd been wrong about her singing ministry.

Most of all, she was grateful that God had led Jay back to her.

DISCUSSION QUESTIONS

1. Jay is furious when he learns Sharon and the rest of their friends are singing an Amish hymn of praise for the *Englishers.* Do you think his feelings are valid? Why or why not?
2. Sharon is heartbroken when Jay breaks up with her. Have you ever had your heart broken by someone you loved? How did you cope with your heartbreak? What Bible verses helped you cope?
3. Jay's father makes an analogy between Jay's criticism of Sharon and the way Jay criticizes his own woodworking. Do you think this analogy is valid? Why or why not?
4. Which character can you identify with the most? Which character seemed to carry the most emotional stake in the story? Jay, Sharon, or someone else?
5. At the end of the story, Jay realizes he misunderstood the effect singing the

Amish hymn for *Englishers* could have. What do you think happened throughout the story that contributed to his changing his mind?

6. What role did the friends' singings play in the relationships throughout the story?

136

■ ■ ■ ■

AMAZING GRACE

■ ■ ■ ■

For Her Royal Highness, Princess Lily Belle, with love and kisses

Featured Characters

Annie m. Emmanuel "Manny" Esh
|
Rosemary
David

Edna m. Harvey King
|
Calvin
Raymond

Louise m. Moses Smoker
|
Jay

Jean m. Merle Detweiler
|
Andrew
Samuel

Feenie m. Ira Lambert
|
Sharon
Ruby Sue

Dorothy m. Floyd Blank
|
Benjamin
Alice

Roselyn m. Alvin Bender
|
Biena
Darlene

Rosemary m. Stephen Lapp
|
Nancy

CHAPTER ONE

Dave Esh stared down at his plate. As if he needed anything else to dampen his appetite, the mid-June, humid air trapped in the Swarey barn smelled stale.

This was another Sunday, another church service, another meal with the men he'd known all his life. His own father sat across from him as lunchtime conversations swirled all around. Yet he felt as though he sat alone.

"Tomorrow we'll finish up that wall in Strasburg, and then we have to start on a *haus* in White Horse," *Dat* said. "It's not far from your *schweschder*'s farm."

Dave nodded but kept his eyes focused on the uneaten food on his plate.

"This will be a *gut* job for you," *Dat* continued as if Dave were interested. "Soon you'll be managing your own crew of brick masons. I think you're ready to take on a more supervisory role in the company. Before you know it, you'll be the boss, and

I'll be retired."

Dave closed his eyes as the familiar, soul-crushing guilt threatened to swallow him whole. He wasn't worthy to be a member of this congregation let alone a supervisor at his family's business. He didn't know why his father still trusted him. Or was he just pretending?

He inwardly sighed. As soon as he'd saved enough money, he'd leave this community behind. That should be sometime this summer, but until then, he was stuck here, drowning daily in the memories of . . . that day.

A new life would never bring total relief from his heartbreak, of course. His punishment would never end, and that's what he deserved.

"Kaffi?"

Dave looked up to see Alice Blank standing behind his father holding a coffee carafe. Was she smiling at him? Dave glanced over his shoulder to see if someone else was there, but the space was empty. She *was* smiling at him.

He swallowed against his suddenly dry throat. Alice looked beautiful in a white apron that covered a pale-green dress, which complemented her reddish-brown hair, mostly hidden by her prayer covering. Her eyes? They reminded him of the color mocha.

He'd always been drawn to Alice. They'd been friends since they were in first grade, and their friendship had always seemed natural. He'd sought her out on the playground, and she'd made a point to include him when they played softball.

When they became teenagers, youth group was no different. They always seemed to find each other, and conversation with her was easy and comfortable. She'd been one of his best friends.

Then last year he realized his feelings for her had transformed into more than friendship, and he'd been working up the nerve to ask her father's permission to date her.

Then the accident happened.

After that, his dream of being Alice's boyfriend was dashed.

"Dave?" Alice pointed to his empty Styrofoam cup. "Do you want me to fill that?"

"Sure. *Danki.*" He handed her the cup.

"How are you?"

He shrugged. "I'm all right. How are you?"

Her bright smile somehow grew even brighter as she poured the coffee. "I'm fantastic. It's a *schee* day, and we're blessed to be here."

"Right." Dave took the cup from her.

"I'll see you soon." Alice turned and moved to the next table.

Dave watched her go. *If only* —

"You need to be ready early tomorrow morning."

"What?" Dave turned toward his father, expecting to see a scowl.

But his father merely studied him for a moment, the same old confusion in his eyes. "I said we need to leave early tomorrow. We have to finish that wall before dark because I want to begin our new project on Tuesday."

Dave sipped his coffee as his father droned on about work. He didn't care about the business anymore. Couldn't *Dat* see that?

When he'd finished what lunch he could stomach, he headed outside, moving past knots of young people discussing their plans. He recalled the days when he'd stand beside Alice as they and their friends decided how they wanted to spend their Sunday afternoon.

Cal King met Dave's eye, but Dave looked away. At one time he and Cal, along with Jay Smoker, had been best friends. Dave used to be able to tell Cal, in particular, anything, but now . . .

Even if he tried to tell Cal how he felt, he

wouldn't understand. No one would. Not his former friends, not his family. No one could comprehend how Adam's death had changed him forever. He was alone, and now on Sunday afternoons after church, he headed home, where he would nap or read a book in his room.

He'd just reached his buggy when he heard a female voice calling his name. Surely she was calling another Dave. Why would any woman in their congregation want to talk to him?

He wrenched open the buggy door.

"David Esh! Don't leave!"

He stilled, then turned to see Alice almost jogging toward him, the ties of her prayer covering fluttering past her shoulders. He gripped the door as he took in her radiant face. Did she have any idea how attractive she was?

Alice gave a little laugh as she approached him. "I've been calling and calling, but I guess you were distracted." She paused and caught her breath. Then she tilted her head and smiled up at him. "Do you have plans for this afternoon?"

Would she ever learn? But he told her the truth. "No, I don't."

"Oh, *gut.*" She gestured behind her, where the others still stood. They were all talking, and he wondered if they knew what Alice was up to.

"We're going to go sing for Darlene's *onkel* who recently underwent a complicated surgery. He's a widower without any *kinner,* and he's much older than her *mamm.* Would you like to join us?" Her gorgeous brown eyes seemed hopeful, and a mixture of longing and anxiety nearly overcame him.

He glanced past her to see Jay loop his arm around Sharon's shoulders, and she leaned into his side. During the past couple of church Sundays, he'd noticed the two of them had grown closer. It was obvious they were dating now.

Dave swallowed as he imagined what could have happened last winter if Adam hadn't died. Perhaps he and Alice would have started dating. Perhaps they would be talking about a future together right now. A family. Children.

He looked down at the ground, shook his head, and fought to remove that painfully unattainable idea from his mind. "I can't."

"Why not?"

He met Alice's gaze and found disappointment in her eyes. He'd seen it there every time she'd tried to get him to join the group in some activity. But today that disappointment seemed . . . deeper.

He'd lie anyway.

"I'm tired. I need to rest. I have a busy week coming up at work."

"Oh." She seemed like she wanted to say more, but she only gave him a little smile. "Maybe you can join us next time, then."

Before she could speak again, he climbed into his buggy. "Have a *gut* week, Alice."

"You too." She waved, then turned to leave.

Relief washed over him.

"What did Dave say?" Sharon asked Alice when she returned to her friends. "Is he meeting us there?"

Alice shook her head. "No. He turned me down again."

She crossed her arms over her chest and stared at where Dave's buggy had just disappeared down the driveway, still contemplating the sadness in his face. Dave was so different now. It was as if he'd lost himself the day the accident happened.

He'd always been one of her closest friends. And he used to be happy, always smiling and joking with Cal and Jay. In fact, the three of them were nearly inseparable in school and then youth group, always trying to outdo each other with silly pranks. And Dave's boisterous laugh was contagious. He was also handsome, with light-blue eyes, light-brown hair, and a friendly face, and he was tall — around six feet, just like Cal and Jay.

For all those reasons, Alice found herself enjoying time with him. They talked about their families and shared their deepest secrets. And she even asked for his advice if she had a problem she couldn't solve on her own.

But now Dave seemed not just unhappy but broken. She hadn't seen him smile since the accident, and he'd completely distanced himself from her and all their friends. It broke her heart to see him so miserable — especially since last year she realized she harbored a secret crush on him. But she'd kept her feelings to herself for fear of ruining their friendship.

She'd encouraged Dave to join them for Sunday afternoon activities for months, but each time he'd said no. She was determined to break through the wall he'd built around himself, but how?

Alice looked at Jay. "You're one of his best *freinden,* right?"

"*Ya.*" Jay looked at Cal. "But I'd say Dave's even closer to you than to me, Cal."

"And he's always been *mei freind* as well," Alice continued. "Cal, do you have any advice for how I can get him to open up to me?"

He blew out a breath and shook his head as his trademark smile flattened into a thin line. "I don't have any advice at all. I'm just as lost as you are. I've tried to talk to him, but he blows me off. So, to be honest, I gave up."

Alice studied him. "You gave up on one of your best *freinden*?"

Cal rubbed his clean-shaven chin and looked away. "Not exactly. It's just . . ."

"It's just that he won't talk to us," Jay chimed in as he held Sharon's hand. Last spring, Sharon had admitted to Alice that, with his tall stature, brown eyes, and light-brown hair, Jay had always had her attention. Now their new dating relationship seemed to be going strong.

"But we can't give up on him," Sharon said. "He's our *freind.* He needs us." Jay gazed down at Sharon, and something reflecting how close they'd become passed between them. Along with Darlene Bender, Sharon had been Alice's best friend since they started school together when they were all seven years old. Alice had always thought Sharon was pretty with her light-brown hair and baby-blue eyes. No wonder Jay had been attracted to her, too, but his obvious care for Sharon made Alice's chest tighten. Would anyone ever look at her that way? She'd thought maybe Dave . . .

"I agree," Alice said. "I'm worried about him, and we can't give up. I don't know how, but I'm going to get him to come back to us."

She turned to Darlene. "Are you ready to go sing for your *onkel*?"

Darlene nodded. With her golden hair and brown eyes, Darlene was attractive as well, and Alice often wondered why she didn't have a boyfriend. But lately, she didn't have much time for a relationship. The Bender family was struggling as her mother received chemo treatments for cancer.

"How is your *mamm* doing?" Alice asked.

Darlene frowned. "She had another tough week." Then she gave them a weary smile. "The Lord is taking care of her, though, right? Even though she can't come to church with her immune system suppressed?"

"Of course he is," Sharon said.

Alice glanced at Andrew, who stood right next to Darlene. His dark eyes seemed to fill with concern. He'd always been the shy one, remaining quiet while Cal and Jay traded barbs at times. He pushed a lock of dark hair out of his eyes. "Would you rather we sing for your *mamm*?"

"No, but *danki.*" Darlene shook her head. "She still doesn't want visitors." She nodded toward Cal's buggy. "But, *ya,* let's go sing for *mei onkel.*"

As Alice climbed into Andrew's buggy, she began forming a plan to get Dave back in their friend group. She was determined to do it.

Confusion plagued Dave as he guided his horse home. Why did Alice keep bothering to ask him to join her and the others? He'd turned her down every time, and the last time he'd been with them was a week before the accident.

He'd always been drawn to Alice, but her nearly relentless invitations frustrated him. Deep down he knew she wouldn't want to spend time with him once she accepted who he really was. At first, Jay and Cal had tried to reignite their friendship with him as well, but they finally got smart. Just as well. Not even the men who'd been his best friends could make any difference in his life now.

Maybe they were all just trying to be good Christians. But didn't they know the truth? When he'd let them and the whole community down, he'd let God down as well.

Dave rubbed at his stinging eyes as his

horse trotted up the driveway to his parents' large, brick house with the sweeping front porch. This was where he'd been born and raised, along with his older sister, Rosemary.

After stowing his horse and buggy, he made his way inside the house. He was relieved to be alone. His sister had a family of her own now, and he'd managed to get home from church before his parents did.

He climbed the stairs to his room, where he changed out of his black Sunday suit and white shirt, then flopped onto his bed. Now he stared at the plain, white ceiling, waiting for the relief of sleep, hoping the dreams wouldn't come.

CHAPTER TWO

"How was your afternoon?" *Mamm* asked as Alice stepped into the family room later that evening. She held a novel in her hands as she relaxed in her favorite armchair.

With the dark hair and eyes Alice had inherited from her *mamm,* her friends often said she was the spitting image of her mother. All Alice knew for sure, though, was that she was grateful for *Mamm*'s special friendship and patient ear whenever she needed advice.

"It was nice. We sang for Darlene's *onkel* Merv." Alice dropped down on the worn brown sofa she'd known all her life. "He seems to be doing much better since his back surgery. Where are *Dat* and Benji?"

"They're checking on the animals."

Alice smoothed her hands over her white apron as her thoughts turned from her father and brother to Dave again. The image of his sad blue eyes had haunted her all

153

afternoon, and she'd completed her new plan on the way home.

"Is something on your mind?" *Mamm* asked.

Alice bit her lower lip. "Well, has Annie Esh mentioned any upcoming quilting bees?"

"No." *Mamm* tilted her head. "Why?"

"It's been a while since we quilted with her, and you're *gut freinden,* right?" Alice had tried to think of any other reason to get together with Dave's *mamm* in case her mother didn't like this idea. But she was sure it would work. "After all, we have quite a few quilts to finish before fall. Before you know it, the tourists will be buying quilts for Christmas gifts."

"But why do you want to quilt with Annie?" *Mamm*'s eyes assessed her, obviously looking for a motive. "What are you not telling me?"

Alice rested her elbow on the arm of the sofa and then dropped her chin to the palm of her hand. "I approached Dave again today, but he still won't join our group activities. Really, he won't even talk to me. He always looks so *bedauerlich.* I want to find a way to minister to him. I miss his friendship, and I'm worried about him."

Mamm clucked her tongue. "That was

154

such a terrible accident, and my heart breaks for Annie Esh's *freind.* Esther Fisher lost her little Adam, just seven years old. But we can't question God's plan for us or for our *kinner.*"

"I just can't take the pain in Dave's face. He used to smile and laugh, and my heart breaks every time I see him. I want to help him find happiness again. I think if we quilt with Annie at her *haus,* I'll have a better opportunity to talk to Dave, and maybe I can convince him to come to a singing with us."

Mamm smiled. "That's a *wunderbaar* idea. I'm certain he needs his *freinden.* I'll give Annie a call this week."

"Danki." Alice stood. "I'm going to change my clothes."

Once upstairs, she started down the hallway to her bedroom. But when she reached the sewing room, she stepped inside and then sank into the chair at the sewing table to look at the pink-and-blue Lonestar quilt she'd begun last week.

She ran her fingers over the stitching as she once again thought about the anguish — not just sadness — she'd seen on Dave's face, especially when he didn't know she was looking. How she longed to replace it with the joy she used to see there.

155

Closing her eyes, she whispered, "Lord, please help me break through the wall Dave has built around himself. I need your guidance so I can show him that I miss his friendship and want him back in my life. Help me show him that I'm still his *freind* and I need him to be mine."

When she opened her eyes, she smiled. A special warmth had filled her, and with God's help, Dave's friendship would return to her and all their friends.

Dave jolted upright in his bed and then glanced around his dark room before wiping away the sweat beaded on his forehead. Despite taking an afternoon nap, he'd been able to fall asleep for the night almost as soon as he laid down. But now . . .

A humid breeze and chorus of cicadas poured through his open window, and the nightmare clung to him like a second skin. He could still hear Adam's screams followed by Esther's wails, and his heart pounded like a hammer trying to break out of his chest.

Pushing himself up from his bed, he grabbed the lantern from his nightstand, then flipped on the light to pad down to the kitchen. Once there, he leaned against the sink as he filled a glass with water, and then his hand trembled as he lifted the glass to his lips and took a long drink. He dropped his head nearly to his chest, taking deep breaths in an attempt to slow his still-pounding pulse.

He lifted the lantern and slipped out to the back porch, where he dropped into the swing, breathing in fresh air, hoping to erase the horrific images and sounds the nightmares tortured him with nearly every night. Rubbing one hand down his face, he forced them all from his mind. He needed to think about something else, anything else. He closed his eyes and tried to conjure a more pleasant and comforting image.

Alice Blank.

Her lovely face. Her smile with those pink lips and high cheekbones. Her sweet voice.

His eyes snapped open. Why was he doing this to himself? This was just another kind of torture. He'd lost any chance with Alice when he'd allowed Adam to die in his care. No one would ever want to be involved with such a careless man, not even her. Alice just pitied him, like everyone else did. He'd seen it in their eyes every day since the accident. He knew they all blamed him too. Oh, he'd heard his friends and family say he wasn't at fault, but deep down, how could they think that? Of course they didn't.

His lungs seemed to freeze, but he forced the air from them as he recalled his brief encounter with Alice after church, replaying the conversation and the warmth in her eyes. She'd seemed to genuinely want him to join them as they sang for Darlene's uncle.

But she was wasting her time. After Adam died, Dave was lost in a sea of guilt and grief. He'd craved love and understanding from his friends — especially from Alice — but he'd known those friendships also died that day.

He needed a fresh start, and that was why he'd leave Bird-in-Hand as soon as he had enough money to sustain him while he searched for a job and a new home. That was also why he had to keep Alice at a distance. Soon he'd leave her behind.

He took a deep breath and then stood. He had to get some sleep before facing another day working beside his father. He loved his parents and Rosemary and her husband, Stephen — and certainly his little niece, Nancy. But they all felt more like strangers than family now. Since the accident, he could tell they looked on him with pity, too, and blame had to be just under the surface no matter how they tried to hide it. Just like everyone else, they were no doubt judging

158

him for his mistake with every step he took. How could they help it?

If only he hadn't let them down.

If only he hadn't let down God.

Dave pinched the bridge of his nose as blame again pummeled his heart.

He grabbed his lantern and empty glass, and after locking the back door behind him, he deposited the glass in the sink and then took the stairs to his room.

Dropping onto his bed, he closed his eyes and tried to clear his mind. But Alice's face floated to the front. He needed to shove away any thoughts of her. After all, once he left, he'd never see her again.

If only he could understand why his heart hurt at the thought of leaving Alice when it was the best choice for his future — and for her.

Alice leaned forward on her gardening cart and pulled another weed from the ripe, red tomato plants. The Tuesday morning sun warmed the back of her neck as she dropped the weed into the bucket beside her and then glanced around her garden, taking in the green lettuce and cucumbers waiting for their turn to be picked. The garden was actually her mother's, but *Mamm* always said she considered it theirs because Alice loved it so.

She tented her hand over her eyes as she heard *Mamm* call her name.

"Alice!" She called again as she came closer.

"*Ya?* Is everything all right?"

"Everything is fine." *Mamm*'s smile widened. "I just checked the voice mail messages, and you had one from Sharon. She's hosting a supper Friday night and wants to know if you can help serve — and also sing. Those meals with the *Englishers* are so popular. It's a great way for families like the Lamberts to teach them about our culture as well as make a little extra money to help their families."

"I'd love to go. Would it be all right?"

"Of course. You'll be interested in another message too. Annie Esh called me back. I mentioned it's been a long time since we've quilted together, and she wants us to come over for a quilting bee Thursday afternoon."

"That sounds like the perfect opportunity for me to talk to Dave once he's home from work." Alice popped up from the cart and hugged her mother. *"Danki!"*

"Gern gschehne." *Mamm* pointed to the tomato plants. "It looks like you could use some help with that weeding."

"I thought you were dusting the down-stairs."

"I'm done." *Mamm* nodded toward the cart. "If I can sit, I'll help you."

"That would be fun." Alice smiled as *Mamm* sank down and started weeding. How she enjoyed the time they spent working side by side. And how grateful she was that *Mamm* was going to help her minister to Dave.

The rays from the sun Thursday afternoon burned through Dave's gray shirt, already soiled from the day's work. Worse, his shoulders ached and his back throbbed as he set another brick on the foundation that would support the basement walls of the house they were building.

He removed his straw hat and swiped his bandana over his sweaty forehead, then glanced around at the other workers. Nearly all his father's employees were Amish, dressed in clothes similar to his — darker-colored, button-down shirts; broadfall trousers; and suspenders.

Dave took a long drink from his bottle of water as he observed his father giving instructions to the newest member of the team. The young Amish man seemed eager to please as he nodded and wore a serious

161

expression.

Not that long ago, Dave had been eager to please his father, too, soaking up everything *Dat* told him about brick masonry. He'd enjoyed using his hands to build homes, fences, and patios. And although he ran the risk of being prideful, he knew he was good at it. He'd felt as if he'd found his calling, and he dreamt of the day he would build his own home in Bird-in-Hand.

But he no longer enjoyed his work. And he was planning to leave the community — and his job. But today, he was somehow filled with a mixture of regret and anxiety.

Dave replaced his hat and set down the water bottle, then rubbed the sore muscles in his shoulders.

"How are you doing here, David?"

Dave glanced over his shoulder as *Dat* approached, his face stern, which seemed to be the only expression he wore at work. He took the business seriously, but Dave couldn't blame him for that. "It's going well. We're making progress."

"Gut, gut." *Dat* looked down at his clipboard. "Well, then, keep going. We have a deadline to meet," he said before walking away.

As Dave turned back to the foundation, he suddenly found himself longing for

162

someone to talk to, someone who would listen and offer the understanding his heart ached to receive. But how could anyone he knew — even Cal, who'd been his closest friend, or even his own father — really care about him after the mistake he'd made? They couldn't. Nor could they ever understand his agony.

He'd just have to follow through with his plan to leave. Maybe he'd make new friends somewhere, with people who'd never know what he'd done. And no matter how much he craved someone's understanding, he'd never risk telling them. Never.

CHAPTER THREE

Gnawing on her lower lip, Alice stood near the window closest to the end of Annie Esh's long, rock driveway and listened for the rumble of a car engine that would announce Dave's return from work. Beside her, *Mamm* and Annie were discussing the heirloom quilt *Mamm* had added to her armload. Annie had asked her if she'd repair it — one of *Mamm*'s special talents.

As she spent the afternoon working on her king-sized Lonestar quilt, she must have peeked out the family room window nearly a hundred times, watching for Dave even when she knew it was too early for him to appear.

The whole time, conversation with *Mamm* and Annie had been mundane, mostly discussing the current health of people in the community, the weather, and sewing projects. But Alice had longed for Annie to talk about Dave, knowing his family had to

164

be dealing with his sorrow too. Several times she'd considered asking her how she thought Dave was handling the tragedy he'd experienced, but such a personal question would be inappropriate. If Annie wanted to discuss her son's well-being, she'd bring up the subject herself.

"I really had a nice time," Annie told them when *Mamm* finally seemed ready to go. "*Danki* so much for coming over." With her light-blue eyes and light-brown hair she bore a strong resemblance to Dave, and Annie could never deny he was her son.

"We had a *wunderbaar* time too." *Mamm* glanced at Alice. "Alice and I have missed quilting with you. We're so glad you were available today."

Alice nodded and then turned as the crunch of tires on rock sounded from the bottom of the driveway. Her heart seemed to flip as the black truck that carried Dave and his father home from work steered toward the large barn she knew housed their equipment and supplies. She hugged her quilt as Dave climbed out and said something to his father and their driver before heading for the barn, his shoulders hunched, his eyes focused on the ground.

She pivoted toward her mother and Annie. "Excuse me. I'd like to go say hello to Dave."

"That would be nice," Annie said.

"Take your time," *Mamm* added.

Alice hurried after him. She wasn't going to let this opportunity slip away.

"Hi!"

Dave spun toward the barn door, and his eyes widened for a split second as they focused on Alice. "Hi. What are you doing here?"

"*Mei mamm* and I quilted with your *mamm* this afternoon." She smiled as she came closer.

Dave tried to shake off his confusion. Once again Alice had completely taken him by surprise, appearing when he least expected it. Why did she keep doing this? If she spent more than five minutes with him, she'd regret it.

"I was just about to go into my workshop."

"May I join you for a minute?"

"If you want."

She followed him, and once inside, he flipped on a couple of lanterns, then dropped onto a stool by his worktable and picked up the latest iron railing he'd created. He ran his fingers over the piece and once again imagined it on one of the steep staircases he helped build.

"That's *schee.*"

Alice hugged a quilt against her black apron and peered down at the railing, her brown eyes glittering in the low light of the lanterns. She looked lovely today clad in a black apron and a dark-green dress that made her hair seem more red than brown.

She leaned over him and touched the railing. He breathed in her scent — some kind of flowery shampoo? — and his pulse strangely galloped as chills nearly made him shiver.

"Did you make this?" she asked.

He nodded.

She scanned his workshop, her intelligent eyes taking in the piles of scrap metal, his tools, and the railings he'd completed stacked in the corner. Then she looked back at him, her brow furrowed.

"I didn't know you made railings."

He shrugged. "It's sort of a new hobby."

"When did you start doing that?"

He opened his mouth to tell her it was after Adam died, but he couldn't form the words.

She sat down on the stool beside him and brushed her long, slender fingers over his work. "This is fantastic. Do you sell them?"

"I've sold a few." *And added the profits to*

the savings that will take me away from here.

"You're quite talented." She smiled at him, and warmth filled his chest.

He looked down at the table to avoid her gaze. "It's just something I do to clear my head after a long day."

"Quilting is like that for me." She looked down at her quilt and ran her hand over the fabric, which included different shades of purple and blue. It was a Lonestar pattern from what he could see, and it looked as if it had been stitched with care. But that was what he'd expect from Alice. She'd always handled her life — and her friendships — with care.

"Whenever I have a bad day, I look forward to sewing. It always makes me feel better." She met his gaze and held it. "Is that what metalworking is for you? A stress reliever?" She watched him as she waited for his response.

He took in her expectant expression, her kind eyes, her pretty face. He could almost feel her begging him to talk to her.

And why shouldn't he talk to her? This was Alice, the *maedel* he'd longed to date. But now as he looked at her, he felt tongue-tied, lost, confused.

Her smile wobbled, and he felt guilty. He needed to say something against the awkward silence that felt like a giant chasm expanding between them.

"Your quilt is *schee.*" He pointed to it. "Is that a gift for someone? Or are you going to sell it?"

"Oh." She seemed surprised by the compliment as she looked down at it. "I'll probably sell it. We send quilts to auction, and we also sell them at the farmers market in Bird-in-Hand." She unfolded part of it and smoothed it onto her lap. "It's a Lonestar."

"The colors are nice."

"Danki." Her smile was back as she folded the quilt. "So, Dave, we're all getting together to help with a meal for *Englishers* and then sing at Sharon's tomorrow night. You could come with us."

He fought to keep the dismay from his face. Serving a meal together would be bad enough, but singing in front of strangers as though they were all still friends?

"You know how the tourists like to book meals in an Amish home so they can learn more about our culture."

He blinked and then shook his head. "Thanks for inviting me, but I have too much work to do." He gestured around the shop, even though his ironwork was more of a hobby than a job.

"It's fun. We started singing for *Englishers*

169

in the spring, and we're trying to get more *freinden* involved. The food is *gut* too. We get to eat the leftovers." She gave a little laugh that sounded more forced than genuine.

Was Alice nervous around him? Before the accident, they could discuss almost anything. But now they were sitting here staring at each other like acquaintances, not lifelong friends.

"Why don't you stop by Sharon's after work, Dave? You might enjoy it."

He raised an eyebrow as he studied her. "Did Cal tell you to invite me?"

"No." Her eyes narrowed. "Why?"

"He used to try to invite me to come to things, too, after . . ." He couldn't finish the sentence. And he'd already said too much. He needed her to leave. "I don't want to be anyone's pet project."

She hesitated. "I don't know what you mean. It was my idea to invite you."

"Why?"

"Because I miss you. I mean, *we all* miss you."

The emotion in her eyes was too much for him. "You should go." He looked down at his workbench.

"Okay." Her voice was small, tentative. "Good-bye."

"Bye." He kept his eyes focused on the worktable until she was gone. Then he blew out the breath he hadn't realized he'd been holding.

He rested his elbows on his knees, chin on his palms, and recalled how close to Alice he'd once felt. If only he could find that level of intimacy with her again.

But even if she were the same, he would never be the same. Never.

Never just felt like such a long time.

"I think that was a *gut* supper," Sharon said as she carried the last empty platter to the counter. Alice had heard her send her mother to the family room, telling her they had plenty of help for cleanup even though Darlene couldn't come, and she deserved to relax.

"*Ya,* it was *gut.* And the food was great." Ruby Sue, Sharon's younger sister, finished wiping down the folding tables as Jay, Cal, and Andrew dealt with the folding chairs. "I love spaghetti and meatball casserole as much as *Englishers* seem to, and the corn, salad, and peanut butter pie were great too. You and *Mamm* outdid yourselves — again."

Alice found the dustpan and broom in the utility room and began sweeping the kitchen floor. As she worked, she hummed "Amazing Grace" — one of the songs they'd sung to the guests — and her thoughts wrapped around Dave. He'd rather rudely asked her to leave his workshop yesterday, but she still couldn't get his sad face out of her mind.

"Alice?"

"Ya?" Alice looked up to where Jay stood beside her, balancing a chair under each arm. "Oops! Am I in your way?"

He gave her a sheepish smile. "I almost walked into you."

"He's being nice," Sharon chimed in from where she stood at the sink, about to wash dishes. *"You* almost walked into *him."*

Alice's cheeks heated as everyone looked at her. "I'm sorry."

"You okay?" Ruby Sue asked as she hung her wet dishcloth to dry.

"Ya." She stooped to sweep a pile of crumbs into the dustpan. "I talked to Dave yesterday. I invited him to come tonight, but he said he couldn't because he had work to do, which I know was just an excuse. I tried to convince him to even come late, but he refused."

Cal stopped folding chairs and looked at her. "Really?"

"He asked me if it was your idea to invite him."

"Huh. Well, like you, I tried to talk him

into hanging out with us after the accident, but he never would. He told me to leave him alone, so I backed off. I know I said I gave up on him when he wouldn't talk to me, but it was more like I didn't know what else to do." Cal returned to the chairs.

"He told me he didn't want to be anyone's pet project. Do you know what he meant by that?"

Cal turned around again. "I'm not sure, but the more I think about it, the more I think maybe I pushed him too hard when he kept telling me he was fine."

Alice fingered the handle of the broom as she again recalled the anguish she'd seen in Dave's face. "I keep getting the feeling he needs me to reach out to him. Like he doesn't want me to give up on him, even though he's pushing me away."

Cal shook his head. "It's nice that you invited him to one of these suppers, but I don't think he'll ever come. When I tried talking to him, he was adamant that he needed space. That accident changed him."

"That's so *bedauerlich,*" Sharon said.

Ruby Sue clucked her tongue as she joined Sharon to dry dishes.

"I feel so bad for him." Jay started folding the legs of the first table.

As Alice returned to sweeping, she silently

vowed not to give up on Dave no matter what. In her heart, she knew he needed a friend, and she would keep trying until he once again allowed her to be that friend.

When the kitchen was clean, Alice said good night to her friends and then started down the street to her farm, a flashlight guiding her way through the dark as fireflies glittered around her.

Above her, the sky was dotted with bright stars, and the cicadas sang their nightly chorus. Her mind still swirled with questions. She'd heard what Cal said, but how could he stop trying to reach Dave when they'd been best friends for years? Couldn't he tell Dave needed his friendship now more than ever?

But at the same time, Alice understood why he might have stopped trying. After all, Dave's rejection last night had cut her to the bone. Perhaps he'd hurt Cal just as much, if not more.

As Alice made her way up her rock driveway, she spotted a flashlight bobbing toward the house. She quickened her steps to catch up with her older brother as he headed toward the porch. With his dark hair and eyes, they were easily identified as siblings despite their three-year age difference. At least, that's what Sharon had once told Alice. Benji was just a few inches taller than Alice, and his broad shoulders boasted his hard work as a dairy farmer.

"Benji. Isn't it late for you to be feeding the horses?" she asked as she fell into step with him.

"I just got home from Joyce's *haus*. Were you at Sharon's?"

"*Ya*. How is Joyce?"

Benji's smile was wide. "She's *gut*."

"Have you proposed yet?"

He blew out a sigh. "You know I need to build her a *haus* first. Maybe in a couple of years."

Alice smiled at the thought of someday calling Joyce Petersheim her sister-in-law. Benji had been dating her for four years now, and even though Joyce was three years older than Alice, she'd always gone out of her way to talk to Alice as if they were the same age. She considered Joyce a friend, and she looked forward to officially welcoming her into the family.

"Could I ask your advice?" Alice asked when they'd reached the top porch step.

"Sure." Benji turned toward her.

"How can I convince someone to trust me?"

Benji smirked. "Could you be a little more specific?"

175

"You know what happened to Dave Esh, right?"

He frowned. "Of course I do. Everyone heard about what happened. Terrible tragedy."

"Well, Dave and I have always been *gut freinden*. But after the accident, he pulled away from me and the rest of our *freinden*." She shared how she and the others had reached out to him, inviting him to join them for activities, but he'd rejected them again and again. "How can I encourage Dave to open up to me? He acts like he doesn't even trust me anymore."

Benji leaned back on the porch railing and rubbed his chin. "I think you need to keep doing what you've been doing. Keep inviting him."

"Even though he keeps rejecting me?"

"*Ya,* don't give up on him. God doesn't give up on us, right?"

"Right."

"Then we shouldn't give up on each other when we're struggling." Benji pointed at her. "If you keep inviting him, eventually he'll realize that you're a *freind* he needs. And someday soon, he'll accept your invitation. Would you like me to ask Joyce what she thinks? Confidentially, of course."

"*Ya. Danki.*" Hope lit in her chest as she

176

entered the house, imagining the moment Dave would finally return to their group of friends, even though she still didn't know why he was so determined to be alone in his sorrow. Until then, she'd seek him out and keep reminding him he was always welcome to join them.

The following Wednesday afternoon, Dave paid for his club sandwich and bottle of water before pocketing his change, taking the paper bag containing his lunch, and heading toward the restaurant exit. He'd been so exhausted this morning that he'd failed to pick up the lunch his mother packed for him. He'd told her dozens of times that he could make his own lunch, but she insisted she was packing one for *Dat* anyway.

"Dave!"

Turning, Dave almost walked right into Cal and his younger brother, Raymond.

Cal's smile was bright, almost too bright. "How are you?"

"Fine. *Gut* to see you." Dave gave them each a nod and then started toward the exit again.

"Hang on, Dave!"

Dave halted and closed his eyes as he bit

back a groan. He just wanted to eat his lunch in peace before going back to the sweltering worksite. He swiveled toward Cal and Ray again. *"Ya?"*

"How have you been?" Cal gave him a tentative smile as if he worried Dave would turn and bolt through the door. "We haven't talked in a while."

"I've been busy." Dave gripped the paper bag tighter. "You?"

"Gut." Cal cleared his throat as he glanced at his brother and then back at Dave. "We've all missed you."

Dave's eyes narrowed as frustration sizzled through him. "So I've heard. Did you tell Alice to invite me to sing at Sharon's supper last week?"

"No." Cal shook his head as his expression seemed to fill with surprise. "That was Alice's idea, but we all would like you to come hang out with us again. I think it would be *gut* for you."

The pity in Cal's face sent Dave's anger surging. "As I told Alice, I don't want to be anyone's pet project."

Cal frowned. "That makes no sense. You're not a pet project. You're our *freind,* and *freinden* care about each other."

"When did you start caring so much?"

Cal leaned in and lowered his voice as

customers squeezed past them. "I've always cared, Dave. You're the one who pushed us all away." He turned to Ray. "Let's go." He looked back at Dave. "We'll all still be here when you realize you need us." Then he turned and strode toward the counter with Ray at his side.

Dave stared after his former best friend for a moment and then headed out to the waiting work truck. As he climbed into the back, Cal's words echoed in his mind. If he *had* pushed his friends away, it was for good reason. He didn't need their pity or their judgment.

Besides, none of them — especially Alice — had any idea what it would be like to spend time with the man he'd become. Maybe they really were just a bunch of do-gooders as he suspected when he told Alice and then Cal he didn't want to be a pet project. They needed to leave him alone. And the sooner he left, the better.

Alice stood at the sink and washed a supper plate later that evening. She'd spent the day cleaning and quilting as thoughts of Dave plagued her. She'd tried to come up with a plan to get him to join them for a singing, but her only idea was to go back to his house for another afternoon of quilting so she could at least talk to him just as Benji advised.

Of course, he might show her the door again, but she was determined not to surrender to his rejections.

"You look so serious. What are you thinking about?" *Mamm* asked as she lifted a handful of clean utensils from the rinse water.

Alice looked sideways so *Mamm* could see she was okay, but, yes, she was serious. "I was wondering if we could plan another quilting bee at Annie's *haus.*"

"So you can try to talk to Dave again? Maybe issue another invitation?"

"*Ya.* I asked Benji for advice, and he suggested I keep trying."

Mamm smiled. "I have an idea. You know that quilt Annie asked me to repair? I'm almost finished with it. What if we deliver it tomorrow night? If we wait until after we've cleaned the kitchen, we'll most likely arrive at their *haus* after Dave normally comes home from work. We don't want to go too early and miss him."

"Perfect! And I can bake something for him." She snapped her fingers. "I think he once said his favorite *kuche* is carrot. I'll take one as a gift."

"That's a fantastic idea." *Mamm* set the

dried utensils in the drawer. "While you bake, I'll finish the quilt."

When they finished in the kitchen, *Mamm* headed upstairs to the sewing room, and Alice opened her grandmother's cookbook. She found her favorite carrot cake recipe and began to gather the ingredients. As she did, she sent up a silent prayer.

Lord, please let this kuche *be a blessing to Dave. Grant me the right words to show him that his* freinden *miss him and we want him back in our lives. Guide my heart as I remind him that you love him and want the best for him.*

Surely God would help her show Dave he needed his friends.

As Dave stepped from the mudroom onto the back porch after supper Friday evening, he breathed in the still-humid June air. The day had been long and exhausting as he and the crew worked on a staircase for a mansion a few counties over.

His back and neck ached, and his knees were sore. But it had been a good day. At least he found himself in a relatively good mood.

His work boots crunched the rocks in the path that led from the back porch to the large barn housing his workshop. Once inside the shop, he flipped on the lanterns before sitting down at his worktable, then picked up a tool and began working on the railing he hoped to sell on their next job.

He was twisting the metal with the help of a vise and two pipe wrenches when he felt as though someone was watching him. He turned toward the doorway, where Alice stood holding a cake container with plates, forks, and napkins balanced on top.

Wearing a pink dress that matched her pretty cheeks, and a black apron, she gave him a sweet smile, and for a moment, he was almost certain that his heart had turned over.

"Hi." Her voice was soft and unsure, as if she were nervous.

"Hi." He spun on the stool to face her. "What are you doing here?"

She held up the cake container. "I remember you once told me you liked carrot *kuche.*" Her dark eyebrows lifted. "Is that still true?"

"It's my favorite." He studied her as a new suspicion nipped at him. "Did you come here just to bring me a *kuche*?"

She came up beside him, and when she set the container on the worktable, the delicious aroma caused his stomach to gurgle.

"Not exactly," she said. "*Mei mamm* repaired a quilt for your *mamm,* and she wanted to drop it off tonight. I thought I'd come along and bring you something special to brighten your day."

He swallowed as his throat dried. Did Alice genuinely care if his day needed brightening? Maybe so, but she probably took cakes to everyone she felt sorry for.

She took the top off the container and revealed the cake, already sliced. Then she used a fork to scoop a piece onto a paper plate. After handing the plate and a napkin and fork to him, she put a second piece on a plate, replaced the lid, and then pointed to a nearby metal stool. "May I sit here?"

"Of course."

She pushed the stool over to him and hopped up on it. Then he watched her bow her head in silent prayer before taking a bite of the cake.

He took a bite, too, and then he closed his eyes as his taste buds danced with delight. He savored the sweetness, and for the first time in months, he felt a glimmer of happiness enter his soul.

"You don't like it."

"What?" His eyes popped open, and he found her staring at him, her lovely face twisted in a frown. "No. I mean, I love it. It's fantastic."

"Whew." She blew out a sigh, and her smile reappeared. "I thought maybe I'd added too much sugar or something."

"It's perfect."

"Gut." She looked down at her plate again.

They ate in an easy silence for several moments, and his shoulders relaxed. Normally, his empty workshop was his sanctuary away from everything and everyone, but now he felt comfort in Alice's company. He still couldn't stop one question from echoing in the back of his mind, though.

"Why are you here?" he asked as he set down his plate.

She shrugged one shoulder. "I already told you. *Mei mamm* wanted to deliver the quilt to your *mamm,* so I decided to come and bring along a *kuche* for you." She pointed her fork at his half-eaten piece.

"That's not what I mean." He took a deep breath as his suspicion returned. "Why are you checking up on me? I told you I don't want to be a project. I can take care of myself."

She set her fork on the plate, then placed them both on the workbench beside her. She folded her hands in her lap, and her brown eyes glistened as she met his gaze.

"Dave, if you think I'm here on some kind of pity mission, then I've been a terrible *freind* to you. I'm sorry I haven't had the right words to say, that I haven't known how to best reach out to you since the accident without you thinking I'm a terrible person."

Her words shocked him, and then guilt overtook him once again.

"No, that's not true." His voice sounded raspy. "*I'm* the terrible person everyone has to hate."

"No, Dave, you're —"

"I'm the one who let Adam die. I couldn't —" His voice cracked, and he covered his face with his hands as emotion threatened to pour out. He took deep, shuddering breaths as he tried to hold back all the blame that had plagued him for months.

The soft touch of her hand on his bicep was just the balm he needed as he tried to keep tears from spilling over.

"It's okay." Her voice was soft and warm near his ear. "I'm here. You can tell me."

He took another deep breath, then wiped his stinging eyes. Where to begin?

He stared at the floor as he spoke.

"*Mamm* and Esther have been *gut freinden* ever since they were in youth group together in Esther's district, and when Esther married — quite a few years after *Mamm* married *Dat* — and moved to this district, the *zwillingbopplin* were born the next year.

"That afternoon, it was Esther's turn to care for her *aenti,* who was *krank,* but her husband was out of town for a week on a job with his boss, and her cousin canceled babysitting for her. Esther called and said Adam and Kevin thought of me themselves since I'd cared for them before. Even though I was older, I still visited the family with *Mamm* just so I could spend time with the *buwe.* They . . . they were the little *bruders* I'd never had.

"When I got there, I asked Esther if I could take the *zwillingbopplin* to the pond right down the street from their *haus.* It was January, and with the cold we'd had, I was" — he swallowed hard — "I was sure the pond was frozen solid. I'd skated there myself as a *bu.*

"The *zwillingbopplin* told me they were *gut* skaters, so I let them take off all around the pond. But Kevin fell, and I skated over to help him up. Then I heard that terrible cracking noise. I can still hear it if I close my eyes . . ."

He'd never told the story like this before, and he didn't know if he could go on.

"It's okay, Dave. I'm listening."

Maybe Alice *would* understand.

"I got to Adam as fast as I could after screaming for Kevin to run to a neighbor's for help. But at first I couldn't find him. He'd hit his head and slipped under the ice. When I realized he wasn't breathing once I managed to lift him out of the water, I did my best to give him CPR, but . . . it was too late. He was dead before we could even get him to a hospital. And I can't get the sound of Esther's wails out of my head. I can still hear her crying for her *sohn.* I can't —"

A knot swelled in his throat, cutting off his words. He held his paper napkin up to his face, humiliation whipping through him as he tried to control his emotions. He wiped his eyes and then jammed his eyelids shut. He didn't want to cry, especially in front of Alice.

The pressure of her hand on his bicep disappeared, leaving a cold longing in its wake. Why did he suddenly crave her touch?

Then loud scraping of metal on the concrete floor sounded, and her hand landed on his bicep again.

"It's okay." Her voice was right next to his ear, sending heat soaring through his veins. She'd moved closer to him, and her nearness was a comfort! "You can share whatever you need to. Get it off your chest."

He shook his head, then cleared his throat past the lump. "I'm okay."

"You can talk to me." Her tone seemed to be pleading with him, and when he looked at her, the compassion on her face was almost too much for him to bear.

"There's nothing else to say. I did an unforgivable thing. Skating on that pond was my idea. I let a *kind* die, and I deserve to be alone."

"No, you don't." She gave his bicep a squeeze. "Maybe you made a mistake about the pond being safe enough, but God still loves you. Your community and *freinden* love you, and so does your family. You're forgiven. Forgive yourself."

"I don't deserve God's grace." He looked down at the floor again. "And I'll never forgive myself, because I broke a family." He closed his eyes as the moments of disaster filled his mind again. "I left a twin without his *bruder* and two parents without their precious *sohn.* I'm a monster."

"You're not, Dave. Listen to me." She pulled her hand away, and she seemed to study him with frustration in her eyes. "You need to stop punishing yourself."

She paused as if contemplating something. "Come sing with us Sunday afternoon. I don't know who we'll sing to yet, but I'm sure Sharon will know of someone. It's a new ministry for her and the rest of us. And

189

I do think it will make you feel better. When I minister to someone else, I always feel as if God is wrapping me in a hug and encouraging me. Singing about his love and forgiveness will help you work through your grief and feelings of guilt. It's just the medicine you need."

She smiled. "Come with us, Dave. Just once. Maybe it's what you need for God to heal your soul."

He shook his head. "I can't." *Not even for you.*

He picked up the plate and forked more cake into his mouth, keeping his eyes trained on the remaining morsels.

"Why not?"

"I just can't." He set his plate back on the worktable. *"Danki* for bringing this. It was *appeditlich."* He pointed to his project. "I need to finish this railing and then feed the animals. I'm sure you have to get home."

She nodded and stood, but he detected disappointment in her expression. "I'm glad you enjoyed it." She set her plate on top of the container. "I'll leave the *kuche* for you. You can share it with your family. I can get the container later."

"Danki."

"Have a *gut* evening."

"You too."

190

As he watched her go, the comfort he'd felt in her presence disappeared, and the familiar loneliness crept back into his heart.

CHAPTER FIVE

"It didn't go the way I hoped," Alice said as she sat beside her mother in their buggy on the way home from the Esh house. She tried to push away the disappointment that overwhelmed her as she looked out toward the cars roaring past them on the road.

"He shared what happened the day Adam died, and he got emotional. I think he even shed a few tears. But he still won't join us at a singing." Her heart had nearly shredded when she'd seen the pain in his eyes. Oh how she longed to take it away!

"That's progress, though." *Mamm* gave her a sideways glance from her place in the driver's seat.

"It is. But we used to talk about nearly everything. Then after the accident, he completely shut me out. He shut everyone out." She turned to face her mother. "Has Annie ever shared anything about how Dave seems to be at home?"

"No. I think it's probably too painful for her to talk about anything related to the accident, and of course, I would never just ask."

"I understand, but I imagine he's shutting out his family too." She sighed. "At first, he seemed to be accusing me of being some kind of interfering do-gooder. I told him I was sorry I'd failed to know how to reach out to him, that I'd caused him to think that about me. Then what he went through that night came pouring out." Alice looked out at the deepening twilight.

"But now it sounds like you are getting through to him." *Mamm*'s smile widened as she guided the horse through an intersection. "I'm so proud of you for not giving up. You're a true *freind.*"

Alice turned back toward her mother. "But I'm not much of a *freind* at all if he still refuses to join me — us. At least on Sundays."

"But he trusted you enough to share what happened that day. Your efforts are paying off, Alice. Keep praying for him and asking God to give you the right words. I know God will give you the keys to unlock Dave's heart."

Alice stared out the window again and hugged her arms to her waist. *Mamm* was right; only God could help her win Dave's trust completely. She just hoped he'd reveal those keys before Dave closed himself off forever — or as she now feared, before he left everyone and everything he knew behind.

"What do you have there?" *Mamm* asked as Dave stepped into the kitchen later that evening.

He set the cake container on the counter and dropped the used plastic forks, paper plates, and napkins into the trash can. "It's a carrot *kuche.*"

"Carrot *kuche*?" *Mamm* opened the lid and examined the remaining pieces of cake. "That's lovely." She narrowed her eyes. "Where did you get this? Did a customer give it to you today — and you hid it in your workshop so you could eat it all yourself?" Then she smiled.

He lifted an eyebrow, unamused, and filled a glass with water. "No. Didn't you see Alice bring it to me?"

"No, I didn't. Dorothy came inside to give me a quilt, saying Alice was going to say hello to you out in the barn." She grabbed a clean plate from a cabinet and dropped a piece of cake on it. Then she forked a bite into her mouth and moaned. "This is *wun-*

derbaar. It's so moist."

"It is *gut.*" He swallowed the last of his water and then started toward the stairs. "I'm going to take a shower."

"Wait. Tell me about Alice."

He slowly turned to face her. "There really isn't much to tell. She brought me the *kuche* and asked me how I was." *And I was moved to tears as I started spilling my guts to her.*

He recalled the sympathy and kindness in Alice's eyes. Was Cal right? Had Dave truly alienated everyone when all they wanted was to still be his friend? Alice was reaching out to him in a new way, and he was beginning to doubt he'd been right about her motives. About all his friends' motives.

"Dorothy told me Alice and the rest of your *freinden* have been singing for *krank* members of the community and for *Englishers* at Sharon's *haus* for suppers." *Mamm* leaned back against the counter as she held up her plate. "She said they plan to sing this Sunday too. Maybe you should go with them. Try getting out of this *haus* and spending time with your *freinden.*" She paused. "Dave, you have to learn to live again."

Renewed fear and frustration boiled in Dave's gut. "How can I live again when Adam will never go home to his family?"

Mamm's eyes widened, and she set the plate on the counter before walking over to him. "You made a mistake, but at some point you have to move on. Forgive yourself."

He shook his head as that familiar ball of grief filled his throat once again, stealing his words.

"Listen to me." She rested her hand on his arm. "You know it's a sin to doubt God's will. Adam may be gone, but you're still here. God still has plans for you. You can't punish yourself forever."

"That's easier said than done."

"Dorothy also said Cal, Jay, and Andrew go to these singings, so you won't be the only man there." She tilted her head. "You and Cal used to be especially close."

"That was a long time ago. Things change." He took a step back and out of her touch.

"Why don't you try to reconnect with him? You need *freinden.*" The concern in her eyes made his chest tighten. "It's not healthy for you to be alone. You're young. You should be dating. You should be enjoying life and thinking about a future. A family."

He took another step back toward the stairs. "I really need to shower." He turned and almost made it.

"David."

He stopped on the bottom step and let his head drop down. With a deep sigh, he faced her again.

"I'm worried about you." She joined him and reached up to cup her hand to his cheek. "I can't stand to see you so *bedauerlich* and alone. Even angry. Please try to reconnect with the community. Your *freinden* can help you. I don't want to see you this way for the rest of your life."

He cleared his throat and looked down. "Fine, *Mamm.*"

"Danki." She patted his cheek and turned back toward the counter. "I'm going to finish this *appeditlich* piece of carrot *kuche*. Alice is a talented baker. You should ask her to make you another one of these."

As Dave climbed the stairs, Alice's face filled his mind. She was beautiful, sweet, thoughtful, and talented. Dave would be blessed to have a woman like her in his life, but surely Alice could gain the attention of any man in the community. Why would she waste her time on a damaged creature like him?

He pushed the thought away. After all, he wasn't planning to stay in the community. He had no right to even think about Alice.

But just the same, she lingered at the edge of his thoughts as he retreated into his bedroom.

"Are we going to go sing for Titus Zook today?" Alice asked as she stood with her friends after church at the Bontragers' place.

"That sounds *gut.*" Sharon leaned against Cal's buggy.

Alice turned to Darlene. "How is your *mamm* today?"

Darlene shrugged. "She had another tough week, but she seemed better this morning. She insisted that *mei dat* and I come to church, though, and Biena stayed home with her."

"Could we sing for her today instead of to Titus?" Alice asked.

"*Ya.* Sharon and I were just discussing how we want to help you and your family more," Jay said as he took Sharon's hand and looked at her. "Weren't we?"

Sharon nodded, then looked at Darlene. "Let's sing for her."

"And we can make her a meal for your family this week too," Alice added.

"No, but *danki.*" Darlene crossed her arms over her yellow dress and white apron. "You all keep offering, and I appreciate it, but she doesn't want company. She insists she would rather just our family take care of her, and we know what she can stomach and can't. She's very private."

"I understand." Alice glanced toward the far end of the driveway and saw Dave walking toward his buggy. "I'll be right back," she told them all before she dashed away.

"Dave!" she called. "Dave! Wait up!"

He turned toward her, and to her surprise, he waved. But his blue eyes were rimmed with dark circles, as if he'd had a restless night. He was still handsome, though, and her heart swelled as she approached him.

"How are you?" she asked.

"I'm okay." He glanced past her and then met her gaze. "I guess you and your *freinden* are planning another singing today."

She looked over her shoulder and found the four of them pretending not to watch them, but she knew they were. She turned toward him again. "They're your *freinden* too."

He folded his arms over his wide chest. "I enjoyed your *kuche.*"

"Oh?" She raised her eyebrows. "Did you share it with your family or keep it all for yourself?"

"Sadly, *mei mamm* made me share it."

A burst of laughter exploded from her lips, and he smiled. The expression lit up his entire face, and she felt . . . happy.

"I hope she enjoyed it too."

"Oh, she did. *Danki* again."

"Gern gschehne." She studied him. "What other kind of *kuche* do you like?"

He rubbed his clean-shaven chin. "I honestly like all *kuche*. I suppose I'm not a big coconut fan, but I like everything else. And I like pie too."

She nodded, making a mental note. "I'll have to bring you another treat when I come to quilt with your *mamm*."

"You don't need to do that."

"I will if it will guarantee me another smile." She knew the words were bold, but she didn't stop them from escaping her lips. Maybe her baking was one key to opening his heart.

He stilled for a moment and then swallowed, never breaking his gaze.

"Please come sing with us today," she said. "We're going to try to cheer up Titus Zook. He's been going for chemotherapy, and his *fraa* says he's been struggling."

He glanced past her again, and then his lips pressed into a flat line. "Alice, you're *schee,* sweet, and thoughtful, but you really shouldn't waste your time on me. I'm not worth a second thought." He paused. "I'm not worthy of God's forgiveness, and I'm not worthy of yours either."

Her heart seemed to break, but then she narrowed her eyes with determination. "That's where you're wrong, David Esh." She jammed her finger into his chest. "You're worth more than you know, to God and to me, and someday soon I'm going to convince you of that."

His mouth dropped open, and then she turned and marched back to her friends to the tune of alternating frustration, disappointment, and heartbreak.

Dave stood in stunned silence as the ties from Alice's *kapp* fluttered behind her.

She'd just told him he was worthy. And he could feel the determination coming off her in waves. Did that mean she really did care about him? That she didn't just feel sorry for him? And was she right about God?

A strange new longing swirled in his chest. He wanted to run after Alice and tell her he'd go with her and their friends, and then he imagined himself standing by her side as they sang hymns for Titus Zook. But he felt cemented in place, his shoes stuck to the rock driveway as if his guilt, sorrow, and grief were as strong as the mortar he used while building walls and stairs.

He remained in place as Alice approached his group of old friends and said something to them. Cal met his gaze and smiled as he waved. Dave responded with a nod. Then Alice climbed into Cal's buggy, and Dave's longing intensified. He not only wanted to go with her to Titus Zook's house; he wanted her to ride in his buggy.

She should be at my side. She belongs with me.

Dave swiped both hands down his face and closed his eyes. He had to stop these thoughts! After all, he planned to leave the community and never look back. He couldn't drag sweet Alice into his nightmare. And he knew she was wrong about what God thought about him.

He climbed into his buggy just as Cal's horse and buggy passed by. He snuck a glance at Alice, who was sitting beside Cal and smiling as she spoke to him. White-hot jealousy roared through him. He had to extinguish these feelings for Alice. They would do nothing but make leaving more difficult. He had to find a way to put her out of his mind for good.

Dave stowed his horse and buggy and then stepped into the house, where he poured himself a glass of iced tea from the pitcher in the refrigerator. He rested his hip against the kitchen counter and savored the cool drink as he tried to force an image of Alice's sweet smile into oblivion.

Then just as he reached the bottom step of the stairs, his parents entered the kitchen.

"David!" *Mamm* called. "Are you home?"

"Ya." He stepped back into the kitchen and leaned on the doorway frame.

Mamm smiled. "What were you and Alice talking about after church?"

Dave bit back a groan as his parents watched him with interest. "Nothing important."

"It looked important to me." *Mamm* sang the words. "What was it?"

Dave raked his hand through his thick hair. "She just wanted to say hello, and she invited me to go singing with her and her *freinden* today." He regretted the admission as soon as it left his lips.

Dat's brow furrowed. "Why didn't you go with her?"

"I've told you before. Nothing is the same now. I don't fit in with that group." He might as well tell the whole truth. He'd be gone soon. He had almost enough money now. "I don't fit in with this community anymore, either."

His parents exchanged a look, their eyes

wide with distress.

"Don't say that." *Mamm* hustled over and took his hand in hers. "You belong here. You're a baptized member of the community, and you're our *sohn.* Tell me you're not planning to leave." She placed her hand on her chest. "Don't break my heart. Promise me you won't."

Dave looked into his mother's panicked face, and he couldn't tell her the rest. He couldn't admit that he thought about leaving every day, especially when he found himself lying in bed at night, so very lonely.

"I'm still here," he said, unable to lie to his mother.

"Don't do anything you'll regret." *Dat* sidled up to him and rested his hand on Dave's shoulder. "If you leave, you'll be shunned. Life isn't as easy as you think on the outside. When *mei bruder* left, he struggled to find a job and make enough money to pay rent. He wound up living in a homeless shelter for a while. You don't want to be destitute." He gestured around the kitchen. "You have everything you need here, and you're a talented brick mason. The company will be yours someday, and you don't want to miss that opportunity."

Dave looked down at his shoes to break his parents' stares.

"And I think you and Alice care for each other," *Dat* said.

Dave's gaze snapped to his father's. "What did you say?"

"You heard me. It's obvious."

Was that a smug expression on *Dat*'s face?

Dave blinked. His father had noticed his attraction to Alice. But he had to be wrong about Alice being attracted to him.

"If you leave, you'll lose the opportunity to date her. You've been close *freinden* for years. You should see how that friendship could develop into more," *Mamm* chimed in.

"Alice might still want to be a *freind,* but she would never be interested in dating me after what I did." Dave's voice sounded raw to his own ears. "Stop trying to force me to go back to my former *freinden,* let alone date a woman in this community — any woman. It won't happen."

Mamm placed a palm on his chest. "Ask God to heal your heart and lead you on the right path."

Dave stepped away. "I'm going to my room."

Before they could respond, he made his way upstairs, then sat on the edge of his bed as his mother's advice rang through his mind.

He'd tried to pray a few times, but he could never form the words. He didn't deserve God's guidance or mercy. He deserved to suffer the same way Adam's family had suffered.

Dave glanced out his window at the beautiful, sunny, cloudless blue sky, and his heart ached. If only he'd saved Adam, then maybe he'd be next to Alice as she sang this afternoon.

But it was only right for him to endure the pain of his mistake for the rest of his life. And despite his parents' pleas, he would leave the community, no matter how much it would shatter his heart to lose Alice forever.

CHAPTER SIX

"Let's sing 'Hallelujah, Hallelujah, Hallelujah,' " Alice suggested as she sat on a folding chair in Titus and Jane Zook's family room that afternoon.

"That's a great choice." Darlene opened her hymnal and flipped to the right page.

Alice and her friends had been singing for Titus for nearly an hour, and Alice was making every effort to keep a bright smile on her face despite the empathy she felt for Titus and Jane as they sat on the sofa across from them.

The treatments had aged this man, and he looked closer to eighty than his true age of sixty. Alice recalled Titus as a large and portly man with a head of bushy, bright-red hair and a matching beard. But now he had only a few tufts of hair left, and dark circles rimmed his faded, once bright-green eyes.

Jane held Titus's hand as they sang, and she seemed to have aged fast too. Alice spot-

207

ted more wrinkles on her face, as well as more gray in her brown hair. Dark circles rested under her eyes as well.

Before they started singing, Alice had silently asked God to help them bring comfort to this dear couple, and she hoped they had.

Sharon cleared her throat and then began to sing.

Alice and the rest of their friends joined in, sharing their three copies of the *Ausbund,* the Amish hymnal, and her two copies of *Heartland Hymns,* a German and English songbook Alice brought so they could sing a variety of songs.

As she sang, Alice's thoughts shifted to Dave for what felt like the thousandth time this afternoon. As much as she kept trying to concentrate on the hymns, he still crept into her mind, and she found herself recalling how he'd said she was pretty, sweet, and thoughtful. Did that mean he cared about her? Her heart took on wings at the idea!

And then she considered his shocked expression when she told him he was worthy and that she wasn't going to give up on him. She longed to know what had been going through his mind when she walked away from him. She was almost certain she could feel his eyes boring into her back. Was he angry? Or had her words finally broken through the brick wall he'd built around his heart?

But if she *had* broken through that wall, wouldn't he have come with her and their friends to sing this afternoon? Instead, she'd looked over her shoulder and seen him jump into his buggy and leave, most likely going home to be alone.

But Alice had a sneaking suspicion that she'd at least made a dent in that wall, and perhaps she'd make more progress if she continued telling him he was worthy of her friendship and God's love.

Sharon began the second verse for the hymn, and her friends joined in as Jane and Titus exchanged smiles.

When the song was over, Jane invited them to have a piece of apple pie and coffee.

"*Danki* so much for coming," Jane said as she walked Alice and her friends out to the front porch. "I haven't seen Titus smile that much in months. You truly brightened our day."

Alice's heart warmed. "I'm so glad we could offer you both some happiness."

"We enjoyed singing for you," Sharon chimed in.

"Could we come again sometime?" Darlene added.

"We would love that." Jane waved. "Be safe going home."

"We will," Cal called over his shoulder as he, Jay, and Andrew headed down the porch steps toward their waiting horses and buggies.

Alice started toward the buggies, too, but Darlene took her arm and gently held her back after Jane closed the front door. "I want to ask you about your conversation with Dave earlier."

Sharon's blue eyes sparkled. "*Ya!* All you said was that he wouldn't come."

Alice glanced toward where the men stood talking by their buggies and then turned back to Sharon and Darlene. She had to quickly summarize her conversation with Dave before the men lost their patience and said it was time to go. "I took him a carrot *kuche* on Thursday."

"What?" Darlene gasped.

"How did that happen?" Sharon asked.

Alice explained the circumstances and how Dave had opened up to her a little, but she didn't share any details. She'd never embarrass him if she could help it.

"Today I tried to invite him to come with us again, but he refused," she said. "I told him I'm not going to give up on him, and

210

I'm not. He said he liked the *kuche,* and he smiled when he told me. So I'm going to make him another dessert and see if maybe I can get him to trust me enough to come hang out with us."

Sharon seemed to study her. "Do you care about Dave?"

"Sure I do." Alice shrugged, trying to sound casual despite her jolting heart. "He's our *freind.*"

"I think it's great that you're reaching out to him," Darlene said.

Sharon nodded. "I do too. Keep inviting him to join us. Maybe someday he'll agree."

Alice was relieved that her friends hadn't realized just how much she cared about Dave. The truth was her feelings for him blossomed like the flowers in her mother's garden every time she saw him. If only he felt the same way . . .

"Are you all ready to go home?" Cal called.

"*Ya,* we're coming." Sharon turned to Alice. "Do you want to ride with Jay and me?"

"I don't want to interfere with your time alone. I'm sure you want to talk."

"No, it's fine." Sharon looped her arm around Alice's shoulders. "You're always welcome to ride with us."

"Okay." As Alice made her way to Jay's

buggy, she hoped someday she'd find herself riding home with Dave in his. But if friendship was all she could have with Dave she'd gladly take it.

Alice climbed out of Jay's buggy and waved to him and Sharon. "*Danki* for the ride. Have a *gut* week."

Sharon gave her a big smile as the horse and buggy started back down the driveway.

Alice breathed in the warm air and glanced at the colorful flowers blooming in her mother's garden. Coming closer, she took in the roses, lilies, marigolds, and hydrangeas.

She smiled. How she enjoyed summer! She glanced at the bench near the edge of the garden and thought about how much she would love to sit there with Dave and talk. If she could just convince him he was worthy of her friendship, but she didn't know how unless he was willing to forgive himself.

She glanced up at that cloudless cerulean sky. Only God could help her do whatever was best for Dave.

When she heard voices coming from the porch, she turned to find Benji and Joyce sitting in the glider. Joyce laughed when Benji said something to her, and then she rested her head on his shoulder. The glider moved back and forth as they held hands.

A renewed longing filled Alice. If only she and Dave could have a relationship like theirs.

"Hi, Alice!" Joyce sat up and waved as Alice came near. "I didn't realize you were home."

"How are you, Joyce?" Alice asked as she climbed the steps.

"I'm great." She pointed toward the garden. "I was just telling Benji that your *mamm*'s garden is so *schee*. I'm sure you've been helping her with it."

"*Danki*. I have." Alice sat down on a rocker beside Joyce and took a chocolate chip cookie from the small table.

"How was your singing today?" Benji asked.

Alice swallowed the bite she'd just taken and sighed. "It was *gut*."

"Really?" Benji squinted his eyes. "You don't look like you enjoyed it."

"I did. We sang for Titus and Jane Zook, and they really appreciated it. I was just disappointed because I couldn't convince Dave to come with us." Alice angled her body toward her brother. "I'm doing everything I can think of to reach him."

"Are you talking about Dave Esh?" Joyce

213

asked. "Benji told me a little something about what you've been trying to do."

"*Ya.*" Alice explained her latest failed efforts.

Benji picked up a cookie. "I still think you just need to keep at it. Show him you care about him and keep inviting him to your group activities."

Joyce leaned forward. "Here's an idea. Tell him how much you need him to join your singings because your group could use another man — to balance out the harmony or something."

Alice smiled. "That's a *gut* idea. I'll try it."

"Let me know how it works out."

"I will." Alice took another cookie and stood. "You two enjoy your time together. I'll talk to you later." She stepped into the house and found her parents reading in the family room. She flopped down on the sofa and took a bite of the cookie.

"How is Titus doing?" *Dat* asked as he set his magazine on the end table.

"He looks so tired and thin." Alice crossed her ankles. "But he and Jane were *froh* that we came."

Mamm peered at her over her reading glasses. "I'm sure you were a blessing to them."

214

"I hope we were." Alice smoothed her hands over her apron and then looked back up at her mother. "Could we please plan another quilting bee at Annie's?"

"Of course." *Mamm* set her book on her lap. "Does that mean Dave refused your invitation again?"

"*Ya.* He wouldn't come with us today." Alice pressed her lips into a tight frown. "But I'm not giving up. I'll keep trying to convince him he's worthy of my friendship and God's forgiveness. No mistake is beyond the Lord's forgiveness."

Dat's brow puckered. "Dave thinks he's not worthy of God's forgiveness?"

"That's what he said." Alice's lower lip trembled. "It just about broke my heart to hear him say it."

Dat nodded. "Keep trying. Don't give up on him." He turned to *Mamm*. "I think it's a great idea to ask Annie if you can have another quilting bee there. Then Alice can take Dave a pie this time and have more time to talk to him." *Dat* looked at Alice again. "You'll be a blessing to him."

Alice sniffed. "Only with God's help."

CHAPTER SEVEN

Alice carried her pie up Annie's back steps on Tuesday afternoon, a week and a half after her parents agreed to support her plan. She looked down at the pie and bit her lower lip, then glanced back at *Mamm* and Joyce.

"Do you think I made a mistake making this frozen banana split pie? I've never made it before. What if it doesn't taste *gut* and Dave doesn't like it?"

Joyce gave her a sweet smile as she touched her shoulder. "Don't worry. It's the gesture that counts, right?"

The back door opened, and Annie appeared. "Hello!"

"I'm so glad you agreed to this quilting bee." *Mamm* smiled as she held the king-sized quilt with the Wedding Ring design she and Alice had been working on. "Alice and I are so *froh* to have your help."

Joyce nodded toward the small quilt

216

folded over her arm. "I brought a quilt too. I've been working on a Spinning Star, but I've had some trouble."

"Well, come inside." Annie beckoned them. "Rosemary is here, too, so we'll have a *gut* afternoon."

"Wunderbaar." Alice had always enjoyed talking with Dave's older sister when she was a member of their church district. After she married John Yoder four years ago, though, when she was twenty-four, she moved to White Horse and joined his church district there. Now Alice rarely saw Rosemary, and it would be a special treat to spend the afternoon with her.

Alice followed Annie into the kitchen, where Rosemary stood making iced tea.

"Hi," Alice said.

"Alice!" Rosemary stopped stirring and gave her a hug. "It's so *gut* to see you!"

"It's *gut* to see you too." Alice smiled up at her. The family resemblance between Rosemary and Dave was just as obvious as it was between Annie and her son. They all had the same light-blue eyes and light-brown hair. Rosemary had also inherited her parents' tall stature, just like Dave. "How's Nancy? It must be exhausting running around after a three-year-old."

"It is. But she's doing well and getting so

tall." Rosemary beamed. "She's taking a nap in *mei mamm*'s room."

"Oh, I hope I get to see her." She glanced down and noticed Rosemary's extended abdomen. It was rude to mention pregnancy, but Alice couldn't hide her excitement.

Rosemary touched her middle and grinned. "We're so blessed."

"That's fantastic," Alice said.

"It's so *gut* to see you, Rosemary. You look great." *Mamm* gave her a hug before Joyce did.

"*Danki.*" Rosemary pointed to Alice's pie plate. "What did you bring us?"

"Oh." Alice hesitated. "I actually made this for Dave."

Rosemary grinned again as she looked at her mother. "You didn't tell me Dave was dating Alice." She clapped her hands. "What happy news."

Alice shook her head. "We're not dating. I just wanted to do something to cheer him up." Alice pointed to the freezer. "May I put my pie in there until he gets home?"

"Of course." Annie opened the freezer. "What kind of pie is it?"

Joyce grinned. "It's frozen banana split pie. Even though it's for Dave, I wonder if I can convince him to share a piece."

"I want a piece too." Rosemary said.

"We can only hope there's some left," *Mamm* added.

Rosemary stepped toward the family room. "Let's get started. I have a new quilt I want to show you all."

Mamm and Joyce followed Rosemary into the family room as Alice set the pie in the freezer.

Then Annie placed her hand on Alice's arm. "*Danki* for trying to get through to my Dave." She heaved a heavy sigh. "He's been so *bedauerlich* since the accident, and now he says he doesn't belong in the community anymore."

Alice's mouth dropped open as her greatest fear took hold. "Has he said he's leaving?"

"Not outright, but I'm afraid that's what he might do." Annie's lower lip trembled.

Alice's blood ran cold as she imagined Dave packing up and leaving — and never seeing him again. "He can't go."

"I pray he won't." Annie gave Alice's arm a gentle squeeze. "*Danki* for being his *freind*. I believe he cares for you, and I think you're the one who can convince him to stay and become an active member of our community again."

"With God's help."

"That's right." Annie gestured toward the family room. "Now, let's enjoy each other's company before he gets home."

Worry and frustration slowed Alice's steps as she followed Annie. If Dave truly was thinking about leaving, she had to convince him to stay — if only at first for the sake of everyone who cared so much about him. But was the love of his family and *freinden* enough when he was so broken?

Dave stepped into the mudroom later that afternoon and heard women talking and laughing. He quickly picked out his mother's and sister's voices, but as he made his way into the kitchen, he realized he heard more voices, and one of them belonged to Alice.

Alice.

An image of her beautiful face had twirled through his mind every day since he last saw her. And at times, he'd considered visiting her, perhaps in the evening so they could sit on the porch and talk like a couple.

He closed his eyes and grimaced. Why did he keep torturing himself with those thoughts?

At the sink, he washed his hands even though he'd cleaned up in his workshop before coming into the house. He opened the refrigerator and pulled out a piece of watermelon, then leaned against the counter and bit into the sweet, juicy fruit as he peered into the family room. He spotted Alice sitting next to Rosemary as they worked on a quilt together. Dorothy and Joyce worked on another quilt beside them.

Nancy sat on the floor, playing with a doll. She was so sweet, and she looked just like her mother. She was an angel to Dave, and soon she would be a big sister. Dave was certain she'd be a good big sister, just like Rosemary had always been to him, and she would be patient as she guided her younger sibling in learning the rules of the house and community.

His eyes found Alice again. She looked stunning wearing a royal-blue dress with a black apron. If only things were different . . .

After finishing his snack, Dave disposed of the watermelon rind and then washed his hands again.

He heard footsteps behind him.

"You got home from work early today."

Dave glanced over his shoulder and found Alice smiling. A strange tingling filled his chest. "Hi, there. I didn't expect to see you today." He pivoted to face her.

"Your *mamm* didn't tell you we were having a quilting bee today?" She gestured toward the family room.

"No, she didn't." He gave her a sheepish smile. "Or she did, but I wasn't listening."

She pointed a finger at him. "I bet that's the truth."

"You're probably right." He was surprised at how easy it was to smile around her. "What are you working on?"

"It's a Wedding Ring design one of *mei mamm*'s customers ordered for her *dochder*'s wedding in the fall. You know how *Englishers* love that design." She tilted her head. "How was your day?"

"*Gut.*" He shrugged. "We finished a basement for another new *haus*. We have to go back and brick the outside once the rest of the walls are up."

"Oh." She nodded but seemed to be contemplating something else. "I bet it looks great."

He shrugged again. "Did you go singing last week?"

He shouldn't have given her an opening to invite him to join them again, but he was interested in her life.

Her expression brightened. "We did. We sang for a couple of members of the congregation and then we sang at a supper at Sharon's *haus* last Thursday." She held up her finger again. "Do you want to come with us when we sing at her *haus* again later this week?"

He shook his head. "You won't be surprised to hear me say no, I don't."

"But you have such a nice voice. When we sang in school, you were the best of the *buwe.*"

He gave a nervous laugh as he rubbed the back of his neck. Her compliments made him feel itchy all over. "I think you're remembering wrong. I always hid in the back when we had to sing. I couldn't stand it when we put on a program for our parents."

"Nope, I'm right." She tapped her temple. "I clearly remember that. Even Teacher Miriam said you had a lovely voice. That's why you should join us. Besides, we need another man in the group."

He looked down at his feet again and shook his head. "*Danki,* Alice, but I don't think so. I really don't belong with you all."

"But you do. You do belong."

He looked into her brown eyes and felt something inside him shift. Then he shook off the feeling. They could never be together. *Never.*

"I just don't think it's a *gut* idea," he said.

"I brought you something." She walked over to the freezer and opened it. "It's my first time making this dessert, so I hope it's *gut.*" She held out a pie plate. "It's frozen banana split pie." She held it up and gave him a tentative smile.

"Wow." Her kindness tugged at his heart.

She set the pie plate on the counter. "I'm sorry if it's terrible."

"I doubt it's terrible." He lifted the lid and studied the pie. It looked perfect. The whipped cream icing was decorated with chocolate sauce and cherries, and it smelled heavenly. He glanced at her. "Will you have a piece with me?"

"Well, it has to defrost for fifteen minutes before we can slice it."

"What if we warm up a knife?" He grabbed one from the block on the counter and ran it under hot water.

"I suppose we could do that." She laughed. "I'll find plates and spoons."

Once he thought the knife was hot enough, he pushed it through the pie and then used a server to put a piece on each of their plates. After Alice said a silent prayer, they both dug in. He closed his eyes and let the sweet, cold taste slide over his tongue and down his throat.

When he opened his eyes, he found Alice studying him, as if praying he'd like it.

"This pie tastes amazing, Alice." He shook

his head as he tried to form the right words. "It might be the most *appeditlich* pie I've ever had." He glanced back toward the doorway. "Please don't tell *mei mamm,* okay? She'd be upset to hear that."

Her smile returned. "Your secret is safe with me. Unfortunately, your *mamm* and *schweschder* have seen it, so you might have to share it. But I can make you another pie." She gave him a coy expression. "If you join us for a singing, I'll make you two more pies."

"I can't, Alice. But I appreciate your persistence." He ate another bite. He wanted to keep talking to her, but he had to change the subject. "Where did you find this recipe?"

She swallowed a bite and then leaned back against the counter. "It's in *mei mammi*'s favorite cookbook. I enjoy going through her recipes, and I wanted to make something different for you."

His heart felt as if it might explode. She chose a special recipe just for him. Why was she continuing to go out of her way for him? In his worst moments, he thought of himself as not much better than a murderer. And his idea of their ever being a couple? She could do so much better than him!

"I'd never made it, but *mei mamm* encouraged me to try." She glanced at the remainder of the pie. "It's not perfect, but it came out pretty well."

"Actually, it *is* perfect." He took a step toward her and set his plate and fork on the counter. *Just like you, Alice.*

She looked up at him, and her eyes widened. He reached for her cheek but then stopped his hand in midair. Her breath seemed to come in short bursts, and his pulse trotted. The urge to kiss her was overwhelming, as an invisible magnet seemed to be pulling him toward her. Then his fingers brushed her cheek, and he leaned closer, close enough to feel her breath on his lips. His heart felt as if it might beat its way through his rib cage.

Footsteps sounded behind him.

"I really had a nice afternoon, Annie," Dorothy said.

Alice snapped to attention, then pivoted away from him and gathered their plates before setting them in the sink.

Dave pushed his hand through his hair as he moved three steps away from her and scooped up their utensils, plus the knife, before setting them in the sink as well, careful not to touch Alice.

"It was nice to get caught up with you," *Mamm* said. "Oh, David! You tried a piece

226

of that pie. How was it?"

"Positively *appeditlich.*" Dave was aware that his voice was a bit too loud. He looked at Alice and found her scrubbing the plates in the sink a little too hard. "I'm going to have a difficult time sharing it."

Dorothy chuckled as she walked over to Alice and touched her arm. "And here you were afraid it hadn't come out right!"

"I'm just grateful Dave liked it." Alice gave a little shrug as she rinsed the dishes. She stole a glance at Dave, and her cheeks were flushed. She looked adorable.

"We should get going," Dorothy said. "It's almost time to make supper."

"I'm glad you could come today," *Mamm* told her. "It was so *gut* to see you all." She pointed at Alice. "You stop washing those dishes. I'll take care of them." She snapped her fingers. "Oh, and I have the container you left here when you brought the carrot *kuche.* I don't want you to forget that." She retrieved it from the pantry.

"*Danki.*" Alice glanced past Dave to where Rosemary stood in the doorway, holding Nancy. "Take care, Rosemary. Your *dochder* is adorable."

"We hope to see you very soon," Rosemary said, her tone sounding as though she was saying something more significant.

Alice looked at Dave, and he longed to ask her to stay so they could sit on the porch until the lightning bugs made their appearance.

"Enjoy your pie, Dave," she said as she took the cake container from his mother.

"I will." He smiled, and she returned the gesture.

Dave said good-bye to Dorothy and Joyce, and soon all three guests were leaving the house with his mother in tow.

"You should ask her out."

Dave turned toward his sister. "What did you say?"

"Come on, Dave. I'm not blind." She set Nancy on her booster seat and then handed her a handful of crackers. "Alice cares about you, and you care about her. You two were always *gut freinden.* I remember clearly how you used to play together at school and how you gravitated toward each other at youth gatherings. She brought you a pie, and I imagine you're the reason her *mamm* planned this quilting bee today."

"Why would you say that?"

"Because Alice kept glancing out the window all afternoon. I'm certain she was looking for you." Rosemary leveled her gaze with his. "So what are you waiting for? If you don't ask her out, she might find someone else."

The thought of Alice with another man sent bile racing to his throat. But that was what she needed — a good, Christian man who hadn't made the mistake he had.

"She deserves someone better than me," Dave muttered as he headed toward the stairs.

"Why would you say that?" Rosemary followed him. "You're a *gut* man with a great future in *Dat*'s company. You'll be a fantastic husband and provider. I know your heart, Dave. You've always had a gentle, giving soul."

Dave spun toward her as fury boiled in his gut. "You know what I did," he growled.

Rosemary blanched. "Are you talking about Adam?" She waited a beat, and when he didn't respond, she added, "That wasn't your fault, and you know it."

"It *was* my fault. I'm the one who thought the pond was safe, and it wasn't. Now, I'm going to take a shower." He started up the stairs.

"David," she called after him. "Stop punishing yourself when God and everyone else has forgiven you."

"If only it were that easy," he whispered.

CHAPTER EIGHT

When the men's after-service meal ended Sunday afternoon, Dave walked beside his father toward the barn exit. Then a woman called his name, and he recognized her voice.

Esther Fisher.

He kept moving forward, stepping into the sunlight.

"David Esh!"

"Don't you hear her?" *Dat* halted and put his hand on Dave's shoulder to stop him.

Dave's throat dried. Adam's mother must be visiting their church service today. Why hadn't he stayed home?

"*Ya*, but I can't talk to her. I won't be able to bear it."

Dat shook his head. "You need to hear her out."

Dave turned around just as Esther caught up with them. He didn't understand why her expression was so . . . pleasant. She had to hate him.

"Dave, why haven't we seen you since the funeral? It's been months."

Why would her family *want* to see him?

"I-I've been busy." He could hardly get out the words.

"Working for your *dat*?" Smiling, Esther divided a look between Dave and his father.

"Ya." He rubbed at a tight muscle in his neck.

"That's *gut.*" Esther seemed to study him, and he longed to hide under a nearby buggy. "You look well."

He shrugged.

"You should come by the *haus*. Kevin misses you."

Dave blinked. "He . . . he does?"

"Of course he does. He and Adam always loved spending time with you."

Hearing Esther say Adam's name as though it was no more difficult for her now than when her son was alive felt like a knife to his heart.

"Kevin wants so badly to talk to you. He feels guilty because the *buwe* convinced you they were better skaters than they were. Then when he fell, you had to help him, and that's when —"

"It's my fault, not Kevin's." Dave took a shaky breath as tears stung his eyes. "You

231

counted on me to keep the *buwe* safe, and I failed you."

"Dave, don't you know we don't blame you for Adam's death?" Esther put her hand on his shoulder. "No one does. You need to forgive yourself. I had no idea you felt this way, or I would have come to you long ago. I wish your *mamm* had told me —"

Dave's breath came in quick bursts as he took a step away from her, evading *Dat*'s attempt to stop him. "I need to go." He turned and ran to his buggy without looking back.

"You never told us what happened when you saw Dave on Tuesday," Sharon said as she sat on her back porch with Alice and Darlene that afternoon.

Alice rocked back and forth as she gazed toward Sharon's pasture, watching the horses play. The sky was a bright azure dotted with white, puffy clouds, and birds sang in nearby trees.

"Well, *Mamm,* Joyce, Annie, Rosemary, and I had a nice time quilting. I took Dave a frozen banana split pie, and when he got there, he and I ate some out in the kitchen."

And he almost kissed me!

Goose bumps raced up Alice's arms, and her cheeks nearly burst into flames at the recollection of how close his lips had come to hers. And oh, how she'd wanted him to kiss her! She'd dreamt about how that would feel. But then the other women had come into the kitchen, and the moment was lost.

"And . . ." Darlene said, prompting more.

Alice pulled at a loose string on the hem of her apron to avoid their eyes. "Well, he loved the pie. And we talked a bit, but he says he won't come to a singing."

"Did you invite him to come here and play games?"

"No. I didn't see him after church today. He must have left early. Did you see Esther Fisher there? I wonder if he saw her and just took off. It can't be easy for him to be around her."

"Oh, maybe he did," Darlene said.

"But he seemed a little happier on Tuesday."

"That's because of you," Sharon said.

Surely Darlene didn't know . . .

Alice shook her head. "No, I don't think so."

"Sharon's right," Darlene chimed in. "I think you've touched his heart."

"Uh, maybe." Alice broke off the string. "I feel like I'm making some progress with him, but . . . it's slow."

"I'm sure you are." Darlene touched her arm. "Don't give up."

"I won't. And I'm going to keep praying for him too."

And maybe he'll call me. Maybe he just needs time.

The following Sunday afternoon Dave smiled as his brother-in-law, Stephen, shared another story about fishing with his brothers. No wonder Nancy had the coloring she did. At thirty, Stephen had light-brown hair and blue eyes, just like Rosemary.

Stephen had always been like an older brother. A hardworking dairy farmer, Stephen took good care of his family, and Dave admired him. Still, even if Stephen told himself their relationship hadn't changed, it had — just like with the other adult members of the family.

Since it was an off Sunday without a church service, his mother had invited Rosemary and her family to visit. Dave took a sip of coffee and smiled as Stephen shared more about his brothers' antics.

"Then Mahlon told Jeremiah his fish was bigger, and soon they were arguing." Stephen wiped at his eyes as he chuckled. "*Mei dat* told them both to be quiet because they were going to scare the rest of the fish away!"

Everyone laughed, and Dave did too.

"It was hilarious. Those two are always in some battle. *Mei mamm* says it's because they're close in age, but I think they're both just stubborn like *Dat.*"

"Oh, and you aren't stubborn, Stephen Lapp?" Rosemary challenged him with a pointed look. "Where do you think Nancy gets her stubbornness?"

She pointed to their daughter, who was sitting beside her on a booster seat, spooning chocolate pie into her mouth. Her face was covered with it, and she smiled as she shoved in more.

Stephen looked at Nancy and then back at Rosemary. "She looks like you, and she acts like you. You should just accept that now."

Rosemary looked as if she might argue with him, but then she laughed, and soon their parents joined in.

Dave held his mug in the air as he watched the love pass between his sister and her husband. How he envied their relationship.

He glanced down at the chocolate pie, and his thoughts turned toward Alice and the delicious desserts she'd shared with him. He'd thought about her all week, wondering how her days had gone, wishing he could have talked to her before Esther tracked him down.

He couldn't think about Esther. She said she didn't blame him for Adam's death, but she was probably fooling herself.

His thoughts turned back to Alice. Had she done any sewing this week? Would she sing for someone with her friends today?

Did she think of him?

Did she miss him?

The last thought tugged at his heartstrings.

"Did you hear me, Dave?"

"What?" Dave looked up and found Stephen watching him from across the table.

"I said you should come fishing with us sometime." Stephen looked at *Dat* too. "You should come as well, Manny. I promise my younger *bruders* won't scare the fish."

"We *should* go." *Dat* patted Dave's shoulder. "That's if the business slows down. Right now we're working six days a week."

"You need to make time for fun," Rosemary said. "Right, *Mamm*?"

Mamm pointed her fork at *Dat*. "She's right, Manny. You've always worked too hard."

Dave held back the urge to roll his eyes. His mother constantly told his father he worked too hard, but that never changed. *Dat* loved the business.

And that truth sent guilt spiraling through Dave. With the paycheck he'd collected on Friday and the sale of another railing, he finally had enough savings to start a new life somewhere else. Now he had to find the courage to actually do it.

He glanced across the table at his precious niece, who hummed to herself as she enjoyed her last bite of chocolate pie. If he left, he'd miss seeing her grow up. He'd miss meeting her future siblings. But would they miss him? Would not having an uncle around, their mother's brother, impact their lives?

Dave looked down at his empty coffee cup. His mistake had put an irreparable wedge between him and his family, no matter what they said. It was time to move on. They would eventually heal. They would survive — even thrive — without him. It just made sense to go.

Once they finished dessert, the women began cleaning the kitchen, and Dave followed *Dat* and Stephen to the back porch. The other two men sat down on rocking chairs, and Dave sank onto the top step and stared out toward his father's fields.

The sun was beginning to set, sending

vibrant streaks of orange and yellow across the sky, and a soft breeze moved the summer night air around his face as he breathed in the sweet smell of grass and flowers.

Despair came out of nowhere. He'd been researching brick mason businesses in Maryland and had even started writing up a résumé. He would have to go to a library and ask someone to show him how to type it up on a computer so he could hand it out when he arrived and began meeting with business owners.

But leaving Alice . . .

His heart crumbled at the thought. She'd brought joy into his life. She made him laugh. Would he ever find such a woman again? He scrubbed one hand across the stubble on his chin.

"Are you all right, Dave?"

He turned toward Stephen, who was rocking back and forth behind him. *Dat*'s seat was empty.

Dave shrugged. "I was just thinking."

"I know. Your *dat* and I were talking for a while, and then he went inside, but you haven't moved. You seem fixated on something." Stephen halted his rocking and leaned forward, resting his elbows on his thighs. "Do you want to tell me what's on your mind?"

Dave looked out toward the pasture again as he considered his response. If he told his brother-in-law he was leaving, he'd feel obligated to tell Rosemary. Then she'd tell his parents, and . . . That was news he had to deliver himself.

"Roe told me she's worried about you," Stephen began. "She said you seemed upset when she was here for a quilting bee not long ago. You said you weren't worthy of dating anyone because of what happened to Adam."

Dave angled his body toward Stephen. "That's true."

"Why do you feel that way?"

Dave picked up a pebble from the top step and tossed it toward his mother's garden, where her colorful, cheerful flowers seemed to mock his somber mood. "Because my mistake took a life and ruined a family."

"But Adam's family doesn't blame you, do they?"

Of course they do. They have to.

"It's time to forgive yourself."

Dave stared out toward the garden.

"Dave, look at me."

He did — reluctantly.

"Adam died that day, but you lived. It's time you acted like it. You should be dating and planning for a future, not worrying about your mistake when you've been forgiven for it."

Dave's eyes narrowed. "You could never understand."

"Then help me understand. I'm listening." Stephen's serious expression challenged him.

The back door opened and then clicked shut as *Dat* returned.

"Where were we?" *Dat* asked. "How are your folks doing, Stephen?"

"They're fine," Stephen said as he shifted in the chair and plastered a smile on his face. "*Mei mamm* is still keeping *mei dat* in line."

"As she should. That's a *fraa*'s job."

"Isn't that the truth?" Stephen said, and they both laughed.

Dave settled back against the railing and sighed, grateful for the interruption. This could be the last Sunday he spent with his family, and he wanted to cherish it.

But in his heart, he felt a tingle of worry. Was he about to take the wrong step?

"Have we thought of everything for tonight?" *Mamm* asked Alice Saturday morning as she washed the breakfast dishes.

"I think so." Alice picked up her to-do list, the one she'd started earlier in the week.

She'd been so excited when Sharon and Feenie suggested she and *Mamm* host the supper for *Englishers* from Lancaster Inn this time. The Lamberts needed a break, although Sharon was still going to come help and sing tonight.

She and her mother had spent all week cleaning the house and sprucing up their garden to prepare for the visitors. This afternoon they would start preparing the meal, and then her friends would arrive. She couldn't wait. How she loved to cook and bake! And singing with her friends was the best part of these evenings.

"Have you invited Dave?" *Mamm* asked.

Alice looked up from her list. "No, I haven't."

"You should." *Mamm* turned back to the sink. "Maybe this will be the night he has a change of heart."

"You think so?"

"It could be." *Mamm* nodded toward the back door. "Go leave him a voice mail message before we get busy with our chores."

"Okay." Alice gave her *mamm* a hug.

"What was that for?" *Mamm* laughed.

"*Danki* for believing in Dave."

"I believe God will change his heart, and he's using you to do it."

"I hope you're right." Alice dashed out

241

the back door, down the porch steps, and to the barn, where she made her way to the back and dialed the Esh family's phone number.

After the beep she began to speak. "Hi. This is Alice, and I'm calling for Dave." She stretched the phone cord as she spoke. "Dave, I haven't talked to you for a while, and I've been hoping you'd call me. But since you haven't, I thought I'd call you. I hope that's okay.

"*Mamm* and I are hosting a group of *Englishers* tonight for supper at our *haus.* We're having roasted chicken, buttered noodles, homemade *brot,* green beans, salad, and then shoo-fly pie and apple crisp for dessert. Our *freinden* are coming to sing, and I'd like for you to join us."

She paused as she gathered her thoughts. Then she took a trembling breath and pushed on, letting down her guard. "You've told me time and again to give up on you, but in my heart I believe you don't want me to. It may sound too forward, but I think you want to be *mei . . . freind,* and I know I want to be yours. So please come tonight. We start gathering to set up around four since the guests arrive at five thirty. I know everyone else would love to see you. In fact, Cal was just asking about you the other day.

I hope to see you at four, or later if that works best for you. I know you might have to work. I miss you. Good-bye."

Her cheeks burned, and her hands shook as she hung up the phone. She'd been too forward, but she had to tell Dave the truth. She did miss him. In fact, she was beginning to wonder if she'd fallen in love with him since he was always there at the back of her thoughts. Could that be love?

She closed her eyes and whispered a prayer.

"Lord, I miss Dave, and I have a feeling he misses me too. I'm beginning to wonder if we're supposed to be together, because I feel such a close connection to him. But if that's true, I don't understand why he keeps rejecting me. Please give me the right words to help him realize he belongs with me and our *freinden.* Please lead him to me if it's your will. And if that can't happen until he forgives himself, Lord, show him the way."

A peace settled over her, and she nearly floated on her way back to the house. With God's help, maybe Dave would decide to come back to his friends tonight.

CHAPTER NINE

Dave's whole body shook, and his heart hammered in his chest as he glanced around his bedroom later that afternoon. The room was bare except for a few books on the shelf.

When he'd arrived home from work earlier than he thought he would, he told his mother he was going to take a shower and then rest before going to his sister's for supper. But that wasn't the truth. In fact, it was a bald-faced lie.

Instead of resting, he'd packed his clothes and few belongings, jamming them into a large duffel bag. Then he'd written a letter to his parents.

"Dave!" *Mamm* called from somewhere downstairs. "Your *dat*'s ready. We're leaving for Rosemary's *haus* now. Are you going to follow us?"

"Uh, I don't think I'll come after all." Dave grimaced as he lied once again.

You're a sinner, David Esh!

"Why?"

He rubbed the back of his neck. "I'm still really tired. Tell Rosemary I'm sorry."

"Oh." *Mamm* hesitated. "Are you sure? Do you need us to stay home?"

"No, no. You go on. Don't worry about me. I just need to get to bed early. I didn't sleep well last night."

"Okay, then. We'll see you later."

Dave stood at the top of the stairs and listened as his parents' footfalls headed outside. Then he watched out his window as they climbed into their buggy before the horse pulled it down the driveway.

He carried his duffel bag down the stairs, then set the letter on the kitchen table and closed his eyes.

You're a coward, too, David Esh!

Yes, he was. He didn't have the courage to tell his parents he was leaving to their faces. Instead, he had to leave them a note and let them believe he was just too tired to go with them.

He took a walk through the downstairs of the house as memories flowed over him like waves. He stood in the middle of the family room and recalled the winter Sundays he'd spent sitting with his parents, talking after church. The summer days when he was a child and his grandparents came to visit. All the family memories he'd keep locked away in his heart forever. His eyes stung with tears as regret stole his breath for a moment. But he had to do this.

Then he walked through the kitchen again, in anguish as the delicious food his mother had served over the years came to mind. He would miss the meals she'd prepared for him with such love, and he'd miss the conversations he shared with his parents as they enjoyed those meals. But his no longer being here was best for them too. They might even be happy for him if he were happier somewhere else, even though he'd be shunned.

Dave stepped outside, then locked the back door and headed to the barn to call for his driver. When he reached the phone, he found a voice mail message.

As Alice's sweet voice filled his ear, he dropped into the chair beside the counter, his knees buckling.

"Alice," he whispered.

As she spoke, tears filled his eyes. She *had* been thinking of him! She missed him. And she wanted him to come to her house tonight despite all the times he'd rejected her.

Maybe she'd even wanted him to kiss her that day in his mother's kitchen.

Was this a sign from God — a sign that he should stay?

No, it couldn't be.

He played the message again, doing his best to commit Alice's voice to memory as heartbreak overtook him. Then he called his driver and asked for a ride to the bus station.

Dave paced in the rock driveway, wringing his hands while he waited, Alice's message echoing through his mind as if on a loop.

Alice wanted to see him.

He wanted to see her too.

A solution hit him. He could see her one last time and tell her he was leaving in person. He owed her an explanation, and he hadn't written her a letter. He couldn't leave without trying to explain why. After all, she was the person who'd never stopped trying to convince him he belonged here.

Was she right?

Dave stopped pacing and looked up at the sky. He longed to pray for God's help, but he couldn't. He'd lost his ability to share his deepest thoughts and emotions with God the day Adam died. God couldn't care about him after what he'd done, and he was on his own.

He just hoped he had the courage to leave once he'd seen Alice — and never look back.

Alice surveyed the four folding tables full of guests who were enjoying their meal. So far their evening had gone smoothly. Alice, *Mamm,* and her friends had all served the food, and the guests all seemed satisfied and happy to be in their home.

Alice filled a few of their water glasses and then walked to the kitchen counter. She set the pitcher down and then glanced through the windows that looked out over the back porch — again. But there was still no sign of Dave, and her heart sank even lower.

"I think everything is going well, don't you?" Sharon asked Alice as she joined her at the counter.

"*Ya,* I think so." Alice began pulling desserts out of the refrigerator.

"Why do you sound disappointed?"

Alice handed her a shoo-fly pie. "I was just hoping Dave would come."

Darlene appeared behind her and took one of the pies. "Maybe he didn't get your message."

"I guess that's a possibility." Alice pulled out two more shoofly pies and then two apple crisps.

"I'll put on the *kaffi,*" *Mamm* said.

"Sounds *gut.*" Alice turned to her friends. "Let's start clearing the tables. Then we can serve dessert and *kaffi* before *Mamm* answers questions and we sing."

"Perfect," Sharon said.

But the night would be perfect only if Dave came.

Dave sat frozen in the front seat of Dustin Henderson's van and stared at Alice's house.

"Are you going to get out?" his family's longtime driver asked. In fact, Dustin had always been a friend.

Dave sighed and pushed the door open. Then he stilled again.

"Do you want me to just take you to the bus station?"

"No." Dave looked at him. "I need to stop being a coward. I might be a few minutes."

"Take your time."

Dave climbed out and closed the door.

"Dave!"

He spun as Dustin leaned out the window.

"I don't know what's going on, but my advice? Listen to your heart."

Dave nodded and then tried to swallow the messy knot of emotion in his throat as he climbed the back-porch steps. But his effort was in vain. He didn't even know if he'd

249

be able to say a word.

When he heard Alice's sweet voice coming through the screen door, he stilled again.

"Now we'd like to sing for you," she said. He imagined her standing in front of the guests.

"My friends and I started singing during these suppers in the spring, and our visitors seemed to like it. We hope you'll like it too. I'd like to start with a hymn you might know. And if you don't, I hope it touches your heart like it always touches mine."

Dave quietly stepped inside the mudroom and watched her through the doorway to the kitchen. She looked like an angel.

She cleared her throat, closed her eyes, and then began to sing. "Amazing grace, how sweet the sound that saved a wretch like me . . ." Her voice was so beautiful, as if she were an angel singing those holy words.

Suddenly he felt all the pain, guilt, and grief pouring out of him. Tears filled his eyes and then spilled over, running down his cheeks as Alice sang.

"I once was lost, but now am found, was blind but now I see."

Esther's words, Stephen's words, his mother's words — Alice's words — echoed through his mind. *Forgive yourself.*

But would God forgive him?

Then he felt as if God were reaching for him, then hugging him, loving him — and yes, forgiving him. God had been there all along, and Dave had been wrong. He'd pushed everyone away, including the Lord. Now he saw the truth, and he opened his heart, allowing himself to pray for the first time since he'd held a lifeless young boy in his arms.

I hear you, God! I hear you loud and clear. I'm so sorry about the mistake I made, and I'll always hurt when I think about Adam's death. Yet I feel your forgiveness. And I forgive myself.

" 'Twas grace that taught my heart to fear," Alice continued, "and grace my fears relieved. How precious did that grace appear, the hour I first believed."

Dave wiped his eyes, and he knew for certain that he belonged — not just in this community and with his friends but with Alice. Leaving would be a mistake. He needed to stay, and he wanted to ask Alice if she would consider a future with him.

As if on cue, she turned her head toward him, meeting his gaze. She gasped, and the room went silent.

Dave stepped into the kitchen, and all the *Englishers* turned and stared at him. Alice, her mother, and all his friends stared too. Then his body shook as he focused on Alice.

This was his moment to tell her the truth. But how would he find the words to share everything in his heart?

Lord, give me courage!

"Dave," she said, her voice barely a whisper as she studied him standing at the back of her kitchen.

Was she dreaming? Was Dave really there, staring at her with tears streaking down his face?

Yes, he was! But he looked as if someone had died, and his tears nearly broke her heart in two. Something was wrong!

A hand grasped her arm.

"Go to him," Darlene whispered in her ear. "I'll take over the singing." Then Darlene cleared her throat. "Through many dangers, toils and snares I have already come . . ."

With her heart hammering in her chest, Alice strode across the room, took Dave's hand in hers, and led him outside to the porch. She steered him down the steps to find a more private place to talk.

She stopped at the top of the driveway when she found his driver's van . . . waiting for him.

"You're not staying?" She searched his reddened eyes. "What's wrong? Are your parents okay? Why are you so upset?"

"Alice, wait. Let me explain." He looked down at the ground, then back at her. "I came to say good-bye." He wiped the tears away with his hand.

"Good-bye?" Panic gripped her. "Are you leaving the community? Are you leaving me?"

"Wait." His expression relaxed slightly. "I was going to leave, but . . ." He rested his hands on her shoulders. "I've been saving money for months. I was going to move to Maryland and start a new life."

She sniffed as her eyes filled with tears. "Why?" she asked. And yet she knew why. He'd told her as much.

"Because I didn't think I was worthy of this community. I thought I needed a fresh start after what happened to Adam. I decided today would be the day. My parents went to Rosemary's for supper, and I left them a letter. I was going to run away like a coward."

He cupped his hand to her cheek. "But then I got your message, and you told me you missed me. I thought I should come say good-bye to you in person."

She let out a puff of air as tears rolled down her cheeks.

"But when I got here, at first I couldn't get out of the van because I'm such a coward. Dustin asked me if I wanted to go to the bus station, but I realized I had to face you. Then, once inside, I heard your voice. And you started to sing 'Amazing Grace.' " He paused, and his blue eyes shimmered with fresh tears. "I realized everything you've been trying to tell me is right. God has forgiven me. The community has forgiven me. I thought everyone here must hate me for the mistake I made, the mistake that cost Adam his life. So I pushed you all away, including my family and *freinden.*"

He jammed his finger into his chest. "The problem was I needed to forgive myself." Tears again rolled down his cheeks, and she reached up and swiped them away.

"I tried to tell you that."

"I know. So did *Mamm.* And my brother-in-law, Stephen, told me Adam died but I didn't. He said I needed to start acting like I'm still alive. I see what he means now. And even Esther told me I needed to forgive myself." He took her hand in his and cleared his throat. "You've never given up on me, Alice. You've tried to show me for months now that I'm worthy of your friendship. And I see how blind I've been, just like the hymn says. I've been blind to God's love for me, and I've been blind" — he swallowed — "I've been blind to my love for you."

Her breath caught, and he wiped another tear from her cheek.

"I love you, Alice. I've always cared for you. In fact, I'd been trying to work up the courage to ask you to be my girlfriend before the accident."

She gasped. "You had?"

He nodded. "You've been my best *freind* for years, but I wanted more. After Adam died, though, I felt like my future died with him. I thought no one could ever love me after I allowed a child to die."

"But you tried to save him. You did the best you could." Her voice trembled as she touched his cheek again.

He closed his eyes as if the memory of that day had seized his mind, then opened them again. "I know that now. And I also realize that leaving you would be the worst mistake I could make. If you give me a chance and your *dat* approves, I'd be honored to date you and explore building a future together."

She nodded and pulled a tissue from her pocket, happiness warming her from the inside out. "I'd like that." She wiped her eyes and then her nose. "I'd like that a lot."

"*Ich liebe dich,* Alice." He cupped both hands to her cheeks, and his words were like a sweet hymn to her ears.

"I love you too."

He leaned down and pressed his lips against hers, sending a new warmth flooding through every cell in her body. She lost herself in the nearness of him.

When he broke the kiss, he touched her lips with the tip of his finger. "*Danki* for never giving up on me. Without you, I would still be lost like a wounded ship at sea. You're the light that led me home."

"I'm so grateful. I've been asking God to lead you to me, and he did." She took his hand in hers. "Why don't you call your parents at Rosemary's and tell them you're here? Tell them not to read that letter, that you're staying. Then can we go sing with our *freinden?*"

"I love that idea."

As they walked together to the barn, Alice glanced at the stars twinkling in the sky and smiled. What amazing grace!

DISCUSSION QUESTIONS

1. Dave is convinced his friends, family, and everyone in his congregation must hate him after a child dies while in his care — especially the child's parents. He feels lost and alone. Have you ever felt that way? If so, how did you cope?

2. Alice is determined to convince Dave to come back to their friend group, no matter how much he rejects her. Do you think her heart is in the right place?

3. Stephen, Dave's brother-in-law, tells him Adam may have died but Dave didn't, and he needs to move on with his life. Do you think his point of view is valid? Why or why not?

4. Which character can you identify with most? Which character seemed to carry the most emotional stake in the story? Dave, Alice, or someone else?

5. At the end of the story, Dave realizes he has been forgiven all along, and he doesn't

need to run away. What do you think contributed to his changing his mind throughout the story?

6. What role did hymns play in the relationships throughout the story?

■ ■ ■ ■

GREAT IS THY
FAITHFULNESS

■ ■ ■ ■

*With love, hugs, kisses, and snuggles for
my sweet Leo, the best cat ever*

Featured Characters

Annie m. Emmanuel "Manny" Esh
|
Rosemary
David

Edna m. Harvey King
|
Calvin
Raymond

Louise m. Moses Smoker
|
Jay

Jean m. Merle Detweiler
|
Andrew
Samuel

Feenie m. Ira Lambert
|
Sharon
Ruby Sue

Dorothy m. Floyd Blank
|
Benjamin
Alice

Roselyn m. Alvin Bender
|
Biena
Darlene

Rosemary m. Stephen Lapp
|
Nancy

CHAPTER ONE

Darlene Bender stood at the kitchen sink and scrubbed a handful of utensils as she glanced out the window and spotted her father disappearing into the barn.

The early-morning sun lit up the clear blue sky, and a cardinal happily ate at the bird feeder near her mother's cheerful garden and its colorful summer flowers. She sighed. The problem was it was filled with clumps of pesky green weeds too. How she loved working in the garden. If only she had more time to tackle those weeds.

Still, Darlene smiled at the bird as she rinsed the utensils and set them on the drying rack.

"I need to go open the store." Biena set three drinking glasses on the counter. "Can you finish cleaning up alone?"

Darlene turned. "*Ya.* Of course."

Biena turned toward the doorway to the mudroom. "I'll see you later."

As Darlene watched her go, she recalled how often strangers asked them if they were twins because they shared the same golden-blond hair and deep-brown eyes, and they were the same — and average — height. But her sister was two years older.

"Biena!" *Mamm*'s hoarse voice barely sounded in the hallway before the bathroom door slammed.

"*Ach,* no. I thought she was feeling better when she woke up." Biena started for the bathroom, but then she spun around. "It's almost eight. Can you go open the store?"

"But it's my turn to take care of *Mamm*," Darlene said, drying her hands with a paper towel.

"I'll take care of her today. Go open the store while *Dat*'s feeding the animals." Biena made a sweeping gesture. "Go on!" Then she hurried off. "I'm here, *Mamm*. I'll get some towels."

Darlene closed her eyes and leaned forward on the sink as the sounds of her mother's sickness filled the kitchen. This latest round of chemo seemed to be the worst.

Please, God. Please heal her. Take away her pain.

Biting back tears, Darlene straightened. She had to be strong for *Mamm*. She had to be strong for the whole family.

She quickly finished cleaning up and then hurried to the mudroom, grabbing the key to the store before she rushed outside and headed down the porch steps.

The August sun warmed her neck as she strode down the short path to the large building that housed Bird-in-Hand Dry Goods, the store her father opened nearly twenty-five years ago. The one-story, white, cinder block structure sat on the busy Old Philadelphia Pike in the heart of Bird-in-Hand, Pennsylvania.

Darlene unlocked the front door and turned the sign from Closed to Open. Then she made her way down the main aisle to the counter at the back, where the battery-operated cash register sat along with plastic bags and other supplies. She breathed in the familiar smells she'd grown up with as she prepared for the first sales of the day.

Then she straightened the items on the counter before checking the displays of greeting cards, books, and small gifts. In the next aisle, she straightened the toys and games. She continued on, checking racks with sewing notions or cleaning supplies, all the while trying to chase thoughts of her mother's illness out of her mind. Yet over and over, they returned.

It was a nightmare watching *Mamm* suffer with ovarian cancer, first with the aftermath of surgery and now with chemo. Ever since her mother was diagnosed, Darlene had prayed daily for her suffering to end and her strength to return.

If only Darlene had someone to talk to about this struggle, someone who would understand what she was going through. But she didn't want to burden her friends — not even her best friends, Sharon Lambert and Alice Blank.

For the past several months, Darlene and her tight group of friends — including Sharon's boyfriend, Jay Smoker; Alice's boyfriend, Dave Esh; Andrew Detweiler, and Cal King — had been singing for members of their church district as well as for *Englishers* who paid to attend suppers at Sharon's or Alice's home to learn more about the Amish culture. The suppers started with the Lancaster Inn and Sharon's mother, but now the managers of several local hotels and tour companies frequently asked both Feenie Lambert and Dorothy Blank to host them. It was a way for them to earn extra income for their families.

During the meals, the mothers answered questions about their culture, and then Darlene and her friends sang. Darlene enjoyed spending time with her friends, but she especially enjoyed the opportunity to share the gospel through the hymns they chose.

Even though I'm struggling with my faith. Another burden I can't share.

Darlene pushed that thought aside.

Although she'd told her mother how their singings had seemed to help others in the community who were struggling with illness, *Mamm* continued to refuse to allow anyone to visit. She'd always been rather private, but not like this. She said she didn't want visitors to see how the chemotherapy treatments had ravished her body and strength. She even refused Darlene's friends, who so often offered to bring food, help with chores, or sing for her.

So Darlene, Biena, and *Dat* pushed on alone, running the store and caring for the house, animals, and her mother. The only living relative they had in the area was her uncle, Merv, but he was a widower and much older than *Mamm,* and not in any physical condition to help. Darlene didn't want to add to anyone's burden by confessing how alone she felt, even when surrounded by her precious group of friends and her family.

Darlene finished straightening another

display and then moved to the gardening supplies. She was rearranging watering cans when the bell on the front door sounded, announcing a customer.

"Good morning," Darlene sang, trying her best to sound cheerful despite her dark mood.

Dat appeared at the end of the aisle. "I thought Biena was going to run the store today."

Although he was in his early fifties, *Dat* seemed to have aged nearly a decade since *Mamm*'s diagnosis. His own light-brown hair was now threaded with gray, and wrinkles had taken up permanent residency under his tired, deep-brown eyes. A constant frown lined his lips, and Darlene missed his bright smile and easy sense of humor. She hadn't seen him happy for months, and her heart ached at the sadness she found in his handsome face.

"*Mamm* is having a bad morning after all, and Biena asked me to open the store." Darlene fingered the end of a cool, metal shelf.

"Oh." *Dat* rubbed his beard and looked down at the floor.

"When do you think she'll feel better?" She leaned forward, holding her breath while she waited for her father to say the words she longed to hear — that her mother would be well and back to normal soon.

Dat met her gaze. "I don't know. We just have to pray and have faith. The Lord will take care of her. He loves her — and us — very much."

"Right." Darlene stood up straight and forced a smile. But inside, her soul was shattering. How could she have faith when her mother suffered so?

Dat pointed toward the front door. "I'm going to go see if Biena needs any help. Will you be okay here?"

"Of course." Darlene pushed the ties from her prayer covering off her shoulders. "I know how to run the store."

"Danki." Dat touched her shoulder. "We'll be just fine, Darlene. The Lord provides."

"I know." Darlene folded her arms over her waist.

Dat started toward the door. "I'll be back to check on you as soon as I can."

"Just take care of *Mamm.*"

Dat disappeared out the front door, and Darlene leaned back against the shelf as she tried to recall what life was like before *Mamm*'s illness had rocked their world. It seemed like years since their lives revolved only around the store and their community. But that all changed when their days were suddenly ruled by doctor's visits, then surgery, chemotherapy, and *Mamm*'s suffering.

Would their family ever go back to normal?

The ring of the store phone broke through her thoughts and sent her dashing to the counter.

Darlene picked up the receiver. "Thank you for calling Bird-in-Hand Dry Goods."

"*Gude mariye,* Darlene." Sharon's voice sang through the phone. *"Wie geht's?"*

Darlene hopped up on a stool and leaned her elbow on the counter. "I'm okay."

"I called to see if you're coming to the supper tonight at Alice's *haus."* Sharon's voice was bright, and Darlene could imagine her pretty smile. "Her *mamm* is expecting a dozen *Englishers* from one of the local tour companies, and we'll start helping her and Alice cook around four. You'll love their menu. It's meat loaf, and —"

"There's another supper tonight?" Darlene looked at the calendar behind her on the wall. "But it's Tuesday."

"We talked about it at Alice's on Sunday." Sharon paused. "Oh, I'm sorry. I forgot you weren't there."

Darlene pressed her lips together as the familiar feeling of despair rolled over her.

270

Not only did she dread watching her mother suffer but she also despised missing gatherings with her friends. And it definitely hurt that Sharon had forgotten she wasn't with them on Sunday.

Guilt replaced despair. How could she worry about missing time with her friends when her mother needed her?

"I'm so sorry. I should have called you sooner," Sharon continued. "Are you free tonight? We'd love for you to join us. We've missed you at the last two singings."

"I can't." Darlene rubbed her forehead as a headache began to throb.

"Oh." Sharon hesitated. "Is your *mamm* okay?"

"She's just having a bad day." The words flowed from Darlene's lips with ease. After all, she seemed to say them nearly every day.

"I'm so sorry. I pray for her and your family often."

"Danki." Darlene sat up straighter. "I hope I can come to the next supper, but I need to stay home tonight."

"I understand. We'll miss you." Sharon paused again. "Do you need any help? Alice and I can come over and cook or clean, maybe while your *mamm* is napping?"

Darlene smiled. How she treasured her friends. *"Danki,* but we're fine."

"You always say that, but I feel we should be doing more for you. Would you tell me if you needed something?"

Darlene opened her mouth and then closed it. How she longed to tell Sharon the worries that burdened her heart. But she couldn't. Not only did she not want to burden her but she couldn't let down her guard. If she did, she might crumble and never recover.

"Of course I would," Darlene said.

"I feel like you're not being completely honest with me. I've known you since we were in first grade. I can tell when you're holding back."

The bell on the front door sounded, and Darlene jumped down from the stool as three Amish ladies she didn't know walked in. Maybe they were visiting Bird-in-Hand.

"I'm sorry, but I need to go. I have customers. Will you tell everyone hello for me tonight?"

"Of course. Have a *gut* day."

"You too. Bye." Darlene hung up and squared her shoulders, pushing her worries away. *"Gude mariye,"* she called out to the women. "How may I help you?"

Andrew Detweiler stepped into Alice's kitchen, where Alice, Sharon, and Alice's mother, Dorothy, scampered around, pulling food out of the oven and gathering dishes. His friends Jay, Cal, and Dave were bringing folding chairs and tables from the utility room.

The aromas of meat loaf and freshly baked bread filled Andrew's senses. He was glad the women always made enough food for them to enjoy when the guests left. He secretly believed eating the leftovers was the best part of these evenings. As far as he was concerned, that was enough payment for his help, but Feenie and Dorothy always insisted on sharing their profits with everyone.

"Andrew! You made it!" Alice called.

Not for the first time, he found himself comparing Alice's — and Sharon's — coloring with Darlene's. Darlene was a gorgeous blonde with brown eyes. Alice had brown eyes, too, but reddish-brown hair, and Sharon had light-brown hair and blue eyes. They were all attractive yet different, although each was an average height for a woman.

One thing different about Darlene was her dating status. Alice had recently started dating Dave, who'd been estranged from their friend group for a while. Andrew was still impressed by how she'd managed to not only persuade Dave to open up to her after he'd gone through a tough time but convince him to join their group for suppers and singings. And Sharon had been dating Jay since last spring. But as far as he knew, with her mother so ill, Darlene didn't have much time for socializing beyond occasionally making it to these suppers or Sunday afternoon singings.

Andrew gave Alice a sheepish smile. "Sorry I'm a little late. *Mei dat*'s furniture store was busy today."

"It's no problem. We're just glad you're here. We've been running behind with the cooking." She pointed to the other men. "Would you please help the guys set up?"

"Ya." Andrew scanned the room. "Is Darlene here?"

"She couldn't make it." Her lips pressed into a flat line. "Sharon talked to her earlier, and her *mamm* was having another bad day."

Andrew shook his head. For some reason, Darlene had been on his mind for the past few days, and he wanted to know how she was doing. Although everyone in their church district was aware of her mother's battle with cancer, Darlene never really talked about it. Andrew couldn't shake the feeling that she could use some emotional support. He knew Sharon and Alice were there for their best friend, but he'd heard them say Darlene had resisted sharing her feelings with them ever since her mother's diagnosis.

"Hey, Andrew," Cal said, breaking into his thoughts. "Are you going to help us set up? Or just stand there like some kind of *dummkopp*?"

Cal was never shy. He stood around six feet tall, just like Andrew and the other two guys, and Andrew supposed he was good-looking. He had golden hair and blue eyes. But he was the jokester of their group and could always be counted on to make a smart remark or offer a witty comeback, enjoying being the center of attention. Andrew, on the other hand, was happy to hover in the background.

"Sorry." Andrew grabbed a chair and unfolded it before pushing it in under a table.

Sharon's voice rose from the counter where she was hard at work, Alice's mother at her side. "We have enough chairs out here now, but Dorothy and I think we need another table, so the guests won't be too crowded together." Andrew could see she was icing a large chocolate cake. She turned and locked eyes with Jay, Andrew noting his were another set of brown. "Would you please get another one from the utility room?"

"Of course."

Alice spoke from across the room, where she was taking a dish out of the fridge. "I was thinking we could sing 'The Old Rugged Cross' and 'How Great Thou Art' tonight."

"What about 'Amazing Grace'?" Dave said before looking at Alice, who gave him a smile that seemed meant only for him.

Andrew looked away. His thoughts once again turned to Darlene. Maybe he'd see her at church on Sunday so he could ask her how she was doing.

" 'Amazing Grace' would be lovely," Dorothy said, turning to display a tray of cookies.

Sharon turned the cake around. "Okay. That's done. What's next?"

"Grab the tablecloths?" Jay asked as he and Dave unfolded the additional table.

Alice deposited the dish next to her mother and then pulled two tablecloths from a drawer and tossed them to Andrew. "We need to get these tables set. The guests will be here before we know it."

CHAPTER TWO

"Let me help you to the kitchen." Darlene tied *Mamm*'s robe around her waist and then held her arm as she slowly shuffled toward the kitchen for some supper. She'd showed little improvement all day, and Darlene knew she'd done the right thing by staying home from Sharon's supper.

Mamm had lost so much weight that she looked as if she might blow away on a windy day. Her dresses hung on her as if they'd been made for a much larger woman, and her thick, golden hair had started falling out in clumps. Darlene had always thought her mother was beautiful, but now her deep-brown eyes had lost their brightness, and her cheeks were sunken in.

It nearly tore Darlene to shreds to see how weak and exhausted *Mamm* was. She would fall asleep while trying to read a book, and Darlene and Biena had to take turns bathing her. Darlene often felt like *Mamm*'s mother instead of her child.

She did her best to hold back tears as she steered the once-strong Roselyn Bender to her usual chair at one end of the kitchen table. "Would you like some pot roast, *Mamm*?"

"No, *danki.*" She touched her blue head-scarf. "Some soup would be *gut,* though."

"Coming up." Darlene retrieved the refrigerator jar of homemade chicken noodle soup she'd thrown together yesterday and poured it into a pot before turning on the propane stove.

Biena carried a large serving dish with the pot roast to the table just as *Dat* came in from outside. He crossed the room to kiss *Mamm* on the cheek. "How are you feeling, dear?"

"I'm *gut,* Al." *Mamm* touched his chest as she gazed up at him, and Darlene took in how tiny and frail her hand looked. She was not well.

She turned her attention to the pot and stirred the soup.

"You just closed up the store?" *Mamm* asked *Dat.*

"*Ya.*" He moved to the sink to wash his hands. "I took over for Darlene so she could make supper." He turned to Biena. "You made my favorite tonight. It smells *appeditlich."*

"Danki." Biena set a basket of rolls on the table.

The soup began to bubble, and Darlene ladled a healthy portion into a bowl, then carried it to her mother.

"Danki." Mamm sounded breathy, as if it took great effort for her to speak.

"Gern gschehne."

"Let's eat," *Dat* said.

Darlene took her usual spot across from her sister, and after a silent prayer, she placed a helping of pot roast on her plate. She glanced at *Mamm* and saw her shakily scoop a spoonful of soup and bring it to her mouth. Darlene bit her lower lip and held her breath, trying to resist the urge to offer help.

Then *Mamm* dropped the spoon, splattering soup outside the bowl, and Darlene couldn't hold back the words.

"Do you need help, *Mamm*?" Darlene pushed her chair back.

"No." *Mamm*'s tone was nearly as sharp as the knives sitting in a wooden block on the counter, and Darlene winced at the tone. "I can do it." She huffed out a breath as she mopped the mess with her napkin. "This illness has taken nearly everything from me. I should be taking care of myself, my home, and my family. The least I can do is feed myself. So, no, I do *not* need help, Darlene." She lifted the spoon again, and this time she managed to slide some soup into her mouth.

With tears stinging her eyes, Darlene turned to *Dat,* who gave her a grave smile and discreetly shook his head as if warning her to not respond.

Dat cleared his throat. "Roselyn, Darlene said the store was busy this morning." He glanced at Darlene and lifted his eyebrows.

"Ya, I did, *Dat."* Her voice sounded strained to her own ears. "A dozen or so customers came in before lunch, and I sold quite a few greeting cards, some books, and some *boppli* clothes. A group of Amish women visiting Bird-in-Hand bought gifts for a newborn."

"Isn't that nice?" Biena's voice sounded a little too perky.

Mamm kept her eyes focused on her soup as if it took all her strength to eat it.

"It was busy when I took over as well," *Dat* said. "Some *Englishers* purchased a few gardening tools."

Dat talked about business throughout the remainder of the meal. He seemed to want to fill any silence. If only his enthusiasm could heal *Mamm.*

Once they were finished with supper, Biena helped *Mamm* return to the family room to sit in her recliner until bedtime.

As her father sat at the table drinking the last of his coffee, Darlene ferried all the dishes to the counter and then filled the sink with soapy water. Her mother's words about how the illness had taken everything from her echoed in Darlene's mind.

"Why didn't you go to the supper and singing tonight?"

"What?" Darlene spun to face her father.

"Why did you stay home tonight?" *Dat* tilted his head and studied her.

"How do you know about that?"

"Biena told me."

Darlene glanced at the doorway leading to the family room and then back at him. Why had she told her sister about Sharon's phone call? She'd shared that news in confidence. She hadn't wanted either of her parents to know about it.

"Don't be angry with Biena." *Dat* leaned back in his chair. "You know your *mamm* and I want you *maed* to continue seeing your *freinden.* You deserve to have social lives. It's part of our culture for young people to spend time with others their age."

Darlene shook her head as she turned off the water. "I just couldn't go tonight. I

281

didn't want to leave you and Biena to take care of everything. The chores, the meal, *Mamm* . . ."

Dat shook his head as he rose and came to stand beside her. "You're just as stubborn as your *mamm.*" He touched her shoulder. "You know I'll support you whenever you want to see your *freinden.* I want your life to be as normal as possible."

Nothing will ever be normal until Mamm *is well.*

"I know you will," she said. But she would never leave her father and Biena to care for *Mamm* on a bad day.

"I'm going out to take care of the animals. Call if you need me."

As Darlene tackled the dishes, she sucked in a deep breath and silently begged God to heal her mother.

A few moments later her hands stilled in the water as she recalled what her father said earlier in the day, that God loved them all. But how many times did she need to ask God for his special touch? She longed to have her beloved mother back.

Another thought caused her to gasp. Would God allow this illness to steal her mother away forever?

After leaving the shop behind the showroom

of his father's furniture store, a large, cinder block building at the end of their long driveway, Andrew climbed the back steps of his family's home and glanced at the setting sun. Taking in the stunning hues of pink and purple, he breathed in the air, grateful that evening would bring at least a slight relief from the humidity of the day.

His shoulders and back ached after working for hours on a triple dresser that was part of a bedroom suite one of his father's *English* customers had ordered. He enjoyed building furniture, but it had been a long Friday.

Glancing down at his trousers, he found them covered in sawdust and sighed. Like always, he should have changed his clothes back in the shop. But he'd been so eager to get home and eat some supper, he'd forgotten.

At the edge of the porch, he began swiping his hands over his trousers, sending sawdust dancing through the air like dandelion seeds on a spring day.

"Andrew?"

He turned to see his mother standing in the doorway. Although Andrew and his younger brother, Sam, had inherited both her dark hair and eyes, they were several inches taller than her as well as *Dat.* But she still commanded respect with her strong, stubborn personality.

"Hi, *Mamm.*" He gave his trousers another swipe.

"What are you doing?"

"I forgot to change my clothes at the shop, so I'm trying to clean up before I come inside." He gave her an embarrassed smile. "I know how you feel about sawdust in your kitchen, and . . . I'm really hungry."

Mamm rolled her eyes. "Come inside. Your supper is getting cold."

Andrew followed her into the mudroom, where he left his shoes and straw hat. Then he entered the kitchen, crossed to the sink, and began to wash his hands.

"You stayed late tonight," *Mamm* said as she pulled a plate from the oven. "Your *dat* and *bruder* are already taking care of the animals."

"Didn't *Dat* tell you? I'm running behind on a big project, so I told him I'd try to catch up."

She set the plate with pork chops, mashed potatoes, and broccoli on the table. "*Ya,* he did. Did you get as far as you'd hoped?"

"*Ya.*" He dried his hands on a paper towel. "I'll start staining it tomorrow."

"That's *gut.*" *Mamm* pointed to the plate. "Sit. Eat. I'll get you some water."

Andrew dropped into a chair and bowed his head for a quick prayer before slicing off a piece of pork chop.

Mamm gave him the glass of water, then turned to the sink.

Andrew chewed as his mind once again settled on Darlene. He still wasn't sure why she'd invaded his thoughts all week, but he found himself more and more concerned about her and her family.

"Mamm," he began, and she glanced over her shoulder at him. "Have you heard how Roselyn Bender is doing?"

She stopped scrubbing a pot and turned to face him. "Why do you ask?"

"Darlene didn't come to the supper and singing we had at Alice's *haus* on Tuesday. Sharon said her *mamm* was having another bad day."

"Ach, I'm sorry to hear that. But I ran into Louise Smoker at the market yesterday. Sharon Lambert told her Roselyn really seems to be struggling with the side effects of chemo."

"Ya. That's the impression we're all getting, although Darlene doesn't like to talk about it."

"It breaks my heart. I've been praying for the family."

Andrew had been praying too. In fact,

while he worked on the dresser today, he prayed for the Bender family frequently. If only he didn't need to wait for Sunday to ask Darlene how *she* was doing. But he didn't want to push her.

Mamm turned back to the sink and rinsed the pot. "Roselyn has always been rather private, but Al used to be much more social. I don't get to his store much, but when I do see him, there or at church, he doesn't say much. I've also heard Roselyn doesn't want any visitors, which makes it difficult for the rest of the church district. Many of us would love to help her and the family."

Andrew nodded. He recalled the many times he'd heard Sharon and Alice offer to sing, cook, or clean for Darlene's mother. Each time, Darlene declined.

"We have to keep them in our prayers," *Mamm* said. "They've been through so much, but we know the Lord will provide."

But as Andrew took another bite of his food, he wanted to do more, to be a better friend to Darlene. For some reason he couldn't pinpoint, he thought maybe she'd talk to him even though she seemed to be keeping Sharon and Alice at bay.

CHAPTER THREE

Darlene stood in front of her mirror Sunday morning and brushed her hands down her favorite pink dress and white apron. Then, after checking her prayer covering, she glanced at the clock on her nightstand and sighed. Her mother wasn't able to attend church anymore — even if she felt like it — because being around a crowd when her immune system was compromised by the chemotherapy was too great a risk. But the rest of the family had to leave within the next hour or they'd be late.

Still, even though her mother had rallied yesterday, Darlene regretted agreeing to leave her home alone. *Mamm* had insisted, though.

Despite her current struggles with God, Darlene closed her eyes and whispered a prayer. "Please help *Mamm* be strong today."

Then she hurried down the stairs, but when she found the kitchen empty, her shoulders wilted as her hope deflated. This meant one thing — *Mamm* had a bad night.

Darlene turned as footfalls sounded in the hallway leading to her parents' first-floor bedroom. Then *Dat* stepped into the kitchen, his shoulders slumping, his mouth turned down. "Your *mamm* is *krank* again."

Darlene's bottom lip trembled.

Biena entered the kitchen from the stairwell and stopped short. "Where's *Mamm?*"

"Bad night." Darlene's voice wobbled as the nearly relentless sadness flooded her soul. She hadn't seen her friends in two weeks, not since last worshipping with the members of her church district. They all had their own lives and responsibilities, and they rarely if ever came into her father's store. For days, she'd looked forward to church and then spending the afternoon visiting and singing with them. And when *Mamm* was better yesterday, she'd thought she'd have that chance.

But now her hope for the day was dashed.

Would her friends really miss her? After all, Sharon forgot she missed their gathering last Sunday. If Darlene stayed away too long, would they just stop inviting her to join them?

She gritted her teeth as guilt raised its ugly head. How could she worry about seeing her friends when her mother was in such bad shape?

"I'll check on her." Biena started for the hall, but *Dat* captured her arm and gently pulled her back to him.

"No. She just fell asleep. Leave her be." He huffed out a breath, and Darlene took in the dark circles under his eyes. He must have been awake all night.

Darlene swallowed against the thickness in her throat. She was disappointed about not seeing her friends while her father had lost sleep. How could she be so selfish?

Biena nodded. "Oh. Okay. What would you like for breakfast, *Dat*? I'll make it."

"Nothing, *danki*. I'm going to rest until she wakes up." *Dat* stepped toward the doorway and then turned. "You two go on to church."

"Why would we when *Mamm* is so *krank*?" Biena asked.

"It wouldn't be right for us to go to church after you've been up all night, *Dat*. You should get some sleep." Darlene pointed toward the family room. "Go rest in your recliner, and Biena and I will care for *Mamm*." She glanced down at her dress. "I just need to change my clothes, and then I'll eat something before peeking in to check on her."

"No." *Dat* shook his head. "Go to church, and then spend the afternoon with your *freinden.*"

Darlene turned toward Biena, who looked just as conflicted as she felt. Then she swiveled back to *Dat.* "But what if you need help?"

Dat scrubbed his hand down his face. "I'll be fine. We have plenty of leftovers in the fridge, and I know how to warm them up. And I'll call on a neighbor to help with the animals. Go enjoy your day. You both deserve it." Then he pivoted and left.

Darlene blinked and faced her sister. "Why doesn't he want us to help?"

Biena stepped closer and rubbed Darlene's arm. "I overheard him talking to *Mamm* the other day, and they were saying they want us to have some sense of normalcy. That's why they want us to see our *freinden.*"

Darlene snorted. "Normalcy? That's what *Dat* said to me too. But nothing will be normal again if *Mamm* doesn't get well."

"Don't say that." Biena's expression grew fierce. "We have to trust in the Lord and have faith. I can't explain it, but with all my heart, I believe his will is for *Mamm* to get better."

Darlene nodded, but her own heart ached.

Unlike Biena's faith and *Dat*'s, hers was dwindling day by day. She didn't know what to believe anymore. But she could never admit that to anyone. Not her family, not her friends. They'd be disappointed in her. No, her doubts were hers and hers alone. Yet she craved the opportunity to be honest with someone about her confusing feelings, someone with whom she could freely share the burdens in her soul.

An hour later, Darlene walked with Biena toward the Bontragers' house. She and her sister had said only a few words during the short and solemn buggy ride there. Darlene's sorrow was slowly eating away any sense of happiness.

"I'll see you in the barn." Biena gave her a weak smile and then left to join some friends standing on the back porch. Darlene looked around to see if any of her own friends had arrived.

When she spotted Alice and Sharon with Dave and Jay, she headed toward them. Alice looked so pretty in a bright-green dress that complemented the red highlights in her hair peeking out from under her prayer covering. And Sharon seemed to glow in her blue dress as she smiled up at Jay.

Alice turned and saw Darlene, and her

expression brightened. She met her halfway and enveloped Darlene in a tight hug. "It's so *gut* to see you. How are you? How's your *mamm*?"

"About the same." Darlene shrugged, and they joined the group. *Mamm* was worse, but she didn't need to dampen anyone else's day with that information.

Sharon hugged her. "We were just talking about you. So your *mamm* isn't doing better?"

She couldn't completely hide the truth. "She had another bad night. That just happens sometimes, but she'll be okay." She forced a smile.

Sharon looked past her. "Is your *dat* here?"

"No." Darlene licked her dry lips. "He wanted to be the one to stay home with *Mamm*. Biena and I offered, but he insisted we come to church and see our *freinden*."

Alice looped one arm around Darlene's shoulders. "We've missed you at our singings."

"I'm glad you're back," Dave offered.

Jay smiled. "It's *gut* to see you."

Darlene's eyes moistened. Maybe her friends hadn't given up on her.

Jay turned to Sharon. "Are we going to sing for someone this afternoon?"

"*Ya,* one of our newer gentlemen is on dialysis, and he's struggling. I thought we could sing for him. His name is Enos Chupp."

"Darlene."

Darlene jumped at the sound of her name, then spun and nearly bumped into Andrew. Embarrassed, she felt her cheeks heat as she looked up at him. "Andrew. Hi."

"I didn't mean to startle you." He gave her a shy smile. "How are you?"

"I'm okay." That was her standard answer. Then she nodded at Cal as he moved past her to join Jay and Dave. They started talking, and she noticed Sharon and Alice were deep in discussion about their afternoon plans.

"Are you really okay?" Andrew asked, his voice a little lower as though he didn't want the others to hear.

She looked into his face, and she was struck by the concern in his deep-brown eyes. Although she'd known him since starting school, they'd never been more than acquaintances. They shared the same group of friends, and they spent time together frequently, but they'd never been close.

Darlene had always admired Andrew's quiet demeanor. Cal was often the loud jokester who commanded the group's attention, but Andrew was his opposite. He never made a fuss. He often stayed calm when their friends were excited about this or that, and his tranquility was comforting.

Yet Darlene couldn't recall a time when she'd had a deeply personal conversation with him. When they spoke, it was usually about mundane subjects, such as the weather or mutual acquaintances.

But now Andrew was studying her, awaiting her response, and she was tongue-tied.

"You can be honest with me," he said.

"I-I appreciate that." And she did. But this wasn't the time or place for her to pour out her heart — to anyone. If she ever did find the courage to bare her soul to someone, it would be in private. And most likely, she wouldn't pour her heart out to Andrew. That would be too awkward and forward.

He scanned the young people around them and then met her gaze again. Something in his eyes told her he understood. "Why don't we talk later?"

"O-okay." She tried to smile, but it felt more like a grimace.

"It's nine," Sharon announced. "Time to head into the barn."

Alice grabbed Darlene's arm. "Let's go."

As Darlene allowed Alice to steer her, she glanced back and caught Andrew watching her. A strange awareness skittered through her veins, but she tried to ignore it and turn her attention to preparing for worship.

Andrew sat between Jay and Cal in the unmarried men's section of the barn. He tried his best to stay focused on singing the hymns and listening to the sermons, but his gaze kept drifting to the other side of the barn, where Darlene sat between Biena and Alice. She seemed to be lost in thought as she focused on her lap.

When he'd first spotted her talking to Alice and Sharon earlier, his pulse had leapt — to his surprise — with actual joy. But as he moved closer to her, he'd noticed the sadness and anxiety in her pretty eyes. She seemed more burdened than ever.

When he'd asked her how she was doing, he could tell by her hesitation and melancholy expression that she wasn't sharing the whole truth. He yearned to encourage her to open up to him. But how?

Andrew closed his eyes, then stared out an open barn window while pondering his sudden interest in Darlene. While he'd always considered her a friend — a good friend, in fact — they'd never shared a heart-to-heart conversation. He'd always appreciated how pretty she was, and she had a sweetness about her that set her apart. But this was different.

Darlene always seemed thoughtful too. When they were in school, he noticed her going out of her way to talk to schoolmates who were loners. And when it was her turn to pick someone for her softball team, she chose students who weren't the best players. She had a kind heart.

Andrew bit his lower lip. Was he developing romantic feelings for Darlene? Was that possible with someone he'd known most of his life?

Andrew joined the congregation for the fifteen-minute kneeling prayer, but when he closed his eyes, he thought about how strong Darlene tried to sound when asked about her mother's illness. But was she only being brave while breaking on the inside?

He couldn't shake the feeling that she needed someone to listen, yet for some reason, not someone in her family or Sharon or Alice.

But was it prideful for him to assume he could be the friend she needed?

When the fifteen-minute prayer ended, he stood along with the congregation for the benediction and then the closing hymn. While he sang, Andrew's eyes moved again to Darlene. To his surprise, she met his gaze, then gave him a shy smile before looking down at the floor.

He made a decision. No matter what, he'd find a way to talk to Darlene after the noon meal. He'd encourage her to go with their friends to sing today if she seemed ready to go home instead. And given the smile she just gave him, maybe she'd even ride in his buggy with him.

Somehow, he'd convince her to open up about how she was truly coping — or not coping — with her mother's devastating illness.

"It's *gut* to see Darlene here today," Andrew commented as he and Cal moved the last of the benches turned lunch tables from the Bontragers' barn. Now he, Jay, Cal, and Dave would wait for the girls to finish helping with cleanup in the Bontragers' kitchen.

"*Ya,* it is." Jay folded his arms over his chest.

"I hope she's going to join us for the singing today."

"What's with your sudden interest in Darlene?" Cal came closer and bumped his shoulder against Andrew's.

"What do you mean by that?" Andrew turned to him. "She's our *freind.*"

Cal displayed an exaggerated shrug. "It

just seems like you've paid awfully close attention to her today. You were talking to her alone before the service, and I saw you looking at her during the service. Then at lunch, you kept peeking at her while she was delivering the food and filling *kaffi* cups." He tapped his chin. "I think you like her."

"I do — as a *freind.*"

Cal snorted. "I'd say you like her as more than a *freind.*"

"So are we going singing?" Dave asked, probably sensing possible friction between friends.

Jay nodded toward the house. "Sharon said they wouldn't be long."

Cal sighed. "But it has been long. I wonder what the holdup is."

Just then Darlene came out the back door, Biena with her. "I'll go see." When they got closer, he could hear their conversation.

"You're going out with your *freinden,* then?" Darlene was asking Biena.

"*Ya,* we're going to play games at Linda's *haus.*" Biena looked up and greeted Andrew, then turned back to Darlene. "Are you going with your *freinden?*"

Darlene turned to Alice and Sharon as they appeared from the house and joined the group. "Are you still going singing this afternoon?"

"*Ya,* we are," Alice said. "We're singing for the man I mentioned before church. Enos Chupp."

"Aren't you coming with us?" Sharon asked.

Darlene turned back to her sister. "Are you taking the horse and buggy?"

Biena nodded. "I thought you could probably get a ride."

"You're more than welcome to ride with me to the singing," Andrew said. "And I can take you home too."

Darlene looked up at him. "Are you sure?"

"Of course."

Darlene gave him a timid smile. "I guess I'm riding with you, then."

"Perfect." Andrew smiled. Now he had the perfect opportunity to talk to Darlene alone.

Darlene found herself feeling strangely calm as Andrew guided his horse down Old Philadelphia Pike, following Jay's buggy. The sun's bright rays streamed in through the windshield, and looking out the window, she admired the lush, rolling patchwork of green pastures dotted with farmhouses, barns, and livestock.

What a wonderful day. I wish Mamm *could enjoy it.*

Andrew's voice broke through Darlene's thoughts.

"I noticed your *dat* wasn't in church today. And I can't remember the last time I saw your *mamm* there."

"*Mamm* can't attend while she's on chemotherapy. It's too risky for her to be around crowds. She might catch something." She kept her eyes focused out the window.

"Oh. I think I've heard you say that

300

before. And how are you feeling?"

She turned toward him, giving him a smile she had a feeling he didn't believe. "Like I've also said before, I'm okay."

He raised his eyebrows. "Are you sure?"

"*Ya.*" She fingered the hem of her apron. "Why?"

"You just seem *bedauerlich* and preoccupied. And you have good reason to be." He halted the horse at a light and then angled his body toward her. "Do you want to talk about it?"

Suddenly self-conscious, she touched the ties to her prayer covering. "I'm fine. I'm not the one going through chemo."

"No, you're not. But you're supporting your parents, and you're under a lot of stress."

Darlene shifted in the seat. Did she have a right to admit how stressed she felt when her mother was suffering? And *Dat* and Biena had to be just as stressed.

She needed to gather herself before she lost control of her emotions. She glanced toward the intersection just as the light changed. "It's green."

Andrew faced the windshield and guided the horse ahead.

Desperate to change the subject, she asked the first question that popped into her head.

"How's your *dat*'s furniture store doing?"

"We're busy, and that's *gut*."

"What are you working on in the shop?"

He gave her a sideways glance. "A bedroom suite. I've been working on a triple dresser for days now. It's going pretty well."

"What will the dresser be like when it's done?"

"It has six drawers and a hutch with four shelves and a mirror." He glanced at her. "I'm going to stain it walnut."

"You said it's part of a suite, right?" she asked, and he nodded. "What are the other pieces?"

"Two nightstands, a headboard, and a footboard. I'm also working on . . ."

As Andrew told her more about his work, Darlene relaxed for the first time in weeks. The knots in her shoulders eased and her always-ready frown dissolved. She was grateful Andrew had asked her to ride with him. He was a good friend, and she liked hearing about his work.

But another tingle of guilt appeared. Why should she get to relax?

She tried to dismiss remorse at having left her parents on their own today, but it was a losing battle.

"Have you met Enos Chupp?" Darlene asked as the horse pulled the buggy up to the Chupp family's farm.

A two-story, whitewashed home sat surrounded by three red barns, and a pair of horses stood in the pasture beside them.

"No, I haven't." Andrew halted the horse. "But if he's struggling with dialysis like Sharon said, I'm glad we're here."

Darlene climbed out of the buggy and joined their other friends by the back porch. Then she and Andrew followed them up to the door, and Sharon knocked.

A woman who looked to be in her midsixties came to the doorway. "Hello?"

"Hi. We haven't met yet, but I'm Sharon Lambert from our church district, and these are *mei freinden.*" She gestured toward them all. "We sing for members of our community, and we'd like to sing for Enos to brighten his day. If that's okay with you, of course."

Darlene lingered at the back, aware of Andrew as he took a step closer to her.

"Oh my." The woman's hazel eyes sparkled. "That would be lovely. What a blessing." She held out her hand, and Sharon shook it. "I'm Hadassah."

"Nice to meet you." Sharon's smile widened.

Hadassah beckoned them to enter. "Please come in."

Sharon stepped forward to lead everyone into the house, but Darlene couldn't seem to move. The remorse she'd felt in the buggy was still with her. She'd wanted to help bring joy to this family's day, but she should be home with her own family. She didn't begrudge Biena spending time with her friends. She just knew it was wrong for her.

She pressed her lips together and closed her eyes as renewed stress took hold. But she couldn't let her friends see it. They already asked too many questions — even normally quiet Andrew.

Darlene felt a hand on her arm, and when she looked up, Andrew immediately let go.

"Hey." His voice was soft and warm. "Are you okay?"

"Of course." She gave him a stiff nod.

"I don't think so. Do you want me to take you home?"

"No, but *danki.*" She started up the porch steps.

"Darlene."

She spun and faced him.

"We can go." He jammed this thumb toward his horse and buggy.

She huffed a breath. "No. We need to sing."

Darlene stepped into the mudroom and followed the voices to the small family room off the kitchen, where her friends were already standing in front of a frail man with graying brown hair and a matching beard, sitting in a recliner. His shirt and trousers seemed to hang on him — just like *Mamm*'s dresses hung on her. His skin had a yellowish tone, and his face was gaunt. Cancer wasn't the only enemy.

Hadassah sat in a wing chair beside Enos and held his hand. "These young folks are going to sing for you. Isn't that nice?"

The man nodded, and his brown eyes looked misty.

Darlene held her breath for a moment as a vision of her mother struggling to stand and walk filled her mind. She should be with her.

Hadassah looked at Sharon. "Would you please introduce your *freinden*?"

"Of course." Sharon shared their names, and they all greeted Enos. Then she asked him, "Do you have a favorite hymn?"

"*Ya.* 'It Is Well with My Soul.' " His voice sounded tired and weak.

"That's a favorite of mine too," Sharon said before pulling four copies of the *Ausbund,* the traditional Amish hymnal, and four copies of *Heartland Hymns,* a German and English songbook, from her tote bag. "We can share the hymnals."

305

Andrew took one of them and quickly found the song.

Sharon cleared her throat and then began to sing. "When peace like a river attendeth my way . . ."

Darlene joined in, trying her best to concentrate on the lyrics instead of her regret at not being home. She glanced up at Andrew, and when he winked at her, confusion smacked her in the face.

What did Andrew's sudden attention mean? Had he decided she needed his pity? No thank you.

They sang four more hymns and then drank coffee and ate apple pie with Hadassah and Enos before heading outside.

"*Danki* again for coming to visit," Hadassah told them as they stood on the back porch and said good-bye. "It really meant a lot to us."

"*Gern gschehne,*" Jay said.

"We'll come back soon," Sharon said, a promise Darlene knew she intended the group to keep.

Hadassah waved and then headed inside.

"We're hosting another supper at *mei haus* Saturday night," Sharon announced as they walked to the buggies. "I hope you all can come and sing."

"I'll come," Alice said with a nod, and

Dave nodded too.

"You know I'll be there." Jay took Sharon's hand in his.

"Sounds *gut*. I'll see you all then." Cal climbed into his buggy and then guided his horse toward the road.

Alice hugged Darlene. "I'm so glad you came today."

"Give our love to your *mamm*." Sharon hugged Darlene next.

Darlene waved good-bye to Dave and Jay and then followed Andrew to his buggy.

"I think Enos and Hadassah enjoyed our visit," Andrew said once they were settled on the seat and headed home.

"I do too."

"How are things at your parents' store?"

"*Gut*." She nodded. Why was he asking so many questions?

"Do you run the store every day? I've worked in our showroom at the store once or twice when *Dat* was in a bind, but I'm not that *gut* with customers."

She turned toward him, and he gave her a warm smile. She realized he was truly interested in hearing about her work at the family business, and that baffled her. And she didn't see pity in his face at all.

"I take turns with *mei dat* and *mei schweschder*. Sometimes Biena stays in the *haus* and cares for *Mamm,* and I run the store. Other times, *Dat* runs it while Biena and I watch over *Mamm* or do chores. When *Mamm* has an appointment, *Dat* always goes with her, and Biena and I take care of everything else."

"Do you like working there?"

"*Ya.* I enjoy talking with the customers."

"What are your favorite items to sell?"

She took in his kind expression and realized something else. She'd never heard Andrew talk this much. Normally his gregarious cohorts overshadowed him.

He gave her a sideways glance and raised his eyebrows again. "Why are you staring at me?"

"You're very talkative today, but you're normally the quiet one."

"Oh." He halted the horse at a red light and then faced her. She was almost certain she spotted a pink blush on his cheeks. "Is that a bad thing?"

"No, it's a *gut* thing."

"That's a relief." His smile was back. "So tell me. What are your favorite items to sell in the store?"

"Hmm." She tapped her finger against her chin. "I suppose it's the greeting cards. We have some lovely ones. I enjoy ordering them from the vendor and stocking the racks. I also enjoy selling art supplies. Lots of Amish women like to make their own Christmas cards, for instance. I love it when they bring in samples of their work." She settled back in the seat, and once again, she felt relaxed — even if she shouldn't. How did Andrew manage to make her feel comfortable?

They spent the remainder of the ride to her house discussing the funny questions *English* customers sometimes asked about the Amish. It was good to laugh, and when Andrew's horse pulled the buggy up her driveway, she was disappointed. She'd love to continue riding around with Andrew, discussing mundane things. What a welcome distraction his company had been.

But that didn't mean she could stay away from home like this again. Not when her parents needed her, no matter what they said.

Andrew halted the horse at the top of the driveway and faced her. "*Danki* for riding with me today. I had a great time."

"I did too." An awkward silence filled the buggy, and she cleared her throat as she pushed open the door. "Have a *gut* night." She climbed out.

"Darlene," he called as she closed the door.

"Ya." She peeked through the window, and his expression was tentative, almost nervous.

"I hope you have a *gut* evening with your family and that your *mamm* is feeling better."

"Danki. Please tell your folks and your *bruder* hello for me." She stepped away from the buggy and waved before climbing the porch steps and entering the house. She found her father sitting at the kitchen table eating a bowl of her homemade soup. His dark eyes looked so tired, and his smile seemed halfhearted as he looked up at her.

"Hi, *Dat,*" she said, glancing around the kitchen. "Is Biena home?"

"Not yet." He wiped his beard with a paper napkin. "How was your day?"

"Gut." She dropped into a chair across from him. "How's *Mamm?*" She braced herself for his response.

Dat sighed and looked down at his bowl. "She was too weak to get out of bed today, but she did eat a little bit without getting *krank.*"

More guilt, hot and sharp, sliced through her chest. She should have insisted on staying home today to help him. And how could she have enjoyed her time with Andrew, no matter how nice he was? She pressed her lips together.

He met her gaze. "Did you go singing?"

"We did. But I should have been here."

Dat shook his head as he reached across the table for her hand. "Darlene, I'll tell you this as often as I have to until you understand. You and Biena deserve time to be like the other young folks in our community. And you work so hard. You need breaks like today."

"But we're family." A few tears escaped her eyes.

"Don't cry, *mei liewe.* Everything will be fine. God is in control, and he is the Great Physician. He'll take care of your *mamm.* Hold on to your faith."

Darlene wiped her eyes with a napkin as her father's words echoed in her mind. She *would* try to hold on to the faith she still had, but some days it felt as cracked and fragile as her heart.

CHAPTER FIVE

On Friday afternoon, the sound of hammers banging and saw blades whirling filled the workshop as Andrew strode toward his father's office, and the familiar heaviness of sawdust and the pungent odor of stain washed over him.

Concerns about Darlene had haunted him all week while he finished the two nightstands for the bedroom suite. No matter how hard he tried, he couldn't get her out of his mind.

Jay had called him yesterday to confirm that Sharon was hosting a supper and singing at her house tomorrow night, and Andrew yearned to know if Darlene was planning to attend. But he didn't want to ask Jay. He did, however, want to give Darlene a ride to Sharon's house so he could talk to her alone. The only way to find out if she was going, though, was to ask her.

And he'd finally decided to call her at the store.

When he reached the office, he leaned against the doorframe and waited while his father completed a phone call.

"That's right. I'll send a truck out for the supplies tomorrow. Thanks, Ron." *Dat* hung up. "Andrew. How are those nightstands coming along?"

"Almost done." Andrew brushed his hands over his trousers. "May I use the phone?"

"Of course." *Dat* stood and pointed to the desk. "Who do you need to call?"

"Just a *freind.*"

"Okay." *Dat* gave him a knowing smile. "I'll go out to the shop so you have some privacy."

Andrew ignored the teasing in his father's grin and slipped the local phone book from the bottom drawer of the desk. Then he looked up the number for the store. He just hoped Darlene was working there today, not inside the house doing chores. His cheeks warmed as he dialed the number.

"Please answer, Darlene," he whispered as the phone rang.

"Thank you for calling Bird-in-Hand Dry Goods. How may I help you?"

Andrew breathed out a sigh of relief as her voice rang through the phone. "Hi,

Darlene, this is —"

"I'm sorry, but this is Biena."

"Oh." Andrew squeezed his eyes shut as humiliation shook his confidence. They were sisters, so of course they sounded alike! "Is, uh, Darlene available?"

"*Ya,* she is. May I tell her who's calling?"

"It's Andrew."

"Oh, Andrew! Hang on a moment."

Andrew dropped into his father's chair and listened to commotion and muffled voices on the other end of the line.

"Hi, Andrew." Darlene's voice was radiant, like the sunshine spilling in through the window. "How is your day going?"

"It's going well. I've made a lot of progress on that bedroom suite I told you about on Sunday."

"Oh, nice."

"So you and Biena are both at the store today? Does that mean your *mamm* is having a better day?"

"*Ya,* she is. She was sitting on the back porch when I checked on her earlier."

A pleasant warmth sifted through him. "That's great news. I'm so *froh* to hear it."

"*Danki.*"

He leaned back in the chair and gathered all his courage to share the true reason for his call. "I spoke to Jay, and he confirmed

314

Sharon and her mother are hosting a supper at their *haus* tomorrow evening."

"Oh, *ya*. She mentioned that on Sunday."

"I was wondering if you're planning to go, and if so, I thought maybe I could pick you up." He held his breath, waiting for her response.

"Oh." She hesitated, and Andrew covered his face with his free hand.

This was a mistake. I never should have —

"*Danki* for offering. That would be nice."

Andrew released the breath he'd been holding and sat up straight. "*Wunderbaar.* I'll be there around four. Sharon always asks the guys to be there early enough to help set up."

"Perfect. I can help with the meal prep. Oh, please hold on a moment."

Andrew heard a whooshing noise, as if she put her hand over the receiver, and then muffled voices again.

"I'm sorry, but I have to go," she said. "A group of *Englishers* just came into the store, and *mei schweschder* needs my help. *Danki* for calling. I look forward to seeing you tomorrow."

"Have a *gut* day." Andrew hung up and then clapped his hands together as his lips spread into a wide grin. Darlene said yes! She was going to ride to the supper and

315

singing with him.

"Looks like your phone call went well."

Andrew turned to find his father in the doorway, smirking. "How long have you been standing there?"

"Long enough." *Dat* gestured toward the phone. "Who was that?"

"I told you. A *freind.*" Andrew started toward the door.

"Sounds like she's more than a *freind.*"

"I need to get back to work." Andrew moved past him.

"Andrew."

Pressing his lips together, Andrew turned toward his father. "What?"

"I'm glad to see you dating."

"I'm not dating, *Dat.*" Andrew pointed toward the shop. "I have to get back to those nightstands if you want me to make the deadline."

As he made his way to his work stall, his father's words sank into his bones. Would he like to date Darlene?

The answer was as clear as the cloudless summer sky. Yes, he would like to date her. But would she want anything more than friendship with him?

Only time would tell.

As soon as the *English* customers left,

Darlene returned to the stool behind the counter and tried not to smile, but that was a lost cause. Hearing from Andrew had been a pleasant surprise, especially since throughout the past week she'd found herself recalling their conversation on Sunday.

When he'd asked her to ride with him to Sharon's house, she'd been so stunned that she wasn't sure how to respond. While she'd decided she did want to spend more time with Andrew, she didn't want to give him the wrong idea. After all, she wasn't looking for a boyfriend.

Not that he wanted to date her.

Biena leaned forward and grinned as she rested an elbow on the counter, her chin on her palm. "What did Andrew want?"

"He reminded me that Sharon and her *mamm* are hosting a supper and singing tomorrow night." Darlene folded her arms over her chest. "And he offered to pick me up and take me there."

"Ooh!" Biena stood up and clapped. "I think he likes you! Maybe he'll ask *Dat*'s permission to date you."

"Stop. He's not interested in dating me." Darlene hopped down and crossed to the greeting card section, where she began straightening what didn't need to be straightened.

"Why do you think that?"

Darlene glanced over her shoulder to where her sister now stood right behind her. "For one thing, I'm sure he realizes I'm not looking for a boyfriend. It's not a *gut* time. I'm too busy working here, sharing all the chores with you because *Mamm* can't manage any, and helping care for her."

Biena grabbed Darlene's shoulder and spun her around. "Are you *narrisch*? Andrew is such a nice guy, and he's handsome too. Why would you miss an opportunity to date someone like him?"

"What about *Mamm* and *Dat*?" Darlene asked as frustration simmered in her gut. "They need us."

"That doesn't mean we can't date. They fully expect us to meet people, fall in love, get married, and build families of our own. We'll always help *Mamm* when she needs us — even when we're dating or married."

"No one is getting married, Biena. Andrew is just giving me a ride." She huffed out a breath. "Right now I'm focused on the family I already have. That's all."

"You really should consider —"

The chiming of the bell over the front door announced customers.

Thank goodness! Darlene hustled toward the door as two more *English* women, about her age, entered.

"Hello! Welcome to Bird-in-Hand Dry Goods. May I help you find something?" Darlene asked.

"Yes," one of them said. "We're looking for Amish dolls."

"Let me show you what we have."

As Darlene led them to the toy aisle, she breathed a sigh of relief. She didn't need her sister's lectures. After all, Andrew was just a friend. And dating anyone would only complicate her life, which was complicated enough right now.

She just hoped Andrew really wasn't looking for more than friendship with her.

"It's okay, *Mamm*." Darlene held back tears as she picked up a clump of her mother's hair from the bathroom floor Saturday afternoon. "It'll grow back. I'm sure of it."

"I'm just so tired, Darlene." *Mamm*'s voice was weak and raspy. "I know I seemed better yesterday, but it never lasts. I want to sleep all the time. This disease and the chemo . . . I know the Lord has a purpose for everything, but I don't know how much longer I can be strong."

Mamm's words stabbed at her heart.

"We have to have faith and trust in the Lord." Darlene repeated *Dat*'s and Biena's

319

words as a messy knot of sorrow nearly choked her. "Let me help you back to bed."

"I don't think I can make it." *Mamm* sat down on the lid of the commode and held on to the sink. Then she stared down at the lap of her white nightgown. "I'll just stay here."

Darlene held out her trembling hand as tears filled her eyes. "*Mamm,* I can get you to bed. Just take my hand."

"Darlene," Biena said from the hall. "Andrew is here."

Darlene looked at her sister. "He's here now?"

"Andrew Detweiler?" *Mamm*'s question came out in a hoarse whisper as she looked up at Darlene.

"*Ya.*" Biena smiled at *Mamm.* "He's giving her a ride to one of Sharon's suppers for *English* visitors." She turned back to Darlene. "It's four." She waved toward the kitchen. "Go."

Darlene shook her head with such force that the ribbons of her prayer covering fanned her face. "No."

Mamm touched Darlene's hand. "Go with Andrew. Have fun."

"She's right," Biena said. "You should go."

"I can't leave." Darlene nearly barked her conviction, then took *Mamm*'s hand. "It's more important that I'm here with my family."

A hand on her shoulder startled Darlene. She looked up to see *Dat*. "You need to go."

"But *Mamm* —" Darlene's voice broke.

"We'll take *gut* care of her." *Dat* nodded toward the hallway. "Go."

Darlene divided a look between her parents and then turned to her sister. Confusion squeezed her chest, stealing her words.

"I promise we'll make sure she's okay," Biena told her.

Darlene felt as if her heart was being torn apart as she let go of *Mamm*'s hand. "I won't be out late."

"Enjoy your evening, *mei liewe*," *Mamm* whispered.

Barely holding back tears, Darlene ran upstairs without glancing into the kitchen. She changed into a yellow dress and fresh black apron, then glanced at the red and puffy eyes reflected in her mirror. Andrew would definitely be able to tell she'd been upset.

She took a deep breath and hurried to the upstairs bathroom, then washed her face with cold water. After she'd straightened her prayer covering, she sped down the stairs, then froze at the bottom and stared down the hall toward her parents' bedroom.

Oh, how she longed to stay home. But *Mamm* had told her to go, and deep down she knew he mother would be upset if she stayed.

She closed her eyes and prayed for the first time in days.

Lord, please guide my heart. I feel as if I need to be here for my family, but they insist I belong with mei freinden *tonight. Where do I belong? Please lead me.*

"Darlene?"

She pivoted toward Andrew as he stepped toward her.

His brow furrowed. "Are you okay?"

She squared her shoulders and lifted her chin. "*Ya.* I'm sorry to keep you waiting." She entered the kitchen and gathered the container of oatmeal raisin cookies and the pecan pie she'd made earlier. The Lamberts and Blanks never expected her to bring anything, but she wanted to. "We need to get going."

She glanced over her shoulder and found Andrew's expression filled with concern. Maybe he could tell she was leaving her heart at home.

Chapter Six

Darlene's hands trembled as she climbed into the buggy. She held the box of cookies and pie on her lap and stared straight ahead as Andrew settled in the driver's seat, then guided the horse toward the road.

Darlene's thoughts spun. She couldn't get the vision of her mother slumped against the bathroom sink out of her mind. *Mamm* seemed weaker and more despondent than she'd ever seen her. She gripped the box of cookies as grief threatened to pull her under.

"Darlene, I apologize if this is out of turn, but you look like you're having a really rough day." Andrew's voice was calm. "Do you want to talk about it?"

She opened her mouth to speak, but a sob escaped her throat and tears pooled in the corners of her eyes. She covered her face with her hands as she tried to control her emotions, but she knew that wasn't going to happen. She'd reached the end of her strength.

The horse and buggy jerked to the right and then came to an abrupt stop.

"Hey, hey." Andrew's voice was close to her ear. She felt the seat shift, and then his leg brushed against hers. "It's okay. Just let it all out."

"I'm sorry," she whispered with her eyes closed. Tears dripped down her cheeks.

"Don't be sorry."

The seat shifted again.

"Here. I found these," he said before his warm hand touched hers. She took the wad of tissues.

"Danki," she whispered as she wiped her eyes and nose.

"You know you can talk to me, right?"

She glanced up at him, and the care and concern in his dark eyes warmed her from the inside out. "I just feel so alone."

"You're not alone." He touched her arm. "I'm right here. And I'm listening."

She nodded.

Silence filled the buggy, and she looked out toward the passing traffic. Andrew had halted the horse at the side of the road.

She turned toward him again, and the urge to share her burdens overwhelmed her. It was as if the compassion in his expression had crashed through the wall she'd kept around her heart. "*Mei mamm* has had such a horrible day."

He rested his arm on the back of the seat behind her and shook his head. "I'm sorry."

She looked down and lifted a piece of lint from the skirt of her dress. "Sometimes it all just gets to me. Watching *Mamm* suffer is torture, and all I want is to take away her pain. But I can't, so I just keep doing what I can to care for her and —"

Darlene's voice broke as a new rush of tears took her by surprise. She covered her face with the tissues and wept.

"You're going through something awful, Darlene." Andrew's soothing voice was beside her ear, sending a chill down her spine. "Just let it out. It's just you and me here." He handed her the box of tissues.

She ripped a handful from the box. After wiping her eyes and nose again, she looked up at him, and she felt safe. It was as if she could tell him anything, and he would keep it a secret.

After a deep breath, Darlene felt her heart open, and truth poured out. "The stress is overwhelming me. And *mei dat* keeps telling Biena and me to make time for our *freinden.* But how can I spend time with you all without feeling guilty?" She looked down at the box of cookies and fingered the plastic top.

"*Mei mamm*'s hair is falling out in clumps, and she can barely walk. I was trying to get her back to bed when you arrived. My family insisted I come with you. So here I am, trying not to sob because I feel like I'm letting *mei mamm* down. I feel selfish and wretched for leaving her."

She looked out the window as a car sped past them.

"Darlene, look at me." Andrew touched her hand again, and a strange awakening stirred in her chest.

She took in his serene expression, and for the first time she noticed just how handsome he really was. And how had she not noticed the kindness in his eyes before? She swallowed against her suddenly dry throat.

"If you'd rather be home, I'll take you back," he continued, not seeming to sense her admiration. "I don't want you to spend tonight feeling as if you shouldn't be at the supper. Your *mamm* is more important than singing for *Englishers,* and I'll tell Sharon it's not a *gut* day. She'll completely understand, and so will everyone else."

The urge to stay with Andrew shot through her. He made her feel protected as she shared her deepest emotions. She needed more time with him — more time to be herself.

He set his elbow on the back of the seat, lifted his hand, and leaned his cheek against it. When he smiled, he looked adorable. "You look like you're trying to figure out a complicated puzzle," he said.

She looked down, trying to ignore her sudden attraction to him. "I still feel torn."

"I understand. But this is your decision. What do *you* want to do, putting aside what anyone else says?"

"I want to spend time with you." She felt her cheeks flame at her admission. "I mean, I want to go to the supper. I think."

He looked at her for a moment, then said, "I think I can help you solve your dilemma."

"How?"

"What if you go with me but then let me take you home early if you still feel like you shouldn't be there? That way you're spending time with your *freinden* to appease your family, but you're giving the evening a chance." He shrugged. "Does that work?"

"It does." And just like that, the tense muscles in her shoulders relaxed. How did Andrew know exactly what she needed to hear?

"Gut." He twisted back in the seat and faced front. Then he glanced at her. "Dar-

lene, you can always talk to me. I promise I'll listen to you — without judgment."

"Danki." She smiled. "I appreciate that."

"Anytime." He guided the horse back into the street. "And I do hope you save a piece of that pie for me," he added with a wink. "It smells *appeditlich.*"

"Of course I'll save you some." She chuckled.

"It's *gut* to hear you laugh, Darlene. I hope to hear that more often."

Warmth surged through her veins as she settled back in the seat. Andrew's friendship was a blessing. She just hoped her strange new feelings for him stayed in their place.

And maybe, someday, she could be totally honest with him. He said he'd listen without judgment. But she wasn't ready to tell anyone the current state of her faith as she watched her mother suffer.

Andrew tried to concentrate on setting up the tables and chairs in Sharon's kitchen, but he couldn't stop his gaze from moving to where Darlene prepared a salad for the meal.

She looked so beautiful in the yellow dress and black apron she wore, and her brown eyes were dazzling as she said something to

Alice and Sharon and then smiled. He kept recalling their intimate conversation in the buggy — how she'd cried and opened up to him, sharing what seemed like deeply personal emotions about her mother's illness.

His heart had nearly shattered when she sobbed, and he'd had to fight the overwhelming urge to pull her into his arms and console her. Although it was inappropriate for him to even think of touching her like that, he'd wanted to take away her pain and tell her she'd be okay.

Instead, he'd handed her tissues and only touched her hand. When their skin brushed, the contact had sent shivers of awareness up his spine. His attraction for her was growing each time he saw her, and he could only pray she had feelings for him too.

"Hey, Detweiler," Cal quipped. "Are you going to take these chairs from me or just stare off into space? What is it with you at these suppers lately?"

"Sorry," Andrew mumbled as he grabbed another stack of chairs from Cal and began unfolding them. Then he pushed them all under the tables, doing his best to keep his thoughts of Darlene from distracting him.

Andrew, Dave, Cal, and Jay set the tables while the women continued prepping the food. They were just finishing when the

Englishers began arriving.

Andrew sat on a stool at the back of the kitchen between Cal and Jay as the women greeted the guests. Darlene smiled as she introduced herself to an *English* couple, maybe in their early thirties. Andrew studied her mannerisms. She seemed more relaxed as she nodded and listened to something the woman said. Andrew hoped she would allow herself to enjoy this evening.

When all the guests had arrived and were seated, Sharon walked to the middle of the kitchen. Her mother had asked her to take the lead tonight.

"Good evening. My name is Sharon Lambert, and I'm so excited that you came for supper. Welcome to my father's dairy farm. I live here with my mother, Feenie." She pointed to her mother standing by the counter. "And my younger sister, Ruby Sue."

Ruby Sue waved, and the group said hello.

"My family and I host these suppers periodically, and we enjoy teaching others about our culture and sharing our favorite meals." Then she introduced each of her friends.

Andrew offered a wave when Sharon said his name, then glanced over to find Darlene watching him. She blessed him with a sweet smile, and his pulse galloped. She was so pretty and special. He longed to tell her how much she was coming to mean to him, but he feared scaring her away. For now, he'd just be the friend she needed and keep his growing feelings for her to himself.

"Let's eat," Sharon told the group. "We'll start with a green salad and a fruit salad."

Sharon and the rest of the women took bowls to the table while Andrew and Cal filled the guests' glasses with water. Once they'd finished their salad, Andrew helped serve the main course — ham loaf, egg noodles, broccoli, corn, and rolls.

"You're *gut* at serving food," Darlene teased after he set a basket of rolls on a table.

She grinned at him, igniting a fire in his veins. How he adored her!

Once dessert was served, Sharon fielded questions from guests, and she shared information about her farm. When a young man who seemed to be a few years older than Andrew asked about occupations, Dave shared stories about working as a brick mason, and Cal spoke about his father's horse breeding and training farm.

"We'd like to sing for you while you finish your dessert and have some more coffee," Sharon announced as her mother began making rounds with her carafe.

"Isn't that nice?" a middle-aged woman sitting near the back said.

"We enjoy singing hymns during our suppers," Alice said as she handed hymnals to her friends. "What would you all like to sing first?" she asked them.

"How about 'Blessed Assurance'?" Ruby Sue asked.

"That's a lovely one," an *English* woman who overheard her said.

Darlene sidled up to Andrew and held out the *Heartland Hymns* songbook. "Share with me."

Andrew smiled down at her. "I'd love to."

Darlene turned to the hymn and then looked up at him. "Sharon asked me to take the lead on the first song tonight. Ready?"

"Always."

Darlene began to sing, and Andrew enjoyed the beautiful lilt of her voice. Soon their whole group was singing along.

Andrew lost himself in the hymns, enjoying standing beside Darlene while they praised the Lord and shared the gospel through song. What a perfect evening!

"That went well," Jay said as he carried a stack of dishes to the counter after the guests had left. "I heard several of the *En-*

glishers say they enjoyed the food."

"I did too," *Mamm* chimed in. "You did a great job, Sharon."

"*Danki.*" Sharon looked at Darlene. "You got quite a few compliments on those *kichlin* and that pie. You didn't have to bring anything, but *danki* again. That gave our guests more variety to choose from."

Andrew carried a handful of forks to the counter and then turned to face Darlene. "Did you save a piece for me?"

"I tried." She bit her lip as she held up an empty pie plate. "But one of the guests took the last piece."

"Oh no." Andrew rested his hand on his chest. "It was that popular. My heart is broken."

"I'll make it up to you. I promise."

Andrew winked at her. "Then maybe I'll forgive you." He turned around and found Cal smirking at him.

"Let's eat," Ruby Sue said. "I'm hungry, and I'm sure everyone else is too."

As they sat down to eat from the bounty of leftovers, Andrew glanced at Darlene again. She still seemed to be enjoying herself, and he eagerly anticipated another conversation with her on the way to her home.

■ ■ ■ ■

"I'm so glad you picked me up today," Darlene said as the horse and buggy headed toward her house. "I probably would have stayed home if you hadn't come."

"I'm glad too." Andrew gave her a sideways glance. "You seem more at ease now. Did the supper give you a break from your worries?"

"I think so. Especially the singing. *Danki* for listening to me." She smiled warmly. "What do you like to do for fun when you're not at work?"

He gave her a surprised look. "You mean like a hobby?"

"Ya."

"Oh." He rubbed his clean-shaven chin. "Well, I like to read."

"Really?" She angled her body toward him. "What are your favorite genres?"

"Mysteries."

They spent the rest of the ride talking about their favorite books, and when her house come into view, Andrew was disappointed. He longed to continue talking. He guided the horse up the driveway and then tried to think of a reason to keep her in the buggy for a while.

He halted the horse, and when he turned to look at Darlene, she said, "Wait here for a moment. I want to get you something." She grabbed her empty pie plate and cookie container, then hopped out of the buggy before dashing up the back-porch steps.

What was she doing?

She appeared on the porch a few moments later holding a pie plate, and he laughed as he climbed out of his buggy.

"I told you I would make it up to you." She handed him the pie when they both arrived at the bottom of the steps. "It's pecan."

He took the plate but then shook his head. "Did you make this for your family? I can't accept it if you did." He held the pie out to her. "I'll get a piece next time."

"No." She took his free hand. "I insist that you take it. I can make another one for my family. I want you to have it as a special thank-you." Her smile faded. "Please take it."

He searched her eyes. "Why?"

"It means a lot that I can share my feelings with you." She released his hand. "This pie is just a small way to tell you I'm grateful you're *mei freind.*"

This time Andrew's heart seemed to completely turn over. "I'm glad you're *mei freind* too."

Darlene took a step back and pointed toward the house. "Well, I want to see if my family needs me. Be safe going home."

"*Gut nacht,* Darlene."

"Bye!" She gave him a little wave and then rushed up the steps.

As she disappeared into the house, Andrew stopped for a moment to look out toward her father's expansive pasture. The sun had started to set, painting streaks of coral across the horizon.

He truly cared for Darlene, and with all his heart, he hoped someday she'd care for him too.

CHAPTER SEVEN

The following Thursday, Darlene heard a late-morning knock on the back door. "I'll get it," she called from the kitchen. She stepped through the mudroom and gasped when she found Alice and Sharon standing on her back porch. "What are you doing here?"

Alice held up a container. "We want to help."

"Help?" Darlene divided a confused look between them.

"Ya." Sharon balanced a casserole dish in her hands. "I made a tuna noodle casserole, and Alice made brownies."

"And we want to clean, do laundry, or anything else you need — if you'll let us," Alice said. "We know you've said you're *mamm* doesn't want visitors, but we're not visiting. We're just here to lighten your load."

Darlene *wasn't* sure what *Mamm* would

think about this. Over and over she'd made it clear she didn't want anyone around but the family. But Darlene was overwhelmed with appreciation as she opened the door, and maybe *Mamm* would be amenable since she was having a good day. "*Danki* so much. Please come in."

"How's your *mamm* doing today?" Alice asked as she stepped inside.

Darlene smiled. "Fairly well. I helped her take a shower, but then she dressed and came out to the kitchen while I made breakfast. She's resting in the *schtupp* now."

"That's fantastic!" Sharon said.

"*Ya*. It's the first *gut* day she's had in a long time."

"Is Biena running the store?" Alice asked.

Darlene led them into the kitchen, where Alice and Sharon set their offerings on the counter. "*Ya*. And *Dat*'s running errands until suppertime."

"Darlene? Is someone here?" *Mamm*'s soft voice called from the family room.

"*Ya*."

Darlene motioned for them to stay where they were, and then she slipped into the family room, where *Mamm* sat in her recliner with her favorite light-blue and gray lap quilt on her legs. A gray scarf covered her head. "Sharon and Alice are here.

338

They'd like to help us today. And they brought lunch."

To Darlene's surprise, *Mamm*'s expression brightened. "How nice. I feel so much better today, and I'd like to see them." She paused. "As for helping . . . As long as you'll help me with personal needs, I'm *froh* for your *freinden* helping you today. You work too hard, and so does Biena."

Still surprised, Darlene brought Sharon and Alice into the family room.

"*Danki* for coming," *Mamm* told them with a smile.

Darlene stood back as her friends sat down beside *Mamm*.

"You look *gut* today, Roselyn. How do you feel?" Sharon asked.

"I actually feel a little like myself." *Mamm* touched Sharon's hand. "How are your parents and Ruby Sue?"

As her *mamm* chatted with them, Darlene smiled. Yes, it was a good day — a very good day. Gratitude for God's blessing rippled through her. Maybe he had been hearing her prayers.

Alice pointed to the kitchen. "If it's all right, we'd like to have a noon meal with you and then help Darlene with chores."

"They brought a tuna noodle casserole and brownies, *Mamm*." Darlene stepped closer and held her hand out to her mother. "Do you feel like eating? Then you can nap in your room while we work."

"Okay." *Mamm* took Darlene's hand, and Darlene helped her up.

After settling *Mamm* on a kitchen chair, Darlene warmed up the casserole in the oven and then took a plateful to Biena in the store. When she returned to the kitchen, she sat down with her mother and friends to enjoy their lunch.

"How's Jay?" Alice asked Sharon.

Sharon grinned, and Alice and Darlene shared a smile.

"He's great." Sharon forked more casserole. "I'm really *froh* dating him. I feel like we get to know each other better every day."

"That's *gut,*" *Mamm* said as she picked at her casserole. "This is *appeditlich,* Sharon."

"I'm so glad you like it." Sharon sipped her water, then turned toward Alice. "And how is Dave doing?"

Alice gave a shy smile. "He's *gut.*"

Darlene lifted her glass. "You two looked happy together at church."

"We are *froh.*" Alice gave Darlene a curious look. "What about you and Andrew?"

Darlene shook her head as she set her glass back on the table. "There's nothing going on between Andrew and me."

"But he picked you up for the supper and singing Saturday," Alice said.

"And you two talked a lot. I noticed you stood together when we sang and then you sat together when we ate." Sharon pointed her fork at Darlene. "I think he likes you. He's always been so shy, but he seems different with you."

"Do you care for him?" *Mamm* asked.

Darlene turned to her mother, and she couldn't stop her smile. It had been so long since she'd had a conversation like this with *Mamm* — one that almost made her forget about what they were all going through. Her eyes stung with happy tears.

"Are you okay?" *Mamm* reached for Darlene's hand.

"I'm fine. Actually, I'm better than fine because you're having such a *gut* day."

Mamm shook her head. "You're avoiding the question."

Alice and Sharon laughed.

"Do you care about Andrew?" *Mamm* asked again.

"Answer the question, Darlene," Sharon said.

Alice clucked her tongue. *"Ya,* Darlene. Answer your *mamm."*

"You're all ganging up on me." Darlene

341

sighed. "I like him as a *freind.*"

Sharon groaned and rolled her eyes.

"What was that for?" Darlene asked, frustrated.

"You two seem so *gut* together," Sharon said.

Alice scooped more casserole onto her plate. "What if he likes you? Will you date him if your *dat* gives permission?"

"If he asked me, then I'd think about it, but I wouldn't want to ruin our friendship. I like talking to him." Darlene turned to her mother. "Weren't you and *Dat freinden* before you started dating?"

"We were." *Mamm* nodded. "Don't rush it. See where the Lord leads you."

As Darlene ate, she tried to imagine dating Andrew. But it was safer not to. She'd meant it when she said she'd never want to lose his friendship.

After lunch, Darlene helped her mother to her room. Then after she and her friends had cleaned the kitchen, they started on the chores Darlene and Biena had trouble getting to with *Mamm* needing so much care. Darlene cleaned bathrooms, Alice cleaned the upstairs bedrooms and sewing room, and Sharon cleaned the family room and mudroom.

When they were done, they sat at the table

and ate brownies as they talked and laughed. Darlene relished their time together.

"*Danki* so much for coming today." Darlene hugged Alice and then Sharon as they stood on the back porch waiting for Sharon's driver. "It was so nice spending time with you, and I appreciate your help. Now all I have to worry about is the laundry, and Biena and I can handle that."

Alice rubbed Darlene's shoulder. "We've been offering to help for a while, and you kept saying no. So we finally decided to just come over without asking permission first."

Sharon shrugged. "We figured you wouldn't throw us off your porch if we were standing here with a yummy lunch and dessert. And we prayed your *mamm* would welcome us. Maybe God prompted us because he knew she was having a *gut* day."

"I'm so blessed to have you as *mei freinden*," Darlene said.

"And we're blessed to have you too." Alice smiled.

A black SUV pulled into the driveway, and Alice and Sharon started down the steps.

"Call if you need us," Alice said over her shoulder.

"Take care," Sharon said as she waved.

Darlene waited until the SUV left the driveway and then walked back into the house, smiling as she thought about the wonderful afternoon spent with her best friends.

Her thoughts moved to Andrew, and her heart danced a little. She hadn't seen him or talked to him since last weekend, and . . . well, she missed him. If her mother's good days grew more frequent, maybe she would see him again soon.

"Darlene!" Biena's voice sounded frantic from the hallway outside Darlene's bedroom later that evening. *"Dummle!"*

Darlene dropped the novel she'd been reading and sprinted to the door. *"Was iss letz?"*

"It's *Mamm.*" Biena's brown eyes widened as she grabbed Darlene's hand and yanked her toward the stairs. "She's lethargic and can't seem to get out of the recliner. *Dat*'s been trying to get her to move, but she's weak and not herself at all. Something's wrong."

"No, no, no." Darlene rushed down the stairs, then halted in the family room doorway. She held her breath as *Dat* stood over *Mamm.*

Dat wiped at his eyes as he leaned down and touched *Mamm*'s face. "Roselyn. Please answer me."

344

Mamm didn't respond. Her eyes remained closed.

"What's going on?" Darlene asked, her heart thumping in her chest.

Dat spun toward Darlene. "I think we need to get her to the hospital."

"I'll make the call." Darlene grabbed a lantern and the key for the store, then sprinted out the back door. She ran into the store and then dialed nine-one-one once she reached the phone in the office. She told the dispatcher her mother needed help and gave him the address.

Her heart sank as she hung up, and as she headed for the house, her knees nearly buckled, and she covered her face with her hands. Tears began to flow. Why had God let this disease ruin a perfectly wonderful day for her mother?

Please, God. Please. Mamm*'s done nothing wrong. Please heal her! She's suffered enough.*

Biena opened the screen door on the back porch. "Is the ambulance coming?"

"Ya." Darlene wiped her eyes.

"Let's wait out here for it."

Darlene joined her, then glanced up at the stars twinkling in the sky, choking back a sob.

A siren sounded in the distance, and

345

Darlene bit her lower lip. Surely God would help her mother. But when? How long did God expect them to endure this nightmare before he stepped in?

And one more time, she wondered if he ever would. She'd heard of people facing a crisis of faith, but she'd never thought one of those people would be her.

Darlene sat in the waiting room and stared at the local news on the hospital television. The hum of quiet conversations filled the large room as other people sat on the surrounding chairs. She glanced at the clock on the wall. They'd arrived nearly three hours ago, and she and Biena still hadn't received an update on her mother other than when *Dat* came out to say they were running tests.

She glanced to where Biena snored softly beside her. It never ceased to amaze Darlene how Biena could sleep no matter how stressful the situation was.

Darlene longed for someone to talk to. How she yearned to have Andrew here, sitting next to her, holding her hand, and telling her it was going to be okay.

But he wasn't here. And she needed to be strong for her family.

Darlene sipped from a bottle of water

346

she'd bought from a vending machine and then looked toward the doors leading to the ER treatment rooms. She'd gone up to the desk to ask about her mother more than once, but the person there just kept telling her she had to wait for her father to come back.

How long did they have to wait? And would *Dat* tell them if *Mamm*'s condition had become so grave that —

A chill zipped through her. *Please, Lord. Please!*

The doors opened with a whoosh, and *Dat* walked out. His eyes were red, and his face was drawn.

No, no, no!

Darlene shook her sister's arm. "Biena, wake up. Biena!"

"Huh?" Biena jumped with a start and then yawned as she looked around. "What's going on?"

"*Dat*'s here."

Biena rubbed her eyes as she sat up straight.

"She's going to be all right, but they're admitting her." *Dat* dropped into the empty seat across from them. "She's severely anemic, and she needs a blood transfusion."

"*Ach,* no." Biena gasped.

Dat cupped his hand to his forehead.

"Can we stay with her?" Darlene asked.

"Only I can. Call my driver again and get a ride home." *Dat* reached out and touched their hands. "She'll have *gut* care here. Just keep praying. God will pull her through this."

"But we're family," Biena said.

"There's only one recliner in her room. I'm sorry." He gave Darlene a quick hug and then hugged Biena. "Please, go home and get some rest. I'll take *gut* care of her. And they think she can go home tomorrow."

"Give *Mamm* our love," Biena said.

"I will." *Dat* gave them a sad smile and then left.

Biena nodded toward the reception desk. "Let's see if we can use the phone over there."

As Darlene followed her sister, she tried to imagine how empty their house would seem tonight without their parents. Worse, she found herself imagining what would happen to their family if her mother never came home. *Dat* said God would get her through this, but would he?

She didn't know what to believe anymore. And she couldn't let anyone in her community know that. Not their bishop or one of the ministers, not her family, not her friends — and even Andrew, despite his expressed willingness to listen without judgment. She was on her own, and she fought back fresh tears.

expressed willingness to listen without judgment. She was on her own, and she fought
back fresh tears.

CHAPTER EIGHT

Saturday evening Andrew stood from the
kitchen table and carried his plate to the
counter. "*Danki* for supper. I'm going out
for a while."

"Where?" *Mamm* asked.

"To see Darlene. I haven't seen her since
last weekend, and I want to make sure she's
okay." *And I miss her.*

Andrew had planned to visit Darlene during the week, but he wound up working late
every evening. She'd been a constant presence in his mind, though.

"Are you dating Darlene?" Sam asked as
he sat between their parents at the table.

Although Sam was eighteen, four years
younger than Andrew, he was already
slightly taller than Andrew, and Andrew
suspected he would keep growing until he
stood eye to eye with one of their six-foot-
four uncles.

"No." *Not yet.*

Sam raised his eyebrows. "Then why are you going to visit her?"

"Because she's *mei freind.*" Andrew waved to his parents. "I'll see you —"

"Wait." *Mamm* jumped up from the table. "I made some sand tarts yesterday. Take some with you for her family." She opened a cabinet and pulled out a container. "And tell her we're praying for her *mamm.*"

"I will." Andrew waved with his free hand and then hurried out to the barn to hitch his horse to his buggy.

As he set off on his journey, he smiled at the idea of visiting with Darlene. He just hoped her mother was well enough for him to be there, and that Darlene wasn't too busy, especially with other guests. He'd run into Alice in town on Wednesday, and she told him Roselyn had allowed her and Sharon to eat lunch with her and help with chores a few days earlier. That was good for Darlene, but he wanted to see how good for himself.

When he reached the Bender house, he tied the horse to a fence and then took the back steps two at a time, the container of cookies in his hands. He knocked and then paced around the porch.

The screen door opened with a squeak, and Darlene peeked out. She was so pretty

351

in a rose-colored dress. She smiled at him, and his pulse raced.

"Andrew. What a nice surprise."

"I was hoping you might have time to visit with me." He held up the container. "I brought sand tarts."

"Well, you had me at sand tarts." She laughed, and it was music to his ears. "And I do have some time." She pointed to the glider. "Have a seat, and I'll bring out some lemonade."

"Perfect." He sank down on the glider as he looked out toward the same green pasture he'd admired the last time he was there.

The sky was a clear, vivid blue, and he could hear birds singing in nearby trees. What a great day. He glanced at the garden and took in the colorful flowers, imagining Darlene and Biena caring for it alone while Roselyn convalesced from her treatments. He was certain the sisters were exhausted from doing all the household chores on their own.

The screen door opened, and Darlene stepped out with a tray holding two tall glasses of lemonade and some napkins.

Andrew popped up and held out his hand. She handed him a glass, and when their skin touched, a shiver danced up his arm. "I was just admiring your garden."

"*Danki.* It's really *mei mamm*'s, but I like taking care of it. It's relaxing to be out in the sun while enjoying God's glorious creation. It's my favorite pastime."

"I can tell."

She shook her head. "I just wish I had more time for it. The weeds grow so fast."

He opened the lid on the container. "So you like sand tarts?"

"I love them. *Danki.*" She took one and bit into it. "This is *appeditlich.*" She eyed him. "Did you make these?"

He chuckled. "No. *Mei mamm* did." Then he sobered. "She also told me to tell you she's praying for your *mamm.*"

"Please tell her thank you very much." She took another bite.

"I saw Alice, and she told me you had a *gut* day earlier in the week. How have you been since then?" He took a sip of lemonade.

She looked down at her lap and then back up at him. Her smile had faded, and a kind of pain entered her eyes. "*Mamm* was better, but then . . ."

Alarm shot through him. "*Was iss letz?*"

She held up her hand as if to calm him. "She's home and doing better now, but she was in the hospital Thursday night. She was so anemic she needed a blood transfusion."

She blew out a deep breath that seemed to bubble up from her toes. "I was really scared. I had to run to the store to call an ambulance. The doctors had a *gut* report when they released her, but I'm still concerned."

"I'm so sorry." He took her hand in his and ran his thumb over her skin. "I wish you would have called and told me. If I'd known, I would have come sooner."

Her whole body seemed to stall at his touch. "I wouldn't want to bother you."

He clucked his tongue. "You could never bother me."

She stared out toward the store as if she were avoiding eye contact with him. He longed to know why.

"Is something else on your mind?" he asked.

She paused, but then seemed to have come to a decision.

"I'm just so confused. I don't understand why *mei mamm* has to suffer so much. I keep wondering if . . . if God has forgotten her."

Andrew tilted his head as he tried to comprehend her words. "Forgotten her? I don't believe God forgets anyone. I just think sometimes we don't understand his plan. But he's always there to guide and comfort us."

She turned toward him, and tears glistened in those coffee-colored eyes. "But why should someone like *mei mamm* suffer like this? She's such a *wunderbaar* person. She doesn't deserve this."

"You know we're not supposed to question God's will."

"I do, but I need an answer." The anguish in her expression nearly shredded his heart.

"I don't have an answer, Darlene. But I do believe God is ever faithful, and I'm certain he's hearing your prayers and answering the way he knows is best."

An awkward silence fell over them as Andrew slid his thumb back and forth along the condensation on his glass and watched a blue jay eat from a bird feeder. Out of the corner of his eye, he could see Darlene examining a cookie. Her emotions seemed to be radiating off her in waves, and he longed to take away her stress. Obviously, her burdens were causing her to say things she didn't really mean. She couldn't really think God would abandon her mother.

"Darlene, God will take care of your family. I pray for you all daily, and I'm certain you're safe and protected in his hands."

She nodded and looked up into his face. *"Danki.* Have another *kichli."* She smiled, but still, her demeanor seemed a bit strained. He sensed she wanted to change the subject, at least for now.

They spent the remainder of his time there chatting about lighter subjects — the book he was reading, her love of the outdoors, their mutual friends. But although she smiled as they talked, Andrew couldn't shake the feeling that Darlene might really believe God had forgotten her mother. But again, that had to be the stress talking. He kept the gentle conversation going until she said she better get inside.

"*Danki* for coming this evening," Darlene said as they stood by his buggy.

"I'm glad you had time to visit with me." Andrew took her hands in his. "Remember, if you need to talk, just call me. If I can't come over, I'll listen on the phone. I'm here."

She swallowed. "I appreciate it. Please tell your *mamm* thank you for the *kichlin.* My family will enjoy the rest of them, and I'll get the container back to you soon. Be safe going home."

He released her hands and immediately missed the feel of her soft skin. Then as he climbed into the buggy, he prayed.

Lord, please show Darlene your love and

comfort her. And if it's your will, please heal her mother from this disease.

Darlene waved as Andrew's horse and buggy disappeared down her driveway, the sun now dropping toward the horizon. She smiled as she thought of their conversation and how she enjoyed the feel of her hand in his. He was so kind and sweet. Oh, how she'd enjoy having a boyfriend like him!

But there was one disconnect between them. He didn't seem to understand her feelings about God. He insisted God was listening, and he couldn't admit it was unfair that her mother had to suffer.

She headed up the porch steps, then picked up the tray with their empty glasses and the container of cookies and went back inside. Biena sat at the kitchen table flipping through a cookbook.

Biena grinned as she faced her. "How was your visit with Andrew?"

"It was *gut.*" Darlene set the tray on the counter, then the glasses in the sink. "We had a nice chat."

"When do you think he'll ask you to be his girlfriend?"

"That again? Never. Even if he wanted to, he won't." She washed the first glass.

"I think he will."

"Why would he? For one thing, I'm too distracted juggling so much here. I don't have anything to offer him right now. He could easily find another *maedel,* someone who can focus on him."

Biena shook her head. "You sell yourself short. If he didn't care about you, he wouldn't spend his Saturday evening here. I still think he likes you — a lot."

Darlene sighed. She was just as confused about Andrew as she was about everything else, especially since his faith was so strong when hers had weakened so much. The only thing she knew for sure? She missed her life as it used to be, and she wanted her mother well more than anything.

She put the clean glasses in the cabinet and then headed for the family room. If only *Mamm* could help her sort through these confusing feelings, but she was dozing in her recliner with *Dat* reading a book beside her.

Dat looked up over his reading glasses and put his finger to his lips, instructing Darlene to remain silent. She nodded and turned for the stairs. How she missed her mother's sage advice.

"Good morning!" Darlene called as the bell above the front door of the store dinged, announcing a customer. She was just putting a supply of bottled water in the cooler under the counter, and without looking up, she said, "Welcome to Bird-in-Hand Dry Goods."

"Gude mariye." She raised her head, and Andrew's handsome smile widened as he removed his straw hat and strode toward her.

"Well, this is a welcome surprise!" Darlene couldn't stop her own smile. During the past two weeks or so, she'd seen Andrew at church and at a singing or two for community members, but for some reason, Sharon and Alice hadn't had any suppers in their homes lately. She still felt a burst of excitement at the sight of him.

Maybe they wouldn't have to talk about faith again until her mother was well. And she had to get well. She just had to.

"I was in the area picking up supplies, so I thought I'd stop by." He glanced to his right, where an older *Englisher* couple perused a display of decorative wooden signs. "You're busy."

"No." She waved for him to join her at the counter. "Come get a drink." She pulled two bottles of water from the cooler. "Here you go."

"Danki."

She sat down on a stool as he leaned over the counter. "I can't believe it's almost September. Summer has really flown by."

"I know."

"So how are you this fine Wednesday morning?"

"*Gut.* You?" He opened the bottle and took a sip.

"Well, even though she had to have that blood transfusion, the doctors allowed *Mamm*'s final chemo treatment. She had a rough few days, like usual, but now she's perking up a little. It's such a relief for her therapy to be over."

"That's great news!" He reached over and touched her hand. "I can tell you're *froh.* What a blessing!"

She felt a thrill at the contact. Oh, how she enjoyed their talks and his affection! If only she knew if that affection came only out of a deeper friendship, nothing more. She longed to ask him, but she'd never risk being too forward, even if she had the courage.

"I picked up a mystery novel last week," she said. "I finally made it to the library since *mei mamm* has been better. I was wondering if you've read it. It's really *gut.*"

"What's the title?" He set the bottle on the counter and rested his elbows beside it.

When she told him, he grinned. "I have read it!"

"No kidding." She enjoyed listening to him talk about the plot and the character they'd both decided was guilty of the crime — before the novel's surprise ending.

"Miss," the woman looking at the decorative signs called. "Do you have more of these? I'd like to buy five as gifts for my coworkers back home."

"I'll have to look in the back." She turned to Andrew. "I'm sorry."

"Don't be. Are you going to the supper at Alice's *haus* tomorrow night?"

She jumped down from the stool. "I plan to."

"May I pick you up again?"

"I'd love that."

A kind of delight seemed to flicker in his smile. "Great. I'll come around four o'clock again." He held up the bottle of water. "*Danki* for the drink. See you tomorrow."

"Bye, Andrew."

She smiled as he headed out the door, elation curling its way from head to toe. Andrew wanted to spend time with her. And even better, *Mamm* was improving. Perhaps everyone else had been right to hang on to their faith.

But was her faith too weak to survive?

CHAPTER NINE

At almost closing time later that day, Sam rushed into Andrew's work stall. "We need to go! *Dummle!*"

"What is it?" Andrew tossed his sanding block on his workbench. "What's happening?"

"*Dat* just called our driver, and then he ran to the *haus* to get *Mamm*. We're meeting *Mammi* at the hospital. She thinks *Daadi* had a stroke." Sam started for the door. "Let's go."

Andrew prayed as they headed to the front of the store.

God, please protect our daadi. *Please stop this stroke from doing lasting damage.*

Sam shook his head as they stood in the parking lot. "He can't die. He just can't." His dark eyes shimmered as he swallowed, his entire body sagging.

"He won't, Sam. Have faith." Andrew squeezed his younger brother's shoulder.

"Just pray." *Daadi* had to be okay! He had to!

"I am praying." Sam sniffed and wiped his eyes with the back of his hand.

Mamm and *Dat* joined them, and *Dat* pointed to the blue van pulling into one of the parking spots in front of the store.

"Stan's here," *Dat* said.

Dat sat in the front passenger seat while the rest of the family piled into the back.

"When she called from the hospital, *mei mamm* said *Dat* was joking with the emergency personnel in the ambulance," *Dat* told them. "She said he was also in *gut* spirits last she spoke to him."

"See?" Andrew whispered to his brother. "Have faith. The Lord will take care of him."

Sam nodded and cleared his throat, but Andrew could see the worry in his eyes.

Andrew stared out the window and thought of Darlene as they moved through the traffic past storefronts in Bird-in-Hand. She'd faced these scary times, too, and she seemed to worry just like Sam did. Andrew closed his eyes and once again asked God to protect his grandfather.

And please, God, protect Roselyn Bender as well.

Andrew sat with Sam in the hospital cafeteria amid hushed conversations.

"We should have heard something by now," Sam grumbled as he picked up his cheeseburger. "We've been waiting for hours." His eyes widened. "What if *Daadi*'s passed away?"

"*Dat* said they had to run a bunch of tests. Just because it's taking a while doesn't mean the worst has happened." Andrew thought of Darlene as he took another bite of his turkey sandwich. How many times had she sat in a hospital worrying?

"How do you do that?"

"What?" Andrew asked. His brother was staring at him through narrowed eyes. "Why are you glaring at me?"

Sam pointed a fry at him. "How do you just assume the best? Why don't you ever worry?"

"I worry plenty."

"When have you worried?" Sam lifted his chin. "Tell me one time when you were actually afraid something bad would happen."

Andrew set down his sandwich and gave him a frustrated palm up. "I'm worried right now. Doesn't that count?"

"No, you aren't. You just automatically assume everything will be fine."

"Trust me, Sam. I'm scared that *Daadi*

might be permanently paralyzed or worse. I just lean on my faith in times like this."

"Huh." Sam shook his head and ate another fry.

Andrew's frustration boiled over. "What does that mean?"

"You don't seem like you're worried at all, and it's annoying."

Andrew sighed. "What will worrying do except upset me? I'm praying, and I trust God to take care of *Daadi*."

Sam shook his head. "I really don't understand how you do that."

Andrew looked up to see their parents walking toward them.

"We have an update," *Dat* announced. "Your *daadi*'s speech is slurred, and he's lost movement in his right arm."

"Is the damage permanent?" Andrew asked, worry twisting his insides.

Dat shook his head. "We're praying it isn't. He'll be moved to a rehabilitation facility tomorrow for physical therapy, and we're praying he'll have a full recovery."

"He survived. Thank God for that." Andrew glanced at Sam, who seemed to be avoiding his gaze.

Sam wiped at his eyes. "When can we see him?"

"Soon." *Dat* sat down beside Sam and

365

Mamm beside Andrew.

"How is *Mammi?*" Andrew asked.

"She's still shaken. She didn't want to leave his room, so we offered to bring her something to eat." *Mamm* reached over and squeezed Sam's arm. "*Daadi* is going to be okay."

"We just need to keep praying," Andrew said.

"We do." *Dat* took one of Sam's fries. "We can lean on our faith in the Lord."

But Sam looked doubtful, and it hit Andrew — Sam didn't know how to lean on his faith in times of need. And neither did Darlene.

The bell chimed above the store's entrance door.

"Good afternoon," Darlene called as she straightened the last row of art supplies.

"Excuse me. Do you have any birthday cards?"

Darlene turned to see Andrew walking toward her, and she tilted her head as she took in the dark circles under his eyes. "*Wie geht's?* Are you okay?"

He removed his straw hat and began turning it in his hands. "It's been a long night."

"*Ach,* no." She pointed to the counter. "Do you want to sit?"

"That would be nice. I came as soon as I could. I really want to talk to you."

Darlene pulled two bottles of water and two stools from behind the counter and gestured for him to sit.

"What happened?" She hopped up on a stool and opened her bottle.

"*Mei daadi* had a stroke yesterday."

"No!" Darlene clapped her hand over her mouth. "How is he?"

"He was in the hospital overnight, and then he was transferred to a rehabilitation facility today. His speech is slurred, and he has some paralysis in his right arm. But there's a chance he can make a good recovery and regain the use of his arm." He opened the bottle of water and took a long drink.

"I'm so sorry." She pressed her lips together and frowned. "I don't understand why bad things happen to *gut* people. It's not fair."

"He's going to be fine. God is *gut*."

She eyed him. "How do you know he'll be fine?"

Andrew sighed. "You do sound like *mei bruder*."

"What do you mean?"

"He was so upset when we got the news, but I just leaned on my faith. He said he doesn't understand how I can be so calm about things like this. And I realized —"

Irritation pricked at her. "I don't understand either. How can you be so optimistic, especially when not everyone comes away saved or healed?"

"Because I believe God has a plan, and he knows what's best."

"Even when his plan doesn't make any sense? The way *mei mamm* has suffered with cancer and treatments, and Enos is struggling with kidney failure. Or the tragedy our *freind* Dave Esh had to face last winter. Or how your *daadi* had a stroke." She fingered her water bottle, and it crinkled in protest. "What kind of plan makes those things all right?"

Andrew's brow furrowed as if he couldn't understand her words. "But we're Christians. That means trusting God, even when we don't understand why he's allowing bad things to happen. It's a sin to doubt him."

She shook her head. "It would make suffering easier if we knew why God allows it."

"But we don't know why, and that's why we must have faith."

She paused, telling herself it was time for the whole truth. Andrew said he would never judge her, and even if she couldn't trust God right now, surely she could trust this man who'd become so dear to her.

"I don't know why that's so easy for you to say, but it's not easy for me. Andrew, everyone, including you, has told me to have faith and trust the Lord. And I've tried. But after watching what this illness has done to my mother — and to our family — I don't understand how that's possible. Yes, *Mamm* is better now that the chemo is done, and I'm grateful for that. And I'd still beg God for healing if I thought he'd listen. But there's no guarantee the cancer is gone or that it won't return if it is. Is that his plan too?"

Andrew blinked, and then a deep frown overtook his face. He set the half-empty water bottle on the counter. "*Danki* for the drink. I need to go." He stood, then put on his hat as he started toward the door. "Good-bye, Darlene. I won't be coming to the supper and singing tonight. You'll have to get a ride after all."

Darlene suddenly felt off-balance. She hopped down from the stool and hurried after him, her heart thudding in her chest. "Andrew! Wait. Please."

He spun to face her, his expression grave. "It feels wrong to debate our Amish beliefs with you. If you're a doubter, I need to keep my distance. I don't think we should see each other anymore."

"You don't want to be *mei freind* because of my doubts?" She felt the blood drain from her face as if he'd struck her.

He scrubbed his hand down one cheek. "I don't know what I want. But I need to go. Take care."

He turned and stalked out of the store as Darlene stared after him, a sick feeling snaking its way through her stomach.

"Darlene?"

She turned as *Dat* came out of his office.

"Was that Andrew?"

She nodded. "He just left."

"Is everything okay?"

She shook her head as her throat thickened. "We had a disagreement, and he walked out. He's upset with me."

Dat pursed his lips. "I'm sorry. May I ask what you disagreed about?"

Darlene hugged her arms to her chest as if to shield her breaking heart. "I'm not ready to talk about it, *Dat.*" What if she told her father the truth? Would he feel compelled to walk out on her too?

Dat nodded slowly. "Okay. Just know I'm here anytime you need me. I'm off to check on your *mamm.*"

As he left, she swallowed back tears. Just when she thought she'd discovered a *freind*

370

with whom she could be honest about her doubts, someone she could tell the truth of her heart, she found herself alone.

She didn't know if she should be hurt or mad, but she acknowledged both warred inside her.

The following Saturday afternoon Andrew sipped a glass of iced tea as he moved back and forth in a rocking chair on the porch of his grandfather's rehabilitation center. He gazed up at the gray clouds clogging the sky as a slight breeze swept over him.

His thoughts turned to Darlene. He hadn't seen her since they'd had their disagreement, but that was for the best. He'd not only skipped the supper at Sharon's that night but he'd chosen to work late at the furniture store to try to take his mind off her.

As frustrated as he was, he still missed Darlene. In fact, his heart had fractured when he realized they could never be more than polite friends. Not with her beliefs so different from his own. Her mother's illness had affected her deeply, but this?

"Penny for your thoughts." His grandfather's words were still slow and slightly garbled, but Andrew caught them.

He glanced to where *Daadi* sat on another

371

rocking chair, smiling at him. "I'm sorry. I was deep in thought."

Daadi studied him. "I could tell. Do you want to talk about it?"

Andrew rubbed his chin. "No. I'll be fine." He forced a smile. "Your speech has already improved, and I'm sure the function in your arm will be next. You gave us a scare."

"I'm sorry about that, but I am feeling a little stronger. What about you? I heard you're seeing a pretty *maedel*. What's her name?"

Andrew shook his head. "I won't be spending time with her anymore, at least not alone. I thought perhaps we could have a dating relationship, but it's over, *Daadi*."

"So soon? I never got to meet her."

"We're too different."

"How so?"

"When it comes to our beliefs." Andrew tried his best to summarize their disagreement. "She said she doesn't understand why God lets bad things happen to *gut* people, and she doesn't understand how I can depend on my faith when those bad things happen — like to you. She thinks God is unfair."

"Why would she say all that?"

"Her *mamm* has been battling cancer and has had a difficult time. So has she."

"Hmm." *Daadi* looked out toward the parking lot. "It sounds like she could use a *freind* like you to guide her heart back to faith."

Andrew shook his head. "Not me. I care about her, but I'm too upset by what she said."

Daadi looked at him with an intensity he hadn't expected. "But do you love her? I have a feeling you do. And if you do, you'll give her another chance."

Andrew swallowed. Did he love Darlene? He missed her so much his heart ached. He longed to see her smile and hear her laugh. But love?

How could he love someone who doubted God?

CHAPTER TEN

"I haven't seen you smile all day today," Sharon told Darlene as they sat with Alice in the Petersheim family's barn. "What's going on?"

Alice picked up a pretzel and pointed it at Darlene. "Not only did you not come to the supper Thursday night even though we know your *mamm* is better, but you looked like you were in your own world during the service." She tapped her chin. "And I didn't see you or Andrew acknowledge each other this morning. Did you have a disagreement?"

Darlene snorted. "You could say that."

Despondency and anger had been her constant companions ever since Andrew marched out of her family's store. She couldn't stop thinking about him, and she'd cried herself to sleep every night. She kept hoping he'd call her or show up, that he'd apologize to her, but she hadn't heard from him.

And when she spotted him this morning before church, he'd turned and walked the other way, sending another knife into her already punctured heart. He'd told her she could share her deepest feelings, and when she did, he'd judged her after all. That's when her hurt turned once again to anger.

"What happened?" Alice asked.

Darlene shook her head. "It's too difficult to explain."

"Well, whatever it is, I'm sure it will be all right," Sharon said. "Have you tried talking to him?"

"He wouldn't even look at me this morning." Darlene picked up a pretzel and then dropped it. Her appetite had evaporated the moment she saw Andrew walking out of the barn without a glance her way. She looked up just as Alice and Sharon shared a glance of their own. "What?"

"Nothing," Alice sang, a little too happily. "How is your *mamm* doing now? We're looking forward to the day she feels up to coming back to church."

The three women made small talk during the remainder of their lunch, and Darlene responded with only one-word answers. She found herself checking the barn door, still hoping to see Andrew seek her out. But he never appeared.

After helping clean the Petersheims' kitchen, Darlene stepped outside and scanned the groups of young people for Andrew, but she didn't spot him. He'd given up on her and their friendship, and the reality hit her like a punch in the stomach, making her shoulders slump as she plodded toward the line of waiting buggies to find her family.

"Darlene!"

She spun and found Alice and Sharon standing with Jay, Dave, and Cal. Andrew was still nowhere in sight.

"*Ya?*"

"Do you have plans for the afternoon?" Sharon asked.

Darlene shook her head. "But if you're about to ask me about a singing, I'm too tired. I'm going home."

"Where's Andrew?" Cal turned and then waved. "Hey, Andrew! Get over here."

Darlene held her breath as Andrew joined them. He met her gaze, and the intensity in his eyes sent a shudder through her body. He nodded, and she responded with a nod. His coldness stabbed at her chest.

"Hi, Andrew," Sharon said. "I was just about to say maybe we could all sing for

Darlene's *mamm* today."

Darlene turned her attention to this news. What was Sharon up to?

"Ya!" Alice said, looking at Darlene with suspicious enthusiasm. "Do you think she'd like that today? We can help celebrate her last treatment."

Darlene nodded, unwilling to keep her mother from visitors. *"Ya,* I think it's okay, since she's feeling better."

"I can't join you," Andrew said. "I'm going to visit *mei daadi.* "

Sharon looked at Alice, and Darlene saw the disappointment in their eyes.

Jay turned to Darlene. "We'll just wait by our buggies while you ask your *dat* if a visit is okay with him."

Darlene lingered, hoping Andrew would take her hand and tell her he was sorry and still wanted to be her friend. But he only slipped his hands into his pockets and said, "I'm glad your *mamm* is doing so well."

"Danki." The word came out in a trembly whisper. "I hope your *daadi* is recovering."

"Danki. He is." He looked down at the ground and then back at her, his lips in a tight frown. "Well, *gut* to see you."

She opened her mouth to beg him to talk to her, but he was already marching toward his horse and buggy. Fighting back tears, she hurried to find her family.

Andrew heard someone call his name as he reached his buggy. He craned his head over his shoulder as Cal approached him.

"What's going on between you and Darlene? And don't tell me nothing, because Sharon and Alice made it clear they know otherwise."

Andrew bit his lower lip. He looked over to where Darlene stood by her father and sister, and renewed frustration and heartache raced for first place.

Part of him wanted to apologize to her, then pull her into his arms. But he couldn't just forget the sinful things she'd said. He couldn't plan a future with a woman who didn't trust God.

Still, he missed her to the depth of his bones. Losing her had left a hole where his heart should be.

Andrew took a breath and worked to keep his voice even. "We're not spending time together anymore."

"Why?"

"It's personal."

Cal's eyebrows rose. "What do you mean?"

Andrew looked at Darlene once again, and

his irritation spiked. "Why don't you ask her?" Then he climbed into his buggy.

Cal leaned in the window. "I don't know what happened, but I think you're being stubborn and prideful if you let her slip through your fingers." Then he tapped the door and walked away.

Darlene slipped into the family room as soon as she arrived home with *Dat* and Biena. She'd asked her friends to wait on the porch until she told her mother they were going to sing, just in case *Mamm* preferred not to have company.

She found her sitting in her recliner, reading a devotional.

Mamm looked up at her and smiled. "How was church?"

"It was *gut.*" Darlene glanced over her shoulder toward the doorway where *Dat* stood, and he nodded, encouraging her to ask her mother for permission to bring in her friends. "We have visitors."

"Oh?" *Mamm* removed her reading glasses and set them on the end table beside her. "Who?"

"You know how *mei freinden* and I have been singing for people?" she asked, and *Mamm* nodded. "Well, we want to sing for you today."

Mamm gaped and then smiled, her brown eyes misting over. "How nice."

"Would you like that?"

"Of course I would." *Mamm* sat up straighter. "What are you going to sing?"

For the first time since Andrew walked out on her, Darlene smiled. "I'll see what they have in mind."

Soon Darlene stood between Alice and Sharon, facing both her parents, who were settled in their recliners. Biena stood with the group too.

Holding up her hymnal, Darlene turned to her friends. "What would you like to sing?"

"How about 'Great Is Thy Faithfulness'?" Biena said, making the first suggestion.

"That's a *schee* one," Alice said.

"I'd like to start," Biena said. Then she cleared her throat and began to sing. "Great is thy faithfulness, O God my Father, there is no shadow of turning with thee. Thou changest not, thy compassions, they fail not, As thou hast been, thou forever will be. Great is thy faithfulness . . ."

Darlene never expected what happened next as she and her friends joined Biena in singing of God's faithfulness. Her heart opened wide, and soon understanding flowed through to her soul. God's love surrounded her, held her, kept her safe. He was there. He'd always been there!

She sang the refrain with joy. "Great is thy faithfulness, great is thy faithfulness, morning by morning new mercies I see. All I have needed thy hand hath provided. Great is thy faithfulness, Lord, unto me."

By the time they were singing the third verse, Darlene could hardly get out the words.

"Pardon for sin and a peace that endureth, Thine own dear presence to cheer and to guide. Strength for today and bright hope for tomorrow, blessings all mine, with ten thousand beside."

As Darlene sang, God's comfort wrapped around her. *God always cares. His will is always the best path — even when I can't see ahead on the road he's put before me or when life is challenging.*

She closed her eyes as she opened her heart to the Lord. *I understand now. You've been with me*, mei mamm, *my family, and me throughout this illness, and you'll always be here. You're constant. You never change even as the world spins around us!*

She sniffed and smiled at her sister and then her parents. She was going to be okay. Her family was going to be okay. God would always provide.

Darlene looked at her friends as they again sang the song's refrain, and the warmth of God's love filled her. He was truly faithful — always, and in so many ways. He'd provided for her through the support of her friends. They would take care of her — even when the worst happened. And although she still didn't understand why bad things happened to good people, faith was a choice. She would *always* choose faith!

After three more hymns, Darlene and Biena served apple pie and coffee in the kitchen, everyone talking and laughing. Darlene tried to participate, but her mind and heart were stuck on Andrew. Even though he'd hurt and angered her, she missed him. And she now understood why he'd been so upset with her. She wanted to talk to him and try to work things out.

Later, she walked her friends outside to say good-bye.

"*Danki* for coming." Darlene hugged Sharon and then Alice. "You really helped cheer up our family. I'm so grateful God has blessed me with *freinden* like you. You've been a tremendous support."

"*Gern gschehne,*" Sharon said. Then she leaned over and whispered, "Don't give up. We're praying for you."

Darlene gave her friend's shoulder a

squeeze. "Thank you for not giving up on me. Someday soon I'll tell you both everything that's been going on with me, but it can wait for another day."

Darlene pulled two apple-cranberry crumb pies out of the oven Friday afternoon. She breathed in the sweet scent and smiled.

"That smells amazing." Biena walked up behind her. "What's the occasion?"

Darlene set them on a cooling rack and then closed the oven. "Alice is hosting a supper and singing tonight, and I offered to bring a pie."

"I hope you leave the other one home for us."

"I will." Darlene set her oven mitt on the counter. "*Mamm* and *Dat* should be home soon. I hope they have *gut* news from the test results."

"They will. I have faith."

Darlene nodded as her thoughts turned to Andrew.

"Have you talked to Andrew?" her sister asked, as if reading her thoughts.

"No." Darlene sighed. "I'm hoping he comes to Alice's tonight so we can talk."

Biena looped her arm around Darlene's shoulders. "I have a feeling he will, and that you'll work everything out. I'm glad you

383

finally confided in me."

"Hello!" *Dat*'s voice rang from the mud-room. "What is that heavenly scent?"

"Darlene made apple-cranberry crumb pies," Biena announced.

"How did it go?" Darlene held her breath as her parents entered the kitchen.

Mamm and *Dat* looked at each other, and when they smiled, Darlene's heart soared.

"Do you want me to tell them?" *Mamm* asked.

"Ya," Dat said.

"The cancer is gone," *Mamm* choked out as tears poured from her eyes.

Darlene and Biena cheered before taking turns hugging their parents, their own cheeks wet with tears.

"Praise God!" Darlene said. "You're in remission!"

"It's a miracle," Biena added.

"It is," *Dat* said, wiping his eyes with his fingers.

"We have to celebrate," Darlene said. "Let me make some *kaffi.*"

"I'll grab some ice cream from the freezer," Biena said.

As they sat at the table, Darlene felt as if she might burst with happiness and relief. She looked down at her half-eaten mint chocolate chip and closed her eyes.

Thank you, God. Thank you. Forgive me for ever doubting you.

When a knock sounded on the back door, Darlene looked up. "Is anyone expecting a visitor?"

Dat shook his head. "No."

"I'll go see who it is."

Her stomach flip-flopped when she found Andrew standing on the back porch, holding his hat in his hand. She pushed the screen door open and stepped out. "Hi."

"Hi." He cleared his throat and pointed toward the glider. "Could we please talk?"

"Of course." Her body trembled as she sat down beside him. "How have you been?"

"Gut." He shook his head and grimaced. "No, I've been terrible. Awful. I want to apologize to you. I was so wrong to treat you the way I did."

Her breath hitched as she studied him.

"I've missed you, Darlene, and that's why I'm here. I want to work things out."

"I do too." She took a deep breath.

"Gut." He straightened his shoulders. "I've been doing a lot of thinking, and I realized I've been a terrible *freind* to you. I offered you my support, but when you finally opened up to me, I rejected your feelings and emotions. I judged you. That was wrong, especially when I told you I

385

wouldn't. I'm sorry. You're entitled to your feelings, even if we don't agree."

"*Danki.*" Tears stung her eyes.

"I've also realized something about faith." He angled his body more toward hers. "When *mei daadi* had his stroke, I told *mei bruder* to have faith, and he got annoyed with me. He accused me of never being scared. The truth is I was scared." He shook his head. "No, I was terrified that we were going to lose our *daadi.* And looking back, I see now that it's easy to tell someone to have faith when they're going through something terrifying, but it's not necessarily easy to have faith when it's happening to you."

She nodded. "Exactly."

"I'm sorry for hurting you and for dismissing your feelings. I hope you can forgive me."

"I do forgive you. And I've learned something too." She took another deep breath. "Last Sunday when our *freinden* came and sang for *mei mamm,* Biena suggested we sing 'Great Is Thy Faithfulness.' The words of the hymn made me realize that the Lord has been carrying my family and me all along. But I was too angry about *mei mamm*'s disease to see it. The hymn pointed out that God provided for me. He gave me wonderful *freinden* to take care of me and my family when things were at their worst. God never changes, even when this world we live in is spinning out of control. He is constant, and faith is a choice."

She pointed to her chest. "And I choose to have faith. God is always with us, and he will provide for us, no matter what. My faith will remain strong in that truth."

"You're so right." He took her hands in his. "But I had no right to judge you. You went through a lot. You had a right to be angry. No matter what happens, we'll face your *mamm*'s illness together."

"But I have news. Today she went to the doctor and learned she's in remission. I'm so grateful to God. He's been with us all along." She gave a little laugh as tears fell. "He healed her, Andrew. He did. And even though it's possible her cancer could come back, I trust him with *Mamm*'s life. I trust him with all my heart."

Andrew pulled her into his arms. "I'm so *froh* for you all, Darlene."

"I am too." She rested her cheek on his shoulder and breathed in the scent of his spicy aftershave. "And I'm so grateful for you." She closed her eyes and savored the feeling of his closeness.

He pulled back and leveled his gaze with

hers. Then he reached out and wiped away her tears with his thumb. "I've missed you so much. I never should have walked away from you in your time of need. I'm in love with you, Darlene."

She blinked as happiness nearly overcame her. "I love you too."

"If your *dat* will allow me to, I want to date you."

She nodded. "I'd like that."

Andrew leaned forward and brushed his lips over hers, sending heat spiraling inside her. When he sat back, he smiled. "I'm hoping you'll ride with me to the supper and singing tonight."

"I'd love to. And I made an apple-cranberry crumb pie to share."

He rubbed his hands together. "Why don't we save that and eat it when we get back?"

She laughed. "I made an extra one."

"Great." He stood and then held his hand out to her.

She took it, and he lifted her up.

"Do you think your *dat* would talk to me before we leave?"

"I do. My parents and Biena are all in the kitchen, celebrating."

"*Gut.*" Andrew gave her hand a gentle squeeze. "I can hardly wait to be your boyfriend."

She gave him a coy smile. "I can hardly wait to be your girlfriend."

Andrew kissed her cheek. *"Ich liebe dich."*

As they walked into her house together, Darlene let out a happy sigh. She was so grateful God brought her and Andrew together when she needed him most.

Oh how faithful the Lord had been.

DISCUSSION QUESTIONS

1. Darlene is convinced God has forgotten her mother as she struggles with chemo. Have you ever been convinced God wasn't hearing your prayers? If so, how did you find your faith again?
2. Andrew is determined to help Darlene through her tough time. What do you think attracted him to her?
3. Andrew believes he should have faith no matter how tough a situation is. He leans on it when others sometimes lose themselves in worry and doubt. Do you think his point of view is valid? Why or why not?
4. Which character can you identify with the most? Which character seemed to carry the most emotional stake in the story? Darlene, Andrew, or someone else?
5. At the end of the story, Darlene realizes God was with her and her family all along. What do you think happened throughout the story to make her change her mind?

6. What role did singings play in the relationships throughout the story?

■ ■ ■ ■

O HOLY NIGHT

■ ■ ■ ■

With love and kisses for
squirming Daisy Mae,
even though Matt's the only one she likes

FEATURED CHARACTERS

Annie m. Emmanuel "Manny" Esh
|
Rosemary
David

Edna m. Harvey King
|
Calvin
Raymond

Louise m. Moses Smoker
|
Jay

Jean m. Merle Detweiler
|
Andrew
Samuel

Feenie m. Ira Lambert
|
Sharon
Ruby Sue

Dorothy m. Floyd Blank
|
Benjamin
Alice

Roselyn m. Alvin Bender
|
Biena
Darlene

Rosemary m. Stephen Lapp
|
Nancy

Lovina m. Abram Lantz
|
Elaine

Mary Liz and Melvin Lantz
|
Levi
Uria

CHAPTER ONE

Elaine plastered a smile on her face as she followed her mother and aunt to the Glick family's back-porch steps. It was a church Sunday, their first in Lancaster County, and the Glicks were hosting the service.

She pulled her black sweater tight across her chest as a cool breeze caused her to shiver. She should have chosen a heavier sweater to wear over her favorite long-sleeved dress — the pink one.

After glancing at the cloudy, mid-October sky, she turned her gaze toward the barn. The middle-aged men had all gathered by the barn before the church service, and she spotted her father talking to his older brother, her uncle, Mel, and nearly sighed.

This was what her father had wanted. A new start in Bird-in-Hand, Pennsylvania. And new friends for her in this new church district. But was she willing to make friends after what happened back home in New

Wilmington?

Elaine straightened her shoulders as she made her way up the porch steps. The women she'd grown up with in Western Pennsylvania always met in the kitchens of host houses before services, and her aunt told them this district was no different.

"Lovina, before we go in, I just want to tell you again how excited we are to have you here," *Aenti* Mary Liz said, one hand on the storm-door handle. "You know Mel has been trying to convince Abram to go into business with him for years. We're so grateful and blessed that he finally accepted."

"Well, God's timing was just right. For the last couple of years, Abram was finally considering selling our dairy farm, and then the perfect offer came in." *Mamm* smiled at her. "We're grateful that a partnership in Mel's shed business was still open, and you're even letting us live in the *daadihaus* where your parents lived. We're blessed as well." She turned to Elaine. "And you were eager for a new start, too, right?"

Elaine slowly nodded. That sounded like *Mamm* had told Mary Liz what happened in the youth group back home. She inwardly groaned at the humiliation.

"*Ach,* don't worry." Her aunt touched

Elaine's arm. "We have a nice group of young folks in our church district. I'm certain you'll quickly make some *wunderbaar freinden.*"

"*Danki.*" Elaine forced her lips into a smile. She'd always thought her aunt was one of the prettiest ladies she knew, and she had a kind heart to match.

"Let's introduce you to the women of our congregation." Mary Liz opened the back door, and a buzz of conversation floated out.

With a deep breath, Elaine stepped through the mudroom to where the women stood in a circle in the kitchen. She once again forced a pleasant expression on her face as her aunt steered *Mamm* and her around the circle, introducing them.

Elaine tried to commit the strangers' names to memory, but she knew it was a lost cause. She could never remember them all this soon.

"Elaine, this is Dorothy Blank," Mary Liz said as they approached a woman probably in her mid to late forties with dark hair and eyes. "Dorothy, this is Elaine's *mamm,* Lovina Lantz. She's my sister-in-law, married to Mel's *bruder,* Abram, and their family just moved here from the western part of the state."

"So nice to meet you," Dorothy said, and

Elaine and *Mamm* nodded.

"Dorothy and her *dochder,* Alice, like to quilt, just like you and your *mamm* do, Elaine. And Alice is about your age." She looked at Dorothy. "How old is she?"

Dorothy smiled at Elaine. "She's twenty-one. And you are . . ."

"Twenty-two."

"How about that?" Her aunt's smile widened. "I'll introduce you to Alice. You and your *mamm* will have to quilt with us. We're making quilts for Christmas gifts and to sell in some of the Bird-in-Hand shops."

Dorothy's expression brightened. "Absolutely! And Alice and her *freinden* like to sing for members of our community. Do you like to sing, Elaine?"

Elaine nodded. "I do."

"Wunderbaar." *Mamm* clapped her hands. "You should join them."

Dorothy pointed toward the mudroom. "Why don't we go outside so you can meet Alice and her *freinden* now?"

Elaine followed them out and then to a group of three young women talking near the pasture fence. Standing close together as they spoke animatedly, they looked like a tight-knit group. They were all pretty, and like her, they were of average height for a woman. But they each had different-colored hair peeking out from under their prayer coverings. One woman was a blonde, the second had light-brown hair, and the third had reddish-brown hair.

Visions of her former friends came to mind, and a niggle of worry crept in. Maybe these young women could become her friends, but would they eventually turn on her too? She could never go through that again.

"Alice!" Dorothy called. "I want you to meet someone."

The young woman with the reddish-brown hair smiled as she took a step away from her friends and joined them.

"Alice," Dorothy began, "this is Elaine Lantz. She's Mary Liz's niece. And this is Elaine's *mamm*, Lovina. They just moved here from New Wilmington, and they like to quilt."

"Wunderbaar." Alice shook Elaine's hand, and her smile seemed genuine as her dark eyes sparkled. She glanced behind her, where her two friends stood looking curious. "Elaine, come meet *mei freinden.*"

Elaine glanced at her mother, who nodded encouragement, almost as if Elaine were a toddler. But her mother knew just how reticent she'd become — and why.

"Okay."

They met the other young women halfway, and Alice first gestured toward the blonde. "Elaine, this is Darlene Bender." Then she pointed to the brunette. "And this is Sharon Lambert. Elaine just moved here from New Wilmington. She's Mary Liz's niece, and she likes to quilt."

"You do?" Sharon asked.

"*Ya.* We had a quilting group where I used to live." *That is, until I was no longer welcome there.*

"You'll have to quilt with us, then," Alice said, and the other two young women nodded.

"Do you like to sing?" Darlene asked, just as Alice's mother had.

Elaine gave a half shrug. *"Ya."*

"We sing for members of the community and for *Englishers* who come to suppers Alice's and Sharon's *mamms* host. We could always use an extra voice. Right?" Darlene turned to her friends as if for their approval, and they both nodded.

"We'd love for you to join us," Sharon said. "We're already talking about what Christmas carols we want to sing starting right after Thanksgiving."

"Maybe I will." Elaine glanced to her left as a group of four young men made their way toward them.

She locked eyes with one of them. He had golden hair, and he was tall, around her father's six-foot height. When he smiled, she felt a flutter in her chest and quickly looked down at the toes of her black shoes, away from his blue-gray eyes.

"Here are the other *freinden* who sing with us," Sharon announced. "This is my boyfriend, Jay Smoker." She pointed to another tall young man, who had light-brown hair and eyes the color of honey. He nodded as he came to stand beside Sharon.

Elaine thought of her ex-boyfriend, Lewis, and her stomach soured.

"And this is Dave Esh." Sharon pointed toward yet another tall young man, this one with light-brown hair and blue eyes. "He's dating Alice."

"Hi." Dave gave her a shy smile before stepping to join Alice.

"And this is Andrew Detweiler," Darlene announced as a young man with dark hair and eyes joined her. He was about the same height. "He's my boyfriend."

Andrew waved.

"Hi. I'm Calvin King. *Mei freinden* call me Cal. I'm the only single member of the group." The young man with the golden hair and alluring blue-gray eyes held out his hand. "I didn't catch your name."

She found it amazing that all four of these men were so tall, let alone so close in height. Lewis was only a couple of inches taller than her.

"I'm Elaine Lantz." She offered him a weak handshake and nearly jumped when his skin touched hers. Her cheeks heated, and she looked away, turning toward where *Mamm* still spoke to Dorothy. "I'm going to catch up with *mei mamm.* It's nice meeting you all."

"It's nice meeting you too." Sharon gave her a wave.

Elaine quickly sidled up to her mother, who was discussing quilting patterns with Dorothy and Mary Liz. When she glanced back at Alice and her friends, she found Calvin watching her. He waved.

She merely nodded in return, and this time a strange shiver of awareness rolled over her skin. If only she could, she'd run and hide without a second thought. After the way Lewis shredded her heart and her trust, she'd rather be alone than give another man a chance to hurt her.

Cal couldn't take his eyes off Elaine as she stood next to Alice's mother and Mary Liz, her profile in clear view. She was beautiful with those striking dark eyes that matched her hair, and he'd never seen a *maedel* with such stunning ivory skin and adorable freckles marching across her nose. But something about her was intriguing besides her looks, something he couldn't quite put a finger on.

"Hey, Cal." Jay smacked his arm. "Are you daydreaming?"

"No." *Yes!*

About a month ago, Andrew and Darlene had finally settled into their relationship, leaving him the only single man in their tight group of seven. He had to admit, having a girlfriend was beginning to sound appealing — maybe. If she could be anything like this woman.

He cleared his throat. "Is Elaine just visiting our district today?"

"No." Alice shook her head. "She just moved here."

He rubbed his jaw. "Really? From where?"

"New Wilmington."

"Interesting." He looked back at Elaine.

"She said she likes to quilt," Sharon said, "so we invited her to quilt with us."

"And she sings too," Darlene added. "We've already invited her to join us at singings."

"Huh." Calvin placed a hand on each hip. "How does she know Mary Liz?"

"Mary Liz is her *aenti*," Alice said. "Elaine's last name is Lantz, so I guess her *dat*'s *bruder* is married to Mary Liz."

"Really? That means Uria, who works with me on *mei dat*'s horse farm, is her cousin."

Alice nodded. "Right."

"Mm. Do you have a sudden crush, Cal?" Jay asked.

Cal turned to his friend with narrowed eyes. "No. I'm just curious. How often do Amish families move here and become members of our church district?"

"Not very," Dave said.

"We unmarried women will invite her to sit with us in church, too, but we should all welcome her with open arms to sing with our group, starting this afternoon," Sharon said. "She's new, and she's our age."

Darlene nodded along with everyone else. "I agree."

Cal smiled. He really was curious about Elaine, and he looked forward to getting to know her.

"Did you like the service?" Alice asked Elaine as they walked toward the Glicks' house.

"*Ya,* of course." Elaine was grateful that Alice had invited her to sit with her and her friends during the service.

406

She'd spent a good part of the time glancing around at the congregation. Her cousins Levi and Uri had been sitting together in the unmarried men's section, and Alice's, Darlene's, and Sharon's boyfriends sat only a row away from them. And, of course, Calvin sat with his friends.

Although she'd tried her best to avoid looking at him, her eyes betrayed her more than once. And she'd found him watching her more than once. She immediately broke away from his gaze, but she'd been caught, entranced by his handsome face.

She chastised herself. Her last relationship with a man had ended in disaster, and this community was a brand-new start for her and her parents. She had to make the best of it and avoid creating another terrible situation. That meant avoiding Calvin at all costs. She had a feeling a man like him *expected* female attention.

Pushing those thoughts away, she followed Alice into the Glicks' kitchen and picked up a coffee carafe. Alice said she'd stay to make more coffee, and Sharon and Darlene each lifted a tray of food.

"I know you just met us," Sharon said as they made their way back to the barn, "but this afternoon we're going to sing for one of our community members who's bedridden, and we'd love for you to join us. Just think about it."

"Josiah Gingerich?" Darlene asked.

"*Ya.* He's had some complications after back surgery."

Alice clucked her tongue. *"Ach.* So *bedauerlich."*

Darlene balanced her tray of peanut butter spread and bread as she looked at Sharon. "Did you tell the guys?"

"I did." Sharon nodded, holding her tray with bowls of pretzels steady as well. "They all want to come with us."

"Gut."

Elaine looked straight ahead. She wished she could come up with an excuse to avoid going, but her parents expected her to participate in the youth group, so she had to go. But it would be impossible to avoid Calvin all afternoon. As outgoing as he seemed to be — and already a bit too attentive — he might offer her a ride home. She didn't want to run the risk of giving him the wrong idea. She didn't need or want a boyfriend.

"Do you have a boyfriend in New Wilmington?"

Elaine halted and faced Sharon, who slowed and turned to face her as well. Had she just read her thoughts? "No, I don't."

Not anymore.

"Oh." Sharon smiled.

Darlene's expression warmed as she stood beside them. "Maybe you'll meet someone here."

"I'm not looking for a boyfriend right now." When she noticed them all sharing a confused expression, she added, "I just want to help my parents get settled. *Mei dat* is starting a new job, and we're still unpacking in a *daadihaus* on *mei aenti* and *onkel*'s farm, where we'll live until *mei dat* finds property to build a place. We have a lot on our plates."

"Right." Darlene nodded. Her pinched brow seemed to illustrate her skepticism, but at the same time, Elaine thought she saw a hint of understanding in her eyes. Maybe she'd had a lot on her plate before dating Andrew.

Elaine started toward the barn again. "I need to serve this *kaffi* before it gets cold."

She stepped into the barn and began moving down the tables, smiling as she filled the men's cups with coffee.

When she came to the table where Calvin sat with his friends, he was laughing at something Jay said.

She stilled for a moment and took in his profile, his face looking as though it had

409

been carved out of a fine piece of granite. He was certainly attractive, but Lewis was too. And he'd not only trampled her heart but destroyed her reputation.

Elaine closed her eyes and fought against the familiar cloud of betrayal and heartache that took up residence in her soul after Lewis broke up with her. Then she squared her shoulders and headed down the table.

When she came up behind Calvin, she forced her lips into a smile. *"Kaffi?"*

Calvin craned his neck to look up at her. "Hi, Elaine."

"Hello." She held up the carafe. "Would any of you like *kaffi?*"

Andrew lifted his cup. "*Ya,* please."

Elaine filled his cup and then reached over to fill Dave's and Jay's. When she allowed her gaze to tangle with Calvin's again, she said, "Do you want some?"

"Of course I do." Those blue-gray eyes sparkled. "How did you like the service?"

"Fine. It was similar to our services back in New Wilmington." She filled his cup.

"Did you know your cousin Uria works for *mei dat?* We work together."

Her eyes locked with his. "Your *dat* owns King's Belgian and Dutch Harness Horses?"

"That's right." He took the full cup from

her. *"Danki."*

"Gern gschehne." She moved on to the next group of men, but her mind was stuck on the information Calvin had shared. Uria worked with him. Would that make it even harder to avoid this man?

If so, her heart might be doomed.

CHAPTER TWO

Elaine again sat with her new friends while the women of the congregation ate their lunch. She did her best to concentrate on the conversation, but her thoughts kept wandering to what Calvin had told her about Uria.

Mary Liz had written her mother about how Levi, who was twenty, enjoyed working with his father and the other carpenters at the shed store, but Uria had asked to pursue another vocation. He'd tried working at the Kings' horse breeding and training farm two years ago, when he turned fifteen. He enjoyed the work so much that he chose to stay.

Now Elaine found herself imagining Calvin and her cousin working together. Were they close, despite what she was sure was a few years' age difference? What if Calvin sometimes came to her aunt and uncle's house to see Uria?

"Have you decided if you're going to sing with us this afternoon, Elaine?"

"Huh?" Elaine looked up at Alice's voice and found all three women staring at her. "I'm sorry. I was lost in thought."

Sharon picked up her sandwich. "What were you thinking about?"

Elaine licked her lips and searched her mind for a response. "Nothing. It was nothing."

Darlene turned toward her. "So will you sing with us today?"

"Please?" Alice asked from across the table.

Elaine wished she'd found an excuse to say no, but she still thought she had no choice. "Okay. I'll go."

Darlene smiled. *"Wunderbaar!"*

After Elaine helped with the cleanup, she made her way toward the line of buggies, where she spotted her parents talking to her aunt and uncle.

"I'm going out this afternoon with Darlene, Alice, and Sharon." Elaine pointed toward where they stood waiting for her. "They're going to sing for a church member who's still recovering from surgery."

"Oh, *gut!*" *Mamm* squeezed her arm. "Have fun."

Elaine met up with Darlene, who'd joined

413

Andrew near one of the buggies. "May I please ride with you to the singing?"

Darlene glanced at Andrew and then back at Elaine. "Of course you can."

"Danki." Elaine climbed into the back of the buggy.

They all made small talk during the short ride to a small, white farmhouse that sat in front of a barn and a modest pasture. Once Andrew halted his horse, Elaine scrambled out behind Darlene — and almost crashed right into Calvin.

"You could have ridden with me," he said with a confused expression on his face. Or was that disappointment?

Elaine shrugged. "I thought I should ride with one of the women since they're the ones who invited me." She looked at the back porch as Darlene and Andrew climbed the steps behind Sharon and Jay. Each woman held two hymnals, and she was sure they were copies of the *Ausbund,* their Amish hymnal, and perhaps copies of *Heartland Hymns,* a German and English songbook. "We'd better get going."

Slipping past Calvin, she caught up with the others.

Sharon knocked on the back door, and an Amish woman with a round face, perhaps in her midforties, appeared in the doorway.

"Hi, Bertha," Sharon said. "We were wondering if we could sing for you and Josiah. We heard he's had some complications since his back surgery."

"Oh, how nice." Bertha's expression brightened as she beckoned for them to enter the house. "We'd love that. Please come in."

Elaine followed everyone into a small kitchen, then through a doorway to an even smaller family room. A dark-haired man sat in a recliner. While everyone else gathered around him, Elaine hung back.

"How are you, Josiah?" Sharon asked.

The man shook his head, and his brown eyes seemed full of pain. "It's been a tough recovery, but I'm holding on to my faith."

"We're all so sorry to hear you're struggling. We wanted to offer our support in person." Sharon turned toward Elaine. "This is our new *freind,* Elaine Lantz. She and her parents just moved here from New Wilmington."

"Nice to meet you," Bertha said.

Elaine nodded and smoothed her hands down her white apron.

Sharon looked at Josiah. "May we sing for you? It might brighten your day."

"That sounds *wunderbaar.*"

Darlene touched Sharon's arm. "Why

415

don't we sing 'Jesus Loves Me'? That lovely arrangement we memorized. I can start."

"*Ya,*" Bertha said. "That's always been one of our family's favorites. It's such a simple yet powerful testimony for believers of all ages."

Alice spun to face Elaine. "Would you come join us?"

"Okay." Elaine crossed the room and stood beside her.

Darlene cleared her throat and began to sing. "Jesus loves me, this I know, for the Bible tells me so. Little ones to him belong. They are weak, but he is strong."

Everyone joined in for the refrain, and Elaine sang along. "Yes, Jesus loves me! Yes, Jesus loves me! Yes, Jesus loves me! The Bible tells me so."

Elaine sensed someone watching her. She turned, and her gaze collided with Calvin's, once again sending heat surging to her cheeks. She looked down at the floor and tried to avoid his eyes for the remainder of the hymn.

After they'd sung three hymns, Bertha served chocolate chip cookies and coffee in the kitchen. They talked with her for a while and then headed outside.

"You have a gorgeous voice," Sharon told Elaine as they approached their waiting horses and buggies.

"Danki." Elaine tried to hide her embarrassment as they all looked at her.

"*Ya,* you do," Alice added. "Your voice blends well with ours. We need you at all our singings."

"Oh, I don't know." Elaine hugged her arms against her sweater.

"Please think about it," Jay said. "You definitely add a lot to our little choir."

"That's very nice of you to say." Elaine turned toward Andrew. "Could you take me home? Maybe Darlene told you I live on Mel Lantz's farm. He's *mei onkel.*"

"Of course. Darlene doesn't live far from there. Let's go." Andrew pointed toward his buggy.

"Good-bye." Elaine nodded her head and smiled at the whole group, then focused on Calvin for a moment. He didn't look happy. She tore her gaze away from his and hurried to Andrew's buggy.

Elaine climbed the front-porch steps of the little, white, one-story *daadihaus* that sat on her aunt and uncle's farm. She grinned as an orange tabby cat trotted toward her. "You're back," she told him. "I've seen you before."

She leaned down and rubbed the cat's ear,

and he purred. "I think I'll name you . . . Arnold."

The cat meowed at her, and she laughed. "I'll find a bowl and bring you some food. Wait here." She stepped inside the house, then into the small kitchen. "Hi, *Mamm.*"

"Hi. Your *dat* will be back soon, and then we'll have our supper. Did you enjoy the singing?" *Mamm* asked as she looked up from a cookbook she'd been reading at the table.

"I did." Elaine glanced around the room, taking in the few cabinets. "Would it be okay if I fed that orange tabby cat that keeps coming to visit us?"

"Sure."

"I just named him Arnold. If it's okay with you, I can give him the cooked chicken in the refrigerator until I get to the store for some cat food."

Mamm nodded, so Elaine shredded the chicken into a small bowl. After she'd filled another bowl with water, she took them to the porch, where Arnold sat waiting. When she set down the bowls, he eagerly began to eat.

"Enjoy." She patted his head and then returned to the house, passing the short hallway that led from the family room area to the home's two bedrooms and one bathroom. Once again she noted how few furnishings the family room could hold — a sofa, one recliner, and one end table. She tried to imagine Mary Liz's parents living there before they passed away. Were they happy in this little house? Most of her family's furniture was stored in the barn, waiting for the house *Dat* would build for them.

"I'm so glad you went singing," *Mamm* said when Elaine returned to the kitchen, finding her father there as well. "Making new *freinden* will help Bird-in-Hand feel like home." *Mamm* opened the refrigerator and pulled out the chicken, mushroom, and spinach lasagna casserole Mary Liz had brought the day before. Then she placed it in the preheated oven and set the timer.

"I know you're right." Elaine ran her hand across the back of one of the four kitchen chairs.

"Rhoda and her *freinden* made life difficult for you, but this is a new start," *Dat* said as he washed his hands. "I bet these nice young folks will more than welcome you."

Elaine studied him for a moment. *Dat* was forty-nine. Most of his hair still matched his dark eyes, but now it was threaded with gray. More than once, Elaine had been told she resembled her father more than her mother. *Mamm*'s hair was light-brown, and her eyes were hazel. She wondered what a sibling would have looked like if her parents had been blessed with more children.

"I'll set the table." Elaine pulled three plates from a box, waiting for their unpacking to resume tomorrow.

Mamm touched her shoulder as Elaine rinsed the dishes. "It will all work out, *mei liewe*. We have a new life here to enjoy."

Dat sat down. "*Ya,* and tomorrow I'll start my first day at Mel's shop. I hope he doesn't regret hiring me."

Mamm chuckled as she lifted a hot pad from the counter. "You know he won't. He's been trying to lure you back here for years. He's relieved you finally came."

"*Ya,* but I'm awfully old to be an apprentice."

"You've always been *gut* at woodworking," Elaine said. "You'll do just fine."

"*Danki.*" *Dat* smiled. "The only thing that matters is we're here together, right?"

Elaine nodded.

Somehow Elaine would find her way in this new community. But only with God's help. As her parents talked about her uncle's shed business, she silently prayed.

Lord, please help me in this new community.

Lead me to true freinden. *And help my parents feel welcome here too.*

"Breakfast looks *wunderbaar* as usual, Edna."

"*Danki,* Harvey." She smiled. "Did you meet the new family at church yesterday?"

"The ones from New Wilmington? No, I didn't. I believe I saw them, but I didn't get a chance to talk to any of them."

Cal glanced across the table at his mother, then nodded as he swallowed a bite of bacon. "I met the *dochder,* Elaine. She seems nice." *And she's pretty.*

"Uria told me Elaine is his cousin," Raymond said. "His *dat* has always wanted his *bruder* to come help him run the family shed business. Apparently, Elaine and her parents are staying in the *daadihaus* on Mel's property. It's been empty since Uria's grandparents passed away a few years ago."

Cal lifted his mug and studied his younger brother. Ray was good at gathering information, and that made him smile. Despite their age difference, Ray's seventeen to Cal's twenty-three, Cal felt close to his only sibling, and he could remember arguing with him only a few times. He also noted, not for the first time, that with his medium-brown hair and hazel eyes, Ray looked more like *Mamm* than *Dat.*

Many times, like now, Calvin thought about how much he admired his father. He was close to fifty, but he still had a twinkle in his gray eyes and hardly any gray in his light-brown hair. He was also still in great shape, sporting a trim waist and muscular arms. He was a few inches shorter than Cal's nearly six feet, but that would never diminish his respect for him.

Dat had a great sense of humor too.

Dat buttered his toast. "That's nice of Mel's *bruder* to come. I've noticed that store stays busy all year round. It's about time Mel had a partner."

"Elaine seems like a lovely *maedel,*" *Mamm* said. "I met her before the service." She pointed her fork at Cal. "I believe she's about your age."

"I think so too." Cal forked a pile of scrambled eggs into his mouth.

"I saw her talking to your *freinden,*" Ray said.

"*Ya.* She also went to Josiah Gingerich's *haus* with us to sing to him. Her voice blended perfectly with ours. I'm hoping she'll join us again soon." Cal immediately regretted this honesty when Ray's mouth dropped open.

"Do you like her?" His brother smirked.

422

Cal picked up another piece of bacon. "Like her? I don't even know her."

Raymond shook a finger at him. "You've already got a crush on her. I can tell. You always get that look when you like a *maedel.*"

"Stop it, Ray. I just met her yesterday." He tamped down the urge to roll his eyes.

"Finish your breakfast, Raymond," *Dat* said. "We have plenty to do today."

Saved by Dat! Cal swallowed a sigh of relief.

But the truth was he'd felt more drawn to Elaine than he would have expected to at first sight. She wasn't like any of the other unattached *maed* in his church district. Most of them flirted with him and laughed at his jokes, and he enjoyed that. But when he introduced himself to Elaine, she barely responded before dashing off. Then she pursued riding to the singing with Darlene and Andrew, a couple, instead of asking to ride with him, a man obviously single. She seemed to be avoiding him, which both puzzled and intrigued him.

Yes, she was different! And he was determined to discover why she was dodging him.

When the family finished breakfast, Cal pulled on his work boots and straw hat in the mudroom before stepping onto the large wraparound porch and breathing in the crisp air.

He knew many people in his community were already looking forward to the Christmas season, and so was he. But fall was still his favorite time of year. He enjoyed the colorful leaves on the trees that surrounded his father's huge farm. He glanced at the line of six red barns and stables and then toward the vast pasture surrounded by a split-rail fence. This had always been his home, and he cherished the aroma of their horses and the sound of their whinnying.

"Are you ready to work?" Ray asked as he moved past Cal and jogged down the steps. "We have plenty of animals to feed and stalls to muck."

Cal grinned as he started after him. "I know. I've worked on this farm longer than you, little *bruder.*"

As they made their way to the stables, Uria's horse and buggy moved up the long rock driveway that led to the road. Cal waved as an idea formed in his mind. He would ask Uria about Elaine and hopefully learn more about her.

And maybe, just maybe, Elaine would be his friend one day. Or maybe more. And that last thought sent an unexpected excitement flowing through his veins.

■ ■ ■ ■

A knock sounded on the front door Thursday morning.

Elaine stopped washing breakfast dishes and turned to her mother. "Are you expecting someone?"

"No." *Mamm* stopped sweeping the floor. "And I know Mary Liz is already out doing errands this morning."

"I'll get it." Elaine dried her hands on a dish towel and then headed to the family room.

She wrenched open the door and found Alice, Sharon, Alice's mother, and a woman who looked just like Sharon behind them holding covered dishes. Elaine blinked and then pulled the door open to the full width of the entryway.

"Gude mariye," Sharon announced. "Alice and I and our mothers thought we'd stop by."

"Oh." Elaine was nearly speechless as she took in their wide smiles.

"Why, hello, Dorothy." *Mamm* appeared behind her. "What a nice surprise."

Dorothy pointed to the woman beside her. "I'm not sure you met Feenie Lambert on Sunday. She and I were talking yesterday

425

about doing something special to welcome you into the community. Then Sharon and Alice suggested we bring you a meal."

Feenie nodded. "You must still be getting settled, and we thought food would be a *gut* way to show you how glad we are you've joined our community."

Alice pointed to her mother. "We brought a hamburger pie casserole and brownies. You can save them for your supper so you don't have to cook tonight."

"*Danki* so much." Elaine smiled, but doubt pricked at her. Would her new friends always be happy she was there? Or would that change like her friendships in New Wilmington had?

"That is so kind." *Mamm* gestured for them to enter the house. "Please come in. This was Mary Liz's parents' *daadihaus*. It's small but cozy. Abram plans to build a *haus,* but he needs some time to look for land."

"Mary Liz mentioned your husband had a dairy farm in New Wilmington," Dorothy commented as they all walked into the small kitchen.

"*Ya,* that's right," *Mamm* said as the women set their dishes on the counter. "Abram and I met many years ago when he came to New Wilmington to visit some cousins on his mother's side. We wrote letters after he came back to Bird-in-Hand. Then he made a few trips out to visit me, and when he proposed, *mei dat* invited us to live with him and *mei mamm* on his dairy farm and take it over someday. My parents passed away about fifteen years ago."

Mamm gave them a wistful smile. "A dairy farm is so much work, and for the last couple of years, Abram had been talking about selling it and finding a new profession. Over the years, Mel asked him more than once to move back here and help him run the family shed business. And since my parents are gone, and I don't have siblings, we thought it would be nice for us to move closer to his family here."

"We know what you mean about a dairy farm," Dorothy said, and Feenie nodded. "The work doesn't end."

Mamm glanced at the dishes they'd brought. "This food smells so *gut*."

"I'll put the casserole in the fridge." Elaine picked up the dish and set it on the bottom shelf of the propane-powered refrigerator.

"We also want to know how else we can help you today," Alice said. "We can unpack or do chores . . . You just got here a few days ago, right?"

Mamm nodded. "Well, we do still have a lot of packed boxes in the small barn

427

outside. They're filled with more kitchen items, laundry items . . ."

"Alice and I can do that," Sharon said. "What else can we do? Maybe some cleaning?"

"Mary Liz cleaned before we came, but with all the dirt we tracked in as we moved furniture and boxes — the doors wide open — we were just about to clean the bathroom, scrub the floors . . ."

"I'll clean the bathroom," Dorothy said.

"And I'll clean the floors," Feenie added. "But we'll both dust first. I'm sure you have other things you need to do, Lovina."

The two women made it clear *Mamm* shouldn't try arguing with them.

Elaine divided a look between Alice and Sharon. "I'll show you where the boxes are."

For the next two hours, Elaine, Alice, and Sharon emptied boxes and washed cookware, and then they further organized the kitchen for maximum use of the few cabinets and shelves, plus the small utility room.

While they worked, Alice and Sharon asked Elaine about her life in New Wilmington. She gave them vague answers. She never shared how, at the end, she'd been on her own in the unmarried women's section at church services, nor how her lifelong friends were so taken in by the lies they'd been told about her that they'd started excluding her from all their activities.

After the three of them broke down the empty boxes and shoved them in a corner of the barn, Elaine asked, "Would you like to stay for lunch?"

"I suppose we could," Sharon said as they turned toward the house.

Alice lifted an index finger. "That sounds lovely, but we should check with our mothers."

When they entered the kitchen, they found all three mothers scurrying around, pulling out dishes, rolls, lunchmeat, condiments, and the iced tea *Mamm* had made earlier.

"Oh, there you are," Dorothy said. "We just finished our chores, and we're going to have lunch together before we leave."

Sharon smiled at Elaine. "I think that answers our question."

Elaine felt a sudden comradery with Sharon, but then she cautioned herself to keep her distance. She'd fallen for that with Rhoda.

"I'm so glad Mary Liz picked up some groceries for us," *Mamm* said as she sliced a tomato. "Elaine, would you please grab those folding chairs and the extra table?"

"We'll help you," Alice said.

"Danki." Elaine led them to the utility room, just big enough for a wringer washer and a couple of shelves. The table and chairs barely fit leaned against the far wall.

Once the food was ready, they all sat down, and after a silent prayer, they built their sandwiches. The mothers fell into a discussion about recipes, and Elaine searched her mind for something to say to Alice and Sharon.

"We're hosting another group of *Englishers* for supper at *mei haus* tomorrow night," Sharon said. "You know, the suppers I told you about when we met? My family and Alice's family both host them quite often for some local inns and tour companies. We enjoy having them, and it's a wonderful way to make a little extra money. I believe we're having a dozen people this time."

"Wow." Elaine picked up her turkey sandwich. "That's a large group."

"We've had larger," Alice said. "We had twenty once at *mei haus.*"

Sharon nodded. "That was just a few weeks ago."

"What did you make for them?" Elaine asked.

Alice tapped her chin. "If I remember correctly, we made a few pans of vegetable lasagna, along with homemade *brot* and a huge salad. Several desserts."

Elaine shook her head. "That's a lot of work."

"It is, but like I said, we enjoy it." Sharon dabbed at her mouth with a paper napkin. "The best part is singing."

"It was your great idea," Alice said, then turned to Elaine. "Sharon started our tradition of singing hymns when a guest asked some rude questions. It was brilliant. She completely redirected the conversation."

Elaine's shoulders relaxed. "What a clever idea."

Sharon picked up a potato chip and pointed it at her. "Do you like to cook as well as quilt?"

"*Ya*, I do."

"You should come tomorrow," Alice said. "We usually get together around four so we have plenty of time to finish preparing the meal and set up. The *maed* cook, and the *buwe* manage the tables and chairs. They've learned how to set each place too." She turned to Sharon. "Did you already go shopping for the chicken pasta casserole ingredients?"

Sharon nodded, then swallowed. "*Ya, Mamm* and I went yesterday. Are you still bringing pies?"

"*Ya.* I'm glad our mothers finally agreed

to let us bring something if we want to. After all, they share the profits with us. Darlene said she's going to make a couple of *kuchen*."

Sharon looked at Elaine again. "We'd love for you to come."

Elaine shook her head. "Maybe next time."

Sharon's smile faded. "But we really could use your help with the singing. You have such a *schee* voice, and our voices blended so well together on Sunday."

Elaine gestured around the room. "We still have a lot to do here."

Alice wagged her finger. "We're not giving up on you, Elaine." Then she turned to Sharon. "Do you think I should make another shoo-fly pie or something different?"

Elaine contemplated Alice's words. Would these women really not give up her? Or were they just being nice — for now?

432

CHAPTER THREE

"It's a shame Elaine didn't want to come tonight," Alice said while wiping down one of the folding tables in Sharon's kitchen.

Cal stopped sweeping the floor and turned. "You invited her?"

"*Ya.* Sharon, our *mamms,* and I went to her *haus* yesterday. We encouraged her to join us, but she said no thank you."

"You went to her *haus.*" For some reason, Cal was stuck on that detail.

Sharon turned from where she washed a serving platter at the sink. More often than not, Alice and Sharon sent their mothers off to put up their feet after they'd all eaten the leftovers once the supper guests left. After all, Dorothy and Feenie usually did most of the cooking and took the lead. And even with Sharon's younger sister, Ruby Sue, visiting a sick friend this evening, they had enough help.

"Alice and I spent the morning helping

433

Elaine unpack boxes and organize their kitchen while our *mamms* cleaned," Sharon told him.

Darlene gathered another stack of dishes from the Lambert family's kitchen table, still shoved against one wall. "I wanted to go with you yesterday; I even made a fruit salad. But I needed to help *mei mamm*. Although her cancer is in remission, she's still so tired some days."

"We understand." Alice smiled at her.

Cal fingered the broom as he recalled Elaine's adorable freckles. "Did she give you an excuse for not coming?"

Alice shrugged. "Not really. We told her we could use her voice when we sing, but she just said she had a lot to do and maybe next time."

"But you promised her you weren't going to give up on her," Sharon added. "And neither will we."

Boy, did he agree with that. He couldn't get Elaine out of his head even though she seemed to be avoiding him. He was determined to get her to talk to him and find out why. He shook his head as he returned to sweeping.

"You okay, Cal?"

He looked up at Darlene. "*Ya.* Why?"

"You seem to be contemplating something." Then her eyes twinkled as she gaped. "You like Elaine!"

"Shh." He glanced around. Thank goodness the other guys were all busy stowing the folding chairs and Sharon and Alice were deep in conversation. "Don't say that too loud."

Darlene glanced around and then took a step toward him. "We all want Elaine to feel welcome here, and we want to be her *freind.* So don't worry. We'll figure out how to get her to join us for singings and these suppers." She lowered her voice even more. "And your secret is safe with me."

"Danki." Cal smiled as a determined hope lit in his heart.

A week after the Lambert and Blank women had come to help them unpack and clean, Elaine strode into the Bird-in-Hand Dry Goods store. A bell chimed above her head. They'd run out of some kitchen supplies, and they needed some art supplies too.

"Gude mariye," a familiar voice sang.

"Good morning." Elaine glanced down the main aisle toward the counter, then gasped when she found Darlene sitting behind the counter. "Hi. Is this your family's store?"

"It sure is!" Darlene rubbed her hands

435

together. "What are you looking for?"

Elaine pulled *Mamm*'s shopping list out of her apron pocket and examined it. "I need some dish detergent and sponges." She tilted her head and pursed her lips. "We also lost some of our stamping supplies during the move, and it's almost time to start making our Christmas cards. Do you have stamps and ink?"

"Oh *ya.*" Darlene waved for Elaine to follow her. "They're in aisle three. And we just got in some stamps for the Christmas season and more green and red ink."

Elaine picked up a shopping basket and then followed Darlene to the shelves packed with everything she could possibly need. "I'm sure you can find what you want here." Then Darlene pointed toward the end of the aisle. "The dish detergents and sponges are two aisles to the right."

"Danki."

Darlene started walking backward. "Let me know if you need anything. I'll be working on paperwork at the counter. For some reason, *mei dat* likes me to do it on Thursdays." She grinned, then swung around and left.

Elaine began examining the stamps, trying to recall what she and *Mamm* had used for their Christmas cards in the past. She'd

436

just gathered most of what she thought they needed when she heard the bell on the door ring again, announcing another customer.

"Gude mariye!" a male voice called.

"Hi." Darlene's greeting sounded warm. "What brings you here this morning?"

"Just picking up a few things for *mei mamm,"* the man said.

"Oh. Well you, uh, picked *the perfect day* to come." Darlene's emphasis seemed strange. And the man's voice sounded kind of familiar.

Elaine stepped into the aisle Darlene said held cleaning supplies — where she collided with Calvin King, slamming her basket into his side. "Oh! I'm so sorry." Guilt came on like a flood, followed by humiliation.

He gave a snort as he rubbed his side. "Fancy crashing into you here."

Knowing her face had to be turning red, she set her basket on a nearby shelf and then reached for his side. But she pulled back. "I didn't see you in time. Are you okay?"

He chuckled. "I will be." He looked down and grimaced. "I might have a bruise, though."

"Ach." Elaine glanced down the aisle at Darlene, who apparently had come to stare

437

at them. "Do you have an ice pack, Darlene?"

"No, no." Calvin held up his hand. "I'm joking, Elaine."

"Are you sure?"

"Ya." Then he smiled, and her pulse fluttered. She could easily lose herself in the blue-gray pools of those eyes. He lifted his golden eyebrows as if questioning her expression, and she looked down at her feet.

"How are you?" he asked.

She met his gaze once again. *Flustered. Anxious. Self-conscious.* "I'm okay."

He looked in her basket. "Making something?"

"Mei mamm and I want to start making Christmas cards for my parents' *freinden* back in New Wilmington." She spotted laundry detergent in the basket at his feet. "Did I hear you say you're running an errand for your *mamm*?"

"I am. *Dat* doesn't mind if I dash out for her once in a while, when we're not too busy with the horses." He picked up the basket. "I didn't see a horse and buggy out front, and there weren't any cars. Did you walk?"

"Ya." She shrugged. *"Mei haus* isn't far from here." She glanced down the aisle and noticed Darlene had disappeared. Calvin's finger brushed her hand, and she jumped

with a start.

"What else do you need?" He stood closer to her now, leaning down as he read the list in her hand.

She breathed in his scent — a masculine, musky scent — and her heartbeat seemed to skip a beat. She had to find a way to fight her growing attraction to him.

"Dish detergent and sponges, huh?" He pointed to the shelf. "Do you like this kind of detergent?"

She nodded, and she was careful to not allow their hands to touch as he handed her the bottle.

"Sponges." He glanced down the aisle. "What size?"

"Those." She slipped past him and grabbed a package. *"Danki."* Then she started toward the counter. "I need to get going. I have a lot of chores to do."

She was aware of his eyes on her as he followed her to the counter, where she set down her basket and smiled at Darlene. "I think I have everything."

"Great." Darlene began ringing up the items on a battery-operated cash register.

Calvin sidled up to Elaine, then set his own basket on the floor before leaning his hip against the counter.

Elaine glanced at his side and inwardly

cringed as she recalled their collision. "Are you sure I didn't hurt you?"

He gave a little grin. "I'm fine, Elaine. Really, I am."

Elaine nodded and then caught Darlene giving Calvin a little smile that seemed to hold a hidden meaning. Was she missing something? Darlene and Andrew were dating, so why was she giving Calvin a look like that? It seemed almost flirtatious.

Elaine's stomach turned as she recalled how her former best friend, Rhoda, and Lewis had shared special looks — no doubt before but certainly after Lewis broke up with Elaine, eliminating the need for secret meetings with Rhoda. She dismissed those thoughts and tried to think of something to say.

"How long has your family owned this store?" Elaine asked Darlene.

"About twenty-five years. *Mei dat* opened it just before my older *schweschder* was born. He'd been working for a construction company, but *mei mamm* wanted to run a business that would keep them both at home. They got a loan from *mei daadi* and took a leap of faith that worked out well." She finished putting Elaine's items in a plastic bag and gave her the total.

Elaine pulled out her wallet and gave her

some bills. *"Danki."*

"Gern gschehne." Darlene handed her a receipt and her change. "I'm so glad you came today."

Elaine slipped her wallet back into her purse.

"Would you like a ride home?" Calvin said.

Warning bells sounded in her head.

"No, *danki.* It's not a far walk, and I enjoy being out in the fall weather. I know a lot of people say Christmas is their favorite time of year, but the entire autumn season is my favorite."

Calvin's grin widened. "Mine too."

Elaine nodded. She turned toward Darlene and was almost certain she spotted another look pass between her and Calvin.

"Elaine, Alice and her *mamm* are hosting a supper at their *haus* tonight," Darlene said. "You should come."

"Oh." What excuse could she make this time?

"It's a lot of fun," Calvin said with an encouraging tone.

"Danki, but I can't. *Mamm* and I plan to start making the Christmas cards I bought these supplies for this evening. It's never too early." Elaine lifted her bag. "It was nice running into you both." She cringed as she

glanced at Calvin. "Not literally."

He chuckled, and she enjoyed both his smile and the sound of his laugh. But when she took a step away from the counter, his smile faded.

"I'll see you both at church," she told them.

"Have a *gut* day, and tell your parents hello," Darlene said.

"I will."

Elaine started for the exit, glad for the easy escape.

Cal's hope deflated as Elaine disappeared out the door.

He'd been shocked when Darlene mouthed *Elaine is here* and then pointed toward aisle three. It felt like a sign from God, telling him he was supposed to talk to Elaine today.

But it had all gone horribly wrong, starting when she'd slammed her basket into his side. The spot she'd hit still throbbed, but he'd ignored it, trying to find the humor in the incident. Then his attempts at starting a conversation had failed, and she'd once again turned down the invitation to join them at a supper and singing.

"Cal," Darlene said, breaking through his thoughts. "What are you waiting for? Go after her."

"Right." He scrambled out the door and down the driveway to the sidewalk. "Elaine. Elaine!"

She spun around. Her pretty brow was pinched, and what was that expression on her face? Frustration? His mind went blank. What did he want to ask her? What was wrong with him? He'd never had trouble talking to women before!

He offered the first thought that came to mind. "Would you like to join me for lunch?" He pointed toward the nearby businesses also located on Old Philadelphia Pike. "A diner with *appeditlich* food is just a few blocks down. We can ride in my buggy, and then I'll take you home."

"Oh." Now she seemed flustered as she fingered a button on her black sweater. "No, *danki*. Like I said, I have chores to do."

"Do you want a ride home now, then?" He inwardly groaned at how eager he sounded. Why was he repeating the same question he'd asked earlier? She'd already turned down his offer. When had he become so desperate to gain a woman's attention?

"No, *danki*." She smiled, but it seemed forced.

They stared at each other for a moment, and he swallowed as mortification swelled in his gut. She didn't like him. And he was humiliated. He'd never felt this way before, and he detested the feeling!

"Have a *gut* afternoon." She turned and started down the sidewalk.

Cal's shoulders slumped as he pushed back through the front door of the store.

Darlene frowned. "I'm assuming it didn't go well."

"Not even a little bit." He sighed as he leaned his elbows on the counter. "I offered to take her to lunch, and when she said no, I offered to take her home — again. She said no to both."

"I'm sorry." Darlene bent down and then reappeared with two bottles of water from under the counter. She handed him one. "We need another plan."

"Why? She just doesn't like me." He opened the bottle and took a long drink. When had he become such a loser?

Darlene tapped her chin as she stared up at the ceiling. Then she pointed her bottle of water at him. "You give up too easily."

"I'm just being realistic." He scrubbed one hand down his face. Why was he so obsessed with a *maedel* who didn't like him? Had he lost his mind?

Darlene snapped her fingers. "I've got it! Sharon and Alice told me Elaine's *mamm* really enjoyed spending time with their *mamms.* What if your *mamm* invited Elaine and her parents over for supper? That would give her parents a chance to meet your parents, and it would give you a chance to spend time with Elaine."

"Hmm." He nodded slowly. "That might be a great idea."

"It *is* a great idea." She swiped at his arm. "It's the best way to get her to talk to you. She can't turn you down if her parents want to go, right?"

"Right."

"*Gern gschehne.*" Darlene's smile encouraged him.

He grinned as he took another drink of water. *This plan just might work.*

"Hi, Arnold," Elaine said as she jogged up the front-porch steps and found the cat sitting by his empty food bowl.

Arnold meowed and blinked up at her.

"I'll bring you something to eat in a minute, okay? I need to get these supplies inside."

She stepped into the house and thought she heard *Mamm* humming "O Holy Night." That carol was a favorite for both of them. The prospect of making Christmas cards must have brought it to *Mamm*'s mind. The tune and lyrics were so beautiful. *O holy night, the stars are brightly shining . . .*

"I'm back," she called, then set her bag on the table when she reached the kitchen.

Mamm appeared holding a dust cloth. "*Danki.* Did I give you enough money?"

"*Ya.* I have your change." Elaine pulled it out, along with the receipt. "It turns out Darlene Bender's family owns that dry goods store."

"What a nice coincidence." *Mamm* put the dish detergent and sponges under the kitchen sink.

Elaine thought of Calvin and felt a flutter in her chest. "I need to feed Arnold." She grabbed a scoop of cat food and a cup of fresh water, then hurried out to the porch.

"Here you go," she told the cat. Then she filled his food bowl and changed his water.

"Did you run into anyone else during your errand?" *Mamm* asked when Elaine returned to the kitchen.

Elaine examined the art stamps she'd bought as she considered telling her mother about Calvin. But what could she say about him? She didn't even know him!

"Elaine?" *Mamm* touched her arm. "*Was iss letz?*"

"Calvin King was at the store," she blurted.

446

Mamm's eyes narrowed. "Who is Calvin King?"

"His parents own the horse farm where Uria works."

"Oh." *Mamm* nodded. "And is there something wrong with Calvin King?"

"Not exactly." Elaine fingered a stamp featuring the words *O Holy Night* in italics. Now, *that* was a coincidence. "He just makes me . . . *naerfich.*"

Mamm's eyes widened as her expression filled with concern. "Why is that? Has he said something inappropriate to you?"

"No, no. It's nothing like that." Elaine sighed as she searched for the right words to explain her conflicting emotions. "He's been nice to me, but there's just something about him. I can't quite explain it."

Mamm seemed to study her. "I know you're hurting after what Lewis and Rhoda did, but you can't keep a wall around your heart forever. At some point you have to let people in."

Elaine swallowed against her suddenly dry throat. "I know."

Mamm pointed at the stamps. "Let's see what you've got there. I'm sure you found the perfect stamps for our Christmas cards."

As they looked over the craft purchases, *Mamm*'s words echoed through Elaine's mind. If only the message in her favorite line in "O Holy Night" permeated all her relationships. *Truly he taught us to love one another . . .*

Oh how she longed to trust friendship and love again. *Please, God, show me the way.*

Chapter Four

Cal walked the length of the stable the next morning, and as usual, the aromas of hay and horses struck his senses. He stopped when he reached the stall where Uria was mucking with the pitchfork.

He'd contemplated his running into Elaine — or her running into him — for hours last night. He couldn't stop envisioning her lovely face and shocked expression when she rammed into him with her shopping basket. He touched his side where a colorful bruise had appeared. Although the spot still ached a bit, he smiled at the memory.

He wondered if he'd used the wrong words when he asked her to join him for lunch. Had he appeared too forward and scared her away? But women had always seemed to enjoy his joking demeanor. Why would it have driven Elaine away?

As he stared at his ceiling waiting for

sleep, it hit him. Good thing *Mamm* had been called away to help a friend for the evening. He still hadn't asked Uria about Elaine, and maybe he should do that before asking *Mamm* to invite Elaine's family over. Perhaps Uria would know why Elaine was so leery of him, of even spending time with his friends. After all, she'd sung to Josiah Gingerich with them after church that first Sunday, and no one had bitten her! Yet Elaine seemed so skittish.

Now Uria stopped his work, turned, and leaned the pitchfork against the barn wall before wiping his forehead with the sleeve of his gray shirt. "Are you here to supervise?"

Cal smirked. "No, you're doing a fabulous job, as usual. I do have a request, though."

"What?" Uria leaned back against the wall.

"Tell me about your cousin Elaine."

Uria lifted his straw hat and raked his fingers through his sweaty hair. "What do you want to know?"

"She seems so reluctant to spend time with me and *mei freinden.* Do you know why?"

Uria brushed his hands down his shirt. "From what I've overheard *mei mamm* and *dat* say, I think she was hurt by a boyfriend."

"What do you mean by *hurt*?" He couldn't

keep his brow from furrowing.

Uria's eyes widened. "Oh, I don't mean physically. I think her ex-boyfriend and best *freind* turned against her or something."

Cal drummed his fingers on the stall door. *Ex-boyfriend.* But the fact that Elaine no longer had a boyfriend did little to erase his concern for her. She'd been hurt, and that bothered him.

"I'm going to ask *mei mamm* to invite Elaine's parents over for supper one night. Do you think she'll come too?"

"Sure. Why not?" Uria shrugged. "They'll probably expect her to anyway."

"Great. *Danki.*" Cal turned to go but then stopped and looked back at Uria. "Don't tell anyone I asked about her."

Uria grinned. "I won't."

Cal smiled. *"Danki."* Then he lifted his chin toward the stall. "Now get back to work."

Uria rolled his eyes, but Cal knew he recognized teasing when he heard it.

"You're as bossy as your *dat.*"

"You know it." Cal headed back into the house, where he found his mother washing breakfast dishes.

She stared at him. "Is it lunchtime already? I just put the eggs away, and I haven't finished these dishes." Then she glanced up at the clock.

"It's not lunchtime." He cleared his throat. "I want to ask you for a favor."

"A favor?" *Mamm* dried her hands on a towel and then folded her arms over her black apron as she leaned against the sink. "This should be *gut.*"

He gathered his thoughts. "Would you please invite Elaine Lantz and her parents over for supper one night?"

Mamm's lips turned up in a smile. "You want to have Elaine over?"

Here we go with the teasing. "It's not what you think."

"Oh it must be. Raymond was right. You *do* like Elaine." *Mamm* gave a little squeal. "I'm so *froh.* It's been so long since you dated."

He held up his hands. "Hold on now. Don't send any wedding invitations yet. I just like her as a *freind,* and I want to get to know her. But at this point, I don't even think she likes me."

"Oh, I'm sure she does, Calvin. How could anybody not like you?"

He shook his head. "I'm trying to figure that out myself."

Mamm clapped her hands. "I'd love to have them over for supper. Would you ask Uria what their phone number is? They most likely share the phone shanty with

Mary Liz and Mel, but I want to be sure."

"I will." Cal kissed her cheek. *"Danki, Mamm."*

"Gern gschehne. This will be *wunderbaar."*

As Cal walked back to the stable to start his own chores, he prayed. *Please, God, encourage Elaine's parents to say yes to* Mamm*'s invitation. And then help Elaine understand I want to be her* freind *and I won't hurt her the way her boyfriend in New Wilmington did.*

"I received an interesting call this afternoon," Elaine's mother announced during supper.

"Oh?" *Dat* filled his plate with a mountain of teriyaki chicken casserole and then passed the dish to *Mamm* as Elaine took a long drink of water.

"It was Edna King." *Mamm* looked at Elaine. "Calvin's *mamm.* "

Elaine began to cough. Then she sputtered and gasped for breath.

Dat jumped up and patted her back until she regained control.

"Are you all right?" *Dat* asked as *Mamm* gave her a worried look.

"Ya." Elaine sniffed and wiped at her eyes. "The water went down the wrong way. What

453

did Edna want, *Mamm*?"

"She invited us to join them for supper Friday night." *Mamm* dropped two scoops of casserole on her plate and then passed the dish to Elaine.

"Why?" Elaine asked, alarm surging through her at a rapid pace.

"How nice," *Dat* said at the same time.

Mamm smiled at *Dat* and then turned to Elaine. "I had a pleasant conversation with Edna. She said she and her husband want to welcome us to the district and get to know us better."

Suspicion threaded through the alarm still there. This had to be Calvin's doing. Why wouldn't he just leave her alone?

"I asked her what I could bring, and she suggested dessert. Would you please make one of your triple-chocolate pumpkin pies, Elaine?" *Mamm* asked.

"Oh, I love that pie," *Dat* said. "I'm certain the Kings will enjoy it. They'll be *froh* they invited us for your dessert alone."

Elaine looked down at her plate, but her appetite had evaporated at the mention of Calvin's name.

"It will be nice to meet the Kings," *Dat* continued. "Mel told me Uria enjoys working on their horse farm. In fact, he wants to own a horse farm someday."

Elaine struggled to maintain a calm demeanor. She would have to spend the evening with Calvin King. So much for her plan to avoid him. He kept popping up in her life like a pesky weed.

Elaine peeked out the window at the rolling pastures of the Kings' farm as her father's horse pulled his buggy up the long, winding rock driveway that led to a large, two-story, brick farmhouse with a sweeping wraparound porch.

She nearly gasped as she took in the long row of bright red barns and the freshly painted, white split-rail fence lining the pasture, where several horses frolicked. The business appeared profitable, and the Kings lived a comfortable lifestyle.

"It's nice, isn't it?" *Dat* said as if reading her mind.

"No wonder Uria likes working here," *Mamm* added.

Dat secured the horse to a hitching post near the front door, and they all climbed out of the buggy.

Balancing a pie plate in her hands, Elaine followed her parents onto the porch, where her mother knocked on the door. Footfalls sounded from inside the house, and Elaine pulled in a deep breath. Her hands trembled as she imagined Calvin appearing and flashing his attractive smile.

The door swung open, and a teenaged boy who looked slightly shorter than Calvin smiled at them. He wasn't blond like Calvin, and his eyes were hazel, not blue-gray, but the family resemblance was clear.

"Hi. I'm Raymond."

"Nice to meet you," *Dat* said. "I'm Abram, and this is Lovina and Elaine."

"Please come in." Raymond held the door open for them. "You can hang your jackets here if you'd like." He pointed to pegs by the door.

Elaine pulled off her wrap and hung it on a peg beside her mother's and father's. Then she followed her parents into a large family room furnished with two sofas, two wing chairs, three end tables, a matching coffee table, and two propane lamps. A recliner sat near a desk in one corner. She glanced toward a steep staircase and imagined how large the bedrooms at the top of the stairs must be.

"Hello." A woman about *Mamm*'s age came in from the kitchen. She was pretty, and her hair and eye color matched Raymond's. She held her hand out to *Mamm*. "I'm Edna. I'm so glad you could come tonight."

Mamm made a sweeping gesture. "This is Abram and Elaine."

Edna gave Elaine a smile that seemed to be just for her. "It's so very nice to finally meet you, Elaine."

Elaine nodded as heat crawled up her neck. Had Calvin talked about her? She brushed away the thought and held out her offering. "I made a triple-chocolate pumpkin pie."

"Oh my." Edna took the pie and sniffed it. "Calvin will be delighted. He loves pumpkin pie. In fact, we all do."

"I'm so glad." Elaine glanced around the room. "Your farm and *haus* are lovely."

"Danki." Edna pointed toward the kitchen. "Please come make yourself at home. Harvey and Calvin should be down soon. They're still cleaning up after working all day."

Elaine stepped into the kitchen and barely swallowed another gasp. Just like the family room, the kitchen was huge. A long table with eight chairs sat in the middle of the room. Cabinets lined an entire wall, and a pretty cabinet full of china and crystal sat at the far end.

The delicious aroma of beef filled Elaine's senses as she looked toward the counter where *Mamm* and Edna now stood. *Dat* and

Raymond were huddled by a window while Raymond pointed as if giving *Dat* a tour of the farm from afar.

"What can Elaine and I do to help?" she heard *Mamm* ask.

"Oh, nothing, but *danki.* I think we're all set. We just need the other two men to join us." Edna looked toward the doorway to a hall and then smiled. "Here they are."

Elaine absently smoothed her hands down her black apron and red dress as Calvin walked into the room just behind an attractive older man.

Calvin said hello to Elaine's parents and then faced Elaine. When he smiled, her heart seemed to come to life.

"I'm so glad you could make it," he said.

He was more handsome than ever in a blue shirt that brought out the blue in his eyes.

"*Dat,* this is Elaine." He gestured toward his father. "Elaine, this is *mei dat,* Harvey."

Elaine walked over and shook Harvey's hand. "You have a *schee* home and farm."

"*Danki.*" Harvey seemed pleased with the compliment. "We're *froh* to have you all over." He smiled at his wife. "I convinced Edna to make steak and potatoes."

Dat rubbed his hands together. "My favorite."

"Isn't it every man's favorite?" Elaine blurted. She turned toward Calvin, who gave a bark of laughter, and then everyone joined in.

"On that note," Edna said with a laugh, "let's eat. Please sit wherever you'd like."

Calvin touched her hand, and warmth rushed to the spot where their skin made contact. "Sit by me."

Elaine found herself captured in the depth of his eyes.

"Let me help serve the meal," *Mamm* told Edna.

"I should help too," she told Calvin.

He nodded. "I'll save your seat."

Elaine couldn't quite suppress a smile as she returned the nod. Then she carried two large bowls of mashed potatoes to the table while her mother filled glasses with water from a crystal pitcher. Edna brought the platter of steak, and Elaine followed with a large tossed salad.

Once all the food was delivered, Elaine took her seat beside Calvin. When her leg brushed against his, she took in a rush of air. She glanced at Raymond and found him grinning at his older brother. What did that mean? She recalled the way Darlene had looked at Calvin in her store. Did everyone know something about Calvin she didn't?

Elaine bowed her head and tried to dismiss confusion from her mind as she prayed.

When she heard her father shift in his seat, she looked up just as Harvey took a steak and then passed the platter to *Dat*. Soon the sound of cutlery scraping plates filled the kitchen as well as voices. Their arms resembled an octopus as they reached for food and passed serving dishes from place to place.

Elaine glanced to her left, where her *mamm* and Edna were already discussing quilting. To her right, *Dat* and Harvey talked about *Dat*'s dairy farm.

"I saw a pie plate on the counter."

Elaine looked at Calvin. "*Ya.* I made a triple-chocolate pumpkin pie."

"Oh." Calvin put his hands to his chest. "My favorite."

"You've had it before?"

He shook his head. "No, but you said my two favorite words — chocolate and pumpkin."

Elaine smiled.

"He loves pumpkin," Raymond chimed in. "This is his favorite time of year."

"It's Elaine's too," Calvin said.

Elaine turned toward Calvin again. "You remember I told you that in Darlene's store?"

"How could I forget?" Calvin sliced his steak. "What do you like about the fall?"

"I love how the leaves change." She scooped a pile of mashed potatoes and dropped it onto her plate. "How the air smells. And how the nights get cooler." She passed the bowl to Calvin and found him looking at her with an intensity that made goose bumps dart up her arms. "What?"

"I feel the same way." He took the bowl from her.

Elaine turned her attention to her meal, all the while trying to stop her pulse from zooming.

Calvin was so handsome, and he seemed to like her, not just be flirting with her. But how could she trust any man after the way Lewis had betrayed her — and with Rhoda? And how did she know Calvin truly liked her when he and Darlene seemed to be sharing secrets? It was just too risky to allow him into her heart.

"Elaine," Edna began, "what do you think of Bird-in-Hand so far?"

After she swallowed a piece of steak, Elaine said, "It seems very nice."

"I love the little downtown area on Old Philadelphia Pike with the shops and restaurants," *Mamm* added. "And everyone seems so friendly in our church district."

"Everyone is glad you're here," Edna said.

"*Ya*, we are," Calvin chimed in.

Elaine did her best to focus on what Edna was saying. But she had a sinking feeling. She'd have a tough time avoiding Calvin but an even tougher time denying how her attraction toward him was intensifying.

CHAPTER FIVE

Cal couldn't take his eyes off Elaine during supper. He studied her long neck and gorgeous profile — her high cheekbones, her pink lips, her cute little nose.

His mouth dried as he looked down at his plate. Though he had no good reason to hope she'd ever like him as more than a friend, he couldn't deny the intense feelings swelling in his heart. And he still wasn't sure she'd ever even consider him a friend.

When they'd finished eating the main course, *Mamm* made coffee and Elaine served her pie. Cal enjoyed the delicious dessert while his parents continued to pepper the Lantzes with questions about their community in New Wilmington.

Elaine seemed shy, almost uncomfortable in her own skin as she gave terse answers to the questions directed at her. She clearly did not like to talk about herself. And he was sure she had no idea how beautiful she was.

When the pie was gone — every piece — and their mugs were empty, Elaine helped *Mamm* and Lovina clear the table.

"Abram," *Dat* said. "Let's go sit on the porch." Then *Dat* turned to Cal and Ray. "We'll enjoy this evening out there."

Cal stood and headed out behind the other men. When he reached the doorway to the family room, though, he stopped and looked back at Elaine. She met his gaze and gave him a bashful smile, causing warmth to spread in his chest. He had to find a way to get her alone so they could talk. But how?

The question spun through his mind as he grabbed his jacket, then stepped onto the front porch, where *Dat,* Abram, and Ray had already chosen rockers. The sun had begun to set, sending brilliant hues of orange and red across the cloudless sky.

He sat in the swing at the far end of the porch, next to Ray's chair. He pushed it into motion as he stared at the horizon, but he felt unsettled and anxious. He wanted to go back inside, take Elaine's hand, and lead her out back, where they could sit and talk on a bench without an audience. But could he do that without embarrassing her? He didn't think so.

"How do you like working in Mel's shed shop?" *Dat* asked Abram.

"Very much," Abram responded. "Our *dat* was a carpenter, and he assumed that both Mel and I would follow in his footsteps. He was surprised and not too *froh* when I moved to New Wilmington and worked on my father-in-law's dairy farm instead."

Dat chuckled. "I bet he was. I was just telling the family I've noticed that shop stays busy all year round."

Cal tried to pay attention while the two older men talked, but it was sweet torture to be stuck out here while Elaine was inside. If only he had an excuse to return to the kitchen.

"Cal," Ray whispered. "Are you all right?"

Cal stopped the swing and faced his brother. *"Ya."*

Ray studied him. "You look . . . twitchy."

"I am." Cal was careful to keep his voice low. "I asked *Mamm* to invite the Lantz family over so I could get to know Elaine. But I haven't had a moment to talk to her alone."

A smirk took over Ray's face. "You do like her."

Cal refused to let his younger brother get the best of him. "*Ya,* I do."

Ray shrugged. "So go inside and get her."

"I can't."

"Why not?" Ray leaned toward him. "Ask her if she wants to go for a walk." He pointed toward the pasture. "Then take her around the farm and —"

"Give her a tour." Cal finished the thought.

"Exactly."

Cal stood as excitement fueled his resolve. "You're brilliant."

Ray shrugged. "I know."

Shaking his head, Cal headed back into the house and peered into the kitchen. Lovina was washing dishes, *Mamm* was drying, and Elaine was wiping down the table.

Mustering every bit of his courage, he strode to Lovina and tapped her on the shoulder.

She looked up at him and smiled. "Calvin. Hi."

"Hi." He nodded at Elaine, who was watching him with curiosity flickering over her face. "May I borrow your *dochder*?"

He glanced at Elaine just in time to see her bite her lower lip and twist her finger around one of the ribbons on her prayer covering.

"So long as she doesn't mind," Lovina said. "We're almost done cleaning up here."

Cal smiled at Elaine. "I'd like to give you a tour of the farm."

"That would be nice," she said.

He was surprised she'd so readily agreed — but he was happy.

He glanced at his mother, and she winked.

Elaine placed the soiled dishcloth she'd been using on the counter next to her mother. "I just need to grab my jacket on our way out."

He waited while she donned her wrap, then he pushed open the screen door and moved out of the way so she could step onto the porch. When he glanced at Ray, his brother gave him a thumbs-up. He glared at him, hoping Elaine hadn't seen the gesture.

"Where are you two headed?" Abram asked.

"Calvin is going to give me a tour of the farm," Elaine told him.

"Enjoy," *Dat* said.

Cal lifted a lantern, and then as he started down the steps beside Elaine, he looked out at the sunset again and smiled. "I love sunsets."

"I do too."

He gave her a sideways glance, noting how the color of her dress made her hair seem darker. "You look *schee* in red."

"Oh." She glanced down and then gave him a sheepish expression. *"Danki."*

As they headed toward the line of barns,

he pointed out which ones held supplies and which ones housed animals. He also pointed to the stables and talked about the horses. She nodded and seemed interested, but he worried he might bore her.

When they reached the edge of the pasture, he gestured toward the bench he'd envisioned sitting on earlier. "Why don't we sit?"

"Okay."

They lowered themselves onto the seat, then silence stretched between them as they both stared toward the far end of the pasture. Cal discreetly took in Elaine's posture, now rigid and tense as if she were sitting next to a complete stranger. He couldn't get a handle on her behavior, but he recalled what Uria had told him. He racked his brain for a way to get her to open up.

"Do you really like Bird-in-Hand?" he finally asked. "Or were you just being nice?"

She turned toward him. "*Ya,* I do like it. Why do you ask?"

He shrugged. "I don't know. I just get the feeling that you don't want to be here. Do you miss your *freinden* in New Wilmington?"

She shook her head. "I don't miss *mei freinden,* but I do miss *mei haus.* I grew up there, and it was bigger than the *daadihaus* we're in now —" Worry flashed over her face. "Does that sound prideful, to compare homes that way?"

"No, it's not prideful. If you grew up in a bigger *haus,* then of course you would not only feel an attachment to it but appreciate its qualities."

More silence filled the space between them. Cal's mind wandered as he recalled how Elaine had refused Darlene's invitation to the supper at Sharon's house that day in the dry goods store. Even if she'd been hurt by people where she lived before, was that enough to make her so reluctant to make new friends?

"I've known all my closest *freinden* since school," he finally told her. "We've grown up together."

She looked down at her lap and picked at a stray thread. "That's nice."

"We especially enjoy our singings for people and at the suppers for *Englishers.* We think they're meaningful too. You really should come. The best part, though, is eating the leftover food once the guests leave."

He grinned, but Elaine's expression was serious when she looked up at him.

"Why are you so determined to get me to go to those?"

He stared at her, stunned at her blunt question. Then he mentally shook himself. "You're new here, and you must be lonely. Everyone needs a *freind.*"

She gave a wry smile and shook her head. "I'm not *gut* at picking *freinden.*"

"What do you mean?" He leaned toward her, hoping she would share what happened to her in New Wilmington, especially if what Uria thought happened did.

She sighed and looked out toward the pasture again. "Back in New Wilmington, I had a boyfriend. His name is Lewis. I'd had a crush on him for a long time, and he finally asked me out last year." She kept her eyes trained on the pasture as darkness crept in around them. "I thought everything was going well between us, but then . . ."

"What happened?" Cal reached down and flipped on the lantern, illuminating her face with a soft, yellow glow.

She looked down at her lap again, and her mouth formed a thin line before she went on. "I thought he cared about me, even loved me, but he decided he wanted to be with my best *freind,* Rhoda. They were sneaking around and seeing each other before he broke up with me."

Cal shook his head in anger. Uria had heard right. "Why would he pick *anyone* over you?"

She looked up at him. "*Danki,* but that's what he did. And it was worse than that."

"What do you mean?"

Elaine shook her head, and he was almost certain he spotted tears in her eyes. "To hide what they'd done, Rhoda and Lewis made up lies about me, telling everyone Lewis had *gut* reason to break up with me. *Mei freinden* not only believed the lies but stopped inviting me to join them in activities. I wouldn't even know about them. I was an outcast." Her voice trembled. "By the time we moved away, I had no one to trust."

He opened his mouth to respond, but no words came out for a moment. "That's horrible," he finally said.

She sniffed and looked away. He felt the urge to touch her, comfort her, but he kept his distance. After somehow earning a little of her trust, he didn't want to scare her away.

"Elaine, I hate that you were hurt that way. But none of those people were truly *freinden* to begin with if they believed the lies and rejected you."

She stared down at the bench. "That's what *mei mamm* keeps telling me, but it still hurts. Like you, I'd known *mei freinden* since school. I still can hardly believe it."

471

"I'm certain it hurts." He took another breath. "I hope you'll give me and *mei freinden* a chance. I promise we'll never treat you that way."

She looked up at him and nodded, but he was almost certain he saw doubt in her gorgeous eyes.

Elaine bit back a groan. Why had she just poured out her deepest secrets to Calvin? She'd allowed herself to get lost in his beautiful eyes and dazzling smile. And now she was vulnerable. Surely he'd wind up hurting her no matter what he said.

Calvin started telling her more about the horses his family bred and sold and then explaining the process of training them. Elaine listened with interest, but at the same time, she resumed her guard.

After they sat on the bench a while longer, Calvin stood and picked up the lantern. "Why don't we head back to the front porch?"

She thought she should probably join Edna and *Mamm* inside the house, but Calvin encouraged her to sit with him on the swing so Raymond could get to know her too. She did, listening to his brother force small talk, until *Dat* announced it was time to leave. They all stepped inside.

"We've had a *wunderbaar* time," *Mamm* told Edna.

"You're always welcome here."

"Danki."

Dat shook Harvey's hand. "I enjoyed meeting you and seeing your farm."

"We enjoyed your company."

Elaine turned toward Calvin and found that same intense look in his eyes. She shivered. *"Danki* for the tour, Calvin."

"Didn't I tell you *mei freinden* call me Cal?" When he shook her hand, he held on for a moment longer than necessary, making her determined she'd never allow herself to think of him so casually.

"I hope to see you soon," he added.

Elaine turned to his brother. *"Gut nacht,* Raymond." Then she followed her parents outside to their buggy and climbed into the back.

"What a lovely evening," *Mamm* said as they pulled away. She was practically gushing. "I really like Edna." She glanced behind her at Elaine. "It seemed like you and Calvin were getting along well."

"Ya." Elaine gave a half shrug, but her heart was screaming. She closed her eyes and rubbed her temple at the truth. She was developing feelings for Calvin — especially after he seemed to understand how much

she'd been hurt. But that didn't mean she could trust him, and she prayed for the resolve to protect her heart.

"So?" *Mamm* asked Cal as the buggy taillights disappeared down the driveway. "How did it go?"

Cal glanced to his right and spotted *Dat* and Ray already entering one of the barns, a lantern guiding their way.

"They're gone. You can be honest with me." *Mamm* looked hopeful.

"We sat on a bench by the pasture and talked a little."

"That's *gut,* right?"

"It is, but she was really hurt by a boyfriend back in New Wilmington." Renewed anger boiled in his gut when he thought about what Elaine had been through. "It won't be easy to earn her trust."

"But she opened up to you. That's a huge step."

"I hope so."

Chapter Six

"Hi, Arnold. Want to help me check the mail?" Elaine asked the orange tabby as he strolled beside her to the mailbox nearly two weeks later.

She shivered in the crisp November air and folded her jacket around her body. She should have grabbed a heavier coat instead. Glancing up, she found dark clouds populating a gray sky, not the clear blue sky she'd enjoyed yesterday. But that didn't mean she wouldn't have a good Wednesday. Any week still held promise in the middle.

The cool, metal mailbox door squeaked as she opened it. Then Arnold plopped at her feet and meowed as she leafed through a pile of letters.

Elaine stilled when she found a white envelope addressed to her. The return address was New Wilmington, and she recognized it. The handwriting looked familiar as well. She ripped open the envelope and huffed when she found the letter really was from Lewis. "Arnold," she whispered. "I can't believe this."

Her eyes scanned the page as she cupped one hand to her mouth.

Dear Elaine,

I visited your great-aunt Thelma yesterday and asked how you're doing. She said your mother included a letter in a birthday card, saying you're doing fine. I hope it's okay that I asked her for your address. I know you might not be happy to hear from me, but I need to get a few things off my chest.

First, I was wrong to betray you. I know you truly loved me, and I've realized now that I've always loved you. If only I'd been mature enough and smart enough to see that.

Sneaking around with Rhoda was not only wrong but cruel, and it was the biggest mistake I've ever made. You are the love of my life. You're pretty, kind, intelligent, and genuine. I was blind when I left you for her, and I regret everything I did to hurt you. You deserve a man with integrity. I'm hoping you can find it in your heart to forgive me. I know I don't merit your forgiveness, but if you'll give me another chance, I promise I'll treat you right and be the man you need.

I broke up with Rhoda soon after you moved away, and we agreed we were wrong. She wants to apologize to you, too, and maybe you've already heard from her.

Please think about what I've said, and if you can forgive me, write back or call. I'll understand if you can't give me another chance, but just know that I am sorry, and I'll spend the rest of my life missing you and regretting what I did.

Always,
Lewis

Elaine blinked and rubbed her eyes before reading the letter again. She glanced down at Arnold, and the cat blinked at her. "This is absurd. I need to tell *Mamm*."

Then as a wave of anger rose with each step, she hurried off and jogged up the back steps. *Mamm* sat in the kitchen making a shopping list.

"You will not believe this!" Elaine slapped the letter on the table, and *Mamm* jumped. "Read this."

Mamm's eyes couldn't have grown much wider. "Elaine. You startled me."

"I'm sorry." She dropped into the chair

across from her mother and pointed to the letter. "This is just . . . Ugh!" She dropped the other letters on the table and shook her head.

The anger warred with both irritation and disbelief as she waited for her mother's assessment.

When *Mamm* looked up from reading, she shook her head and removed her reading glasses. "I'm speechless."

"I know!" Elaine threw her arms up in the air. "He cheated on me with my best *freind. And I regret everything I did to hurt you,* he said, not even being specific about it. He turned all *mei freinden* against me, and now he has the nerve to beg for my forgiveness." She tapped the letter with her finger. "And he says he's realized I'm the love of his life." She took a breath. "And no, I have not heard from Rhoda. I wouldn't be surprised to find out she's the one who broke up their relationship, for some other man."

Mamm's lips twisted as she looked down at the letter. "Well, you know it's our culture to forgive, but you certainly don't need to give Lewis another chance. And right now I don't know what to say about Rhoda."

"Why would I give either of them another chance?" Elaine stood and crossed the floor to the counter. "I need some tea."

"*Gut* idea."

After filling the kettle, she set it on the stove and turned on the burner, then grabbed two tea bags and two mugs, her mind swirling with confusion. *The nerve of him!*

"Do you realize we've been here nearly a month now?" *Mamm* asked.

Elaine glanced at the calendar hanging on the wall. "I guess that's right."

"And you still haven't settled in with the young people here." *Mamm* assessed Elaine with her hazel eyes. "You haven't mentioned Calvin since we had supper at his *haus.* Have you spoken to him at all?"

"Only in passing."

"Why is that?"

Leaning back on the counter, Elaine crossed her arms over her waist. *Mamm* had no doubt decided Calvin was interested in her daughter, especially when he asked to give Elaine a tour of his farm. "I admit he's been very nice to me, but I don't want to get attached to him or any other man. I've been hurt enough, and I think my heart needs a break."

To her surprise, *Mamm* nodded. "I think that's a *gut* plan, but you still need *freinden.*" She pointed at her. "That's why we're going quilting at Dorothy Blank's *haus* tomorrow afternoon. Alice and Sharon will be there too."

Elaine groaned. "Why do I have to go?"

"Because you need to get out and make *freinden*. It's not healthy for you to spend every day here with me."

"But it's where I want to be, *Mamm*."

When the kettle began to whistle, Elaine stepped back to the stove. After pouring the water, she carried the mugs to the table and sat down. They sat in silence as they sipped their tea.

Elaine studied her drink, her mind churning. Could she allow herself to at least grow close to Sharon and Alice? And what about Darlene?

She sighed and rubbed her temple. Why was life so complicated? Would she always feel like a stranger here?

Please God! Guide my heart! I'm so confused.

"Elaine," *Mamm* finally said, reaching across the table to place her hand on Elaine's. "I understand you're afraid to trust anyone after what Lewis, Rhoda, and your other *freinden* did to you. But it's not fair to punish the people you've met here for the sins of others. I was grateful when your *dat* agreed to finally sell the farm and move here. I prayed for God to give you a new start to help heal your heart."

Elaine leaned forward. "You did?"

"Of course I did. I was so angry you'd been hurt, and it broke my heart to watch you suffer so. I didn't want you to spend the rest of your life living among people who'd betrayed you. You deserved a new start, but I couldn't give you that unless your *dat* sold the farm. It all came together perfectly when your *onkel* once again offered him a partnership plus this place to live. Then we found the perfect buyer for the farm. It was all God's will."

Sniffing, Elaine wiped her eyes with a tissue drawn from the pocket of her apron. "I hadn't thought of it that way, *Mamm*."

Mamm gave Elaine's hand a gentle squeeze. "That's why I believe you need to give these young people the benefit of the doubt. You don't have to start dating right away. But try to at least make a few close *freinden*. Alice, Sharon, and Darlene seem to really like you, and Dorothy invited us to quilt with them at her *haus*. Why not give them a chance?"

Elaine nodded. "You're right. They've been kind to me."

"*Gut.*" *Mamm* took another sip and then glanced at Lewis's letter. "You should forgive Lewis, but that's all. And you should forgive Rhoda, too, even if you never hear from her."

"I know, and I will." Elaine picked up the letter, folded it, and stuffed it back in the envelope.

Elaine hugged a quilt to her chest as she and *Mamm* climbed the Blanks' back-porch steps the following afternoon.

The door flew open just as they reached it, and Alice appeared in the doorway. "I'm so glad you're here. Please come in. We're in our *schtupp.*"

Elaine and *Mamm* followed Alice through the mudroom and kitchen and into a large family room, where Sharon, Feenie, Dorothy, and Ruby Sue all sat working on their quilts.

Elaine smiled and waved as everyone greeted her, and then she settled in a wing chair.

"What did you bring to work on?" Alice asked.

"It's a Log Cabin quilt I started a few months ago." Elaine opened it and ran her fingers over the gray, blue, and pink pattern. "I'd like to send it to *mei* great-*aenti* Thelma for Christmas."

"It's lovely," Sharon said.

"It surely is," Alice added.

482

"Danki." Elaine smiled as she recalled her mother's words. She had to try to make friends. "Would you help me work on it?"

Sharon and Alice both nodded, and Elaine's shoulders relaxed as they turned their attention to her quilt. Maybe God had blessed her move to this community. Maybe she'd find true friends here.

The bishop had started his sermon, but chagrin stole Cal's concentration as he watched Elaine just stare at her lap.

Why did his efforts to drum up a conversation with her only result in curt answers? Worse, when she was invited to join his friends for . . . anything, why had she rejected the idea every time, saying she was too tired or busy — or giving no excuse at all?

He pinched the bridge of his nose as the ongoing confusion scrambled his brain. He couldn't understand Elaine. He'd been certain they'd become friends the night her family had come to his house for supper, but she still behaved as if he was just some acquaintance, someone who didn't matter much at all.

Then again, maybe she regretted sharing what happened to her in New Wilmington that day they talked on the bench. She had to feel vulnerable after what this Lewis had done to her.

How could he fix this?

He closed his eyes in disappointment. Maybe he'd come on too strong? But what could he have done differently to show her he truly wanted to be her friend?

"Cal?" Andrew whispered. "Are you okay?"

"Ya." He opened his eyes. Then something inside him seemed to crack open. He needed advice.

He leaned toward Andrew. "I can barely get Elaine to talk to me, and it's driving me crazy."

A young man Cal didn't really know turned from his seat in front of him. He glared, then whipped around to face the front again.

Andrew gave Cal a little grin and shook his head before leaning closer.

"I *knew* you liked her," he whispered. "Don't give up. I didn't give up on Darlene, and it worked out for us."

Cal nodded slowly, then looked back at Elaine, taking in her beautiful face as she now studied the bishop. Renewed determination took hold. No, he still wouldn't give up. And with God's help, maybe Elaine would not only agree to spend time with him and his friends today but be willing to ride with him to their planned gathering.

Cal waited until Elaine finished helping with lunch cleanup, then hurried to where she stood talking to Darlene, Sharon, and Alice near their hosts' back porch. He stood a little taller, gathering all the courage he could muster.

Elaine saw him, and to his surprise, a smile — albeit tentative — took over her lips. "Calvin, hi," she said.

"You can call me Cal," he said, losing his focus for a moment. Then he pushed ahead with his plan. "Did the girls tell you? We're all playing games in Dave's barn this afternoon. Will you ride with me?"

Elaine glanced at Alice as if for permission, which sent a flame of doubt through him. But when Alice nodded, Elaine smiled. And then she turned that smile toward him.

"I'd love to," she said. "Let me just tell my parents I'm going."

He felt off-balance for a moment, and he blinked. *Danki, God.* "Okay. I'll get my horse and buggy ready."

As Elaine hurried off, Cal felt someone clap him on the shoulder, and he looked over to see Andrew.

"How long have you been standing there?"

Cal asked.

"Long enough." Andrew grinned. "I told you not to give up."

"You were right," Calvin said. *Danki.*

Andrew nodded and then held his hand out to Darlene. She threaded her fingers with his, and envy pricked at Cal as he watched them walk away hand in hand. Maybe he and Elaine would be holding hands soon.

As Elaine headed toward Cal's buggy, a familiar war developed in her heart. Had she just made the wrong decision, agreeing to ride with him? Deciding to give him a chance, not only as a friend but — she might as well admit it — as a potential boyfriend, a relationship she suspected he wanted to explore?

She wanted to trust Cal with her heart, and he'd given her no real reason not to. She'd realized neither Darlene nor Cal would ever betray Andrew. Their relation-ships were all solid and true. But she still feared what could happen if she trusted Cal beyond friendship. She'd seen the way some of the single young women in their church district looked at him. He could date anyone he wanted, and after what Lewis had done to her, she was afraid — nearly terrified —

of being hurt again.

But the wall she'd built around her heart seemed to be crumbling just a little.

CHAPTER SEVEN

Happiness bubbled through Cal as he guided his horse toward Dave's house. After much praying and hoping since Elaine's visit to his family's farm, she was finally riding in his buggy beside him.

Now he just had to say and do the right things to encourage her to really trust him. He swallowed back a groan. The pressure nearly seemed too much!

The *clip-clop* of his horse's hooves, the whir of the buggy wheels, and the roar of passing traffic filled the space between them. He had to think of something to spur a conversation between them, crashing through this awkwardness. And he might as well be bold about it.

"Have you heard from anyone back in New Wilmington?" he asked as he gave her a sideways glance. He really did want to know.

She hesitated but only for a moment.

"*Ya,* I have. Lewis wrote me. I got his letter on Wednesday." She said the words almost as casually as if she were ordering a burger in a restaurant.

Cal thought he'd probably just blanched. Had he heard her correctly?

"Lewis?" he asked, and she nodded. "Your ex-boyfriend?"

"Correct."

"He wrote to you." He kept his words as measured as possible.

"*Ya.* I was surprised too." She shifted in the seat and crossed her arms. "He visited my great-*aenti* Thelma and asked her for my address. Then he wrote me a letter apologizing for everything he did and begging for my forgiveness. He said he realizes now he made a mistake, and I'm the love of his life."

Cal gripped the reins with such force that pain shot through his wrists.

She snorted. "As if that makes up for what he did. He wanted me to forgive him and give him another chance. He asked me to write him back or call him."

"Are you going to?" He braced himself for her answer.

She gave a little laugh. "I've forgiven him, since it's our way to forgive, but I won't give him another chance. Why would I open

489

myself up to be hurt like that again?"

"Right." He nodded slowly as his hands relaxed — slightly.

She shook her head as she looked out at the passing traffic. "If he truly cared for me, he would have treated me better. I don't see why he thinks he can make up for it now."

Cal stared straight ahead, worried. Even though Elaine said she wasn't planning to give Lewis another chance, he couldn't help but wonder what the man would do if he were determined to win her back.

The thought sent more anxiety twisting up his insides.

"I'm stunned he's making such an effort now," she continued. "He said he broke up with Rhoda, but I think Rhoda broke up with *him.* He's probably just lonely."

"Maybe so." He tried to smile, but his lips refused to cooperate.

"How has work been for you?" Elaine asked. "How are all the horses?"

Though his thoughts were jumbled, Cal managed to answer her questions about the farm during the remainder of the ride to Dave's house. When they arrived, he tied up his horse and then walked with Elaine to the large barn where the ping-pong tables were set up.

They spent the afternoon playing, drinking hot cocoa, and eating cookies. Elaine seemed relaxed. She blessed him with her beautiful smile more than once, and she even teased him when he missed hitting the ball for a serve.

When it was time to go, they both said good-bye to everyone, and he was thrilled Elaine walked with him to his buggy without question. He'd been afraid she might ask someone else for a ride.

"That was so much fun," Elaine said as she settled back in the passenger seat. "I haven't laughed like that in a long time."

Cal smiled. "I'm glad to hear that. Everyone really likes you."

She looked at him. "You think so?"

"I know so." *I like you a lot.*

"*Danki* for including me."

"*Gern gschehne.* I'm not planning on giving up on you." He held his breath, awaiting a rejection, but she just smiled and looked out the windshield. "What are your plans for this week, Elaine?"

"I'll have my usual chores. You know — laundry, dusting, mopping, sweeping, darning." She shrugged. "I also have some Christmas gifts to work on. I'm making some quilts and a few other items. I'm also getting together with Darlene, Alice, and Sharon to make Christmas cards. *Mamm*

491

and I finished ours, and we'll mail them before too long. Alice particularly wants to borrow our stamp that says 'O Holy Night.' That's my favorite Christmas carol."

"Mine too. There's another thing we have in common."

"I guess so! I'll have to make you a card with it."

"I'd like that. Tell me about your cards. What do you use besides stamps and ink to make them?" He smiled inside. This conversation was so easy, so natural. Surely she felt it too.

As he pulled into her driveway, a thought occurred to him. Maybe it was time to ask Elaine for a date! The idea sent warmth to every cell in his body. He would have to talk to her father, of course, but first he wanted to ask her if she even wanted to date him. He'd do that when he walked her to the house.

Please, God, give me the right words to show Elaine how much I care.

When they reached the porch, Cal felt something brush against his leg, and he halted. He chuckled as a large, orange tabby blinked up at him. "Who's this?"

"This is Arnold." Elaine grinned as she leaned down and rubbed the cat's ear. He responded with a purr as he closed his eyes.

"He seems to have adopted me."

"It's nice to meet you, Arnold." Calvin rubbed the cat's head.

"I'm hoping he'll come with us when we move."

His gaze snapped to hers. "Move? What do you mean?"

"*Mei dat* just found some land. He's about to buy it, and then we'll build a *haus* in the spring. It's not far from here, so we'll stay in the same church district."

"Well, that's *gut* news! And . . ." His pulse galloped as he searched his heart for the right words. "Elaine, I really care about you, and I'd like us to get to know each other better. Will you give me a chance to prove I'll treat you right, that I won't hurt you the way you've been hurt in the past? If your *dat* agrees, I'd like to date you."

Elaine stared up at him, her eyes widening with what looked like . . . panic?

"Calvin, I do like you." She took a step back. "I'm just not ready for another boyfriend, and I don't know when I will be. I need space and time."

Cal didn't know how to respond, so he just nodded and shoved his hands in his pockets. "I understand," he finally sputtered. "Maybe we can be *freinden* for now?"

She opened the back door. "Of course. I

493

had fun today. Be safe going home. *Gut nacht.*"

Then she hurried inside and closed the door in his face.

Cal stared after her, his head spinning. Then he kicked a porch post with such force that it sent pain radiating from his toes to his shin. He didn't believe she had no interest in a boyfriend. She just didn't want to date *him.*

When he heard a meow, he looked down at Arnold, again blinking up at him. "I don't know what I'm doing wrong. Do you?"

The cat meowed again and then jumped off the porch before trotting toward a nearby barn.

Calvin descended the steps and then looked up at the sky filled with dark, ominous clouds that reflected his mood. Elaine had splintered his hopes and left him to pick up the pieces. Yet she'd trusted him enough to share about Lewis's letter. And she'd been happy spending time with him all afternoon.

Then she'd wholly rejected the idea of dating him. It didn't make sense.

Did she still love Lewis?

The notion sent a knife slicing through his heart. He needed help, and not just from a friend.

He again looked up at the sky and opened his heart to the Lord.

"God," he whispered as he took slow steps to his buggy. "I'm so confused. I feel as if you're leading me toward Elaine, and to the depth of my bones, I think you intend for us to be together. But every time she seems to be getting a little closer to me, she pulls away. Am I wasting my time? Does she still love Lewis even though she claims it's over between them?"

The last words tasted bitter on his tongue.

"Lead me down the path you've chosen for me. I need your guidance, Lord. I can't figure this out on my own."

And then, with a shaken spirit, he climbed into his buggy and headed home.

"All right, Cal," Sharon announced after they'd finished setting the tables for a group of *Englishers* at her house Friday night. "We have a few minutes before our guests arrive, and *Mamm* and Ruby Sue are upstairs changing. I haven't seen you smile or tease anyone tonight. Why are you so mopey?"

"I was going to ask the same question," Jay said, and the rest of his friends agreed with nods.

Cal shrugged and glanced toward the doorway to the mudroom, still hoping

Elaine would walk through it.

"Is this about Elaine?"

He turned to Darlene. "Are you reading my thoughts now?"

She frowned as she shook her head. "No, it's just kind of obvious. You two seemed to have a connection on Sunday, but she didn't come tonight even though we invited her when we were making Christmas cards yesterday. I've been wondering if something happened between you after you left Dave's barn."

"She turned me down." Cal turned around a folding chair, then sat on it backward, leaning forward. "When I took her home Sunday, I asked if I could date her, and she said no. She said she's not ready for a boyfriend, and she needs time and space. But I think that just means she's not interested in dating *me*."

His friends studied him, wide-eyed, and he rested his elbows on the back of the chair, his hands clasped. "I've prayed about it, and I still feel like God is leading me to her. But why would he do that if she's not interested?"

Darlene sat down beside him. "Maybe you're supposed to help Elaine through something. Maybe she's having a hard time."

Calvin nodded as he studied his hands to avoid his friends' concerned expressions. He didn't want their pity, and he couldn't tell them what happened to Elaine in New Wilmington without her permission. Obviously, she hadn't told even the women in their group, which confused him even more.

He just wanted to spend more time with Elaine. But she didn't want to spend more time with him.

Alice chimed in. "I don't think it's just you. When we invited her to join us tonight, I thought she'd agree since she seemed to have so much fun with us on Sunday. And I thought she liked singing with us at the one supper she came to. But she said no."

"It's as if she wants to be our *freind* yet for some reason she's struggling," Sharon said. "I get the feeling she's been hurt."

"She has," Cal said. "I can't tell you specifics, but I thought I was helping her trust people again. Then she seemed almost panicked at the idea of spending more time with me. I backed off about dating, of course. But I think she'd come to more of our activities if she could just stop being so scared we'll hurt her."

"You are helping her, Cal," Andrew said. "Like I told you, don't give up. Even if she wants you as only a *freind* right now, she might change her mind about dating you later. And we'll all try to make her feel safe when she's with us."

Cal nodded. He'd be Elaine's friend, of course. But what if she kept avoiding him? He wasn't sure how much more rejection his heart could take.

Elaine dashed to the mailbox the following Friday afternoon. She zipped up her jacket and shivered against the late November chill, surprised the coat still fit after all the food she'd eaten at the family's Thanksgiving dinner the day before. She'd helped *Mamm* and her *aenti* prepare an enormous meal, and it was so delicious.

She heard a meow and smiled as Arnold scurried to her side. "Hi there, buddy. How are you today?"

Arnold replied with another meow and rubbed against her leg.

"You can help me get the mail."

She riffled through a stack of letters and fliers, then stopped when she found another envelope from Lewis. She groaned as she took in his familiar handwriting.

"You won't believe this, Arnold, but Lewis wrote me again," Elaine grumbled. "He sent me another letter last week, too, but it's still unopened on my desk. I don't want to hear any more from him." She shook her head. "Why won't he give up?"

Arnold meowed again before plopping down beside her.

"Don't get comfortable. We need to check messages." Elaine shifted the letter to the back of the pile and then walked toward the phone shanty, her shoes crunching the rocks as Arnold scampered beside her. Last night the first frost had descended upon Lancaster County, and the ground was still white.

Elaine punched in the code for voice mail, then settled back on the one chair and drew circles across the notepad on the desk. As she waited for the messages to start, Arnold sat outside the shanty, licking his paws.

A voice came through the line, and her jaw dropped when she realized who it was.

"Elaine. This is Lewis." He paused. "I've written you several letters, and I haven't heard back from you. I assume you received them, because they haven't been returned to me. And I guess I can't even put into words how sorry I am that I hurt you, but please know I'll do anything to make things right between us. What I did was inexcusable. I've begged God for forgiveness, and I've even talked to the bishop about confessing in front of the congregation."

The line went silent for a beat, and then

he continued. "I just want to make amends, and I'm willing to come there to see you. In fact, if you don't call or write me soon, I will. I'll get on a bus or I'll hire a driver. I'll come to Bird-in-Hand to apologize in person."

Elaine shook her head as disbelief nearly overwhelmed her. "Lewis has lost his mind," she said aloud as if expecting Arnold to agree with her.

"I just need to hear from you, Elaine," Lewis continued. "I want your forgiveness and, if possible, another chance. I'll treat you the way you deserve to be treated if you'll just let me try again. Please, Elaine. Please tell me it isn't over. I love you. Goodbye."

Elaine groaned as she deleted the message. Then she listened to the remaining messages, then returned to the house.

"*Danki* for bringing in the mail. Were there any voice mail messages for me?" *Mamm* asked as she sat at the table sipping tea.

"Two for you and one for *Dat.*" Elaine handed *Mamm* the pieces of paper. "And there was an interesting message for me."

"Really?" *Mamm* pointed to the chair across from her. "Tell me about it."

Elaine dropped into the chair and relayed Lewis's message as *Mamm* stared at her in amazement.

Mamm blew out a deep breath. "Well, Lewis is awfully determined for you to respond to him. Are you going to?"

Elaine shook her head. "No. I've forgiven him in my heart — and everyone else involved too — but I don't have anything to say to him."

Mamm clucked her tongue. "I'm not sure that's a *schmaert* decision. If he doesn't hear from you, he might actually come here."

"He won't. I think he's just trying to force me to speak to him, and I refuse." Elaine stood and pushed her chair under the table. "I'm going to clean the bathroom."

As she headed toward the utility room for supplies, she pushed Lewis out of her mind. He didn't deserve a second thought.

But then Calvin King popped into her brain. She'd been thinking about him a lot. When he'd asked her to date him, she'd panicked despite her attraction to him. And she really wasn't ready for another boyfriend. But she should at least be a better friend to him. She'd make sure of it the next time she saw him.

And maybe she was ready to be a better friend to all the others too.

CHAPTER EIGHT

On Sunday afternoon, Cal smiled as Elaine sat down next to him in Sharon's kitchen and handed him a cup of hot chocolate.

"I hope you like a lot of marshmallows, Cal," she said. "That's how I like my hot chocolate."

"I do." He took a sip. "It's perfect."

He'd been surprised when Elaine agreed to come when Sharon invited everyone to her house after church. But now she smiled at him as they sat surrounded by their friends, and she seemed . . . comfortable. She'd finally become one of them.

She'd also called him Cal. Did that mean he hadn't completely scared her away? He could hope.

"Elaine," Sharon said as she set a fresh plate of iced sugar cookies in the center of the table. They were cut into the shapes of Christmas stars, bells, and angels. "I'm so glad you came today. We've been missing you at our suppers and singings. We still really need your voice, and we'd enjoy having our new *freind* there." She grinned. "What better time to add an angelic voice to our group than Christmas?"

Elaine returned the smile — but shyly. "I have been thinking about going. I . . . I think I'm ready to . . ."

Elaine pushed a tie from her prayer covering behind her shoulder as she turned toward Cal. He gave her a slight nod, and she didn't take her eyes off him as she continued.

"You all have been so nice to me, unlike some *freinden* back in New Wilmington who hurt me quite a bit."

Her words seemed to be spoken only for him, sending his hope soaring. Oh how he wanted to be Elaine's boyfriend! He'd just felt something shift between them, and maybe now was the time. Maybe she wanted him to ask again.

"I'm glad to hear it," he told her.

One by one, their friends offered Elaine their support.

He'd talk to Abram next weekend. Then he'd ask Elaine to date him, and he prayed she'd say yes this time.

Elaine set a serving platter laden with fried

503

chicken and a basket of rolls in the center of the kitchen table Friday night. Then she added green beans and salad.

"That chicken smells *appeditlich*," *Dat* said as he entered from the hallway.

Elaine smiled as she filled their glasses with water. *"Gern gschehne."*

"I think that's everything," *Mamm* said, pulling out her chair.

Elaine sat down just as a loud knock sounded on the front door. She turned to her parents. "Are you expecting anyone?"

"No." *Dat* shook his head.

"I'll go see who it is." Elaine hurried through the family room to the front door, past the poinsettias she'd picked up in town a few days ago. She wrenched it open, allowing the cold December air into the warm house. Her stomach dropped when she found Lewis standing on the porch. "What are you doing here?"

He looked the same with his dark-brown hair, piercing bright-blue eyes, and handsome face, but she'd rather be seeing almost anyone else.

"Elaine." He held up his hands. "Please don't slam the door in my face. I hired a driver to bring me all this way to talk to you."

"Hasn't my silence been enough of a hint

for you?" She ground out the words. "It's over, Lewis. And I have nothing more to say to you. I forgive you, but I'm not interested in giving you another chance. You need to let me go."

"Just listen." He took a step toward her. "I'll regret hurting you for the rest of my life." He reached for her hand, but she snapped it out of his reach. "*Danki* for forgiving me, but I want to restore your faith in me. I love you, Elaine. I want to start over. I want to show you I know how to be a *gut* man and a *gut* husband."

"Husband?" She barked a laugh, and he winced. "Are you kidding? Do you think I'm a *dummkopp*?"

Lewis glanced behind her and smiled. "Hi, Lovina."

"What a surprise."

Elaine spun and glared at her mother. *Mamm*'s tone had been just as forced as her smile was now.

"Why don't you come in out of the cold, Lewis," she added.

Had *Mamm* lost her mind? Why would she want this man to even step foot into their house?

Mamm's eyes narrowed with a warning. "We should at least invite Lewis in for supper, Elaine. Then we'll discuss sending him

505

back home." She turned to the intruder. "Let's get your coat and hat off."

"Fine," Elaine snapped before stalking into the kitchen. *Dat* sat there with a bewildered expression. "Lewis is here," she whispered. "We're going to feed him supper and then send him on his way."

"Why is —" *Dat*'s question was interrupted by Lewis and *Mamm*'s appearance.

"Hello, Abram." Lewis approached *Dat* and shook his hand. "It's nice to see you."

"Oh . . . hello." *Dat* shot *Mamm* a confused look but then smiled at Lewis. "Have a seat and join us for supper."

"*Danki.*" Lewis washed his hands at the sink and then sat down.

Elaine brought him a plate, utensils, and a glass, resisting the urge to slam them onto the table to properly convey her annoyance. After Lewis's place was set, Elaine took her usual spot, across from him, and bowed her head. She asked God to bless the food — and help her get Lewis out of there!

As they filled their plates, Elaine kept her eyes on her plate and hoped her parents would carry the conversation.

"So, Lewis," *Dat* said, "how is your family?"

"*Gut. Mei schweschder*'s wedding is coming up in a few weeks, so she and *mei mamm*

506

have been busy making final plans. And of course, everyone's been getting ready for Christmas."

Elaine peeked at him. Maybe the man was just caught up in his sister's excitement about getting married.

"Oh, how nice," *Mamm* said. "Is Lydiann marrying Paul?"

Lewis nodded. "*Ya,* she is. They've been together four years now. *Mei dat* says it's about time."

Her parents laughed, but the laughter sounded just as strained as this awkward conversation. Elaine's food tasted like sand in her mouth. She wanted Lewis to leave, to go back home, to leave her alone. Oh, what a nightmare it was to be stuck at her own kitchen table with him!

Elaine glanced at her mother, who gave her a look of encouragement. Hopefully, the meal would soon be over, all the mundane small talk set aside, and then she could send Lewis back where he belonged.

Cal guided his horse up the rock driveway leading to the Lantz *daadihaus,* and as his heartbeat matched its lively *clip-clop,* anxiety tumbled around in his stomach.

Tonight was the night! He'd ask Abram for permission to date his daughter, and then, assuming he gave his permission, Cal would ask Elaine to be his girlfriend.

He climbed out of the buggy before tying the horse to a fence, and in moments he was jogging up the front steps of the house, light glowing from its family room windows. He smiled when he found Arnold lounging near the door.

"Hey, buddy. Nice to see you again. I guess you're not too cold out here." He rubbed the cat's head and then knocked on the door. He could see his own breath in the night air as he rubbed his hands together and waited for someone to answer.

The inside door opened with a squeak, and as Elaine pushed open the storm door, she greeted him with a look of surprise.

Wearing his favorite red dress, Elaine seemed nervous as well as she glanced behind her and then stepped out onto the porch. She pushed the storm door closed, and Cal could tell something was wrong before she even said a word.

"Cal. Hi." She hugged her arms to her chest. "I didn't expect to see you here."

"I was hoping to talk to —" He looked behind her, into the house. "Is now a *gut* time?"

A pained look darted across her face. "I'm sorry, but it really isn't."

Alarm shot through him. *"Was iss letz?"*

"It's complicated." She gave him a forced smile. "I promise we can talk soon, okay?" Her regret seemed genuine. "I'll tell you everything when the time is right. I just can't right now. You have to trust me."

Cal studied her for a moment, trying to decode what she was saying. He glanced past her just as a man about his age — but shorter — appeared in the doorway behind her. He pushed the door open and joined them. Cal had a bad feeling about this.

"Hello." The guy held out his hand. "I'm Lewis Byler. And you are . . ."

Cal took a step back as the porch floor seemed to drop out from under him. Lewis had come back for her after all.

His stomach knotted as the breath rushed from his lungs. He'd been fooled. He was going to be sick.

"I have to go." He turned and dashed down the steps, then toward his buggy.

Cal thought he heard Elaine calling him, but he kept going, unwilling to even look back as he guided the horse away from her.

"How could you do this to me?" Elaine said through gritted teeth, infuriated as tears streamed down her cheeks. "You have no right to show up here and disrupt my life."

She sniffed and brushed away the tears. "Who is he?"

"Cal King." She looked out toward the road as the buggy's taillights disappeared into the dark. "He's *mei freind.* In fact, he's my best *freind* here in Bird-in-Hand."

He hesitated and then said, "And do you care for him as more than a *freind?*"

The truth hit her like a punch to the stomach. "*Ya,* I do. I care for him very much, and I think you just ruined any chance I had with him."

She stood straighter as her anger spilled over. "Call your driver and ask him to pick you up now. Then go home. You're not welcome here. In fact, you're not welcome in my life."

She turned toward the road again, feeling more helpless than ever. She had to find a way to get Cal back before it was too late.

Cal climbed Andrew's porch steps and knocked on the door. Disappointment, heartache, and regret all stirred in his chest as his mind kept replaying that scene — Lewis standing on Elaine's porch.

He'd come to see her, just like he told her he would. And Elaine had obviously let him back into her life.

Cal needed someone to talk to. And his

first thought was to go see Andrew. He'd been through a lot with Darlene before they'd worked everything out.

The back door opened, and Andrew's mother smiled.

"Hi, Calvin." She pushed the door open. "How are you?"

"I'm fine, Jean. Is Andrew available to talk for a few minutes?"

"Of course. Come on in." Jean led him into the kitchen. "Would you like some *kaffi*?"

"That would be nice. *Danki.*" He sat down at the table and tried to stop his leg from bouncing up and down.

Jean poured coffee in a mug for him and then called upstairs. "Andrew. You have company in the kitchen!" Then she poured coffee into another mug. "He'll be down in a moment. I'll just set this here for him. There's cream and sugar already on the table if you want them." Then she set the mug down before disappearing into the hallway.

Andrew came down the stairs and gave Cal a surprised look — the second he'd received tonight. "Hi. What's going on?"

"It's Elaine."

"What happened?" Andrew sat down across from him and grabbed the handle of his mug.

"I had it all planned out. I went to her *haus* to ask her *dat*'s permission to date her." He pointed to the wooden tabletop for emphasis. "Then I was going to invite her to go for a buggy ride and ask her to be my girlfriend. But when I arrived . . . You'll never guess who was there."

"Who?" Andrew gave him a palm up.

"Her ex-boyfriend from New Wilmington." Without telling Andrew exactly what Lewis had done to Elaine, he shared how he'd hurt her, then recently written her, wanting her back. "But Elaine told me she wanted to avoid all contact with him. She misled me, Andrew. Do you think she was trying to play both sides? Keep her options open?"

Cal rested his head in his hands as a dull pain began to throb behind his eyes. "I'm so humiliated. I'm such a bad judge of character. I really thought she cared about me."

"I don't know, Cal. 'Playing both sides' doesn't sound like Elaine."

"I thought God had led me to her, but I think I've completely misunderstood."

"You might be wrong."

Cal dropped his hands from his face and narrowed his eyes. "How can I be wrong?"

512

"I don't know." Andrew shook his head. "I just have a feeling Elaine might have a *gut* explanation. Maybe you shouldn't give up so easily."

"She said she'd explain, but I can't do this anymore." He slumped back in the chair. "She's rejected me too many times."

"Just wait. Maybe things aren't as they seem."

"No. I've tried too hard, and all she's done is hurt me." Calvin sipped his coffee and wondered how he'd put his shattered heart back together.

CHAPTER NINE

Elaine rushed into Bird-in-Hand Dry Goods Monday morning, hoping Darlene would be there.

"Hi, Elaine." Darlene waved at her from the counter. *"Wie geht's?"*

"Are you busy? I need your help. I've had a misunderstanding with Cal, and he's upset with me."

Darlene nodded slowly. "No one's here but me. What happened?"

Elaine took a deep breath and started from the beginning, explaining everything about Lewis, Rhoda, and her friends in New Wilmington, then about how Lewis had written her letters before leaving her a voice mail message, threatening to come to Bird-in-Hand if she didn't call or write him.

"I told Cal weeks ago about what Lewis and Rhoda did to me, and I also told him I never wanted to see Lewis again." She took another deep breath. "Then Lewis showed up Friday night."

"No!" Darlene gasped.

"*Mei mamm* insisted we invite him to stay for supper before sending him on his way. Then Cal showed up, and Lewis followed me out to the porch and introduced himself. Before I could explain, Cal took off. I've called his farm a few times and left him messages asking him to call me, but he hasn't." Her eyes filled with tears. "I want to tell him what happened. I need him to know I don't care about Lewis."

Darlene smiled. "You care about Cal."

"*Ya,* I do." Elaine wiped at her eyes. "I've cared for him for a while, but I was afraid to trust a man after what Lewis did to me. But Cal has been so patient, never giving up on me. Now, though, I think he has — for good."

Darlene touched her hand. "He's cared for you for a long time."

"He has?"

Darlene gave her a knowing smile. "Remember that day you came into my store and he was here? The day you two collided?"

"*Ya.*" Elaine sniffed.

"He'd just told me he liked you not long before, and he asked my advice about how to get to know you better since you seemed so reluctant."

Elaine stilled. "That's why you two were sharing looks as if you had a secret."

"*Ya*, our secret was that he liked you. He's been interested in you ever since you came to your first church service in our district. You avoided him, even turned him down over and over. He's been trying to figure out how to prove to you that he really cares."

"*Ach.* I've made so many mistakes, and I've hurt him." She wiped away her tears, but more sprinkled down her cheeks.

Darlene rubbed Elaine's arm. "We can fix this."

"How?" Elaine heard the desperation in her voice.

"We're having a supper Thursday night at Sharon's *haus.* Why don't you come tell him how you feel? Explain everything, just like you explained it to me. I'm sure he's hurt, but I know he'll understand and forgive you."

Elaine prayed as she made her way home. *Please, God. Help me find the right words to tell Cal how I feel about him. I know he's hurt, but please help him forgive me.*

Thursday night, Cal stepped into Sharon's kitchen and froze when he spotted Elaine standing by the oven, talking to Alice as she

516

pulled out a baking dish.

His stomach soured despite the warm and delicious aroma of cookies, and he turned and strode back outside. Then he jogged toward his buggy, a frown twisted on his face.

"Cal!" Andrew called after him, chasing him the length of the backyard. "Wait!"

Ignoring him, Cal opened his buggy door.

Andrew caught up with him, panting. "Hey, you need to give Elaine a chance to explain. You have it all wrong about her and Lewis."

"That's doubtful."

"Cal, please. Hear her out, and then make your decision."

Cal suddenly felt as if God were holding him in place, telling him not to leave. "I'll give her two minutes."

"*Danki* for stopping him, Andrew. Two minutes should be plenty of time for what I need to tell him."

Cal looked past Andrew and found Elaine staring at him. She pulled the coat around her shoulders tighter and gave him a tentative smile.

Andrew patted his shoulder. "Just be patient. You'll be glad you were." He nodded at Elaine and headed back to the house.

"Cal, I want to explain what happened

last week. It wasn't at all as it seemed."

"I'm listening." He leaned against his buggy.

Elaine took a deep breath. "Remember how I told you Lewis had threatened to come if I didn't call or write him?"

He nodded.

"That's why he was there. He just showed up unannounced. I was stunned. While I was telling him I had nothing to say to him, *mei mamm* came out on the porch and invited him to stay for supper." She took a step toward him, her voice trembling. "I didn't want him there. It was awkward, and I was furious with him. I was planning to tell him to leave right after supper, and then you came."

She shook her head. "I didn't want to hurt you, but that's exactly what happened. And I'm so sorry."

"And after I left?" He asked the question, but he dreaded the answer.

"I told Lewis he had no right to be at *mei haus,* disrupting my life and ruining my relationship with you. I made him call his driver and go home."

Relief flooded him. "So you really don't care for him anymore?"

"Cal, I meant it when I told you he didn't have a second chance with me." Her dark eyes misted over. "One thing I learned by seeing him, though, is that I'm *completely* over him. I don't feel anything for him, but I do feel something for you. You're my best *freind* here. You've become special to me. You've never given up on me, no matter how many times I turned you away. You've been the most loyal and patient *freind* I've ever had."

Calvin swallowed. "I don't want to be your *freind.*"

Her eyes rounded as she stared at him. "You don't?"

"I want to be more than a *freind.* I always have. I want to be your boyfriend."

The panic on her face transformed into a beautiful smile. "I would like that very much."

His heart took on wings at her words. "I came to your *haus* Friday night to ask your father's permission to date you. If he said yes, then I was going to ask you to go for a ride so we could talk about dating."

"Would you consider asking *mei dat* now?"

He nodded as he moved closer to her. "*Ya,* I would." He touched her arm. "I care deeply for you, Elaine."

Then he leaned down and brushed his lips over her cheek. The contact spread warmth throughout his chest.

Elaine looked up at him. "Why don't we go help set up inside? We can talk more later, maybe over some Christmas cookies." She smiled.

"I'd like that. I heard we're going to sing carols tonight, and I'm always up for that." He threaded his fingers with hers, and they strode toward the house as contentment filled his heart.

"Why don't we sing another carol?" Elaine asked as she sat surrounded by her friends in her family room on Christmas Eve. Poinsettias and greenery decorated the shelves as the delicious aromas of hot cocoa and sugar cookies filled the small house. *Mamm* had made sure everything was perfect before her parents stepped out to visit with her uncle Mel's family.

Cal brushed his shoulder against hers as he sat beside her on the sofa. "Elaine, you should pick one this time."

"*Ya*, I think it's your turn," Darlene said as she sat on the floor next to Andrew.

"How about 'O Holy Night'?" She looked at Cal. "It's our favorite, right?" *Yes, I remembered.*

He smiled.

"Perfect," Sharon said. "You start."

Elaine found it in her hymnal and began

to sing. "O holy night! The stars are brightly shining. It is the night of the dear Savior's birth. Long lay the world in sin and error pining, till he appeared and the soul felt its worth. A thrill of hope — the weary soul rejoices, for yonder breaks a new and glorious morn . . ."

Everyone joined in. "Fall on your knees! O hear the angel voices! O night divine, O night when Christ was born . . ."

Elaine lost herself in the words as joy rolled over her, anticipating her favorite line in the carol — *Truly He taught us to love one another.* With God's help, Cal had given her another chance, and she'd never been so happy.

She turned toward Cal and smiled as his deep, rich voice sounded beside her. How she loved her new home, her new friends, and her wonderful new boyfriend! And how grateful she was for God's love and peace.

Mamm had been right — moving to Bird-in-Hand had been the new start she needed and a blessing from God.

"Led by the light of faith serenely beaming," Elaine sang, beginning the second verse, "with glowing hearts by his cradle we stand. So led by light of a star sweetly gleaming, here come the wise men from Orient land. The King of kings lay thus in lowly manger, in all our trials born to be our friend . . ."

When they finished singing, Elaine stood. "Why don't I get more hot chocolate and Christmas *kichlin* for us?"

"I'll come with you. Just let me get something from my coat." In a few moments, Cal had followed into the kitchen, and then he touched her arm. "I have something for you."

"I have something for you too." Elaine hurried down the hallway to her room, then returned with a large, wrapped package. She handed it to Cal. *"Frehlicher Grischtdaag!"*

"Merry Christmas to you too." He held out a wrapped box.

"Danki." She opened it and found a framed heart with a Scripture verse etched in italics. She read it aloud, " 'Love is patient, love is kind. It does not envy, it does not boast, it is not proud.' " Her eyes filled with tears as she looked up at him. "It's gorgeous. I love it."

"I'm so glad. I wrote something extra on the back of the frame. Turn it over."

When she did, she found the words *Truly He taught us to love one another* inscribed.

"Cal, how did you know that's my favorite line in 'O Holy Night'?"

"It is? I didn't know. I just thought after

everything you went through in New Wilmington . . . well, they seemed like just the words you needed to hear this first Christmas in Bird-in-Hand."

"I love it."

He opened his gift and smiled as he ran his hand over the blue-and-gray Lone Star quilt. He was the perfect recipient.

"This is so *schee,* Elaine — especially because I know you made it."

"I hope it keeps you warm this winter." She took his hand. "This is my best Christmas ever. Bird-in-Hand has been such a blessing to my family and me. I'm so grateful for my new *freinden* — and especially for you. *Danki* again for never giving up on me. No matter how I pushed you away, you were determined to show me that I could trust you. I thank God daily that he brought us together."

"I do too." He set the quilt on the counter, then took both her hands in his and drew her to him. "I'm so grateful God sent your family here for a new beginning."

She looked up at him, and the intensity in his eyes sent a shiver dancing up her spine.

He leaned down, and she closed her eyes as his lips brushed hers.

Then he cupped his hand to her cheek. "*Ich liebe dich,* Elaine. I love you just like the Scripture verse I gave you said. And just like God's Son taught us."

"I love you too." She glanced up through the kitchen window and smiled. "Look."

Stars shined brightly in the clear night sky, just as she envisioned they'd shined on a holy night so long ago.

DISCUSSION QUESTIONS

1. Elaine is afraid to trust the young people she meets when she first moves to Bird-in-Hand. She thinks anyone she makes friends with could betray her like her friends in New Wilmington did. Do you think her fear is valid?
2. Cal is determined to prove to Elaine that he can be trusted as a true friend. Do you think she deserves his loyalty despite the numerous times she rejects him?
3. Elaine's mother believes their move to Bird-in-Hand is an answer to her prayer for a new start for Elaine. Do you think her point of view is correct? Why or why not?
4. Which character can you identify with the most? Which character seemed to carry the most emotional stake in the story? Elaine, Cal, or someone else?
5. Toward the end of the story, Elaine realizes she can trust Cal and cares for him.

What do you think happened throughout the story to make her change her mind?

6. What role did singings play in the relationships throughout the story?

ACKNOWLEDGMENTS

As always, I'm grateful for my loving family, including my mother, Lola Goebelbecker; my husband, Joe; and my sons, Zac and Matt.

Special thanks to my mother who graciously proofread the draft and corrected my hilarious typos. Thank you to Susie Koenig for her help researching *Great Is Thy Faithfulness* and also for helping catch those typos.

I'm also grateful for my special Amish friend who patiently answers my endless stream of questions. You're a blessing in my life.

Thank you to my wonderful church family at Morning Star Lutheran in Matthews, North Carolina, for your encouragement, prayers, love, and friendship. You all mean so much to my family and me.

Thank you to Zac Weikal and the fabulous members of my Bakery Bunch! I'm so grateful for your friendship and your excitement about my books. You all are awesome!

To my agent, Natasha Kern — I can't thank you enough for your guidance, advice, and friendship. You are a tremendous blessing in my life.

Thank you to my amazing editor, Jocelyn Bailey, for your friendship and guidance. I'm grateful to each and every person at HarperCollins Christian Publishing who helped make this book a reality.

I'm grateful to editor Jean Bloom, who helped me polish and refine the story. Jean, you are a master at connecting the dots and filling in the gaps. I'm so happy we can continue to work together!

Thank you most of all to God — for giving me the inspiration and the words to glorify you. I'm grateful and humbled you've chosen this path for me.

LYRIC CREDITS

In *Hymn of Praise*

"The Old Rugged Cross" was written by George Bennard in 1913.

"This Little Light of Mine" was written by Harry Dixon Loes in the 1920s.

"Das Loblied" ("Hymn of Praise") is a centuries old traditional Amish hymn found in the *Ausbund* and translated into English by John Beiler in 1933.

In *Amazing Grace*

"The Old Rugged Cross" was written by George Bennard in 1913.

"Amazing Grace" was written by John Newton in 1779.

In *Great Is Thy Faithfulness*

"It Is Well with My Soul" was written by

Horatio Spafford in 1873.

"Great Is Thy Faithfulness" was written by Thomas O. Chisholm and published in 1923.

In *O Holy Night*

"Jesus Loves Me" was written by Anna Bartlett Warner in 1859.

"O Holy Night" was written in French by Placide Cappeau in 1847 and translated into English by John S. Dwight in 1855.

ABOUT THE AUTHOR

Amy Clipston is the award-winning and bestselling author of the Kauffman Amish Bakery, Hearts of Lancaster Grand Hotel, Amish Heirloom, Amish Homestead, and Amish Marketplace series. Her novels have hit multiple bestseller lists including CBD, CBA, and ECPA. Amy holds a degree in communication from Virginia Wesleyan University and works full-time for the City of Charlotte, NC. Amy lives in North Carolina with her husband, two sons, and four spoiled rotten cats.

Visit her online at AmyClipston.com
Facebook: @AmyClipstonBooks
Twitter: @AmyClipston
Instagram: @amy_clipston

The employees of Thorndike Press hope you have enjoyed this Large Print book. All our Thorndike, Wheeler, and Kennebec Large Print titles are designed for easy reading, and all our books are made to last. Other Thorndike Press Large Print books are available at your library, through selected bookstores, or directly from us.

For information about titles, please call:
(800) 223-1244

or visit our website at:
gale.com/thorndike

To share your comments, please write:
Publisher
Thorndike Press
10 Water St., Suite 310
Waterville, ME 04901